CONNECTIONS: BOOK ONE

THE SWITCHBOARD

CHRISTINA K. GLOVER

Cover art by Plustime001
Cover design by Lies and Bees

First edition 2024, Printed in the United States of America

No AI was used in the creation of this book, its cover, or any component. Content warnings can be found on the publisher's website.

Lies and Bees Press
www.liesandbees.com/books

To Abi and Chu,
my past, present, and future:
This is your fault.
(affectionately)

TABLE OF CONTENTS

SWITCHBOARD

switch·board
/ˈswiCHˌbôrd/
noun: switchboard; plural noun: switchboards
An installation for the manual control of telephone connections in an office, hotel, or other large building.

- Oxford Languages

ONE

STORMS

At least the magic is working this morning.

Henley Yu rubbed the bridge of his nose, pushing his silver-framed glasses out of the way in the process. The steady drum of rain against the canopy he sheltered beneath brought oppressive humidity that glued his collared shirt to his torso. Even his hair was too heavy. The general sense of discomfort added to his troubles as his neighbors to his left and right shuffled their feet.

The patch of sidewalk they stood on ended in the flooded parking lot of his apartment building. Murky water covered the yellow lines that framed the parking spaces and curbs, tricking his mind into thinking the sidewalk had fallen into the water. A few wise residents had driven onto the walkway to keep their engines out of the deluge. The unwise—or unlucky—would find their cars flooded to the seats.

"Next will be the first floor," Laurie said. She twisted a set of keys in her hand, adding a background jingle to their conversation. Her chain-store apron was stuffed in her tote bag, one of the strings blowing in the occasional gust of wind. "If the bayou overflows, we'll be trapped. I have to get to work. I can't afford to lose this job."

"Gonna be a dozen cars totaled out of this lot alone." Charlie's South Texas drawl came with the tapping of a soft pack of cigarettes against his thigh, unlit out of respect for the others. His oil-stained coveralls were as weathered as his lined face. "There's no way we can fight Mother Nature. How much would it take to clear the water—a hundred percent? Probably more."

"No." Henley dropped his hand from his face. The view of the parking lot was no less depressing, but his headache had receded enough to let him think. The awning protected the trio from the rain as well as the eyes of the non-magical witnesses, so he only had to keep up half of his usual appearances. "We can do it in sixty and keep the water from getting higher." The smile he offered pulled at his stiff lips, as if his entire face resisted his positivity. "I know it's been a long week and we're all tired of the rain, but Houston was built for flooding. We just need to make sure the infrastructure is clear to do its job."

"Sixty," Charlie said, the word flat, as Laurie echoed the same.

"Sixty?" She shook her head in slow disbelief. "How? I'm not very strong. I can't manage as much as Charlie, much less you."

"I'll carry the bulk of the weight. Look." Henley pointed to the center of the parking lot where a lazy spiral of fallen oak leaves marked an ineffective drain. "That's our main culprit. Clearing the drain will empty the parking lot. A guiding spell will keep it from being blocked again. Then all we have to do is keep the main outfall into the drainage channel in the back flowing. We can do it together."

Laurie furrowed her brow tighter, but Charlie was listening. "I'll guide you," Henley continued. "Can you manage as much as ten percent?"

She swallowed. The pavement scuffed beneath her sturdy sneakers as she turned to stare at the drain. "I can do ten, but I have to work at it."

"You're better off than you think because you know your limits," he said. "You'll be fine." Laurie was older than Henley by at least ten years. Her potential as a mage had settled decades before, and she struggled when working alone, but her shoulders relaxed under his encouragement. *There we go. That's right, trust me. Trust yourself.* When she nodded, he smiled, the expression a little easier than it had been a moment before. "I want you to do two sets of five to clear the drain. Charlie, can you handle twenty to keep it clear? I know that's high—"

"It's fine, and the garage is closed today anyway." Charlie stuffed his cigarettes into his breast pocket. "Don't worry about me when you're taking *thirty* for yourself. You sure you're gonna be alright?"

When had thirty percent last been a challenge? When he was fourteen, maybe, during his second ranking exam. They didn't need to know he'd used that much to make sure his car wouldn't flood in its usual parking spot the day before, then another small percentage to dry out his shoes when he got home. "I'm fine," he said, tucking his hands into his slacks. "I've done so many memory drills I could fuel the whole city for a day."

"Sure, it's only thirty percent of your life force." Laurie's attempt at a joke faltered on the final word. Henley answered before he could stop himself.

"Thirty percent of what I'm capable of," he corrected. "A mage's life force isn't under threat until at least a single seventy-percent cast. Even then, full recovery is possible with enough rest and—"

Laurie's eyes had glazed over, and Charlie was watching him with a frown. A warm flush crawled up Henley's hairline and added to his general sense of discomfort. "Sorry. Sometimes I open my mouth and my father comes out."

Charlie waved a hand between Henley and the soaked environment. "Why don't you skip the theory and get to the practical? Garage is closed, but you and Laurie have somewhere to be."

"And I'd really like to get coffee before I have to log in to work," Henley agreed. "Assuming I can get anywhere, of course. Are you ready, Laurie? Try it in two pushes. Picture the drain as clogged with leaves and trash as you can, then the water surging through it to shove all of that out of the way. Then do it again. Your first cast will probably break everything loose."

"Okay." She held her elbows tight to her body and raised her hands. Henley's body ached in sympathy with the tension she held in her thin frame. A few deep breaths that lifted her shoulders settled her nerves.

Leave it to a single mom to keep her head straight when it matters. The energy around the trio shifted, twisting as it was pulled, and Laurie began her spell.

"Five percent, *Clear Drain*. Get all that mess out of the way and let the water go where it should go."

Henley preferred a more disciplined casting, but the sense of Laurie's magic wobbled out from the group and the water surged. Floating leaves spun away from the drain under the influence of frothing bubbles, catching on fragments of mulch that had washed out of the flower beds tucked against the apartment building.

"Good," he said. "You've started the process. One more time."

Laurie chewed on her lower lip. "I need another memory. Um..."

"My dog's name is Jover," Charlie offered. "Schnauzer. Likes to take up half the sofa when I want to watch the game. He'll take your fingers off if you don't put his food down fast enough."

Laurie's breath caught with a soft laugh. She closed her eyes, then repeated the spell. When her magic rushed into the water again, the debris blocking the drain broke free, and a whirlpool spiraled out from the center of the parking lot. Henley nodded with approval. Charlie patted Laurie's shoulder hard enough to make her stumble.

"Very clean," Henley said. "Charlie and I can take it from here if you want to head to work." Her face had lost a little color. Tiny creases tightened the corners of her eyes. Henley leaned closer to examine her pupils. "Make sure you get something to eat if you feel lightheaded."

"I will. Let me know if there's anything else I can do to help." She gave the men a smile before she hurried down the dry stretch of sidewalk. Henley watched her splash across the submerged crosswalk before he glanced back at Charlie.

"I didn't know you had a dog."

The mechanic met his stare. "I don't, but she won't remember it now and it served a purpose. Listen, I know ten percent is a drop in the bucket for you, but thirty is substantial. You sure you're gonna be alright? You don't have to keep up appearances for an old man like me."

"You have a responsibility to the mage community," the memory of Henley's father lectured, the stern voice dragging across his nerves with the grace of a rusted nail. *"You must be an example. Those with less training or strength will look to you for guidance. Mind your words and your bearing."*

"I'm fine, really," Henley said. "I've been doing exercises all week to balance my energy, and I've stopped using small spells as much as possible. I promise." He raised his hands. "My family deals in public shame if anyone related to us overextends themselves. If I do anything to impair my ability to help if something really bad happens, the entire Gulf Coast Mage Council will hear about it. I'm exercising all due caution."

A gust of wind blasted the pair with a burst of fresh rain, forcing a retreat into the protective hall that led between two blocks of apartments. Charlie turned his frustrated stare in the direction of the offending breeze.

"Fine. Go on with what you need to do, then. I can manage the spell to keep things clear of the drain. You really gonna go get coffee in this weather?"

"Even if it takes another five hundred percent," Henley said with a nod. "I haven't had coffee for three days. I'm miserable. Besides, the news says Westheimer is mostly clear, and I can make it without hitting high water as long as I stick to the feeder roads on the beltway."

"Suit yourself. Drive safe."

They parted ways. Henley left Charlie behind as he ducked through the open hallway, then skirted the community mailboxes on his way to the back of the complex. The overhang ended long before his destination. The need to conserve his magic and his lack of foresight had the rain soaking through his clothes as soon as he was in the open.

Next time, umbrella. His short black hair tangled around his fingers as he raked the strands out of his face. Beyond the wrought iron fence that surrounded the complex, shaded by the heavy branches of oak trees twice his age, the water level of the drainage ditch threatened to exceed its banks. Overflow from the parking lot poured into the channel to add insult to injury. Half a mile of apartments, townhomes, and retail centers stood ready to flood if the water continued to rise.

He curled his hands around the cold bars of the fence. The road that bordered the eastern side of the complex was just within view. A small bridge passed over the rushing water, the concrete supports obscured in part by broken branches and tangled blackberry vines.

More out of sight beneath the surface, for sure. The breath he drew into his lungs was thick with summer heat, familiar and wild. He fixed his eyes on the bridge and opened himself up to the invisible world. The magic uncurled around him, visible to the caster, glittering in strands of energy that sparked when they encountered the natural paths of magic in his environment.

The existing ley lines were too dangerous to be touched. Instead, he sorted through his memories, seeking an appropriate offering. Thirty percent required an intense memory, or one with all sensory layers. Just as he now noticed the weight of the humid air, he had taken note of every piece of his surroundings for the past twenty years. He chose the memory of a traffic jam on a busy afternoon, adding the scent of exhaust from a lumbering dump truck and the surge of adrenaline as an impatient sports car cut into his lane, almost clipping his front fender. The hard bounce of his palm against the horn. The brazen sound that followed. The shared look of resignation with the dump truck driver, both shaking their heads in wonder that someone could be so inconsiderate.

"Thirty percent," he said. "*Clear Passage.* Remove these obstacles from the path that water must take and prevent them from forming again." The bridge was one of five between him and the nearest reservoir. The bulk of his focus was on the first, but each successive structure received a touch of his intention. He visualized the water flowing without hesitation, the levels low enough to allow even a surge of drainage from the neighboring buildings. When the image was locked into his mind, he fused his magic to one of the glittering threads and set the memory free.

It disappeared, pulled from his mind by an invisible force that tasted of dry earth. Somewhere beyond the barrier between worlds, an Ethereal accepted the memory and offered magic in return. Raw power filtered into his body and simmered under his skin with an artificial fever. Henley didn't know what the elemental spirits wanted with his memories and he didn't care—the loss was negligible in comparison to the energy he received. He sent the magic out from himself. The branches and vines broke free of the bridge in a rush of water that had the drainage channel levels dropping within seconds.

With the release of the spell came renewed pain at the back of his skull. Rolling his head back and forth only softened the ache. Coffee would help—coffee and information from his preferred source. He left the fence and trudged through the rain back to his apartment. The no-slip stripes on the wet stairs caught under his shoes, and a patch of paint flaked away under his hand as he climbed to the second floor. A large moth had taken refuge near the ceiling of the second-floor landing. Henley filed each detail away for a future casting.

He paused at his door and dripped for a moment. Drying himself would take at least ten percent. His temples throbbed, and he sighed as he pushed open the door and reached for the towel he had left on a chair just inside. When he was less likely to make a mess in his entryway he stepped into the apartment, attention caught by the lit screen of the cell phone he had left on a small table. Three missed messages waited.

From "Work": *The Regency Creative Solutions office is closed for the rest of the week due to flooding. Please work on your projects as much as possible from home and we will keep you updated.* No surprises there. The laptop bag on the floor next to the chair had everything he needed to stay busy.

From "Dr. Yu": *Water in the street but not in the house. Can you get to work? Be careful on Memorial Drive.* The perfect middle child, the surgeon, the mother of the grandkids. Somehow, she still had the strength to worry about her older brother while she juggled school closings and the energy of his niece and nephew.

From "Dad": *Meeting at Kim Son restaurant at 5 p.m.* As if Henley were part of the older man's magical workforce. As if a graphic designer could do much for the struggling city. As if they were speaking.

The last message doubled the intensity of his headache. He left the phone where it was and threw his wet towel at the nearby closet that held his washer and dryer with unnecessary force. By the time he returned from changing into dry clothes, he had relaxed enough to pick up the towel and hang it on his drying rack—but not enough to answer the messages.

The sheltered walk from his apartment to the parking garage helped clear his head. His preparations the day before had kept the garage from flooding, and the way out and onto the street was clear. Rain or no rain, Houston was a big city, and people found ways to get to work. He was grateful for every mile he didn't have to test his black sedan's limits in the high water that pooled to the middle of the road. The rapid pulse of his windshield wipers added to the tension in his lower back as he focused on the road.

Fine Ground was tucked into the strangest corner of a trendy shopping center filled with boutique shops and expensive stationery stores. A parking garage separated it from the main avenue, and another backed it, framing the coffee house in shadow and concrete. The magical signature of the place called out across Henley's senses with a warped, dreamlike energy. Only moments passed before the familiar scent of coffee that spiraled out from the location seeped into his car.

What wasn't familiar about his favorite coffee shop was the shadow of black uniforms he could see through the window, gathered around the bar. The Observers, the local mage-police, didn't linger around small businesses. He parked and spared a moment to finally reply to his sister's message with one of his own. *Not flooded, working from home this week. Turn around, don't drown.* The city's mantra was an easy response. His father's message could wait.

With his responsibilities managed, Henley braced his hands on the steering wheel. "One percent, *Quiet Interruption.* I would like to enter, if your business is not private." The memory of what he'd eaten for breakfast was barely out of his mind when one of the black-coated figures inside turned to face the windows.

"Enter." The bare minimum of a response, curt, and the man's voice was sharp with annoyance. At Henley? Not likely. There was no way the Observers were displeased with the quality of the coffee.

Elryk, what have you gotten yourself into?

He timed his run from the car with a pause between gusts of rain. The pavement scraped under his feet as he darted from his curbside parking spot to the sheltered doors of the coffee shop. Heavy drops soaked through his shirt. The rough rug by the door didn't do much to gather the moisture that had puddled around the entrance, but he had other concerns as he was faced with the scrutiny of four Observers.

Fine Ground wrapped around him like a warm blanket. The dim lighting of the coffee shop was augmented by hanging Tiffany lamps that glowed gold. All the furniture was wood, with leather cushions. The old concert posters and mysterious relics on the walls had faded with time. In that comfortable environment the Observers were a jarring discord of faint hostility.

"Name and affiliation?" The demand came in the same voice that had permitted him to enter, spoken by a short man with graying hair.

"Henley Yu, Gulf Coast Mage Council." He tucked his keys and phone into his pockets to free his hands.

His questioner frowned. "Yu, as in the leader of the council?"

The stiffness of Henley's headache seeped into his smile. "My father. Is something wrong?"

"Nothing you need to concern yourself with."

The speaker turned back to the counter. One Observer had kept her eyes on the lanky, brown-skinned man wearing a black apron on the other side of the aged cedar bar. Elryk Seldriksen's thin frame could have used a couple of hamburgers, and Henley was never sure if the man was older or younger than forty. His habitual smile was nowhere to be seen.

"Are you going to let me get back to my business, or ask me more pointless questions?" Elryk knocked his knuckles on the counter. "I told you, I don't have anything to do with the magic failures. As you can see, there's nothing wrong with this area—nothing more than the usual issues with the leyline convergence. I don't need magic to make good coffee."

"No mage in their right mind sets up shop on a leyline crossing without reason," the lead officer replied. "We've had reports from this area that say the magic has gone in and out for the last three days."

"The rent's cheap, and I like the challenge of the twisted magic. Most of my customers are mages. What's the point of me making them miserable?" Elryk braced his palms on the wood. "You're wasting time here instead of finding real answers."

Maybe it was the tone his friend was using. Maybe it was the way the Observers stood, feet braced and ready for a fight. Maybe it was his headache or the rain. "Do I need to fill out a character statement?" Henley asked, earning himself the immediate attention of all four officers.

The leader turned at the question and narrowed his eyes at Henley. "Does the Gulf Coast Council usually interfere with Observer business? Think twice before swinging your father's weight around."

"I'm not the one who brought his name into this. I don't need the backing of the council to know that harassing private citizens with no proof of wrongdoing is against Observer regulations." Henley nodded in Elryk's direction. "Either you have a case to bring against him, or you don't. I'd like to get my coffee before the roads flood and I can't get home."

The officer bristled. One of the others leaned close to whisper something that made the man straighten his shoulders. "Fine. We're done here—but don't think we won't be watching." The last words were said with a significant stare at the coffee shop's owner. His threat delivered, the Observer led his group out into the rain, leaving Fine Ground drained of warmth for several minutes.

Henley stared after the dark coats until a groan of relief sounded behind the bar. "Damn, I'm lucky you showed up," Elryk said as he pulled a fresh cup from under the counter. "Thought they'd never leave. I appreciate it, but you don't need to get on their bad side for my sake."

"If questioning them gets me on their bad side, I'm not the problem." The vintage wood floor creaked under his feet as Henley crossed the room. He didn't need to make a specific request after three years of placing the same order at least five times a week. "Everything alright?"

"Most people don't have the confidence to bully the Observers out of a coffee shop." Elryk turned to the antique coffee urns against the back wall and tapped a spigot to send bubbling coffee pouring through the glass tubes and into the cup. "Eh? Oh, I'm fine, shop's fine. They're grasping at straws. They like to tangle me in things I've got no business in, since 'no mage in their right mind' would keep a shop on a leyline convergence." He closed the valve, caught the last drops of coffee in the cup, and then slid the drink across the counter. "Sorry to cause you trouble when I know you're not just here for coffee."

"I might be." Henley took a seat on one of the stools at the bar. The black coffee, darker and richer than anything he could find within five miles, was the perfect temperature for sipping. Even his headache couldn't linger when the warmth spread down his throat and into his chest. "I missed this more than I want to admit, but...I did want to see what you've heard."

"Hmm." Elryk braced his elbows on the counter. The room was still too cold. With an exhaled breath, he pushed the chill out and flooded the space with warmth. Henley averted his eyes from the wordless casting, the same way he ignored Elryk's pointed ears or the eyes that were more gold than brown. Keeping friends sometimes meant keeping their secrets. Normal magic didn't feel like it was being dragged from the fabric of the world. Elryk had the touch to do whatever he wanted, and Henley ignored that, too.

"The losses are accelerating," Elryk said as the temperature of the shop settled. "There have been more dead zones in the last three days than in the six before. France is being hit the hardest right now, but Guatemala had some strange activity last night. I'm not happy with how this particular episode is dragging out." He drummed fingertips stained with coffee grounds on the bar. "The magic will right itself in time. I can't give you anything more specific without breaking a dozen restrictions."

"It's fine. I appreciate anything you can tell me. I'd come to the same conclusion about the acceleration, but I can't get a feeling for what I should be doing next."

Elryk shrugged. "Helping as much as you can locally, I'd guess. What have you heard?"

"The council is organizing volunteers to help move the flood waters along in the worst-affected areas. We've all given up on stopping the rain." Henley sipped his coffee. "Dad wants me to report to his response group tonight. I can't think of anything I'd avoid more than working with him in person."

Elryk's chuckle made a sound like gravel in the back of his throat. "But you'll go anyway, won't you?"

"Of course. People need help, and I still have the energy to assist. I'm going to pretend I've never met him, though." The light tone of the conversation fell flat beneath the pounding of the rain. "Are you going to be alright here? You have plans if the water rises?"

"I may not like the water, but it won't kill me. Spend your care on yourself." Elryk looked to the rain-scoured windows, then back at his customer, lines of tension creasing around his eyes. "You need to be careful. There's something ugly in these storms."

The break in his relaxed demeanor sent a stab of unease through Henley. "How bad is this going to get?"

"Depends on who does what, and how fast. I can promise you that whatever happens, this mortal realm can only ride out the waves, helpless to the tide." Elryk gave him a tight smile. "It doesn't take a great man to do great deeds. Play nice with your father. If you feel the need, get you and yours to higher ground as fast as possible."

Henley didn't think Elryk was talking about the flooding. He gave the coffee man a slow nod. "I'll keep that in mind."

"I expect as much from you. Go on, don't risk the high water—coffee's on the house today."

Two

Apprehension

A world away from Henley and his saturated city, the rush hour frenzy of requested magic rattled through the Switchboard in a dizzy spiral of voices and cables snapping into receiving ports. The voices of the operators attending their panels rose and fell, a steady chorus free of panic. Magic flowed through the aging wooden building, surging from realms beyond, fed to mortals seeking power in exchange for memory. In pauses between calls, operators congregated around wooden desks, flirting or trading stories or taking bets on the next day's connections. A handful of clerks punched out reports on typewriters that clattered and rang with every return.

"Terminal G31, contact 77004, connecting three percent. 'Dry clothes.' Do they not have umbrellas in Houston?" Chief Operator Kittinger asked, pulling a plug from the bottom of the huge panel before him, jostling a small stack of detective dime novels with faded covers. They in turn upset the top-heavy cup of chewed pencils. He steadied it with his free hand out of habit as he punched the cable into the port labeled G31.

"Couldn't tell you, Kit. Feels like I've been getting nothing but rain-related calls for days. Do you think it's a hurricane?" Kelley's voice drifted from behind Kit where his relief was leaning against his desk, nursing a mug of coffee.

"Could be. It's the right time of year. We don't usually see so many requests for so long, though." Kit tilted his head, listening through his bulky headset as the request completed and sent a memory across his nose. It filled his sinuses with the scent of fresh laundry and the warmth of a blanket against his face. Then the sensations were gone, delivered to an Ethereal lord as payment for energy delivered through the cables. Kit pulled the plug and put it back into its home port on the bottom row, this time weaving the cord between a few crumpled balls of paper and a dirty plate from lunch.

A handful of operators carrying bowling bags eased past them and toward the big double doors at the front of the building. Kit waited until they had passed to turn in his seat, making sure not to catch the well-stretched, twisting cord of his headset on his chair. His long hair, a shade of pinkish-blond, was held in a bedraggled bun by a metal pin and wrapped with a length of the same cable plugged into his panel. The pin waved over the top of his head like an antenna.

"Aside from the rain, the requests aren't much busier than normal," he informed his relief. "You'll have a peaceful night. Have you made up your mind to ask that waitress out to dinner?" Long-fingered hands plucked at his simple working-man's shirt, doing a poor job of straightening the wrinkles from a day spent sitting. The shirt, like his pants and laced-up brown boots, was faded in color, threadbare, and fit loosely on Kit's underfed frame. Only his eyes were vivid: gleaming silver, metallic if he turned his head the right way, clear gray even in the worst light. He grinned, spinning his chair back and forth.

Kelley flushed. The other operator was taller than Kit's six foot one, trim and handsome, always neatly pressed with his long hair in an orderly braid over one shoulder. He hid his face as he sipped from his mug, his voice muffled.

"I'm still thinking about it. I don't know how she'd feel, with me being on the night shift." A request crackled through Kit's headset. The other man paused as Kit turned back to his panel and made three connections in quick succession. When Kit turned back to him, Kelley resumed his train of thought, both men accustomed to the constant interruptions. "What if I get transferred?"

"You won't get transferred. We need more operators here, not less, and I'd deny the Reassignment anyway. I'd have to teach someone else to handle my connections—can you imagine? I'm tired just thinking about it."

"Well, I appreciate the thought. Maybe I'll ask her to lunch. That's less serious than dinner, isn't it? Maybe she won't be as nervous."

"Are you worried about her being nervous, or you?" Kit laughed at him, the amusement softening the thin lines of his face. "Take her to that drugstore with the fancy soda fountain. Then it's just a drink and some conversation. She's going to think you aren't interested if you keep—"

Kit thought the sharp noise that broke his thought was an incoming connection at first, before his mind caught up with the tone. He fell silent and held his slender body still. Across the large, open room, separated by several rows of identical desks, another operator was on his feet.

"I don't have enough magic—I can't make the connection!"

The operator's voice was raw, frayed with effort and strain. On the edge of failure, Kole yanked cords from his panel and stabbed them back into new ports, the order haphazard and erratic. Chairs grated backward across the worn wood floor. One by one, the voices of his fellow operators died as they ended their connections and rose to watch with sick expressions. The quieter the open room became, the more the air filled with tension.

Kit ripped off his headset and vaulted out of his chair, dislodging dried-up pens, slips of paper, and a few empty boxes of chips from the cluttered surface of his desk. His steps added to the wear on the thin carpet in the aisles as he cut through three rows of panels, ducking between onlookers who scattered like dried leaves.

"How much do you need?"

His voice broke through the panic. Kole threw a pleading look over his shoulder. The operator was an older man with stooped shoulders and calloused hands, experienced enough to know how to handle his own emergencies until they were *real* emergencies.

"One hundred sixty-five percent, Chief." The room went cold, whispers of fear hovering in the air. "It's the Ben Taub emergency room! There's been a major accident, I've got multiple doctors requesting—"

"Kelley, watch my panel," Kit called over his shoulder, sliding into place next to Kole. "Is anyone else missing connections?" A chorus of negative replies answered. "Kassim, get me ten percent on a long cable. I need twenty percent in small connections, all of you—give me everything you have! Kole, give me your cutters."

The operator's face went white as a hiss of breath rose throughout the room. The other operators were in motion, but everyone stared in Kit's direction at his words. He threw out an impatient hand, making grasping motions. "Come on!"

"You're insane, splitting the flow now," Kole said, but he obeyed, offering out the wire cutters with their well-worn handles. They were heavier than Kit's, but his were buried at his panel under a month's worth of take-out dishes and crumpled paper.

"Gather the other cables as they come in. We'll fix it after the casting," Kit replied. He looked over Kole's panel and spotted the thick cable where it had been plugged into the connection. The light next to the port glowed the red of "insufficiency" before Kit snatched it with long fingers, killing the connection completely. The pulse of raw magic throbbed against his fingers, turning his skin fever hot.

"Forty seconds!"

Kit ignored the call. With a ruthless twist of his wrist, he tore off the head of the cable and split the inner wires apart. The copper frayed under his hands into a starburst. "Kassim?"

"Here!" Kassim shoved a thinner cable into Kit's view. He snatched it and gave it the same treatment, binding it to several of the first cable's strands. The operators held out more cables for him, but they were thin and weak in the face of the magic he needed. He kept his expression still and serene as his heart pounded. Every small cable took precious seconds to strip and add into the feed. Through the burning wires, he heard the voices of the casters, building their spells. Panic edged the words as they weren't met with the energy they expected. "Kole, prep me a new head."

The other operator fumbled in his drawer. Kit twisted and twined copper wire in his fingers, making each little connection feed into the larger. The Switchboard didn't have cables thick enough to transfer one hundred sixty-five percent in one cast, but Kole's panel could usually make the connection in smaller lines. Kit's theft from the other panels was ruthless.

He grabbed the new connector head as it was offered. His fingers had been pricked in several places by the wire, and they smeared blood on the copper. Given that Kit's soul was bound to the Switchboard, the blood was only going to help.

"Ten seconds!" Whoever was counting down yelled out with a shaking, high-pitched voice. Kit fed the wires into the head one by one, precise, disciplined, patient, and hyper-focused by adrenaline. The rising voices of the substation faded from his ears. The last wire fit into place, and he twisted the head. A dozen threads of energy surged into one.

"What's the terminal?"

"F21!"

Kit shoved Kole out of his way and jumped onto the man's chair. It rolled under his feet, and Kit windmilled his arms to catch his balance before several hands braced his legs. "More cable! It's too short!" he cried. A flurry of movement met his words. The clustered bodies surged, hauling the tangled cables. Furniture groaned as they dragged entire desks closer. With a cry of triumph, Kit stabbed the connector head into the terminal labeled "F21." The port light lit up red, then orange, then yellow, then a brilliant green. With his hand on the cable, Kit could hear the voice of the healing doctor on the other side, the focus of half a dozen other mages.

"I give myself to this working and bind my blood to the blood of the fallen. Let light and spirit fill their veins, let the threads of fate be rebound."

In awe, the operators stared as the energy poured through the cable, a major casting even on a busy day. A full minute passed before the transfer was complete. Operators drifted off one at a time as they were called to make their own connections; those remaining were spellbound by the experience. Kit stared at the glowing green light, licking the blood from his fingers. The glow finally died.

"What happened?" Kit asked, accepting Kole's help getting down from the stool. Kole looked like Kit's desk: worn and in a natural state of disarray.

"I reached for the feeder connection and the cables were dead," the other operator answered, shaking his head. "I tried to borrow from others nearby and they came up empty, too. I could feel the void in the wires. It was cold. With the demand from the storms, the incoming magic is so thin. If we've lost that connection . . ."

"We'll find other connections," Kit replied as he began dismantling the cables he had bound together. They came apart in chunks, but the ends had to be cut apart, the copper fused together by the heavy magic expenditure. "The Ethereals will never stop wanting to trade with the Actuality. What else can we do? We made it. We always make it. What a story, right? One sixty-five on a split feed! I haven't seen one of those in a while."

"I never would have tried a splice in the middle of a major cast," Kole replied, shaking his head. "Without core connecters? Thank heavens your fingers are quick enough!"

"My fingers are always at your disposal." Kit grinned and handed off the smaller cables to their operators to be fixed. Kole's was the last, the usual head replaced with a deft twist of Kit's wrist. Kole took it back and returned it to its dormant position. With his hands suddenly empty, Kit gave his fingers a rueful look. "They're a mess now, though. No good work without consequences. Is everyone else alright? No other new problems?" The operators back at their desks answered in a chorus of negative replies, bringing a smile to Kit's lips.

"Alright. Good work everyone, that was exciting but efficient. I'll put in the report." He patted Kole on the shoulder as he returned to his panel. The small desk was surmounted by a huge interface with hundreds of labeled connection ports, four times the number on any other panel in the room. Cables crossed all over it, some resting in the grounding ports on the bottom rows, several connected to points across the board. The grounding ports were almost hidden behind the general mess, but his connections were pristine, clear, and perfect, if he did say so himself.

Careful of the order, Kit pulled the connections free and lined them back up in their home terminals. The messy surface caused him to debate sweeping the whole pile into the trash, but he never knew when he'd need something from the clutter.

"Anything you need connected while you report, Kit?"

"Nope, thanks, Kelley." Kit gave his relief a smile. "Just about done here, are you ready?"

Kelley nodded as he took his seat at the desk behind Kit's. Kelley's panel held a clean, steaming mug of coffee, not a cold mug aged with dark stains. A small stack of papers rested at his right elbow. The remaining surface was immaculate.

"Ready. Have a good night, Kit."

"You too. And—pick up."

"Got it."

A quarter of Kit's incoming requests went silent as they lit up Kelley's board, the remaining dispersed to other panels nearby. Kit unlocked his silver panel key from the center of his terminal and the panel went dark. Hanging the key's cold chain around his neck, Kit headed out of the open room and down the front hall.

Switchboard Substation No. 28 was an empty place outside of the main Switchboard room, not frequented by visitors outside of the operators. Enough magic had washed the nails and timbers to make the place pulse with lingering energy. The building was old and the walls sagged, but Kit felt the weight of its reverence as he walked.

When he passed the main doors, a small office waited in the foyer. The desk in that area did not contain a panel, but it held a mug just as stained as Kit's and a pair of propped-up boots. The stocky young Shield officer on guard duty grinned at Kit over the top edge of his newspaper as he leaned back in his chair.

"Heading out, Chief?"

"I am, Sandoval. We've lost another connection, though. Nearly didn't make a one hundred sixty-five percent connection."

"Surprised you can make that kind of connection on any day," the Shield replied, dropping his feet to the floor and straightening in his chair. Sandoval folded the paper to keep his place, and the light caught on the gold buttons of his black patrol uniform shirt, tucked into black slacks. Newsprint smudged his pale fingers. He'd smeared a streak of gray across his button nose. "That's too much for a mortal, isn't it?"

"I think I heard seven mages total. With the storms, we're seeing more mages take risks, but this group was being careful." Kit stepped closer to the desk as Sandoval rummaged in the drawers. "I hope the Order gets this under control soon."

"You know we will, Chief. Can't keep the Between together if the connections keep falling apart." Sandoval produced a folded diagram of the substation panels, crumpled around the corners, and spread it on his desk. "Which connection is it, then?"

"He was feeding into F21, so . . . here." Kit tapped a position on the layout. For a moment the pair of them stared at the multitude of other small marks littering the paper.

"How many more this week?"

"Just this one from our station," Sandoval reassured him, scribbling a circle on the spot with a chewed pencil. "It seems like a mess, but there's hundreds of connections in every substation, you know? These are only a handful of what's really available."

"What about Gainesville? And Durango?"

Sandoval's eyebrows drooped like the ears of a chastised puppy. "Come on now, Chief. We're doing the best we can. Last thing we need is to have you disappointed in us, too. Just be patient a while longer, yeah?"

"I know, I know, I'm sorry." Kit raised his hands, gathered sleeves puffing around his elbows. "It's nerve-wracking, and everyone is frightened. Can you give me anything to help calm the others?"

"Well . . ." Sandoval scratched his chin, fingers making a rough sound against his stubble. His brown eyes lingered on the paper and its scribbled marks, a disquieting reminder that all was not well in the Between. "Don't let this get too far, alright? I'm not supposed to be talking about it without official backing from Headquarters, but I heard Pleasanton came back online yesterday. The higher-ups are really fighting to get things under control."

"That's amazing." The tension left Kit's shoulders, releasing some of the ache in the back of his neck. "Thank you. I'll keep it quiet aside from those who need to hear it. I don't doubt the Shields, but it's a nightmare for us operators."

"I know. And I know you're doing your best, too." The officer smiled, settling back in his chair once more. "Go home and get some rest. I'll send in the report and get us added to the map."

"Thanks, San. I hope I won't have any other lost connections for you to report."

"All in a day's work," the Shield replied, tugging his uniform straight before settling his feet back on the desk. "See you in the morning."

"Good night."

Kit left the foyer and stepped onto the wide platform deck in front of Substation No. 28. The Between opened up before him. To either side, he saw nothing but miles and miles of flat building faces. Above him, layers of storefronts and blocky buildings stretched up to the heavens. Below him, the same shapes, extending under his feet into infinity. To all sides, the world was limitless.

Only the space in front of him was different. Between him and gray nothingness, hundreds of Fetters floated in every direction, following currents of gravity that pushed them into a semblance of order. Individuals drifted past, as well as small clusters of people and larger carts carrying crates and small businesses. The sound of voices struck him, loud after the murmur of whispered connections in the substation. The chime of traffic bells and the bray of food sellers produced a familiar cacophony and a tightness in his chest.

High above him—always high above him, no matter where he stood—floated the glowing beacon of Paradise. It cast the brightest light in all the Between. Kit watched as dozens of individuals and a few larger trollies drifted to and from the glittering platform. If he listened hard enough, he could hear laughter, jaunty music, and the shower of winning coins.

Smiling, Kit walked to the edge of the platform and let himself fall backward into the flow. The moment his feet left the stained wood planks, his body became weightless. As he dropped, he flitted between passersby, turning his shoulders and kicking his legs just enough to guide his passage and keep himself in motion. The Between was a dim place, and lamps glowed as the pervasive gray darkened into evening. As he fell, he zipped through fragments of conversation, music, and sounds of industry. The ever-present din was quieting in the twilight hours.

A familiar red awning pulled him up short. Ignoring a disgruntled scolding from the Fetters who had been following close on his heels, Kit darted to the side, catching the edge of the floating cart and dropping down on its small platform. Gravity returned. Several other patrons occupied the stools lined up at the counter. From the tiny kitchen crammed with cookware, steaming pots, and jars of supplies, a small toad of a man beamed.

"Chief Operator Kit! Off duty? You must try my spaetzle. I've just perfected the texture." The chef wore a shirt with so many colors Kit struggled to look him in the eye.

"Half of the Between is afraid the world is ending, and you're making new dishes. Is that German?" Kit asked, his tone light. The covert gazes of the other patrons were heavy on his shoulders. He didn't recognize any faces, but they recognized his title and the key around his neck.

"German, yes." The chef shoved a small clay tasting bowl under Kit's nose, full of small pasta and a thick brown gravy. "Has the world ended today? Did I miss it?"

"You don't miss anything, Noodle." Kit slurped the spaetzle out of the dish, skeptical until the warmth rested on the back of his tongue. "Mmm. That's good. You're happy with it?"

"Happy enough to feed it to you! Have a seat, I'll make you up a bowl."

Kit sat. As Noodle worked, the other patrons went back to their conversations, eventually leaving a few coins on the counter and drifting off. Noodle's back was still turned as he chopped mushrooms. His movements slowed, losing some of their bustle.

"Are you faking that smile, Chief Operator?"

"A little." Kit stared down into his empty tasting bowl. The oil from the gravy clung to the sides, pooling in the bottom. "It's been a very trying time lately, with the erratic connections. My people are tired."

"It's not your job to fix everything, you know." Noodle scraped the bottom of one of his big pots with a metal ladle. "The Between will right itself. It always has."

Kit's stomach twisted. The smell of pasta was suddenly so strong in his nose he couldn't breathe. "If it does, we won't be here anymore."

"Part of us will be, and I'll still be cooking. Can't imagine you'll ever start, so we'll meet again regardless!"

With a forced laugh, Kit spun the little bowl on the counter and nodded. "That's true. Your food is so much better than mine, anyway. How is the ramen coming?"

"You know, I thought the marinara was difficult, but getting depth in the ramen broth is even worse. Worse!" Noodle dumped a ladle of spaetzle into a bowl, then a different ladle of gravy. With a wooden lid slapped onto the ceramic, and after he wrapped it in a square of cut flour sack, the meal was safe for transport. Noodle hoisted himself up onto a step stool and slid the bundle across the counter.

"I see you fretting, Chief Operator Kittinger." Noodle had kind, if beady, eyes. "We don't decide our Purpose or our lifetime. Make the best of what you have, hmm? You can worry yourself to death, or face every day like a roaring lion. Come on! Let me hear you roar!"

Kit twitched his lips. With both hands on the counter, he pushed himself up and leaned forward.

"Roar," he said in the chef's face, and Noodle cackled.

"Good enough! Go home and get some rest. Make sure you eat all your dinner—and bring those dishes back to me someday."

"I promise I'll bring you a box next time I see you."

"Heard that before. I'll put it on your tab."

Kit lifted the bundle in one hand. The other he used to stroke the counter, feeling the marks of decades of customers scratched into the wood. How many years had he spent among them? For a moment, the breath was tight in his chest.

Before he could lose himself, he pushed away from the cart. Noodle waved, then turned back to his stove. Within a few minutes, Kit could barely see the awning in the steady stream of traffic. Holding the spaetzle to his chest, he resumed his journey, lost in thought until he arrived at a familiar balcony.

His apartment was small. Every home was, in the Between. They had infinite space but infinite Fetters to share it with; his neighbors were close enough for him to hear their voices when they were home. Kit had been lucky to secure a spot between Fetters who worked at night. Wood planks creaked on the tiny porch as he reached for his door handle. The door stuck. He shoved his shoulder into it out of habit. The inside was dark and silent.

"I'm home," he called out, hurrying to put the spaetzle down on his kitchen table and climb onto his bed. The front room was half-kitchen and half-bedroom, with his bed wedged into the space between the front and bathroom walls. The bed was under a window, and that was where Kit reached. He pulled the small potted plant into his arms, a soft smile creasing his cheeks.

"A little dark, huh?" he asked, turning the pot this way and that. The round, broad leaves of his little friend were a bit wilted. Awkward, he scooted off the bed and carried the plant to the small table by the front door, where a lamp waited next to a miniature version of his Switchboard panel. When the pulled cord produced a bright pocket of light, he set the plant down and fussed until it seemed to be in the best position.

"That should help."

He traced his fingertips across one leaf for a moment before he sighed and turned back to the bundle. *We don't decide our Purpose.* Noodle's words echoed in his mind, mingling with his sense of unease.

Kit left the spaetzle where it was and went back to his bed. His boots thudded against the floor as he unlaced and kicked them off, exposing his threadbare socks to the world. The blankets were as old and as worn, his flattened extra pillow not providing much solace as he clutched it against his chest.

"I'm just tired," he said to the ceiling, and squeezed his eyes shut. His ears still rang with requests for connections, the din of a full day's work. He began his nightly routine, attempting to recall every request from morning until evening. With each connection, his eyes grew heavier, until the words trailed off in his mind.

"Clear Passage, terminal C12, contact 77079, connection at thirty percent. 'Remove these obstacles . . .'"

Three

Escape

Kit faced the next morning in better spirits. He darted through the rush hour traffic with light steps and kicks off convenient trolleys, greeting faces he recognized, waving to others who called out to the Chief Operator as he passed. The murky gray of the Between was shifting into the muted glow that signified the beginning of "day." Traffic made up of floating people and drifting trolleys picked up with the morning rush, accompanied by a steady din of voices as Fetters got to work. Weren't his concerns so very small? The Between was a massive place, with thousands of connections and amazing residents who stood ready to protect their home. Nothing so dramatic as the end of the world disturbed its normalcy.

He smiled as he settled on the substation platform, walking in with the other operators on the morning shift. They said their greetings, a few lingering worries in their eyes, but without the whispering panic Kit feared. Sandoval gave him a small salute from his desk. Inside the substation, the Switchboard hummed along, the air throbbing with magic and the burbling hum of voices. It was a far cry from the devastation his imagination could conjure.

"Good morning, Kelley," he said to his counterpart after weaving his way through the tight-packed rows of Switchboard panels. Lifting the heavy silver key from around his neck, he lined it up with the keyhole and gave it a firm turn. His panel glowed to life, every connection registering dormant until he took over from his backups. "Anything interesting happen last night?"

The other man yawned, running a hand over his hair. "Kinney lost that bet about the Rotterdam connections. He'll have to make cookies for No. 11 next week, but that's about it. Think he'll bring any for us?"

"If he knows what's good for him!" Kit laughed, hunting around on his desk. Three piles of notes and papers hid his forlorn tea mug, still half-full from the day before. "I'll be right back."

Kelley waved and went back to his connections as a new request came through. The smile stayed on Kit's lips as he walked to the small kitchen, easing his way between pairs of operators discussing the night's work and changing shifts. There was a line against the faded paneled wall for the coffee pot, but not the tea kettle. Kit dumped out his cold tea in the tiny sink, sniffed the mug, and shrugged before pouring a new cup. Someone had left a basket of muffins on the counter.

The Chief Operator eyed the basket, considering the previous day's events and his resident Shield's determined words. The muffins were still steaming, and the scent of lemon and poppy seed filled the kitchen. Sandoval loved baked goods. Kit plucked one from the basket and walked around the corner to the foyer office. His shoulders bumped against those of one of his fellows. His neck began to ache with pressure, and a sense of something amiss rose in the back of his mind. *Did I forget something? An appointment?* He didn't have appointments unless they were with the High Spirits, or the rare occasion he was forced to retreat to Paradise. He lifted the muffin, giving first it, then his tea mug, a sniff. Both were bright with the scent of citrus. Three more strides of faded carpet passed under his feet before he slowed. It had been several minutes since an operator entered the substation, and there were too many people in the substation entrance.

The press of bodies and black police uniforms drew him up short before he crossed the threshold to the front area. They clogged the foyer and beyond, crowding onto the substation's landing platform. He had never seen so many Shields in one place if there wasn't a parade. They hadn't been there when he arrived. No one was looking in his direction, giving him time to take note of their serious faces and the way they clustered together. One of them wore a trench coat over his uniform with a pair of winged collar pins. Kit had never seen the Captain of the Order at No. 28.

Where is Sandoval? He hadn't seen any of these officers in recent memory. Every one of them was armed with a baton, and their coats were open to display their service pistols. Firearms! In the Between! He leaned close to listen as the Captain's commanding voice rose above the others.

"Move quickly. The less time we take here the easier it will be to control. Take the operators to Headquarters for questioning; tell them we're investigating the outages." The Captain was taller than most of the other Shields by several inches, his short blond hair gleaming in the humming electric lights. He turned once his orders had been delivered, blue eyes piercing the officer at his elbow, restrained by two of their peers. "As for you, Major Sharaz, give me one reason I shouldn't open a portal and feed you to the Ethereals."

Sharaz had styled his hair to fall in an attractive wave over his eye, but the style couldn't hide the raw apprehension on his face. "He wasn't going to cooperate, Captain Shaw. A few more minutes and he'd have made a real scene."

The response did nothing to alleviate Shaw's disapproval. Kit had always liked that about Shaw; the man took no nonsense from anyone. "Half a dozen Shields at your back, and you chose violence over restraint? You allowed your *impatience* greater respect than the life of one of our brothers."

Everyone else on the scene shifted away from Sharaz as Shaw's voice rose to a thunder. The offending officer had gone pale and stammered over his defense. "He wasn't—I thought—"

"Do you understand why we are here, Major?" The Captain spread his arms out to his sides, indicating the clustered Shields crowding the substation lobby. "What we do now, we do for all Fetters, not just the Order or those who actively participate in our work. That young man was an innocent caught in your sights, and now his life is gone, just like that." Leather gloves muffled the snap of his fingers. "He spent his entire life in service, and now he will never know freedom. That is what you have *taken* from him, Major. He was worth ten of you on his worst day."

Sharaz took the smartest option available to him and gave a stiff nod. "I understand Captain. My behavior is inexcusable."

"You may deliver your apologies to officer Sandoval's corpse." Shaw held Sharaz's eyes with his icy gaze for a long moment before he took a deep breath. The mug in Kit's hand listed to the side, the tea dangerously close to spilling. Shaw jerked his head at the officers who held Sharaz's arms. "Take his badge and secure him at headquarters."

"Yes, Captain."

The floor by Shaw's boots was wet and red. Kit followed the line of liquid with his eyes to the small desk area and saw a man's hand dangling from the chair. Sandoval's shape sagged limply to one side. Shaw removed his peaked uniform cap and bowed his head. "You will not be forgotten," he said, without the poison he had reserved for Sharaz. He took the folded newspaper from Sandoval's desk and raised his voice. "Proceed, *without* further casualties."

Kit's heart was beating too fast. Shields crowded around Sandoval's body, their faces grim as they covered the lifeless form in a blanket. More fabric soaked up the blood behind the Shield's desk. The smell reached him: heavy, metallic, and sickening.

Shaw replaced his hat and turned his back on the cleanup efforts. He opened one gloved hand and held out a palm full of clear gemstones to a female officer with a long, narrow nose. Her expression was sour, a perpetual state that went with her constant sniffling. The gems were faded to Kit's awareness, dull and empty of magic. For the moment. "Shemi, you're in charge of collection. Be careful when handling the raw energy. If it doesn't feed properly into the stones, back away and ask for support. I don't want any more incidents." He continued after she nodded. "We need to establish a procedure for future substations."

Kit's palms were slick with sweat. With his elbow, he lowered the bar that secured the door from the inside. When he looked over his shoulder, he saw old friends milling about, most of them unathletic. The big room was cramped with shift change, half of the occupants tired from a full shift, half still waking up. They would be sheep to the slaughter against the well-trained Shields.

"Fire," he whispered, unable to put force behind the word as his head spun. A staccato drumbeat pounded in his head, driving him to flee. He took another breath, then yelled at the top of his lungs, the pitch of his voice rising as he got it out. "FIRE! Everyone, take your keys and go to the back exit! Hurry! Drop all your connections and relocate to No. 18! FIRE!"

Fires weren't uncommon in the Between. The buildings were crammed too close together, and the wood that formed most of the construction burned easily. There had never been a fire at a Switchboard substation, but the operators didn't question him. Hands flashed as they yanked their keys from their panels, ripped off headsets, and began running for the rear of the building.

Something heavy hit the door behind him. With a yelp, Kit tossed the muffin aside and grabbed for the nearest panel desk, hooking his free hand around a table leg and dragging it in front of the door. The desk wasn't heavy enough to stop anyone for long, and he stumbled over the trailing cables as he started to run. The Shields began slamming into the door as the operators streamed out of the substation.

He had just rounded the corner of his row when the door burst open. "Waffle noodle *biscuit* muffin," he swore, and ducked under someone else's panel. The desk was too open and it was no place to hide, but he pulled the chair in front of him. From his position he could see his panel, tantalizingly close, his silver key gleaming brightly in the hanging overhead lamps.

"Seal the exits!" the Captain ordered. He didn't sound as smooth anymore. "Find any operator still in the building. This isn't a complete loss yet!"

Kit's hand shook and tea sloshed over his knuckles. He smothered a hiss of pain against his raised knees. Heavy boots stomped through the area, the floor vibrating under their weight as they checked every station. There were a hundred panels in the substation, divided into five rows. Kit's panel was close to the back wall.

His mind flashed back to the gems in the Captain's hand. *We need to establish a procedure for the other substations*, Shaw had said. Kit drew a deep breath.

When the first officer came close, he shoved the chair back, straight into the man's legs. The Shield yelled and went down in a heap. Kit sprang out of his hiding place, tossing his mug at the woman following the fallen officer. She screamed as the hot tea splashed across her face. With their chaos granting him a few precious seconds, Kit sprinted down the row to his panel.

The key ejected easily when he yanked on its chain. The panel itself was more difficult. From above, thick cords trailed down to his station, feeding the others around him. The magic was stronger. More vulnerable. Thousands of threads glittered at the edge of his vision, near-invisible lines connecting every panel, every object, stretching out of every door and window. He was panting, and he couldn't hear anything. The distance seemed too far to cross as Kit climbed up onto his panel and wrapped his arms around the cables. Then he kicked off his desk and fell backward, tearing all the cables down with him.

The Switchboard shuddered and went dark. Not just Substation No. 28. The *entire* Switchboard. A warped tear in the fabric of the world split open where the magic bled into the room, flickering with views of strange places and people he had never seen.

Kit barked a hysterical laugh as the Shields dissolved into confusion. The magic rippled through the air, bleeding into the Between in twisting waves. It burned where he touched it, and cooled and healed and caused him incredible pain.

"Stop the Chief Operator!"

The magic beckoned. Kit rolled to his feet and threw himself blindly into the flow.

Four

Something in the Cabinet

Late in the evening, Henley made his way home through pounding rain, exhaustion dragging down his shoulders. The quick meal the volunteers had grabbed at the restaurant wasn't enough to restore his energy after hours of channeling heavy percentages and clearing more drains. *At least Dad was working too hard to make polite conversation.* He'd only seen the elder Yu once before he'd gotten to work.

Traffic flowed at a crawl. Too many cars still filled the streets with those too stubborn to believe they could be stopped by the rain. The big pickup trucks so beloved by Texas's population swamped his sedan as they mowed through the water. Henley was forced to the highest center lanes. Seven stoplights were flashing red as he eased through traffic. They and the snail's pace added two hours to his drive.

By the time he reached the apartment his shoulders and neck ached, and the morning's coffee felt far away. The safest parking spaces in his apartment complex were crowded with those who had returned home early or been smart enough to not leave in the first place. There was no subtle spell to shove the cars aside and give him a decent spot. Henley was forced to park on the other side of the complex in what he hoped was a safe area, then trudge through the rain to the main building as the wind fought him for his umbrella. His phone vibrated with endless group messages from family and another text from his father that he didn't want to read.

Step after step brought him to the glass doors, damp slacks plastered to his legs. Rainwater drenched the carpet at the entrance. A few other residents nodded as Henley passed, but conversation was sparse as he took the elevator instead of his usual stairs. His keys slipped from his fingers once before he could unlock his apartment and step into darkness, the only light coming from the occasional flash of lightning through the balcony door. He dumped his bag by the door and toed off his shoes, promising himself that he would put them away later. That was the limit of his available energy. *Maybe I'll watch TV and—*

Did something just move in the kitchen?

From the door, he had line of sight down the hall, past the study, and into the kitchen and living room. He had no pets. There was no reason something should be rolling across the countertops, especially with the clean state he had left them in that morning. Henley didn't hit the light as he eased forward. The umbrella was still in his hand, long enough to be useful at that moment. Each step was a slow creep as he hunted for an intruder.

The tall aluminum cylinder that held his wooden spoons and spatulas lay on its side, with the utensils scattered in disarray across the gray-speckled granite. As he watched, the cylinder rolled again, amplifying the sense of wrongness. The canister was recently disturbed. One of his lower cabinets was cracked open.

Henley took another step. Another. Adrenaline surged in his veins, warring with the panic that clenched his stomach. He stood before the cabinet door and braced himself, drawing a few unsteady breaths. A foreign, acrid scent in the air burned his nostrils. Within the cabinet, small shifts of movement jostled his glass casserole dishes.

Why now? Is it someone escaping the storm? Is it some drug addict looking for money? Am I about to be a crime statistic? Wild thoughts spun through his head, chaotic even for a man trained to discipline his mind. The intricate wards he had spent days placing around his home no longer tingled across his arms. Had he made an enemy of another mage?

What could they possibly want or gain from breaking into Henley's apartment?

Whatever had intruded on the apartment was big—enough to be dangerous. Enough to cause serious injury. Henley didn't like pain. He liked being afraid even less.

With a shaking hand, he reached out to curl his fingers around the edge of the cabinet door. Then he yanked it open and stabbed his umbrella into the space, flinching at the screech he summoned from the dark interior.

"STOP! STOP, I'm not going with you, I'm not going, I'll fight you, I'll bite your face—"

The threats were comical, but the voice was flustered with panic. Henley pressed back against the island. The light over the sink snapped on when he fumbled for the switch with one hand. The skinny figure somehow wedged into his cabinet on top of the pots and pans stared up at him with wild, pale eyes.

"I won't go back," the stranger cried, hands up to protect himself. "I won't participate in whatever you're doing!"

"Get *out* of my cabinet right now," Henley ordered, breathing hard, his body tense and waiting for his insane visitor to act with unexpected violence. "Or I'll call the police. Who the hell are you?"

The intruder stared at him, then cast a wild look around the apartment—what he could see of it from his position. "Are you alone?" he asked, and Henley gritted his teeth.

"Of course I'm alone, this is *my apartment* and no one else lives here. Including you." He pulled his phone out of his pocket. "Five seconds before I call the police."

"Alright, alright! I'm sorry, I'm coming, please don't call anyone."

There was more of him than Henley expected when the intruder crawled out of the cabinet. He had long limbs and a slender, lanky figure. He was also wearing a vintage outfit of puffed pants tucked into boots, with a baggy working-man's shirt, all in shades of brown. His hair, long and light pinkish, was in a messy bun with a long pin and what looked like a length of audio cable stuck through it.

Henley rubbed both hands over his face.

"Start at the beginning. Who are you? What are you doing in my apartment—how did you even get in?"

The stranger gave him an uneasy nod. His gaze was clear enough that Henley's immediate assumption of drugs went out the window. The fear in his eyes was out of place in the still apartment. As he gathered himself, the intruder smoothed his hands down his shirtfront, and his clothes changed. In a breath, his outfit changed to a modern version of the same, and Henley strangled a sound of surprise in the back of his throat.

"Wait, wait, wait—what did you just do? *How?* You didn't say a word!"

"Ah—I'm sorry, was that bad? The Between is still in the 1920s. I thought my clothes were a little out of date." The stranger's hair was still a disaster. He pushed a strand of it back behind his ear and gave Henley a nervous smile. "My name is Kit and I, um . . . I ran here. I ran away *to* here. Because your spell was the last connection I made."

"That doesn't make any sense," Henley said, his tone flat.

"I don't even know how you can see me," Kit replied. "You shouldn't be able to focus on me or remember I was here. Honestly, it's better if you don't. I should go before they come after me. I thought they would, it's only been a few minutes, and I was sure—"

"*Who?* Who is coming after you?"

"The . . . the Shields." Kit looked back at him with somber eyes that reflected silver when he turned his head just right. "They killed Sandoval, and they captured some of the other operators. I saw gems. They were going to take the magic."

"What do you mean, 'take the magic'?" Henley gripped his umbrella tighter, shoulders hunched. "Like the magic outages?"

"Mmhmm." Kit gave him a jerky nod. He had wrapped his arms so tight around himself that the fabric was taut under his nails. A silver machine key hung around his neck, bright and shiny. "I've never used it myself, but I know magic can be stored in stones. It's very valuable, because it doesn't have a personal price then, you know? They came for the magic. The Captain said once they took my substation they would move on to others—I couldn't let them have it. Substation No. 28 is the core of the Switchboard. They could do terrible things with that much magic."

"That sounds bad, but still confusing," Henley said. He looked around again, expecting threats from the lingering shadows outside the range of his kitchen sink light. *Where are they? How would they get in? How much time do I have?* "So you came here by magic, fleeing someone who was stealing magic. Why are you still here? Are they going to follow you?"

"I didn't know how to get out," Kit explained, hunching his shoulders. "From the Actuality, I mean. I can't get back. The magic ripped open, and I could . . . direct it a little, but I can't tear open another portal without a significant flow of magic. And I can't use magic. And nowhere else is safer than this place if I don't have anywhere to go." He swallowed. "I don't know if they can follow me. Probably. They can do lots of things I can't."

"Transportation magic is incredibly difficult—if they can use it then you're in big trouble. It takes hours to set up that kind of spell." Henley paused. "It would take *me* hours to set it up. What are you, again?"

"An operator, but I'm actually a Fetter, we—"

Before Kit stopped talking, Henley felt the energy of the room twist. He didn't need the intruder's widening eyes or muffled curse to know the layers of materiality were peeling back, opening a portal into his living room. Portals took time. He turned to face the glowing crack in midair, bracing his feet. When he reached for the magic he found nothing.

He reached again. The whisper of energy that had answered him since his first determined spell at five years old was gone, like a noisy room abruptly silenced. Adrenaline poured into his veins.

"There's no magic," he said, and backed away from the portal. As it began to open, several figures wearing black World War I-era military uniforms waited on the other side, braced and ready to attack. He was defenseless—and then Kit grabbed Henley's free arm. The magic surged into his skin without being called.

"Try again!"

"Twenty percent, *Barrier*!" Henley yelled, fingers spread, palm flat toward the portal. "Deny my foes and their machinations, resist all advances upon this, my sanctuary! Within these walls—" He sucked in a breath. The magic flowed out of him without him finishing the incantation or offering an appropriate sacrifice. It was wild, bucking his control and fighting his grasp. He bit his lip until it bled, using the pain to focus his mind as he built the barrier, enclosing the apartment in a shield that couldn't be penetrated without a specific assault. An array of translucent, glittering geometric shapes fell into place, locking together like a puzzle, their differing composition thwarting any attempts to break the shield.

The portal closed. One of the soldiers glared at him with anger and frustration, and then they were gone. The only sound in Henley's pristine apartment was the clatter of rain against the balcony.

"Wow," Kit said, still gripping Henley's arm. "That was *beautiful*."

"Get off me." Henley yanked his arm free from Kit's grasp and stepped away, still breathing heavy. Sweat itched along his hairline. The barrier hummed around them, much stronger than Henley would have normally managed at twenty percent, but he couldn't bring himself to feel safe. "What happened to the magic? Do you have anything to do with the outages? How long until they try to break the barrier?"

Kit eased away, wrapping his arms around himself again. "They caused the outages. I think. If they've been attacking substations then that explains why we've been losing connections. But there's no magic because I took the Switchboard down. All of it. The magic can't get to the mages anymore."

The words were so calm, so casual, that Henley took a menacing step forward. "Do you have any idea what that means? Do you know how many people rely on magic—how many lives are at risk because they can't cast? What do you mean you took it *down*?!"

"What could I do?!" Kit took a step back from Henley but met his eyes without guilt or hesitation. "If I didn't, they would have gotten what they wanted. All of the magic would have eventually been gone anyway—at least now they don't have it!"

Every breath out of Hen's chest was tight and rough. "We're coming back to this conversation. How long until they come back for you?"

"For us. I'm sorry, but you're an accomplice now." Uneasy as he was, the intruder's eyes were clear. "Maybe an hour. Your barrier is really secure, but they know how to get around any spell. I'll go on my own—tell them that you were startled and I broke into your house. It's true! They should leave you alone."

Henley raised both hands, silencing Kit before curling his fingers into his palms. Every breath was harsh in his throat. Thunder rumbled outside, a fitting counterpart to his mood. His phone vibrated again in his pocket. *I should call Dad—*

He rejected the thought and dropped his hands.

"You just told me these people killed someone. *Then* you told me I was an accomplice. I'm not waiting around to see what they do next, and *you* aren't going anywhere I can't keep an eye on you." Henley made rapid strides across the living room to his bedroom.

"What are we going to do then?" Kit asked. He had followed, hovering in the bedroom doorway. His eyes roamed the room, taking in the details. "There's so much *space* here . . ."

"We're going to stay somewhere overnight and figure out a plan when we're safe." It took moments for Henley to grab a bag and throw in a change of clothes and a few personal items. With the bag slung over his shoulder, he manhandled Kit back into the main area.

"Walk. We're leaving right now."

FIVE

SHIELDS ON THE HUNT

"Bring in the auxiliary generators. Has anyone heard from Substation No. 37? Do we have confirmation of all stations down?"

"No reports yet from Paradise! No repercussions reported in the Between except for the confused operators."

"Get Unit 2368 out of standby and on active duty. Where can we put them? We need every hand!"

The Order of the Bright Shield was in chaos. A person couldn't move without elbowing a uniformed officer in the ribs or spine. Stoic faces on all sides were damp with sweat. The few Shields who had brought prisoners in for lockup went about their business with single-minded focus, their heads bowed over the work-worn wooden desks that divided the open central chamber into sections. The Switchboard was down and panic reigned.

"What are we supposed to do with the reports? Who gets them?" A harried young officer clutched an armful of paper against his uniformed chest, one skinny, scared face in the center of the mob. The noise of jumbled voices bounced off the high ceiling and absorbed into the gathered figures before it could echo again off the tiled floor.

Lieutenant Solene stood just inside building's doorway, jostled by the press of incoming officers, without the physical presence to claim the space where she stood. It was as if every Shield in the Between was gathered in the Order's mustering chamber. Her foot had been crushed by anxious officers three times in the last ten minutes. It was a small distraction as she absorbed the noise and gathered details. "Everyone—" she began, but even those closest didn't hear her voice. "I need everyone to—"

Still no response. She clutched her clipboard against her chest with dark-skinned fingers that were pale at the knuckle. The frustration caused tension in her shoulders, and her tone was sharper than usual when she pulled out her most forceful voice and bit into the din.

"Captain Shaw needs everyone's reports!" Around the open room, Shields quieted and turned. The young officer with the papers flinched and tripped over a trash can. The flash of her deep brown eyes finally forced those closest to her to move back and give her the space she needed to be seen, though they traded inscrutable looks. It wasn't the first time she'd had to fight to be heard, and it wouldn't be the last.

"Savoy, organize the reports. I want them by section and priority. We still have work to do, regardless of how the job gets done." Someone helped Savoy up from the ground. Solene was reaching them; their expressions grew focused, the panic easing. "Shelm, go to Paradise and wait for word from the High Spirits. I want you to assure them that we are moving, and we'll have the Switchboard back up as soon as possible. Somberg, put Unit 2368 in Auxiliary Camp 6."

"Yes, ma'am." Several salutes were offered. The Shields she had identified grabbed their people and hustled out of the station. A few officers with idle hands began helping Savoy sort his stack of reports. She nodded with approval.

"Lieutenant? What about the rest of us?"

The question came from her shoulder. Solene wasn't a tall woman, even in her practical heels, and the man towered over her.

"Maintain your normal routines as much as possible if you aren't under direct search orders. We must comfort the population. Answer questions with as little detail as you can but remain positive and reassuring."

He nodded and got out of her way. Most of the Shields still stared at her, clinging to the hope that someone would make sense of everything. Deep red lips pursed, she stared back.

"Captain Shaw is aware of the situation and is working to locate the Chief Operator. We all understand how grave this crime is and how severe the consequences must be. However, if we panic, we will lose sight of our mission and our cause. You must keep your heads clear. If you have nothing else to do, then get out on the streets and talk to the people. Remind them that the Between has existed for millennia, and one criminal will not bring it to its knees. We are the protectors of everyone who touches magic, and we will not let them down."

She didn't wait to see the impact of her words. She heard it as she turned to walk toward the offices, long skirt swishing around her calves. The voices picked up again, less fearful, and the Shields got moving. At least she could do that much.

The station was a large facility, big enough to house most of the Shields at once when necessary. Like the Switchboard, the Order had substations, but most of the operations were carried out in the main building. Her heels clicked across the floor past office after busy office, conference rooms of clustered officers, and desks with deadpan radio operators conveying messages. She presented a calm face as she reached the largest back offices. Solene gave the final waiting door, its glass frosted and painted with SHAW in gold letters, a crisp knock.

"Captain?"

"Come in, Lieutenant."

She pushed open the door, stepped inside, then closed it behind her. The blond man at the desk didn't look up. Shaw's office was carpeted. The dense threads soaked up the noise of the station. Within the space, lamps were few, the window blinds were closed, and garish noise had been forbidden. Two chairs waited across from Shaw's handsome mahogany desk. Solene didn't take either.

"The Shields are disorderly, but they're getting back to work. Did you have any specific orders you needed assigned?"

"Not at the moment." Shaw capped his fountain pen and leaned back in his chair. The paper in front of him looked official—an arrest warrant. His penmanship dripped across the page in elegant swoops and curls. "You have such skill with organizing people. I appreciate you keeping everyone focused."

"Thank you, Captain, but they take kicking. Five years isn't enough to make them adjust to my orders."

"I warned you it wouldn't be easy when I assigned you to lead the Between Division. I would hate for you to get bored."

"Boredom is a problem for the uncommitted."

The Captain gave her a tense smile. It was still a smile, and Solene pushed her luck.

"Sir, are you sure we can find him?" His expression clouded, but it was too late for her to take the words back. Months spent under his direct mentorship kept her from offering a hasty apology. "Without access to the magic our entire operation is in limbo."

"Do you think I'm not aware?" The Captain pushed to his feet, tossing his pen onto the desk in a way that would make a certain mess the next time it was opened. Shaw was broad-shouldered and Grecian handsome, with the charisma of a great leader, but it was his infamous temper that made Solene straighten her spine and plant her feet. "The *idiot* Chief Operator gets in the way, and it isn't just our plans that have gone awry. The entire damn Between is now at risk! If we don't get this under control, it will force a rewrite of the Between, and every Fetter within will be chained to this cursed fate for another eternity! Say goodbye to all our ideals and justice then!"

The Captain had begun to raise his voice, and he realized it right before he got too loud to hide their conversation and cut himself off. He breathed in through his nose, filling his chest and lifting his shoulders. The room was washed with his rage, ricocheting around them, the air singing with tension. He deliberately sat back down.

"I'm sorry, Solene, I don't mean to snap at you." A few seconds ticked by on the clock mounted to her left. Solene stood unyielding.

He breathed in again, then continued. "I appreciate your concerns, and I promise, I share them. What do we know about where the Chief Operator ran?"

She waited two careful seconds before speaking, giving him more space to gather himself. "The apartment was empty when we managed to break through the barrier, and he's leaving no magic trace. We'll have to use Actuality methods to track him; it will take hours to demand access to the security camera footage. The mortal police are always so possessive about their jurisdictions." Her words came easier as he made the effort to calm himself.

"And the footage will be poor thanks to the storms, but it's more than we have right now." Shaw flicked his hand in disgust. "Anything on the mage that was with him?"

"He's been identified as the owner of the apartment, Henley Yu. An S-ranked mage from a reputable family, son of the Gulf Coast Council's leader. We don't know for sure that he and the Chief Operator are working together, but both were gone, so we must assume Kittinger has an accomplice or a hostage. How do you want us to handle them when found?"

"Unrestrained force on the Chief Operator and whatever courtesy we can offer to the mage if he cooperates. They should know better than to resist an arrest. Henley Yu is unimportant—dump him on the nearest substation. We can't spare the time to deal with interference from the Actuality." Shaw leaned back in his chair and clasped his hands behind his head, ice-blue eyes distant. "As for the Chief Operator, subdue him and bring him to me. We will compel him to fix what he has broken."

"And if he doesn't? If he can't?" Solene relaxed her strained grip on the clipboard with concentrated effort.

Shaw gave her a smile as grim as his black uniform coat. "We have methods of forcing his cooperation. The Chief Operator knows every-thing about the Switchboard—he can fix it and he will." The Captain got to his feet once more, the chair bouncing upright behind him, and circled his desk. When he stood before her he was several inches taller and broader, blocking the light in a protective shadow. He rested his hands on her arms and squeezed.

"Don't waver, Lieutenant," he told her in a low voice. "This is what we've been working for all this time. In the end, these sacrifices will be worth the cost—we will all have our freedom from our Purpose. You aren't fighting alone." He gave her a little shake. "As soon as I get approval from the High Spirits, we will summon the Lineman to track him down."

Like everyone else in the Between, she needed the reassurance, and Shaw had never failed to provide. His last words, however, unraveled her acceptance. "What?"

"The Lineman." Shaw smiled, almost boyish in his pleasure, and let her go. "You don't look excited."

"Captain, the Lineman is a legend. I don't think we're going to get very far in this chase relying on the boogeyman."

"What do you know about the Lineman, Lieutenant? Go ahead, tell me the wildest stories you've heard."

He was far too cheerful for Solene's comfort. She studied the Captain, wary, but humored his request.

"I've heard the Lineman lives in the dark corners of the Between. He sleeps until he senses wrongdoing. Then he wakes and chases down the Fetter who crossed all that's right and good, hacking them to pieces and spraying the walls with blood. He carries a giant pair of scissors and uses them to cut the heads off the wicked."

"Gory, I like it. It's not completely inaccurate, but it does sound greatly exaggerated." Shaw stepped back, leaning against his desk. The scene could have been from ten or fifteen years before, when he guided Solene as a young officer learning to command her first unit. "Have you ever heard of him actually getting someone?"

"No, Captain."

"That's because it's been a very long time since we had a high-profile need for his services. There have been smaller issues, however. He's a subtle spirit. He's summoned, he hunts his target and brings them to justice, then he returns to his rest." Shaw looked over his shoulder and nodded to the warrant on his desk. "I've signed several dozens of those Writs. The High Spirits approve the request. Then I summon the Lineman and he finds the target, bringing them before the Spirits and the Arbiter."

Solene narrowed her deep brown eyes at the man. "If he's so subtle, why does he have such a terrible reputation?"

Shaw's lips pulled back from his teeth, a white shark's grin. "Because if the crime is terrible enough, he raises his ugly blade and cuts the thread of the miscreant in question, severing their connection to the Between. Depending on the crime, their spirit might be shredded, never to return or be reborn. Everyone who ever knew them forgets they existed, leaving only an emotionless record in the Order files."

Her body went cold. When she stood still, she could feel her own thread, the warm pulse of life and magic that connected her to her home. Solene swayed on her feet. Her skirt brushed against her legs in gentle whispers. Her mouth was too dry.

"Who decides if he cuts the thread?"

"The High Spirits, after consideration of the case presented by the Captain and the Arbiter. I can't imagine he won't have his thread cut, if he continues to run. This is a great crime against the Between."

"Even if his crime is fleeing *our* crime?"

He met her eyes and nodded. His smile was gone.

"The High Spirits will weigh his testimony, but the crime of what he has done far outweighs any reasoning he might have. If his thread is cut, then a new Chief Operator will be named, someone who can fix the connections. If the Between is too deteriorated at that point, the Lineman will cut the thread that binds all the Between, and we'll be rewritten." He lowered his voice. "It's not hopeless. If that happens, we can trap him at the Main Line and stop the rewrite. We can end the cycle without having to gather any more magic. We'll be free."

"Is this what you wanted?"

Something flickered in his eyes at her question: sadness, maybe, or regret.

"It's not exactly what I planned, no. I didn't want to sow chaos. I had hoped that we would operate clandestinely, acting in small doses at a time, until we had what we needed to take control. This will be much bigger than one of those small hunts. Because Kittinger has jumped worlds, the Lineman must be empowered to cross the boundaries between realms, and that will take the whole department. All the Between will know he's been summoned."

He lifted a hand, placing it over his heart. "I swear to you, this hunt will be successful. In a matter of days, we will have everything we fought for. Can you have faith a little longer?"

She took a deep breath. It filled her chest and pushed back some of the fear, but not the growing sense of dread.

"Yes, sir."

"Good. I need your focus and attention to detail." Shaw straightened up from his desk and tugged his cuffs down. "Keep control. Keep looking. Give me everything you can, and we'll let the Lineman do the rest. And get Savoy to bring me some coffee, please."

"Yes, Captain." She offered a crisp salute, tucking the clipboard against her opposite side. Then she stepped away from him, telling herself she wasn't fleeing from the heavy air in that dimly-lit office.

Six

Explanations

It was *raining*.

Kit had seen rain only a few times in his memory. Like cell phones and amusement parks, it was something he knew about from his limited connections with the Actuality but had never experienced himself. As Henley had driven through the rising water and pounding storm, Kit used his fascination with the weather to push back the terror that lingered in the back of his mind. The rain he'd seen through the eyes of mages was nothing like the torrent that made their drive a crawl. The Chief Operator was eager to put space between them and the apartment, but the fear of being caught couldn't overwhelm his wonder at experiencing real *rain*.

When they arrived at the enormous hotel, one with an actual lake in front of it, Henley parked valet. While Henley was getting his bag out of the back seat, Kit stood in the rain just outside of the canopy and let it slam into his body, breathing in the fresh, wet, humid scent. *Everything is so green. What does the grass feel like?* Caution warred with curiosity. He hovered close to the protection of the doorway, yearning for time he couldn't risk.

"Let's go, Kit." Henley hadn't warmed up to Kit during the drive. He never stood closer than a few feet, and his shoulders remained tense. Even though he was reluctant to leave the rain, Kit was motivated to follow his new companion when given the command. Henley seemed to always know what he was doing. His well-tailored slacks and shirt were a kind of uniform; his confident stride and manner earned him the hotel staff's attention when he approached. The open lobby with its two-story ceiling suited the mage, a clean environment of black marble and silver trim accented with the luxury of water features and live plants. Kit slogged behind him, leaving a trail of rainwater that dripped from his sleeves, his boots, his hair, and his nose.

They took an elevator up to the third floor after Henley obtained their room keys from an otherwise empty front desk. The elevator walls were made of glass, letting Kit stare at the river of koi and lush plantings inside the lobby as long as possible. He didn't touch the glass, but he left a new puddle on the elevator carpet. The walls closed in on them when they disembarked, making everything boring again.

Except that it isn't boring. The hotel was the fanciest, most beautiful place he'd ever seen aside from Paradise. The hushed hallways were comfortable and secure. Henley ignored the environment in favor of following the signs that led to their room number. Once the door had been located, the mage opened it with a plastic card, yet another wonder to someone used to metal keys.

"Are you hungry?" Henley asked, his tone full of clipped courtesy rather than care.

The hotel room beyond the clever door was more like the amount of space Kit was used to having. Though spacious, it contained a spartan two beds, dresser, and desk, all in better condition than the furniture of his house. The *window*, though. He skirted the two queen beds and went to the window, distracted enough by the view of the wind-tossed trees below that Henley had to ask the question twice. His tone didn't get any sweeter.

"Yes, a little," Kit admitted, looking over his shoulder. "Is there tea here? Are we safe inside?"

"Tea is right there," Henley replied, nodding to a small contraption on the table that held the phone. He had a leather folder in his hands, turning the pages held within. "Do you like salad? What do you eat?" He narrowed his dark eyes at Kit. "I have no idea if we're safe. It depends on the people who were trying to get into my apartment—but it won't be easy for anyone to track us here without magic."

"Ah . . . of course. I think we have some time for the moment. I eat pasta, mostly. Almost every day. I just tried spaetzle, and it was very good." The rain was enticing, but Kit needed the tea. He moved toward the table, getting away from the fragile glass barrier, clothes still dripping on the thin carpet. The Chief Operator gave the mage a wide berth, not wanting to give Henley any new reasons to be annoyed. Kit didn't ask his questions either. *What if the Shields come through the window? Can they reach such a height? Should I hide under the bed? Could we make it to the door? What if they came from the hall—*

"I'll order something for you," Henley replied, oblivious to the Chief Operator's urgent inner monologue.

"Thank you." Kit stopped his fearful thoughts as best he could. He picked up the device that was supposed to produce tea and turned it over. It had a cord, so he knew it should be plugged in, but it was very small for a tea kettle and didn't even have a pot. Holding the receiver of the phone against his shoulder, Henley grabbed one of the individually wrapped cups and tore off the plastic.

"Yes, I'd like to order one grilled salmon with rice and vegetables, and one pasta carbonara. Yes." Henley held the cup out to Kit and pointed toward a small cabinet that held two bottles of fancy-looking water. *Fill it up*, he mouthed. Kit put the strange kettle down and accepted his mission. The caps were flat, not ridged, and he didn't have a bottle opener. It took several seconds for him to realize they twisted off.

"Yes. Bottled water and extra tea bags. Green and black. Thank you."

Henley hung up as Kit returned with both the filled cup and one of the water bottles. Henley wasted no movement as he plugged the device in, poured the water into the back, and set the cup in front.

"Every hotel is different. You need a degree to make coffee in a new city."

"Coffee? But I wanted—"

"It makes tea, too." Henley opened a small packet and dunked a tea bag into the cup as the device began to sputter and produce hot water. "Dinner should take about half an hour. Start talking." His tone was firm, and he wasn't smiling. Kit wasn't sure the man could smile.

"Okay." He swallowed, staying right where he was and not giving up his claim to that cup of tea. He stuck his damp hand out. "Hello. I'm Kittinger, Chief Operator of the Between. I'm assigned to Substation No. 28."

Henley had said "please" and "thank you" to everyone they had met so far and had held the door for Kit twice, even before he ordered food for the man who had gotten him attacked in his own apartment. His eye twitched behind his glasses, but he took Kit's hand and shook it with a steady grip. "Henley Yu, graphic designer. You're going to have to start at the beginning, because I don't understand anything you say."

The burbling noises of the unfamiliar teakettle stopped, and Henley handed Kit the cup before starting to make a second. The paper was too warm in Kit's hands and the cup too small to be satisfying, but he took what he could get.

"I'm sure," he replied. "You shouldn't know anything about the Between. I guess I'll start there."

He looked around, then walked over to sit on one of the beds. A constant draft blew from the box by the window, cutting through the thin shirt that stuck to his skin. He knew hot climates had internal air conditioning, but he hadn't expected them to be so cold. Henley stared at him with his lips pressed thin, then disappeared into the bathroom. When he reappeared, he had a pair of pristine white towels. Kit took them when offered, juggling the fabric and his tea to fold one in half to cover the wet spot he'd left on the bed before he sat back down.

The tea was hot, at least, and not terrible when he took the first sip. The heat easing down his throat helped him to gather his thoughts. Kit was certain Henley wouldn't appreciate a scattered explanation. He tapped one foot on the floor to indicate the room where they sat. "This is the Actuality. Your world. Where mortals live. This is the place that uses the magic, but it doesn't have any of its own that can be manipulated. The ley lines are too unstable, right? They flood the world with enough magic to sustain life, but they don't obey when you call. That forced mortals to adapt to other methods. Mages like you are born knowing how to *reach* for the magic."

Henley carried his own cup of steeping tea to the other bed, sitting on the edge where he could face Kit. He wasn't glaring, at least. "Not too far off from what I was taught. I'm with you so far."

"The magic comes from a plane called the Ethereal," Kit continued with a nod. The tea bag was stale and the flavor was weak, but it was *so good*. "You can't reach the Ethereal by yourself. You'd have to know how to speak the languages of the elements, and the Ethereals would take advantage of you. They're very demanding. Unreasonable if you let them be, really, so greedy for—"

Henley raised his eyebrows and frowned. Kit hurried back to the subject.

"So there's a world that acts as a buffer between the Actuality and the Ethereal—that's the Between. The spirits in the Between are called Fetters. We *bind* the worlds together, we *connect* them. Operators like me can pull magic from the Ethereal and send it to the Actuality. We facilitate the negotiations between places, you might say."

"That's why I could cast when you were holding on to me?" Henley sat forward, elbows on his thighs, hands wrapped around his steaming cup. His short black hair was neat, aside from a few damp locks that insisted on falling into his glasses. Kit appreciated the minor imperfection. Henley seemed so "together" otherwise.

"Mmhmm. I just fed magic straight into you, rather than through your requested connection."

"Requested?"

"Yes, you 'request' when you cast. 'One percent, *Create Fire*.' That's when you *reach*, but you're not reaching to the Ethereal. You reach to the Between, and we bring the magic to you." Kit smiled, comfortable in his expertise. "That's managed by a Switchboard. I get a call from someone like you, and then I pull one of the plugs on my panel"—he mimed the motion—"and I put it in the port of the requested connection. There's hundreds, thousands of operators, all across the Between. My substation is No. 28, which is all of Texas. We're very busy."

"You know about our states?"

"I know all of your geography and all of your languages. It really changes how a spell is cast, you know?"

"I suppose so."

He must have been a very good student. Henley was listening with such focus, not allowing their panicked flight to disturb his reasoning. There was something very steadying about the way Henley hadn't disregarded anything he'd been told. Kit leaned forward as well, huddled around his cup of tea, burning his mouth with each careless sip.

"The Between has existed almost as long as mages here have been using magic. It's changed a few times, rewritten itself to keep up with the accelerating population and the way history has changed the world." Kit's smile faded. "That's what I think is coming. We've been losing connections for months, spotty patches of magic that stopped responding. I didn't know why, what was happening, but then . . . the Shields came to No. 28."

"Who are the Shields?"

"The Order of the Bright Shield—our police, or military. That's who chased me to your apartment. We had an officer assigned to us at my substation . . . his name was Sandoval. He used to ask me for help with his crossword puzzles." Kit stared ahead with unfocused eyes, seeing that dangling hand, the fingers stained with newsprint. "He's dead. I saw his blood all over the floor."

Henley stared at Kit. Then he got to his feet and stepped closer, grabbing the second towel and draping it around Kit's shoulders. It had a faint chemical smell but it cut the chill of the draft. "I'm sorry," he said. When Kit looked into Henley's eyes, the frustration and hostility in the mortal's gaze had faded.

"Thank you," Kit said, and took a steadying sip of tea. Henley sat back down. He didn't say anything as the Chief Operator got himself back under control.

"The Shields had gemstones—diamonds, it looked like. Do you know how gemstones are used?"

Henley nodded. "They can store magic for later use; we consider them a standard tool for emergency planning. Mages here have been using them up daily as they fight the storms."

"That's most of what they are," Kit replied. "Gemstones are used to store magic to be used without having to bargain with the Ethereals. They can be extremely valuable and equally dangerous in the wrong hands. I think the bad Shields are trapping the latent magic in the switchboard panels and using it for their own purposes. Just the magic of a single substation could destroy all of Texas or sink New Zealand into the ocean. We've never lost a whole substation before. I don't know what they're planning but I knew it had to be *bad*, and I couldn't let them succeed, so I did the only thing I could do."

Henley exhaled a breath that steamed from the heat of his tea. "You disabled all of the magic in the world."

"Yes. I disconnected the planes." Kit met the mage's eyes, but in his mind he replayed the tension, the fear, the loud voices, and the light reflecting off the pool of Sandoval's blood. "I'm the Chief Operator for all of the Between. My panel is the main conduit to the Ethereal. All other panels feed through it, even the ones that route to other substations. I . . . I ripped all the wires out. There's so many no one else can sort them out and fix it." He dropped his eyes to stare down into his half-empty cup. "It's not gone forever, but if it's restored and the Shields come for it again, the same thing will happen."

"Isn't there a backlash? Raw magic is dangerous to handle, and you basically tore open the protective insulation."

"Not for me. If anyone who isn't an operator touches the wires, they'll be badly burned, but the magic can't go anywhere unless it's drawn through the panel and directed."

"But I could do magic if you held my arm. That didn't require a panel."

"That's different." Kit smiled a little, then dropped the expression when he looked up to see the frown on the mage's lips. "I'm the Chief Operator. I can call the magic and connect it anywhere; it responds to me even without full access to the Switchboard. That's why I know I can fix it. Taking the Switchboard down gives me time to figure out what should happen and how to keep things from getting worse."

"And in the meantime, my world—the Actuality—starts to fall apart." The mage's black eyes were cold glass. He gave a sharp gesture with his chin toward the window. "All that rain out there? It's not normal. Patches of magic have been disappearing for months. There have been violent storms, earthquakes, tsunamis. We were seeing the effects before, but now the disasters will get worse. On top of that, the mages who do good work won't be able to function anymore. Houston has a huge medical center, and half of our mages work in that industry. People are going to die because they can't do their jobs. Why does the lack of magic affect us like this?"

Henley's fingers were buckling the sides of his cup. His shoulders were set and his expression a step shy of a glare. Henley was right. The Actuality wasn't meant to exist without magic; the flow of energy helped to keep the world stable. Every word out of Henley's mouth was the truth, but Kit met his gaze without flinching.

"It's because the added flow of magic has been in the Actuality so long that it's become part of the natural order. The Ethereal will be affected as well, because there's too much magic building up. The Between will eventually cease to exist if there's no magic flowing through." Kit gripped the edges of his towel tight, the fabric digging into his palms. "If I had any choice, I would have done something else. It goes against my Purpose to have the magic inactive."

"You could have let them take the magic and run away to find help. If they knew what was happening, every mage in the Actuality would have stepped up to do something."

"If I let them take the magic, the mages wouldn't be able to do anything," Kit countered, the bed shifting under his narrow hips as he leaned into the words, willing Henley to listen. "There would be no magic for them to use to fix the problem. You shouldn't even be able to see me right now. The Between is supposed to be hidden from mortals. It must be something to do with the bleed from the severed wires—"

"You said the Between can be rewritten, right? Would that fix it? Can it be forced?"

"You have no idea what you're asking!" The response was pulled from Kit before he could censor himself, the words hitting him like thrown bricks to his stomach. His chest was tight, so tight, his body rejecting the concept on every level. His hands shook so hard his remaining tea splashed in his cup.

"Of course it would fix everything, that's what the Between does, it *fixes* itself, but the costs are so high. The operators wouldn't *exist* anymore—not as the people we are. No one would remember us. All our lives, our memories, everything ceases to exist and starts over. Whoever we are in the next life, we won't recognize each other, we won't remember where we lived or how the food tasted—"

"Kittinger!"

Henley's sharp voice cut through the torrent of words, and Kit dragged himself to a halt, realizing his voice had risen. His tight chest restricted the flow of air. The Chief Operator took a rough breath.

". . . You can call me Kit."

"Okay. Kit."

The room was silent again as Henley brooded over the words. The sounds of quiet voices and closing doors came from the hallway. A muffled world continued to move around them, held at bay by the neutral walls and heavy room door.

"When I found you in my apartment, you were scared, but you weren't this scared. The Between being rewritten scares you more than people who might kill you?"

"Even if I die, someone will remember me," the Chief Operator said, the words shards of glass in his throat. "I remember Sandoval." He lifted his head, brows knit, eyes locked on his companion. "I don't want to be forgotten."

"Alright."

A knock on the door made Kit jump and huddle protectively around his cup. Henley got to his feet and answered the door, then carried in a tray of food. He set it down on the table and brought a bowl and fork over to Kit. The silent minutes while he handled their dinner knotted Kit's shoulders.

"I understand." Henley kept his voice low, his words careful, easing Kit away from his panic. "This is very serious—and I don't know how to handle it. I think we need help. Tomorrow we'll call the police responsible for local magical issues. We'll figure out what we need to do to protect the magic and get these corrupt Shields under control. Will you cooperate, and help figure out how to stop them?"

Kit set his cup on the bed next to him and accepted the bowl. Henley snatched the cup and moved it to safety on the bedside table. The bowl was warm in Kit's hands, and the pasta smelled like bacon. His stomach growled a mundane counterpoint to his fears. *What can the Actuality police do against Shaw? What if they all die like Sandoval?*

What if the Shields kill Henley?

"Okay," he agreed. "I don't know what else to do. I'm sorry about the magic. I'm sorry about the storms and the doctors."

"Apologies work best when paired with action." Henley patted his shoulder, then went back for his own plate. "I still can't believe any one person could make the magic just stop. There must be a way to restore the magic and keep it from being misused. We'll find it."

Kit nodded, keeping his eyes on his food. The pasta wasn't as good as Noodle's, but it was flavorful and hot. It formed a hard lump in his stomach. The silence that ruled as they ate eventually proved too much for Henley; he set his half-empty plate aside and thoroughly cleaned his hands on a napkin.

"Have you ever been here before?" he asked. With his hands clean, he rummaged in the bag he'd thrown on his bed and pulled out a small black journal with an attached mechanical pencil. When he flipped through the pages, Kit saw that they were plain white and covered in notes and sketches.

"I've been to the Actuality before but it was a very long time ago, to help investigate a problem with the flow. That must have been um . . . forty or fifty years ago. It feels very strange. In the Between we travel up and down, not side to side as much. Everything is so flat here."

Henley paused with his pencil hovering above a blank page. "Up and down?"

"Yes," Kit said around a mouthful of pasta. The serving size was huge, enough for three meals, but it comforted him so much he kept eating when he should have stopped. "All of our buildings are in a vertical alignment. If the Actuality and the Ethereal are two sides of a coin, the Between is the thin middle of the coin."

The pencil had begun to scratch across the page as Henley's hand moved in sharp, neat strokes. Within a few seconds the sketch began to take shape, a coin on its side, buildings growing out to the right and left, with a vertical city in the narrow center. "Something like this?" Henley asked. Kit surrendered his bowl to the nightstand and leaned forward, eyebrows raised.

"Yes, that's amazing. The Between seems to go on forever, but your world is vastly bigger. I don't know how you find anything here."

"Like you said, it's flat." Henley moved his hand to a new spot and started drawing again, this time in small rectangles and long lines. "This is my apartment. This big road is the freeway—I-10. We're here at this hotel. Tomorrow morning, if we're not flooded in, we might have to go to the police station. That's here, down Dairy Ashford." He added small shaded areas to give the drawing depth. Kit tilted his head, still confused, until Henley held the notebook upright. "I guess in the Between this route would be up and down, not side to side."

"Oh. Yes, that's right. And you don't fly."

"*Fly?*"

"Your vehicles wouldn't work very well, driving up our walls."

"No, but—flying as in airplanes, or flying as in magic?"

"Magic." Kit's cup was empty. He rose and crossed the room to the small coffee maker, needing only a couple of small reminders from Henley to start another cup brewing with his used teabag. "Your airplanes are hard for me to imagine. We have large trolleys that float up and down, carrying people or small shops or food carts. We don't have—"

A strange buzz broke through his words. The Chief Operator looked around, then returned his eyes to Henley as the mage reached for his cell phone on the nightstand. The screen had lit up with a notification. "What is that?"

"Phone. You keep talking about a switchboard, and your clothes were pretty out of date. You've never seen a wireless phone, have you?"

"No, but I've heard of them." Fascinated, Kit leaned close to stare at the screen. A long message floated in the notification window. "Is that an email?"

"It's just a weather update." Henley swiped his thumb across the screen and opened the full message. "The mayor is advising people to stay home. Fewer people to get in the way when we leave the hotel."

"How convenient. If I need to send word to all of my operators I can contact them through the Switchboard, but if they've gone home I have to send runners. Does everyone in the Actuality have a phone like this?"

"Not everyone, but most people. We're very connected now."

"That must be wonderful." Kit perked up as another message appeared on the screen, this one labelled 'Dad.' "More work?"

Henley's expression shuttered. A flick of his thumb dismissed the notification. "No." He looked up, past Kit's shoulder, as a gargle of noise rose from the desk. "Your tea's ready."

The Chief Operator straightened, eyebrows raised as he took in Henley's tense shoulders and the new lines around his mouth. When he had taken a step away from Henley to retrieve his tea, he ventured a response. "I see. Is being very connected sometimes unpleasant?"

"Sometimes. What were you saying? The Between 'doesn't have . . .'"

"Oh, distance, in the way you have it here. So we haven't developed means to travel as extensively as the Actuality has. Sometimes it's easier to not do the flying yourself, or you want to sit and chat with someone, so we ride on the trolleys. My favorite food cart is a pasta maker who comes by my substation every day at lunch and dinner. He makes dishes from all over the Actuality, with recipes he trades from operators who have seen your memories."

That brought Henley's head up. A flash of lightning illuminated his face and rendered his glasses opaque; when the light faded, his eyes had narrowed behind the silver frames. "You see the memories we sacrifice for magic?"

"Yes, that's how I know about cell phones." The firm mattress barely shifted under Kit as the Chief Operator resumed his place on the towel. Tired of being chilled, he set his tea aside and started to use the towel around his shoulders to rub at himself and pat his damp hair. "We don't get to keep them, though. We see them for a brief moment, and then they pass through to the Ethereal. This morning—"

He smiled, pausing to lower the ends of the towel. "When you cleared the way for the water. The scene with the cars was so interesting. How do you decide which memories you'll send?"

"Usually it's memories we can easily replace, or memories we don't want to keep. I'm a little uncomfortable with the idea of you seeing every memory; some of them are personal."

Kit tilted his head, considering his answer. Henley put his sketchbook back in his bag, trading it for a thin white cord. This he plugged in on the nightstand, then connected to his phone. Some of his tension eased once the device had left his hands.

"I think that's why we see your memories," Kit said. "Because they are personal, because they're important. They remind us that the ones requesting the magic are people who can be hurt or frightened and that it's vital we complete our work with efficiency and precision. Besides, some of the memories you send are personal, but only when you need a large percentage of magic." The Chief Operator's smile softened his thin features. "Mortals deeply value those emotional connections. If they are lost, how you interact with each other changes."

"That's true." Henley's eyes strayed to his phone. Then he raised his hands to unbutton his cuffs and roll his sleeves, a restless movement that pulled Kit's thoughts away from the direction they'd gone. "If we're so important though, why was it so easy for you to cut off the magic?"

"Henley, what's the highest percentage you've ever requested?"

A single dark eyebrow was quirked in response. "I was part of a large-scale heatwave mitigation several years ago when we had major power outages after a storm like this. That was six hundred percent, but there had to be fifty mages involved."

"And that's a very large expenditure of magic," Kit agreed. "I remember that; we don't see many of those. Very nicely planned so it didn't overburden anyone. I can't identify how much power could be drawn from a substation in one pull, but I would say at *least* a thousand percent. Maybe two." He fixed his silver gaze on the mortal. "What do you think someone would want with that much magic?"

Henley removed his vest and set it aside. A new wave of rain clattered against the window, filling the silence while he thought through the question. "Nothing good," he finally conceded. "I don't even know what that much magic could do. My first thought is that someone's trying to make a weapon."

"Exactly. I can think of many terrible things that can be done with magic; I've watched great atrocities over the years. Operators don't get to decide what magic they connect. Even in those horrible times, however, it was never this great a percentage. Since this happened in the Between, I had the chance to stop it and prevent a great tragedy, even if I didn't know what that tragedy was. It was my responsibility."

Dry enough, Kit set his towels aside and pulled the blankets up around his shoulders. The room around the pair was still and the atmosphere fragile as Henley pulled off his glasses. Henley rubbed his face. He exhaled a breath. Then he looked up at Kit again with a somber gaze.

"Do you really think you can fix all of this?"

"I don't know," Kit said, choosing honesty over reassurance. "It's badly broken right now. The Shields are out of control. All I can do is try, and I'll keep trying until . . . something changes."

The power flickered and died. Kit's sharp inhale was loud in the sudden silence. Freezing himself in a tight ball, he held his breath, listening for the stomp of boots outside or the twist of incoming magic. Neither appeared. The rain pounded against the building, obscuring anything outside of the window.

Another burst of lighting illuminated Henley as the mage rose to his feet. "It's okay. The hotel should have . . ." He paused as the power returned. The lights came back on, and his phone lit up as it began to charge again. "Generators," he finished with a nod, and slid his glasses back onto his nose. "These storms are severe, but the city is prepared for hurricanes. Are you okay?"

"Yes . . . yes. I'm okay. I'm fine. It's just hard to relax when anything happens right now."

"You look exhausted, and I'm at my limit for the day. I think we should get some sleep. It sounds like we need to be fully alert tomorrow morning." The rain drew his attention for a few deep, careful breaths. His calm gave Kit a rock to cling to in the chaos. "I'm going to change. Sorry I didn't think to grab any clothes for you—are you dry enough?"

"Yes. It's alright, this room is very comfortable. Thank you, Henley."

Henley hesitated in his movement toward the bathroom, then looked back. "It's my responsibility."

He grabbed his bag and finished his walk. The soft blankets and hot tea provided a strong barrier against the Chief Operator's fear, but the mortal mage was the real reason Kit had managed as much as he had. Out of habit, he pushed aside the knowledge that they would part the next day and he would likely never see Henley again except to hear his voice over the occasional request. It was more connection than he'd ever had to any mortal. When Henley returned dressed in soft pants and a

T-shirt, Kit let himself enjoy the pleasantry of having someone wish him a good night.

Kit's last view of the night was of Henley's phone illuminating the darkness, the tension in his face again as he read the last text message and then locked his phone without sending a reply.

Seven

Bad News

Henley hadn't been able to sleep in since his early-morning university classes. The storm didn't help. He had been too exhausted the night before, but in the early hours the thunder crackled through the air, almost a physical presence. The drapes were open. The light from the window was dim, but it was enough to let him watch Kit sleep.

The Chief Operator was on his side, facing the middle space of the beds, curled into a tight ball. He looked the same age as Henley, somewhere in his early thirties, but his flightiness and overexcitement made him seem younger.

He's not a younger sibling in need of protection, Henley. You have enough to worry about to protect yourself.

He shoved the blankets back and rolled out of bed, moving as quietly as possible. Bag in hand, he closed himself up in the bathroom for a hot shower and several minutes of introspection. The hot water always helped clear his head. As it washed away the remnants of sleep on his skin, he leaned his head against the cold tile wall and thought hard. The magic had been cut off, and the storms raged. Eventually, "climate change" wouldn't be a satisfactory explanation, and people would panic.

The cities would struggle to keep up with the damage. He remembered the intense power and water outages of previous hurricanes and having to use someone else's shower for two weeks. It would make all the difference in the world to his city if they could find a way to restore the magic.

I have to get Kit to the police and make sure he can restore the magic. The eventual solution wasn't his job. Henley was just a graphic designer, not even a mage profession his father could be proud of. He would hand Kit off to the police and get back to work or go to his sister's house to help her sandbag the doors.

Exhaling a breath, he finished his business in the shower and got dressed. The hotel towel was rough on his skin and smelled like bleach. His glasses were too fogged up to use, making his reflection a fuzzy blur in the mirror. As rejuvenated as he felt, he was in no more control of his situation than he had been half an hour before.

The door didn't creak as he opened it, and the carpet silenced his steps, but Kit was sitting up in bed. He had made himself another cup of tea, using the same worn-out teabag from the night before. Dark circles hung under his eyes as he glanced up at Henley in the dimness, but he still offered a tired smile.

"I'm sorry about the rain, but it's so amazing. We don't have rain in the Between."

"Why not?" Henley asked, shoving his dirty clothes in the hotel laundry bag.

"It's not made that way in this edition. There's no trees, no grass, no weather, and the temperature is always the same." The Chief Operator was huddled in his robe and the blankets. They doubled his size, making a bulky lump silhouetted by the gray light. "I have a plant though. A little one from the Ethereal, that I got as a prize. We go on vacation sometimes to Paradise, where you can play games and win things and listen to music. It's exciting."

"It better be, with a name like Paradise." Henley shook his head. Kit's hands poking out of the blankets to hold his tea looked small and delicate, even if he was taller than Henley by an inch or two. "Do you want to take a shower? You don't have any clean clothes—"

"Oh, it's okay. I was soaked in the rain, after all. A shower sounds good." Kit began to untangle himself from the blankets. The metal pin holding his hair caught on the sheet for a moment, tugging his head backward before he freed himself. "Is it too early to make the call?"

"A little. We need about half an hour more before we can call and anyone will pick up. Go ahead and shower, I'll find us some breakfast and make a plan."

"Thank you." Kit let the blankets fall, his rumpled clothes and hair in contrast to the quiet earnestness of his silver eyes. Henley stepped aside to let Kit get to the bathroom, then ran a hand back through his damp hair after the Chief Operator was gone. There was no good energy about their meeting, which was plenty cause for regret. This was a chance to learn about a world he'd never known existed, and to understand the true nature of his magic.

Maybe Kit is just a nice person in better times. A nice person who likes tea and plants and doesn't bring calamity down on the unsuspecting population.

Shaking himself, Henley grabbed his hotel key and headed down to the lobby. Every TV in the area was turned to the news, and clumps of people stood around watching the reports roll in. The list of closed schools had gotten longer. Henley had picked the hotel because it was close to his apartment and he could make it through the freeway underpass, but every street in the area had since flooded. The Harris County water rescue equipment was in high demand. That wasn't his problem, either. All he cared about was if the phones were still working, and no reports indicated that the lines were down.

The hotel gift shop caught his eye, and he ducked inside to make a purchase before stopping by the small coffee shop next to the hotel restaurant. A barista who looked like she'd slept at the hotel in her uniform made his dark roast coffee and tea for Kit without looking him in the eye. Her attention was on the TV screens. She needed to be reminded twice what size drinks he had requested, but Henley tipped her double his usual amount anyway. If she was the only employee able to make it through the storm, she needed the support.

With two large drinks, a small package of cranberry orange muffins, and his gift shop bag, he juggled his purchases into the elevator. New texts from his father waited, but the police call was a good distraction.

I'll call home later. I won't text. Maybe I'll go to their house, after Kit is settled, instead of Lianlian's place. Mom's got to be worried, and I can talk to her instead of Dad.

The thoughts distracted him as he made his way back up to their floor. The hotel key was in his pocket, and he managed to get his hip high enough to trigger the lock on the door. Once it flashed green, he pushed the door open with his elbow, carefully balanced as he made his way inside. The room was still dark, battered by the rain. He'd had enough. Henley set his armload on the room's desk, then turned on every light in the room. He closed the curtains. Kit would have to live without the view of the rain.

A twinge of guilt met the thought. It would take time for the police to get to them and pick up Kit. *Maybe I'll take him back down to the hotel entrance for a few minutes after the call, so he can experience the intense wind and the trees and the grass.* It sounded like even the potted flowers framing the hotel entrances were a big deal in the Between.

He retrieved his cup and sipped the coffee. Not half-bad, considering it wasn't made by his favorite shop. Henley sat at the desk and scribbled notes in his sketchbook. The room was almost cozy with all the light and the sound of someone else moving around, like it was a home. In the margins of his notes, he sketched a rough, smiling, soaking-wet Kit. Was the drawing accurate? He'd seen very little of the Chief Operator's smile. Maybe—

Henley caught the direction of his thoughts, frowned, and went back to writing. By the time Kit emerged through clouds of fresh-scented steam, Henley had made an organized, bulleted list of details to tell the police.

"Everything is so big here," Kit marveled. His hair was wet, unbrushed, and had been put back into its ragged bun. *No wonder he always looks a mess.* Henley pushed aside memories of brushing tangles out of his sisters' hair. "So much space just for a bathroom. I could dance in there."

"Don't. If the floor is wet, you'll fall and hurt yourself." Henley leaned back in his chair, offering the drink he'd gotten for Kit and a muffin. "I'm ready to make the call when you are."

Kit took the tall cup, a puzzled look on his face as he investigated the plastic lid. The smell of tea put brightness back in his eyes. His clothes looked identical to the day before, but they didn't look slept in. Whatever magic he held over his attire was still in effect. The Chief Operator settled on Henley's bed, closer to the phone, with his breakfast cradled in his lap.

"I'm ready. I want to make everything better." Kit hesitated. "Henley, what do your police do exactly?"

"There are two kinds of police: the mundane officers who are unaware of the magical world like most of the population, and the Observers. We're calling the Observers. They investigate misuse of magic, fine people for being reckless or careless, and charge people so they can be judged in our courts. Why?"

Kit bit into his muffin, his words muffled around the pastry. "The Shields have connections to the mortal police, so I'm just . . . nervous. I hope it will be alright, but please be careful."

Henley narrowed his eyes behind his glasses. "Understood."

Kit cleared his mouth with a sip of tea, and Henley dialed. The phone rang for several seconds before a small click sounded and the ring changed. Three rounds of noise later, the call finally connected.

"Observers, this is Sauda. We are aware of the magic outage, and we are working to get it restored. Please be patient while we put our agents in the field." The harassed-sounding male voice paused for breath. "Anything else I can help you with?"

"My name is Henley Yu. I'm calling about an incident that happened when the magic went down. A home invasion. No injuries to report."

"Henley . . . Yu?" Sauda asked. "A home invasion? Let's start a report. Where are you located right now, Mr. Yu?" He paused, his overall tone much more alert and interested than before. "You're not still in the home, are you? Where can we send an officer for the report?"

Henley opened his mouth to speak but stopped when he felt a hand wrap tight around his arm. Kit had leaned forward, brows knit, silver eyes intent. Henley stared back at his companion, eyebrows up. *What?* He mouthed. Kit nodded to the phone.

"That—won't be necessary," Henley replied. "Over the phone is fine. I don't want anyone out in the storm without reason."

"The Omni Westside, is it?" Henley tensed. "What room number, Mr. Yu?"

I don't like this. The combination of the officer knowing so much and Kit's uneasy expression didn't sit well with Henley.

"You know what, actually, I'll wait until after the storm's cleared. Just forget about it, thanks."

"You don't have to go along with this, Mr. Yu." Sauda's voice was confident, reassuring. "We understand you've gotten involved with something unpleasant. We're going to help you—"

Henley hung up the phone, and Kit sagged back with a sound of concern. Henley stared at the phone as tension crawled up his spine, then detangled Kit's hands from his arm.

"Sounds like the Shields told them you're here."

"That was *them*," Kit said, hands back around his tea. "His name was Sauda. All the Shields have names that start with *S*, like all the operators start with *K*. He knew where you were, he wanted to come and get you."

"That's so much speculation that I don't know what to do with it. I'll admit it's problematic that they've gotten this information from the Shields, but that doesn't mean they would arrest us outright or something. We need help, Kit! You've said over and over again how serious this issue is, and now you've rejected the people who can help?"

"Before last night you didn't even know about the Between," the Chief Operator replied, one hand up as if to weigh the evidence. "Now you don't believe me? Do you know of any other police-type agency besides the one you just called?"

"...No."

"And what do you call them?"

"We call them Observers. That's what they do, they observe the use of magic and monitor related crime." Henley rubbed the bridge of his nose. "We abbreviate it as OBS."

Kit leaned closer.

"OBS—as in, the Order of the Bright Shield?"

"That sounds like an awfully convenient explanation."

"Of course it's convenient. It's true."

"Jesus." Henley pinched the bridge of his nose harder. "Alright then, now what do we do if we can't trust anybody?"

Kit relaxed as Henley stopped arguing. "Well, I did think about it a little in the shower. Showers are good for thinking, right? Maybe all the steam makes it harder to see your problems and get distracted." Kit gave his companion a tense smile. "Anyway, the Shields do have to answer to someone. The High Spirits. They live in their Palace above Paradise and they rarely see anyone, but they're the final source of our justice. I'm sure if we contacted them and told them what was going on, they would take action to protect the Between."

"Alright, let's say I go along with this. You said you don't know how to get back to the Between—how would you contact these High Spirits?"

"I need to go through an operator, they're the only ones who could hear me. I'll call Kelley, my backup, and get him to carry the message. To reach him I'll need a place where the barriers between the worlds is very thin." Kit chewed on his lower lip.

Henley didn't like where the conversation was going. "You're talking about a ley line convergence, aren't you? I might have a place, if we can get to it," he replied, drawing out the words. "What would you have to do—what are you planning? I don't want my friend to get hurt or caught up in this."

"Your friend? You have friends?" Kit raised both hands in apology at Henley's glare. "Sorry, sorry, I didn't mean it that way. I just need to get to the place, then I can reach Kelley. The operators must all be at home with the Switchboard down. He can tell me what's going on and help me get a message moving."

"Alright. You might have to give me some magic for us to get there without flooding out the car. Is that going to be a problem?"

Kit shook his head. "The magic doesn't come from me, it comes from the Ethereal, so I'm not going to run out. I used up my favors last time though, so you'll have to complete the transaction from now on."

"Favors? What does that mean?"

"You didn't pay any price, right? Your memory sacrifice. Otherwise there's nothing in it for them, you know?"

Curiosity ate at Henley until he couldn't hold back the question. "What happens to those memories? What do the Ethereals do with them?"

"Consume them, mostly. I think." Kit smiled. "Most of the memories are tastes or smells or feelings, things that are easy to replace, right? I don't really know anything else, but I know they can be sold. Certain sounds are extremely valuable."

"Amazing." Henley sat back in his chair. "I wish I could ask you a thousand questions, but I think we should get moving. I don't like that the Observers know where we are. Once we're out in the storm they'll have a hard time tracking us again."

"Agreed." Kit rolled off the bed and up to his feet, stuffing the remainder of his muffin in his mouth. Henley got moving as well, neatly storing all his possessions in his bag. As he reached for his coffee, he saw the gift shop bag and grabbed it instead.

"Here. You always seem cold, so I thought you could use this."

He offered the bag. Kit took it, eyes wide and eyebrows up. When he pulled the pile of knitted fabric out of the bag, his fingers curled into it, and he gasped.

"Henley?! It's so soft . . ."

"It's just a sweater, Kit. Calm down. There's no reason for you to be cold all the time." The cream-colored cardigan was too heavy for Houston on a normal basis, and the price tag had a red "Clearance" sticker. The chunky knit cables gave it a nice texture. When Kit gleefully stuck his arms into the sleeves, it wrapped around his thin body and made the Chief Operator look like someone out of a fall advertisement.

"Thank you," Kit said, hugging himself as if he feared Henley would take the gift back. "No one's ever given me anything before that wasn't food. You're so kind, Henley."

"Like I said, it's not that big of a deal." Henley turned away to get his coffee and caught a glimpse of his reddening cheeks in the mirror. With a soft grunt of annoyance, he threw the strap of his bag across his chest. "Let's go."

They checked out of the hotel despite the hotel staff urging them to stay where it was safe. Even the protection of the covered hotel driveway didn't block the storm. The valet, soaking wet after retrieving Henley's car, looked at them as if they were crazy when he handed over the keys. Henley and Kit were liberally splattered with heavy rain by the time they were secure.

"This rain is aggressive."

"This isn't even tropical storm–level wind. You should have been here about a month ago—we're almost out of storm season now." Henley pulled out from under the cover of the hotel entrance and onto the driveway. The rain was too heavy for his windshield wipers to be effective. He parked the car right where the driveway met the main road, and the high water lapped at his tires.

"Alright. We're going to need some pretty heavy magic to get through this weather. I'll minimize the magic needed by focusing on the car and not the rain."

"So efficient." Kit had no respect for seatbelt safety; he was sitting sideways in his seat, cross-legged. "You mortals are so smart. No one in the Between or the Ethereal gives you enough credit."

"You can keep up the flattery after make it through traffic." Henley gave the Chief Operator a stare over his rain-splattered glasses. "Can you give me what I need?"

Kit tucked his hands under Henley's. His palms were warm and delivered a small electric shock. "Whatever you need," he affirmed.

Henley closed his eyes. He centered and rooted himself in place, steady against the currents of magic that would buffet him through the spell. Then he opened himself up. Once again, he felt nothing from the world, a dry emptiness that left his mouth and throat parched. From their joined hands, however, came a rush of heat and humming energy.

"Twenty percent," he said. His voice was barely audible over the roaring magic in his ears. He remembered Kit's comments about what the Ethereals did with memories and sifted through his own. The night he had tried buffalo steak at Brenner's was snapped up by the magic, along with the clink of tableware and the sound of his younger sister's giggle as she fished her napkin out from under the table. The taste wasn't enough, but the experience, the atmosphere, the sensations were a solid cluster of memory.

"*Unhindered Movement*. Let my steps be free and my way undeterred. Let the torrent part like a curtain and the floodwaters flee from my path. Let me find the way I seek without difficulty."

This time he was focused. The ruptured dam of energy that threatened to drown him was Kit's, not his own; he resisted it, keeping his mind fixed on the purpose of the spell and the eventual result. Even so, it was hard to ignore the glow of ecstasy and awe that filled his chest.

One hundred percent would be nothing if I was drawing on Kit.

That heretical thought sobered him. Henley opened his eyes, looking around the car. The rain and wind still pounded, but the immediate space around them showed heavy rain that wasn't impassable. He had lowered his hand as he worked; Kit held it in both of his, wrapped with care around the curl of Henley's fingers.

"So efficient," the Chief Operator sighed. "You're so clear about what you want, and you never use too much magic for the spell. Where did you learn to cast?"

"From my father." Henley frowned and pulled his hand free, making sure his own seatbelt was buckled. "Cross your fingers and hope the place we're going to is open. I've never seen it closed, but I can't imagine he's doing much business in this weather."

Kit made a small noise of agreement, then shifted in his seat to face forward, doing his best to mirror the mage's use of the seatbelt. Henley could feel those silver eyes on him as he drove the car onto the feeder road. In Houston, even hurricanes didn't keep people off the streets, but the traffic was limited to a handful of vehicles. None of them could move as fast as Henley and Kit with the magic protecting them from the worst of the storm.

The drive was easier, but it wasn't *easy*. If he moved too fast, they encountered high water, especially at the intersections. If he moved too slow, the water crept back around them, and the spell didn't have an infinite timeline. Fortunately, his apartment and the hotel weren't far from the coffee shop. As long as he kept his foot steady on the gas—wincing with every red light he ran—the spell did its job.

Kit was quiet support in the passenger seat. He didn't talk or offer distractions. When they crossed a particularly dangerous area of water or avoided something that floated into the street, the Chief Operator reached over to softly pat Henley's arm. Henley hadn't been touched so much since he'd moved away from home. Each pat helped remind him that he wasn't alone, and that the magic would keep them safe.

"Just a little more," he said as they drove under an overhead tangle of freeway ramps. The rain cut off in short bursts as the ramps blocked the water, making Kit stare up at them in fascination. A deep pit of water waited for them as they reached the shopping center. Henley gritted his teeth and drove right into the depths. The water curved away from his sedan, and they passed unscathed. He forced out a breath through his teeth.

"This center is pretty new, so it's on a higher elevation than the other areas we've been. We should be okay now." Most of the surroundings were dark. Many stores were locked up despite the normal business hours, with signs in their windows apologizing for the inconvenience.

At the far end of the center, however, tucked against a parking garage, Fine Ground glowed with golden light.

Henley put the car into park once they made it to the coffee shop and relaxed against the seat. "I do not want to do that again any time soon," he muttered, then glanced at Kit. "What do you have to do here?"

Kit struggled to unbuckle his seatbelt, sitting forward on the edge of his seat. His attention was held by the wooden doors in front of them. "I just need a little time to focus. This place feels so strange—like everything is twisted. Is it really safe for mortals? How can you stand to be around something like this?"

"Just gives me a headache on bad days. I can't use this kind of magic. We'll be safer here than anywhere else in the city—the owner is a friend. He makes the best coffee, too. Don't say or do anything weird if there's anyone else in the shop. We don't want people taking note of us when the Observers are on the hunt."

"I don't really know what you consider weird," Kit replied, and Henley pretended he hadn't heard as he got out of the car with his bag slung over his shoulder. His spell held for the short walk to the door, but it was designed only to make sure their path was unimpeded. The rain battered his clothes and left his glasses soaked by the time they made it inside.

The amused comment that had always greeted him at the door didn't reach his ears. Henley shook the water from his hands and shoes as Kit closed the door and dragged his hair out of his face. When Henley looked for the proprietor, Elryk was behind the bar in his usual place, staring at them.

Staring at Kit.

"Did you run out of coffee with the rush?" Hen asked, ignoring the streaks on his glasses as he walked to the counter and took his usual seat. Kit followed, gazing around the room with the curiosity Fine Ground deserved. "I'm going to be upset if I can't get a cup after what we just drove through."

The shop was empty of more than just people. It felt "off," the heavy atmosphere broken into dry patches. When Henley walked through them, his throat would feel parched, though the next second his steps felt light. Ignoring the strangeness of Fine Ground's location was no longer an option.

Elryk reached across the bar and took the mage's glasses off his nose, wiping them with a clean cloth. His eyes were still on Kit when he returned the glasses to his customer. "I can't run out of dark roast—it's all I've got," he drawled. "Who's your friend, Henley?"

"This is Kit. He needs to contact someone and the magic's a little broken. Kit, this is Elryk Seldriksen. He owns the shop."

The coffee man gave a slow nod. "All the magic is broken. Must have been something really dramatic to change the natural order like that. Can't imagine it will be long before someone gets it fixed, but time's so relative—long for who? The world or a human lifespan?"

"Not that long," Kit said, and he shrugged when the other two looked his way. "I mean, it can't go on that long, right? The storms, the people who will be hurt . . . if it doesn't stop, the damage to the world will be irreversible."

"Good enough point." Elryk examined Kit for another long second before he nodded to the back area of the shop, a door with a sign that read 'No Man's Land.' "There's a space back there for whatever you need to do, if you're confident. Have you ever worked with a nexus node before?"

"I haven't," Kit said. "But I don't need anything complicated, just a quick message. A few minutes."

"Longer than that and the convergence will warp your mind. Be quick."

Kit nodded. He hadn't taken a seat, and he disappeared into the back room as fast as he had arrived. The other two stared after him until Elryk slid a glance in the mage's direction.

"What have you gotten yourself into, Henley?"

Henley set his bag on the floor, and then folded his arms on the counter. *How much to say?* The question answered itself when he found himself talking, the words breaking past his better judgment.

"He's the one who stopped the magic. He said there was an attack, so he took down the Switchboard." He lifted his head, watching Elryk's reaction. The coffee man didn't look confused, only grave. Years of half-formed suspicions fell into place. Henley had always known Elryk was much more than a normal mage.

"Who attacked?"

"He calls them the Shields. Is that the same thing as the Observers?"

"Mostly. They're more militant on the other side, where they only have one government to answer to." Elryk braced his hands on the bar, hanging his head to stare at the floor. "Who's he calling?"

"He's trying to get a message through to the High Spirits."

"Not a bad idea, if he can manage it. Henley, do you know who he is? *What* he is?"

"He explained the Between to me, a little. I know he's the Lead Operator. I can still do magic if he's holding my arm."

"*Chief* Operator. If he's at odds with the Shields, the Between is in real trouble." Elryk raised his head to lock serious eyes on his customer. "You need to get out of this, Henley. However you got into it, you need to turn around and walk right back out. This isn't made for mortals."

"He came through a portal into my apartment, and the Shields chased him. They know he's with me. When I tried to call the Observers and get help, they pinpointed our location at the hotel and said they knew what I'd gotten into." Henley pulled off his glasses to rub his face. The familiar environment was no comfort when someone he trusted showed that much concern. "He said they killed someone at his substation. What will they do if they get their hands on me?"

"Interrogate you, detain you 'with cause,' ruin your reputation if you don't cooperate. Hurt your dad's political chances. They have far-reaching authority that dwarfs anything in this world, but they probably wouldn't kill you." Elryk lowered his voice again, leaning close. The light caught his deep brown eyes, making them shimmer gold and red. "You don't have to make his problem yours."

"It doesn't take a great man to do great things."

"Be serious, Henley. This is no game, and I can only see it ending badly if you continue forward."

"It's my problem too, Elryk. I'm already in this. The least I can do is help him get in contact with some higher power. It's the *right* thing to do if someone evil is trying to kill him." Henley frowned and sat up straight. The stool creaked under him, the old wood protesting his movement. "I can't let him go on his own if there's a chance he could die or be in danger."

Elryk exhaled a grunt. "You've adopted a puppy."

"That puppy's got as many secrets as you do, but I keep coming back for the coffee anyway."

The darker man averted his eyes, then pushed away from the counter. The machines behind him were still hot despite the fractured magic. Maybe they were working on electricity that day. Maybe. "I never brought killers or the police to your door. I can't do much to help you. As knowledgeable as I am, I don't have power or connections."

"I'm pretty sure you could do anything you put your mind to, but I'm not asking for favors. Once Kit's done with his call, we'll figure out where we're going next."

"I appreciate your discretion. I promise I won't let you walk off a bridge into the void, if I can help it." Elryk set a cup of familiar brew in front of Henley with enough care that no ripples marred the surface. "What does he drink?"

"Tea," Henley replied, and Elryk rolled his eyes. "Just put up with us a little longer. I don't want to bring this down on you, either."

"Probably too late for that," Elryk sighed, and turned back to his machines. Henley knew the tea he made would have an aftertaste of coffee, but the man made it just the same. "I can handle the Observers. If this gets to be too much, I want to know about it, alright? Maybe I can do something to get you out of it."

"You'll be the first to know."

EIGHT

BAD NEWS, PART TWO

The weight of Elryk's eyes followed Kit through the coffee shop, across the well-worn hardwood floors much older than the building implied, past the hanging relics that bled magic from a hundred different countries, and into the shadowed back area. The door looked innocent and practical from afar. Up close, it crackled with protective spells and warnings that made him fear putting his hand to the surface. They were unaffected by the lack of magic and the twisted flow of the ley lines.

Shoulders up and fingers clenched in preparation for a shock, Kit pushed on the door. It opened without incident. He narrowed his eyes at the aged wood and stepped through as quickly as he could manage. It closed behind him so fast it almost caught his sweater.

Kit curled his fingers into the heavy knit as he looked around the room. The softness, warm with the consideration of the giver, protected him from the unknown. Just the smell of the dye in the fibers made Kit breathless. It was *new*, it was *his*, and someone had *given* it to him. What an astonishing feeling it was, to be remembered.

He didn't need much protection from the space behind the door. It was a small office, with shelves against one wall full of coffee supplies, an aging sofa that sagged in the middle with a crocheted blanket across the back, and a desk against the far wall. The desk had the same air of history as the rest of the shop. A laptop sat to one side, gathering dust. Several uncut gems were scattered across the desk's surface, shards and small fragments. None were diamonds. All echoed with the same cardamom-flavored energy he felt from Elryk. Kit knew what Elryk was, and he knew Elryk knew the same about Kit.

He rubbed the center of his chest as he took a seat on the sofa. He would deal with Elryk later, as necessary. The man had allowed him into the office, where the magic hummed at an almost-stable level, raw and open to the Actuality like a wound or a geode. They were friends for the moment. Kit wanted to cause as little trouble for Henley as possible.

The sofa was so low to the ground that his knees stuck up in front of him. A spring under his rear end made him shift to the side, only to find two more.

"You've got too many happy memories," Kit muttered to the furniture, and took a deep breath. He let his hands fall loose into his lap. The ceiling and walls were paneled wood, golden and faded with time. He stared up at the planks, following the grain, letting his mind empty.

"Requesting connection," he said, and the magic yawned open in front of him. It was strange and electric, bubbling and fizzing, not the smooth energy he knew. He didn't use the magic the way a mage would, sending his request instead within the lines of energy that bound the worlds together. "Direct line. Operator, Substation No. 28, 'Kelley.' Red sequence." He'd never used a red sequence on a personal call. The connection clicked into place so fast he didn't realize the line was solid and sat in silence for a few seconds before the clearing of Kelley's throat came through his mind.

"Hello? This is Kelley?"

Kit drew a startled breath. *"Sorry, Kelley, that was so fast. Are you alright? How is No. 28?"*

"KIT?!"

The cry was loud and Kit would have held the phone away from his ear if he'd had a handset.

"Yes, I got a little lost running. I'm fine, sorry I haven't been in touch—I don't have much time."

"Several operators are missing. The count was five before you called. Sandoval is dead. There was so much blood, Kit." Kelley drew a deep

breath, as if he were afraid of the words. *"And the Switchboard is down, aside from direct lines within the Between. I tried to fix it. The Shields have been so good to us, reassuring us, escorting us home. I can't figure out how the entire Board went out, and I don't feel safe. What happened to you? I remember you shouting and then everyone ran. The Shield Captain said you saved everyone when you had us evacuate, but there wasn't any fire. Did . . . you see what happened to Sandoval?"*

Kit swallowed around the knot in his throat. He smelled the blood, mixed with tea and fresh baked muffins. *"I did. I can't talk about it. That's why I waited to call until now—I've been too scared to do anything else."*

"Why is this happening Kit? Who could do this? Can the Shields even protect us if the killer took one of them down?"

Kit lowered his head against his closed fists, digging his nails into his palms. He thought about his counterpart's neatly braided hair, his clean desk, the way Kelley talked about the new lady he'd been seeing and how much he wanted to try making candy someday when he had time. He thought about the Shields chasing him, and how they would hunt Kelley down if the other operator showed signs of knowing the truth.

"Try not to worry about the what-ifs. We're just operators, Kelley. We're not meant to fix things that are broken."

"But you can fix the Board, right? Where are you?"

Kit huddled deeper in his cardigan.

"I can, but I'm at the other end of the Between. It will take time for me to get back. I'm sure everything will be fine, Kelley—you just need to keep your guard up. Don't trust anyone. I need you to—"

"I know, and I'm being very careful. I'm sure it won't take long. The Shields are summoning the Lineman to catch the killer. Can you believe it? Everyone is so relieved. Sorry, I cut you off there, what did you need?"

The world spun to a halt. Kit didn't hear Kelley's apology. He was staring into the space in front of him, unable to see the shelf full of office supplies directly ahead. The magic of the room, the sound of Kelley's voice, the fabric under his fingers, all of it was wiped out of his mind.

"The Lineman?" he whispered.

"Yes, so don't be afraid to get back here. We'll be safe."

"Okay. Don't worry about anything, I'll see you soon. Disconnecting."

"Kit? Didn't you need something? What—"

The thread of connecting magic broke, and a scream clawed at Kit's throat. The walls closed in. The sofa seemed to hold him, trapping him in place. His skin was hot and his breathing was short. Possessed with mad energy, he threw himself out of the sofa, then tore out of the office as if it were on fire, running straight past the coffee bar and out into the rain. *I have to run. Have to get away and disappear. If I'm caught—*

The storm slammed into him, unhindered by any spell. The wind almost blew him off his feet. He hit the wall of the closest building and bounced, scraping his fingers on the brick, then kept running. He stumbled over a curb and went down to his knees in the street. The pooled water soaked the legs of his pants and the sleeves of his cardigan. He staggered up and forced himself onward.

The path he took led him to a dead end. Fine Ground was in a weird place, tucked behind dumpsters and maintenance fences. With the parking garage on one side and the artificial stucco walls of the shop on the other, Kit found himself with nowhere to run. He tried climbing the walls, only to be pulled backward. He fell. Henley yanked him around and shook him. The mage was soaking wet.

"What happened?" Henley yelled over the roar of the storm. "What are you doing?!"

"He's coming for me!" Kit replied, struggling against the mage's grip. "The Lineman—he's coming—I have to run or I'll be caught—"

Henley shook him again, squinting through the rain, then dragged him back toward the shop. Kit fought him with every forced step. The doorway provided little protection, but it blocked the wind and let them hear each other without shouting.

"What does that mean?" Henley demanded. "Who is the Lineman? What does that have to do with you?"

"The Lineman is the judge and executioner," Kit told him, gripping the front of Henley's shirt. The fabric pulled and bunched in his grasp as he tried to shove Henley into action. "He never stops until he finds what he seeks. He's a mindless, emotionless killer. If they've released him, that means—means—I'm gone! I'll never be me again! He cuts threads, the spirits he executes are torn from the Between—"

"Okay! Okay, calm *down*." Henley grabbed Kit's shoulders and shielded his companion's body from view against Fine Ground's door. Kit huddled between the man and the wood, ducked down as if hiding would make any difference. Henley was cold. Everything was cold. Kit didn't think he could feel warm again.

"They were already after you. What difference does it make who is chasing you and how? It's the same problem."

"No," Kit said. He rested his head against the mage's chest and felt the scrape of Henley's shirt buttons. "He'll find me. Nothing can stop him. He won't stop, he won't listen. If he gets to me before I can contact the High Spirits, the Between will *definitely* be rewritten because the Switchboard can't be fixed—"

Henley was patting Kit's hair and back, tense and awkward. "How do we get him called off, then? How do we stop him from coming at all?"

Logic wasn't Kit's forte on a regular basis, less so when he was upset. "We can't, nothing can stop him, he's going to—"

"*Kittinger!*"

Henley barked in his ear and gave the Chief Operator another forceful shake. "Who calls him?" he continued. "Who sends him out?"

"The—the Shields do. The Shields summon him when there's been a severe crime."

"So we have to stop the Shields, which means contacting the High Spirits. Did you have any luck with your call?"

"N . . . no. I disconnected when I heard about the Lineman, but the Shields are everywhere. I don't think the other operators can do anything without being watched."

"Damn." Henley swore, looking around. They were so wet that the rain didn't matter, even as they both shivered. "How else can we get through?"

Kit looked up at him. Henley had pushed his drenched glasses up into his hair, which stuck out at odd angles where the rain made it clump. The mage's frustration made his breath hot, the only warmth in their little circle.

"We would have to go to the Between."

"Alright then, how do we get to the Between?"

Kit pushed Henley away, staring at his companion with disbelief.

"You can't go to the Between! You're a mortal, mortals can't even survive the magic flux, you don't have a Purpose or an Assignment. You would die!"

"Can I *get* those things?"

Kit's words died in his mouth. Water dripped from his tangled hair and down the back of his neck. His cardigan was so heavy with the weight of the rain.

"When a spirit first manifests into the Between, they have to get Assigned. There's a process for that. Even the High Spirits can't summon or create a new spirit with an Assignment in place. But if the process takes too long, if they realize you're mortal, if we do *anything* that tells the Shields where we are—"

Henley reached up, gripping Kit's shoulders again with strong hands.

"Kit, do you want to die or not?"

"I don't want to disappear," Kit ground out between clenched teeth, before he even fully processed the question. The world spun in his peripheral vision.

"Then we have to go to the Between. Stop thinking about why we shouldn't, and start thinking about how we can do it."

"Why are you doing this?" The words were almost lost in the noise of the storm. The smell of rain filled Kit's nose, humidity and hot concrete. "You could die. At the worst you'll be killed, at the best you'll be arrested.

You don't have to do any of this, you don't even have to know about the Between."

"Because it was my kitchen!" The words were forceful, and Henley glared at the taller Chief Operator. "Because you showed up in my kitchen cabinet, in my city, in my storms, and I can either do something about it or stick my head back in the sand like a damn ostrich. We can't go to the police. All the magic here is broken. What else should I do? Just let you give up?"

"I don't know!" Kit grasped at the air between them, elbows banging against the door that was hard against his back. "If I take you there, if we both die then what was the point? What if the Lineman gets me, and you can't go back home?"

Henley grabbed Kit's wrists. The mortal stood in front of him, framed by the pounding storm. His gaze was as intense as his voice, if a little unfocused without his glasses.

"That's my problem," Henley said. "You don't get to make that decision for me. If something bad happens, I'll handle it. If I get caught, I'll deal with the consequences. I'm not going to stand by while this happens to you and my city. Besides, they're coming for me, too. I have family here, friends that might get caught up in this. If the Shields are already killing people, I don't want to give them an easy target. Right now my family doesn't know anything, and I can protect them by getting as far away from here as possible."

It didn't make sense. Kit could think of a hundred arguments, a hundred ways for Henley to disconnect himself and back out of the situation. The Chief Operator's fear clouded his mind.

What is one mortal going to do against the Lineman? What am I going to do by myself?

Kit dropped his eyes to the ground, watching the waves of rain get blown against the back of the mage's legs. Henley's fancy leather shoes were holding water around his dark socks. Kit had no idea how they would ever get dry.

"Okay," he said, giving a little nod. "I'm scared. I don't know what else to do so please . . ." He looked up, putting every bit of desperation and urgency he could into his eyes. "Help me."

NINE

ELRYK TOLERATES NONSENSE

At least when Henley and his friend had entered the shop the first time, they hadn't brought half the rain in the door with them.

Elryk had heard the yelling through the door, though not the details. Something had upset the Chief Operator. He was the excitable type, all wild gestures and big expressive eyes. Henley now, that was a different story. Elryk hadn't seen Henley get so passionate about anything in their five years of acquaintance. On the other side of the door, Henley's shoulders were tense. Fire flashed in his eyes, causing echoes that spoke to some of the artifacts hanging around the shop.

"Beautiful," Elryk murmured, watching the sparks as they floated around the room. The shop felt a little warmer, which it could use in that weather. Still, the sparks came with a twisting feeling in the back of his head.

When the pair re-entered the shop, they were both soaked and sloshing across the floor. Kittinger was still cowering from whatever had run him out of the door, but Henley stepped up to the bar like a man with a purpose.

"I'm not going to like this," Elryk told him before he could speak. "The shit just got deeper, and you're stomping both of your cute feet into it. Better men than us have died from that sort of thing, Henley. Died or lost everything."

"Noted," Henley said. He gave Elryk a smile, that same smile he wore when he'd committed to New Years at his parents' place or agreed to extra hours at work. The smile that told the coffee man his favorite customer wasn't going to be back for a few days. "We need to use your back room again."

"And?"

"And we're using it to ground a portal."

The situation keeps getting worse. "And?"

"And I need you to tell my sister if something happens to me."

Elryk looked up at the ceiling, asking for grace. Then he looked back at the pair, pointed at Kit, and pointed to the far corner of the shop.

"Find somewhere to be, Chief Operator. I've got things to say to this one."

Kit was smart, Elryk acknowledged, because he hurried to the table in question and sat without complaint. He did trail water all over the floor. Elryk supposed he couldn't have everything.

"El—"

"I said I had things to say to you, not the other way around," he said when Henley opened his mouth. He leaned on the counter with both elbows, staring into Henley's gleaming black eyes. *A man could get lost in eyes like those, wondering what was happening behind them. Humans are marvelous.* Elryk lowered his voice.

"There are places in this universe mortal men aren't meant to go," he said. "Systems in place, barriers that are made to protect. You're taking huge risks for a pretty face, Henley."

"That's not what this is about, El. People are trying to kill him."

"And what qualifies you to help, Mr. Graphic Designer? Think you can do some damage with your typefaces?"

"No one else is going to believe him."

"He found one fool."

Henley made a sound of frustration and ran his hands back through his hair. Elryk reached out to grab his glasses before they fell, cleaning them off again. Henley thanked him and put them back on.

"We're out of options. Plan A failed. There's only one other plan. Things aren't going to get easier because I wish they would."

"The thing you're about to do scares me, and I take a lot of scaring. I would never dare what you're proposing." Elryk met his eyes again, lowering his voice to the faintest whisper. "Your spirit is weak. Can you find enough strength, fast enough, to survive?"

"I'll figure it out."

Elryk exhaled. He stared at the door, holding back the relentless rain.

"I'm going to be a sad man if I don't get to make you coffee anymore," he said, feeling his age. Henley, with all his energy and determination, felt so young. *Maybe if I just close the doors and put them to sleep—*

The ground shifted under his feet. It was a tiny vibration, unnoticeable to a mortal. Elryk straightened up fast, grabbing a small paper napkin and slapping it down on the bar with a pen from his apron.

"Give me your sister's number." He raised his voice. "Chief Operator, you'd better get busy. Don't make a mess."

Kit leapt out of his chair and darted into the back. Elryk revised his opinion upward again.

"Elryk? What's wrong?"

He looked back at Henley and tapped the bar twice. "*Number.* Don't think there's no magic in the world just because you can't feel it."

Henley grabbed the pen and scribbled a number. Elryk snatched the napkin as soon as he could and stuffed it into his apron. "Go. You haven't got long. Come *back*, Henley, in one piece."

"Thank you."

He didn't look at Henley as he said the words, waving a hand at him with his eyes locked on the door. Henley disappeared into the back, leaving only his puddles of rainwater behind. Pleading for the mage's safe return died in Elryk's throat.

He pressed his lips to a thin line as the front door opened again. The uniformed officers who stepped in ignored him at first, searching the shop with their eyes. A hazy aura around the group identified them as true Shields, not the Observers that plagued him on a regular basis. These officers were sharp enough to notice the water. They tried to keep ignoring Elryk as they headed for the back areas, which was just plain rude.

"Now, now, gentlemen and ladies. This place doesn't belong to you."

The ground ate their feet in a rush of loose earth that rose from between the cracks in the aged hardwood floor. Elryk wasn't ruining it after all the decades he'd occupied that space. The dirt clawed up their legs and solidified into stone, making them stumble and stagger.

"Your residence in the Actuality depends on your cooperation," the leader said. He was a skinny man with a big nose and too much flash on his collar pins. His face was turning an ugly red as he tried to fight the earth.

"Fine for refusing entry is fifty percent," Elryk replied, picking up Henley's forgotten mug of coffee. He took a sip from the black depths and felt the familiar shiver of pleasure. "I'm refusing entry. Full stop. You can come back with a Writ of Search."

"I don't need a writ to—"

"Yes, you do," Elryk cut him off, agreeable but implacable. "I predate your rules. Get your Summons, buy a coffee, or get out."

The magic ripped. The flow might have been stopped but the ambient magic still existed in the world, evidenced by the ley lines and the nexus they created. Someone—Kit, presumably—had stuck his hands into the flow and torn it open. It gave Elryk a splitting headache. Three of his relics fell from the wall, one drained of magic. The lead officer pulled his service weapon and brandished it at the coffee man.

"You'll release us right now or I'll have you on charges of interference!"

Elryk smiled over the rim of his mug.

"Go ahead."

The earth slithered back beneath the floorboards. Free, the officers raced into the back office and bounced off the heavy wards Elryk had put into place. They could open the door, but not enter. Their sounds of frustration confirmed that Henley and Kit were gone.

"We won't forget this, Maker."

Elryk lifted his head to stare at the leader as he stomped past. He saluted with his coffee mug, feeling the heat of fire oozing into his skin, his eyes, his hair. His presence filled the room with force.

"Neither will I. Get out."

They recoiled from him and left. He took a seat on his stool behind the counter and stared into his mug, wishing he could be sure Henley was ever coming back.

TEN

ARRIVAL AT THE SWITCHBOARD

The first thing Henley noticed when they arrived in the Between was that the portal wasn't at floor level. He had thrown himself into the swirling, glowing crevasse Kit had torn in midair, expecting to step through to the other side. The five-foot drop meant he landed hard on a different wood floor. Then Kit followed and fell on top of him in a heap, knocking the wind out of his lungs. They stayed motionless for several seconds, listening.

The portal closed. The space around them was dark and silent.

Kit rolled off him and to his knees. Henley sat up, wet clothes pulling at his skin. The place where they had arrived was warmer than Fine Ground, almost stuffy, without the circulation of central air conditioning. The floor under their bodies didn't have the smooth polish of Elryk's hardwood. Instead, it was dry, warped, and cracked.

"It's so quiet," Kit whispered. "I've never heard the Switchboard quiet."

"You're sure we're in the right place?"

Kit took a deep breath. Henley did the same and sneezed.

"Oh yes," the Chief Operator said. He rose to his feet and shuffled around. With the sound of a metal pull chain, he turned on a small desk lamp that gave Henley his first view of the infamous Switchboard. When his eyes adjusted, Henley saw shadowed rows and rows of desks with single wooden chairs, each facing a tall panel full of bulky ports and wires. The wires ran up the backs of the panels and connected in a vast web to the ceiling. Some of the chairs were knocked over, others pushed back. Papers and pencils were scattered across the floor.

Kit reached out to the closest panel and unplugged three wires crossing its surface, then plugged them back in along the bottom row. His face was still pale from his earlier outburst, and his breathing was still unstable. As he settled into his familiar environment however, the Chief Operator's distress calmed. His hands were gentle on his tools.

"Didn't you say the Shields were everywhere?" Henley gestured around them to the stillness. "Why aren't they here now? As a side note, I think bringing us back to the scene of the crime was a questionable move."

"Sorry. I'm not a mage. All I could do was use the same connection path that took me to the Actuality." Kit shook his head. "If Kelley—that's who I called—couldn't fix the Board, then no one could but me. They could make it worse. They probably secured this place so no one could tamper with it."

"They must not have let any of the operators trying to fix the Board clean up," he added, wrapping his arms around his thin body. "All of the connections are still in place—if the Board came back up now it would send magic bursting out all over the Actuality. I bet it's the same at all the substations."

Henley got to his feet and looked around. The chairs were small, the desks cramped but dotted with small pictures, trinkets, and mugs. A few comfortable sweaters hung over the backs of chairs. Dozens of panels were lined up around the room in a labyrinth of rows, sectioned off with strips of worn green carpet. The small, high windows kept the room dim, but the personal items added cheer. A stabbing pressure behind his eyes made it hard to think.

"Why is the air so thin?"

"Because you don't belong here," Kit replied, turning back to face him. His clothes were still the soaked, modern look, out of place among the 1920s furnishings. "If you didn't have the ability to use magic, the

Between would reject you completely, but as it stands you're just 'out of place.' Don't push yourself too hard until we get you Assigned."

"Time for you to explain that process. What are we getting into?"

Kit nodded but beckoned for Henley to follow him through the desks. Henley did, keeping his steps slow. Kit didn't complain.

"I want to see what they've done before we leave," the Chief Operator said, taking random turns at openings between the desks. They left their small circle of light, and Kit lit another lamp. One rested between every pair of desks on heavy metal arms, and none were powerful. Several minutes later, when Henley looked back, a dotted line of soft golden glow marked their path through the room. A large, open aisle led a straight line from a pair of double doors to the back wall. A lonely muffin rested forgotten on the floor to one side. Kit paused to stare at the doors.

"That's the entrance," he said. "That's where they killed Sandoval."

He shook himself before Henley could offer comfort, then kept walking past an open kitchen and the smell of burned coffee. The personal effects on the desks changed but the panels didn't, a sea of matching stations left in a state of panic. Their destination was to the back of the room. As Kit bent to retrieve a large mug from under a chair, Henley slowed his steps and stared at the desk in front of them. It had a chair and panel like the others, but the wires that hung from the ceiling were thicker, more numerous, and their ends were exposed and broken. The panel itself had four times as many ports and ten times as much wear.

"This is your desk?"

"Mmhmm." Kit set the mug on the desk, finding a spot under a pile of papers and empty cookie tins.

"Why is it different from the others?"

"Different?" Kit blinked, then looked up at it with a smile. "Because it's mine, as the Chief Operator. Because I've been here the longest and I know the most. No. 28 is the core of the Switchboard, and this is the center of No. 28."

Henley stared at the frayed cables, then at his companion. The wires were nightmarish in the limited light. "Is the Chief Operator very powerful?"

Kit let out a nervous laugh. "What? No, no, every operator is equal. I just know more, I can do more, faster, so I have more space to work. I fix problems and figure things out. But when I'm not working, Kelley takes over some of my connections, and the rest are dispersed." Kit patted the chair of the desk behind his own, clear of paper and dusted clean. He pointed to a thick wire hanging lower over his desk.

"They tried to fix it, but they couldn't. After that they probably stopped so they didn't risk setting all of the connections on fire. If you don't know what you're doing, you can make a real mess."

"Can you fix it?"

Kit stared up at the broken cables for a long second, then nodded.

"Mmhmm. They all kind of look the same, but I know what the wires are. They just have to be reconnected properly."

"How difficult is that?"

"Not at all. Once I know it's safe, when the Shields can't take the magic, I'll restore the connection right away."

Kit stepped up to his desk again and brushed soft fingers over the cables waiting to be used.

"I'm so sorry," he whispered. "I'll make it right, I promise."

Henley gripped his shoulder and gave it a squeeze. "Let's get moving, Kit," he said. "The faster we do what we came here for, the faster everything goes back to normal."

The Chief Operator exhaled and nodded. He looked around, as if he could take the details of the place with him when they left.

"We need to hide, first. The Switchboard generates so much magic that the area around it is warped; the Shields couldn't have sensed our arrival. However, they probably know we left the Actuality, and there's only a few places I would go, so they'll be here soon."

Henley sucked in a sharp breath, which lead to a coughing fit. "Seriously?" he replied when he could breathe again. "How are they able to use magic if all of the magic is gone? Let's go?!"

"It's not magic," Kit replied as he set off again. "They're like me, but they have different powers to move from one world to another. Even if they didn't, they've got gems full of stored magic they can use."

He didn't turn on any more lamps, leading Henley into darkness where he found several sharp corners on which to bruise his legs and several chairs to trip over. His quiet cursing and the pace of their transit aggravated his condition. The world began to spin, and he had to grab the nearest wall for support.

"Just a little more," Kit said. The Chief Operator had altered his clothing to dry himself, but still smelled of rain. "Careful, there's stairs."

Stairs meant a railing at least, and Henley clung to it as they made their way up to another area. This one was dustier and had even less light. Kit pulled him sideways and through a doorway while Henley was caught in another coughing fit. He closed the door behind them.

"We're a little safer here," the Chief Operator said, releasing his grip on the other man. "This area is used for storage and not well known. We have to get you ready to go. How are we going to hide you from anyone? You're a mortal! You're weak! Everyone is going to know!"

His voice had begun to rise once more, and he dug his fingers into his messy hair. Henley rubbed his face. Focusing on anything was difficult when he was struggling to breathe, and his head felt like the inside of a drum.

"Kit, you've got to calm down."

"I know. I know. I'm sorry. It seems so impossible. There are so many ways for everything to go wrong."

"You got us this far." Henley felt around; the room was stuffed with stacked boxes. He found one low enough, sturdy enough, and sat. "Tell me how you would do it if you were writing a fantastic story."

"A story? What kind of story?"

"The kind you'd tell a child or some friends you wanted to impress."

"Um."

The Chief Operator shuffled around as he thought. When he pulled the chain on the dangling bulb in the center of the room, Henley saw that the bottom of the door had been blocked with another box to prevent light from escaping. Kit still wore the cardigan, but was otherwise back in the outfit he'd worn when they first met, simple clothes in tones of sepia that blended with his faded environment. Everything in the Between had an air of age.

"If I wanted to impress someone . . . I'd tell them I got through the Bureau without having to wait in line. I'd tell them how I bossed all the clerks around and how they hated it but had to listen to what I said. I'd, um . . . I'd say . . ."

"Start a little earlier. What's the Bureau?"

"It's where you get your Assignment. You come to the Between with a Purpose, and the Assignment confirms where you'll work and what you do. I mean, you sort of *appear* in the Between when the High Spirits decide you're needed. You wake up and you're there at the Bureau, and you have to get in line. It's awful. If you get transferred you have to do the same thing. That happens when the population of mages shifts in the Actuality and we need more operators in a certain place. If you don't have your Assignment then you can't work, and then you start to get sick."

"Sick?"

"Mmhmm. I can feel it in the back of my throat . . . the cough, the nausea." Kit raised two long fingers to touch his pulse at his neck. He didn't wear any jewelry aside from the heavy silver key. The chain caught on the neck of his shirt. "I can't work because the Board is down so I'm denying my Purpose. It happens sometimes when you're being Reassigned and there's a delay in your transfer. Not having an Assignment is twice as bad. Eventually you get so sick you can't move anymore, and you fade away—but that almost never happens."

"Is that what will happen to all of the operators if you don't get the Switchboard fixed?"

Kit turned to face him with eyes more storm gray than silver. "Yes."

"How many days until people start to fade?"

"A week, probably. Since they're trying to work but something else is keeping them from their positions."

Henley gave him a tight smile. "We already knew it was important. Now it's even more important, so we need to get to work. Keep telling me your story."

"Okay, well . . ." Kit raised his hands in frustrated gestures, starting to pace. The floor creaked under his laced brown boots. "It's really about speed, getting through the lines and the departments fast enough. And I can't go with you, because I have my Assignment."

Henley's stomach dropped. He bowed his head, taking deep breaths.

"Okay. It's not impossible, just difficult. We can handle difficult. How do we make your story real? How do we bully the clerks and skip the lines?"

"Well, we can't, the clerks are . . ."

Kit trailed off and touched the key hanging heavy around his neck. "What if . . ."

Henley raised his eyebrows, leaning forward a little, and beckoned for his companion to keep talking. "What if what?"

"Operators always have priority. Even now that should hold true. If we say you're not new, you're transferring, then you'd already have your key. Operators get their key when they're given their first Assignment to the Switchboard. You'd just need your paperwork moved. Since the Switchboard is down, they couldn't get your paperwork, and they'd have to put you into a special queue." Kit licked his lips. "You'd have to talk like an operator. You'd have to make a scene."

The last time Henley had made a scene, he'd been six years old and crying because someone had mistaken him for an apple in the school parade instead of a tomato. The pit in his stomach deepened.

"What happens if we don't do it this way?" he asked, cringing at his own cowardice.

"You'll be there for hours, maybe even days," Kit said, somber. "And you'll get weaker and worse. Right now your body is relying on your inherent magic to stay grounded, but you're using it up. Without an Assignment, the Between won't support you. You're in the same shape as everyone else but deteriorating twice as fast. The longer it takes, the more likely someone will realize you're mortal."

Henley pushed tomatoes and apples to the back of his mind. He sat up straight again, rolling his shoulders when the wetness of his clothes stuck the fabric to his body.

"Then we have to do it this way. I can handle it. You just need to make me look and sound like an operator."

"I'll try." Kit motioned for him to stand. "Hold out your arms. I should be able to fix your clothes."

Henley pushed himself up, bracing his feet when the world spun. He lifted his arms. Kit stepped in close—*very* close, and wrapped his arms tight around him, pressing their bodies together. Henley raised his eyes to stare at the far corners of the room, doing his best to not think about the warmth.

Don't lie to yourself. Being hugged after all this insanity is comforting.

Before he could think of an appropriate response to the thought, fabric slithered across his skin. The sensation was like having clothes steamed on his body, hot and damp, pulling and loosening in areas he didn't expect. As soon as it began, it was over, and Kit stepped back.

"That's good," the Chief Operator muttered, and nodded. "How do you feel?"

Henley patted himself. His clothes were dry. The pants were looser, lower, the vest new and tighter, all in shades of white or dark gray or black. He had armbands around both biceps. His glasses hadn't changed, but they weren't speckled with rain.

"My underwear is still damp."

"I had to convince your clothes that they were mine to make them change." Kit smiled a little. "Getting your underwear to do the same seemed a little personal."

"Point taken." His hair was dry as well, and a little longer on the sides. *How does that work—is hair considered clothes?* He didn't feel quite like himself in his skin, adding to his general sense of misery. He thought back to Kit's arms around him and wished he could lean on the Chief Operator and sleep like a child. "Now what? How do we get to the Bureau?"

"We just go. You're going to have to trust me, Henley, and stay calm—the Between isn't much like the Actuality. You're going to be scared."

"I'm already scared." Henley offered a hand to his companion. "We're doing this together, Kit. I trust you. I know we can handle this. Just talk to me as we go and get me ready."

Kit stared into his eyes, and some of the Chief Operator's desperation seemed to fade. He took Henley's hand and squeezed. "Thank you. I couldn't do this without you, really. Once we finish this stage we can get to work."

"That's the idea. So scare me, let's get this over with."

"Yes, but first—"

Kit dropped his hand and lifted the heavy silver chain from around his neck. The metal glittered in his shaking hands as he placed the chain over Henley's head with reverence. "Please be careful with it," he said. "I'm sure you will. I'm sure it will protect you."

"You'll be okay without it for a while?"

"Mmhmm. It's not my Assignment—without the Board working, it doesn't have any use. It's just precious."

"I'll give it back as soon as possible."

Kit nodded, settling the chain and straightening the key against the mage's chest with a soft pat before he stepped back.

"Okay. We're going out the back way, but there's still an open drop. I'll hold your hand the entire time. I promise I won't let you go—just don't scream. People are usually delighted by the way we move around."

"Sounds exciting. I'll smile really big to cover my screaming."

Kit gave him a concerned look, then a nervous smile when he realized Henley was joking. He didn't gain confidence as he turned off the light and unblocked the door. When Henley could see the Chief Operator's face again, the tension had settled back around Kit's frame and tightened his mouth.

Henley was led a different route, down the same dark hallway and out a door that opened on a small wooden pathway between buildings. The air of the Between hit him in a rush. A strong draft blew through the narrow alley, forcing the pair to hold on to the railing. Henley felt the change in gravity as his steps lightened and the wind tried to pluck him from the platform walkway. The air was full of raucous calls from unseen sellers, the distant groan of factory machinery, and chatting clusters of people just out of sight. Every color was muted, the sky in perpetual overcast.

People were flying at the end of the alley.

He paused, and Kit looked back when Henley tugged his hand. He stared as figure after figure drifted up or down, each holding their own personal gravity that kept their clothes and hair going the same direction. The alley darkened as a large floating trolley glided past, blocking the light and bringing the smell of food. The shadow passed, and Henley realized he couldn't see anything but gray past the floating people. The Between had no horizon.

"The Between is limitless, up or down," Kit said in a low voice. "Once we're out there, you can stop yourself at any time. You can't fall. Nothing will happen to you when we start moving. Will you be alright?"

"I have no idea," Henley said, accepting the truth. "We're going to find out." His grip on Kit's hand was tight, but the Chief Operator didn't complain.

"Okay," Kit replied. "Try to listen as we move, and I'll tell you what I can. You can look miserable, since you're supposed to be sick, but don't scream." He walked them to the end of the alley, waited for a clear spot in the flow of people, and pushed off on his toes into midair.

Henley didn't scream as they leapt into the open gray sky, but he almost broke Kit's hand as he was pulled into empty space. Adrenaline surged through his veins and twisted his stomach. He was gasping for breath as the endless depth stretched out below them. Every instinct screamed that *HE WAS GOING TO DIE*, making his body shudder in preparation for the fall.

I'm never going to eat dumplings again. I didn't clean out the refrigerator. I left clothes at the dry cleaners—

But he didn't fall. Tethered to Kit, he was pulled through the flow of traffic, following others ahead. When he looked over his shoulder, he could see a trio of businessmen flying together, having an argument about a paper one kept brandishing. Below, a young woman checked a shopping list as she scanned the buildings they passed. She stepped out of the flow like a dandelion seed, alighting on a platform that smelled like spice and fresh bread. The buildings were floating sections of ordinary shopfronts with antiquated lettering painted across the windows. He saw no plants, animals, or children. Fixating on the details was much easier than thinking about the endless drop beneath them.

"Operators respond to magic," Kit said. "So your knowledge of spells is really helpful. We're always complaining about the way people use magic and abuse it, asking for too much or making sloppy requests."

The buildings were all flat-fronted, with porches that ranged from small landings to wide decks. Sometimes an alley would appear between buildings, like the one they had left. Everything was made of wood, with foggy glass windows and small electric lights sporadically placed on the face of larger establishments. Sometimes he heard strains of ragtime music that rose in his ears and were quickly lost behind them.

"We work long shifts and most operators don't socialize much, so no one knows much about us. We all know how important our work is, so we don't get distracted. We take vacations to Paradise but it's so rare. We really only go when we're burned out and exhausted." Kit looked up, then out toward the gray. "That's Paradise—the bright lights."

Henley followed the direction of Kit's pointing to stare at the lights, arrayed in levels like a massive chandelier. For a moment Paradise distracted him from his agoraphobia, until he noticed how small the figures were that came and went, tiny black specs in the distance. Paradise was *very* far away. Bile rose in the back of his throat. Kit pulled him sharply to the left to avoid an oncoming trolley—an actual trolley, with no wheels or overhead cables—which added to his disorientation. He wasn't sure if his trouble breathing came from the shock or the fact that he didn't belong in the Between, but it made him gasp as sharp pains bloomed in his chest.

"Shh, it's okay, you're okay . . . close your eyes if needed." Kit pulled him closer, linking their arms together. The position was more stable than their tenuous clasped hands. "You're doing fine. I almost cried when we were in your car, people kept zooming so close."

"Houston drivers set a bad standard," Henley wheezed, closing his eyes as instructed. It didn't help the feeling of floating, but it did help to not see the endless drop below. He took a deep breath.

"I hope so, that was terrifying. You can mention cities and locations by the way, we know about them, but we've never seen them. Our grasp of your geography is quite strong. Our fingers get sore and pricked if we're very busy, from making all the connections. All magic has a flavor, a sensation depending on what kind is requested. And we see the memories. Sometimes we try to make the recipes, but we're usually bad cooks."

The headache still threatened to crack his skull, but the mage's stomach was settling in small stages. The air was so thin and so cold in his lungs, even though the ambient temperature was pleasant.

"We don't have families, and we don't have children, Henley. That's very important. Everything will be over if you mention that."

Henley's feet met something solid. He opened his eyes, staring down as they settled on a big platform. Other figures came and went from a large, dreary building with few windows. His knees buckled, and Kit supported his weight.

"It's okay to look sick," the Chief Operator whispered. "Everyone is sick. Try to cough more than any other symptom. Stay strong. I'll be nearby, even if you can't see me. You're going into that door and you'll get in line, and then tell the first clerk that you're a transferring operator to No. 28. You need your new Assignment card. After that . . . push them until they want you gone."

"You're leaving? Now? Already?"

"We can't wait. You don't have time." Kit made sure the mage's legs were stable, then stepped back. He smiled, but tension ruled his silver eyes. "Be careful," he said, clasping the cuffs of his cardigan in tight fingers. "I'll see you soon."

Then he took a few steps back, pushed off on his toes, and soared away.

Eleven

The Bureau

Henley had plenty of time to calm down and conserve his energy. The endless line for the clerk snaked through a maze of dusty velvet ropes. The room was crammed with bodies. Shelves around the wall held ledger books that bore thick layers of grime and cracked covers. The low ceiling enhanced the air of claustrophobia. Not everyone was sick, but he heard coughs and the occasional wet-sounding sniffle from every corner of the room.

The petitioner at the counter walked away, and the line shifted forward a step. Henley kept his hands stuffed in his pockets and his head down. The only conversation was a few muttered comments about hating the place. Henley had only been there ten minutes and he hated it too. Standing still and waiting was agony after the urgency of their arrival to the Between.

What if Kit leaves me here? What if this is his way of washing his hands, so he can escape and hide?

The thought didn't strike Henley as accurate. He wanted to believe the best of the Chief Operator—and he didn't have a huge amount of faith in Kit taking care of himself. He'd seen the state of Kit's desk. He was uneasy about the tea mug he'd left behind. Had it ever been washed?

And he's so afraid.

Henley could distance himself from many things. Drama at work, politics, his disapproving family. Kit's eyes had been different. That strange silver gaze, clouded with terror in the rain, afraid for his life.

The way he had clutched at Henley like a branch in a raging river. The horrible certainty in his voice and the frantic way he had run out of the coffee shop. Henley couldn't find distance in the face of so much need.

I'm not dying for it. Nobody's dying. I won't accept it.

The line shifted, and Henley took a step. He glared at the floor, rubbing his aching chest. He'd never considered himself a hero or revolutionary. He had chosen a safe path. Being a mage could lead to dangerous or prestigious work, but he had chosen neither. He *chose* Kit. He chose to stand between the Chief Operator and the coming danger. Maybe Kit would do the same for him if things went south, but if not, Henley wouldn't go out with any regrets.

The line shifted.

Henley took a step.

For the next two hours.

By the time he reached the first clerk, he was feeling weak, from a lack of food or from the onslaught of the Between. He shuffled to the window, breath short, worn down by the waiting.

"Operator," he said, and coughed. It wasn't hard to fake. "Transfer to No. 28."

"Papers?" The clerk was a pretty young woman with nice eyes and an ugly shawl. Henley cleared his dry throat.

"Don't have any. Switchboard's down."

Her expression soured. "You'll have to go to the back of the line and wait for another clerk."

Back home, Henley had a River Oaks-area customer who had too much money and not enough humanity. He leaned forward and channeled that woman's menacing, offended tone. "I'm an *operator*. I have to get to *work*. I need my Assignment! Do you even realize what's happening right now?"

"Sir—"

"The whole BETWEEN could be gone in the morning and you want me to *wait for another clerk*?" He felt bad as she cringed back, but he didn't let up. His mother would have been mortified by his behavior. He was mortified. He silently apologized to everyone in the service industry. "You have to get me out of here. I'm sick, it's so hard to breathe—" he coughed again, feeling it echo in his chest. It hurt. "We need every hand. The longer this takes—"

"Sir—!"

"—the more everyone will start to suffer!" He grabbed the key and waved it in her direction as he leaned over the counter. It was stained with decades of oily fingerprints, and he wished for a can of Lysol. "What do you think comes next? First the Switchboard and then—how is the Between going to keep going?"

Now she was looking scared, and murmurs had started up in the line behind him. A handful of people—the other coughers and sniflers—were pushing to the front of the room. They started clamoring with him, holding up their own keys. He'd started a small rebellion. The line got louder.

She gave in, snatching a notecard from a stack and stamping it before shoving the card in his direction. "Okay, okay! Go to the third floor and tell them you're a special Assignment case. You, too? All of you?"

He took the card as she faced the other operators. In quick succession, each was given their own notecard, and the small pack began trooping toward the room's exit. The operators were all different ages, genders, and ethnicities, bound together by their keys and coughs and complaints. Henley struggled to keep up with them. His legs felt too heavy, and a sharp pain formed in his ribs.

Having other people in front of him, however, meant he saw someone float up the "elevator" shaft before them and didn't have to figure it out. He followed on his turn, pushing off from the edge to float upward, digging fingernails into his palms to keep from panicking as the ground fell behind him. At least the shaft in the building was contained, without the open-air terror of his first flight. When they arrived at the third floor in a shoebox-sized waiting room, he elbowed his way to the desk and brandished his card. "Special Assignment. I'm an operator with no papers, transferring. I need this resolved ASAP!"

This clerk was older and less inclined to be pushed into panic. He rubbed a hand over his dark, bald head. "You and everybody else, Operator. Have a seat. We'll get to you when we're done with the Shields."

Oh, Christ.

The waiting room was packed with other people, none of them looking as urgent or miserable as the clump of operators. No familiar, unsettling uniforms. Henley assumed the worst.

"What are the Shields doing to get the Switchboard back online?" he replied, taking off his glasses to wave them at the long-suffering clerk. "I don't have time to—" He broke off as a very real coughing fit choked him for several seconds. When he recovered, he was panting, and his face was hot. "I don't have time to wait for them to hold up the process," he croaked.

"Sir, if you want to tell them that, I'm sure the sergeant would like to hear it. In the meantime, you'll have to wait like everyone else."

"Let me talk to the sergeant then!" Henley barked back. He folded his glasses and tucked them into his vest pocket, then ran both hands through his hair, tugging at the strands. The more deranged he looked, the better. "I'm fading as we speak! I'd like to see the sergeant lose his Assignment!"

"Is there a problem here?"

A door opened, and a uniformed figure leaned out. Henley squinted, unable to make out the details of the face. He was at least sure it wasn't the officer he'd locked eyes with at his apartment.

In for a penny. His palms were sweating, his heart beating too fast. He channeled his younger sister in full spoiled-brat mode.

"Officer!" he said, stepping forward with Kit's key in hand to identify himself. He leaned heavily into his words, forcing the whine out of his chest. "They're holding us up because of whatever you're doing. We don't have Assignments! We need to get to work! Look at us, we can barely breathe!"

The Shield sighed.

"Come in here, then, one at a time. We'll interview you one by one. Answer all of the questions truthfully and quickly, and you'll be done soon."

"At least someone's doing something," Henley replied, stomping across the room to walk past the Shield. The movement helped to hide his shaking hands and unsteady knees. His depth perception faded in and out, making the hallway beyond the door seem long, then short. His activity had worsened his condition.

"This way," the Shield said, grabbing Henley's arm to direct him into a side room. Several other officers in their dark coats were inside, talking to more clerks. The room was an open bullpen of desks and smelled of old paper. "Sergeant, there are operators causing a commotion in the waiting room."

"They can't help themselves, can they? Have a seat, operator. We've got some questions for you."

Henley was more than happy to collapse into the chair. His shirt stuck to his back and chest with sweat. He had to concentrate to keep his breathing relatively even.

"Just make it quick, please. This is terrible . . ."

The sergeant's fuzzy silhouette moved closer.

"You look like you're in pretty bad shape for a transferee, operator."

Henley cut his eyes to the side. Every question was a landmine, and he placed his feet with great care.

"Well, I transferred in yesterday, and there were Shields all over the substation. I thought it'd get fixed and I could get my papers, so I stayed with a friend of my little brother last night, then went back, and it still wasn't up so I came here."

"A friend of your what?" The sergeant bent over him as the room fell silent. Henley barely caught the shift before he opened his mouth. Kit's voice was a distant memory.

We don't have children or families.

"My little brother," he wheezed. "Panel next to mine at the old station. Can't handle Russian connections worth a damn. I help him all the time, and he buys me lunch. He's good, just not all that sharp in Eurasia."

The tension eased. Slightly.

"And what substation did you transfer out of?"

Henley aimed low. "Number 17. Glad to be away from all the weather requests—mages get demanding when they get uncomfortable."

"If you'd ever experienced snow, you wouldn't blame them." The sergeant was still leaning over him, close enough now that Henley could make out the details of his face. He had deep bronze skin and golden-brown eyes that caught the light. He looked far too smart for the mage's comfort.

"What's your name, operator? What's the highest connection you've ever made? To where?"

Kittinger. Kelley.

"Kenley," he replied, and rubbed his face. The world pushed in on him too hard, making him fight to stay upright in his chair. He dug into memories of the news shared among mages. "Highest? Five hundred percent. Dam broke, a real big mess. I was connecting to the Spirits of Air, pushing the water out—no one in particular, the mages wanted anything they could get."

The sergeant was silent, examining his face. Henley let himself be more pitiful.

"Ugh, my chest, it hurts—are we done here?"

The Shield straightened.

"Operator Kenley has suffered enough. Get him Assigned so he can get back to work."

"Uh, yessir—this way, operator."

One of the clerks spoke up, shoulders hunched and hands clutched in front of their chest. Henley pushed himself upright, swaying on his feet. The sergeant caught and supported him.

"Next time go straight to the Bureau no matter what's happening at the station, operator. You just cause yourself more discomfort."

"Yes, sergeant. Thanks for your help. Hope you get the Board back up soon," Henley mumbled. The sergeant stepped back.

"So do we, operator."

The clerk took his other arm and guided him back into the hallway. Across the hall was a small, spartan room that held only a tall wooden box in the center of the room. The clerk fumbled with the box, and the top shifted. Henley wasn't sure what had been on top before, but it changed to hold a large keyhole.

"Just put your key here and turn. We'll get you settled once you connect to the Ethereal."

Twelve

Flight

Kit left Henley and pushed himself into the air. It felt so good to be back in the Between where he knew everything he was supposed to be doing. The food smelled right, and the air was easy to breathe. The air in Houston had been so humid and thick. Even the light nausea was an improvement. As long as he was working to restore the Switchboard, the Between treated him with more kindness than Henley was experiencing.

Stay focused, Kit.

He left the area, then doubled back, sneaking closer to the Bureau through the back routes. He gave himself a floppy hat. It helped to cover his face, even if it conflicted with the pin that held his hair.

The back door of the Bureau was unguarded. Kit eased himself inside and started taking stock of the floor plan. He had been in the Bureau many times himself, directed and redirected through a hundred different doors and hallways. If Henley made it, he would go to the Special Assignment offices on the third floor.

It took time, but Kit found the directory shaft that would take Henley to the Special Assignment office. The shaft held no purpose except to shuffle Assignees to a few different departments, and none of them were higher than the fourth floor. Kit floated above that exit and waited, staring down at the people who traveled through the shaft, hiding himself in the shadows.

He'll make it. He has to make it. He's smart. He's clever. I need him.

He didn't really need the mage. He could survive alone, in hiding, running for the rest of his life—maybe. Until the Between was rewritten. Until everyone he knew suffered too much and they all lost everything that made them who they were. Until the Lineman—

Henley made him think he didn't have to run. Henley wasn't afraid.

I have to believe. Please, please, be okay.

He never feared that Henley would make it to the front of the line. He feared that Henley would begin to fade and need to be carried out. Kit counted heads. Thirty-six Assignees floated out of the lobby waiting area and to the second floor, the Standard Assignment level. Some of them even reappeared, redirected to another area. When one moved to the fourth floor, Kit pressed himself against the ceiling of the shaft. No one noticed his presence.

He exhaled. He waited.

After a wait—*not that bad a wait considering the Bureau*—he started to hear noise. Raised voices. One voice was so familiar he almost darted into the open. He wrapped his arms around himself as he waited for the Shields to take his companion. The Shields didn't come, but a sudden handful of people burst into the shaft. One by one they flowed to the third floor, and Kit almost yelled when he saw Henley among them.

So weak. So pale.

As soon as they were gone, Kit drifted to the fourth-floor exit. This hallway was long and full of a hundred numbered doors, none of them open. He found the secondary directory shaft and made his way to the back areas of the third floor. He didn't expect the Shield that stopped him.

"Who are you? What are you doing here?"

She was tiny and chubby, with beautiful red hair. Kit pointed to one of the doors. "Dropping off some papers. I'll only be a minute."

She frowned at him, hands on her hips. Even her low-heeled shoes couldn't bring her higher than his chest. "Make sure you come through the main shaft next time."

"Alright, so sorry."

She waved him on, and he fled through the nearest door. He knew where he needed to get to, but not the route. It took several minutes for him to sneak past the open offices and close to the Assignment Room. The energy of it pulsed through the floor, calling him like a magnet. He'd never been Reassigned, but he knew the process. He peeked into another hallway just as Henley was escorted into the room. With a gasp, Kit pulled back, pressing against the wall and breathing deep. The air wasn't thin, but his body wasn't happy that he wasn't working.

Not by choice. How I wish I was working a normal shift.

"Put your key here and turn," he heard the muffled voice say. Easing back around the corner, he crept to the door and opened it enough to peek inside. Henley wasn't wearing his glasses. He was as handsome without them as with, but he was dripping sweat and flushed with fever. Henley stared at the clerk. Then he gave the pedestal a resigned look and pulled the key off over his head.

I won't let you fail.

Henley turned the key. Kit closed his eyes, reaching out to that familiar point, and opened the connection to the Ethereal. It responded to his command and magic flooded the room, crackling like lightning around the walls. The complete circuit glowed. The clerk gave Henley a look of respect. Henley straightened bolt upright, hand still on the key, as if someone had pulled him up by his strings. His flush was gone.

"No wonder you were in such a bad way. Strong, aren't you? Here's your Assignment card—"

The clerk was talking to Henley as the door across the hall burst open. Shields poured into the hall. Kit swore and threw himself into the Assignment Room.

"That's him!" a dark-skinned man yelled. "The Chief Operator—he took down the Switchboard!"

Kit ran to throw his arm around one of Henley's. "Time to go!" he screeched. The mage had his card in one hand and the key in the other; Kit snatched the key. "Fire, Henley! Take us straight through the wall to your left!"

"Holy shit," Henley breathed. Together they backed away, rushing to the farthest corner of the Assignment Room. "Ten—no, fifteen percent, *Command Flames*! Come to me great Lords of Fire, direct my strength and bend the world to my will, fill it with your destruction—"

Kit squeezed his eyes shut and established the connection. The Ethereal opened to him, filling him with heat and brilliant flame. He fed it Henley's sacrifice, hearing a snippet of amateur flute music and the still silence of an auditorium before the sound was gone. Without the Switchboard the fire surged through his body like a living conduit, a raging inferno that barely stayed within his skin. It exploded out of Henley's fingers and took the entire wall with it. Open air waited. Shots rang out, and bullets slammed into the wall behind them, showering the pair with flying splinters of wood paneling.

"*Go!*"

Kit followed as Henley threw himself through the smoldering frame. Henley yelled, flailing his arms and legs before Kit snatched him out of the air and kicked off the side of the building. The wall was weak with the fire, and he didn't get far on the first kick, but the second propelled them into the flow of traffic. Fliers cried out in surprise as they were jostled by a pair of wild miscreants and the surge of Shields that followed.

"Hold on tight, I'm getting us out of here!" Kit yelled at his companion. He pulled Henley close and let the mage transfer his desperate handclasp to a more stable position with both arms tight around Kit's waist from behind. The fire had burned the scent of rain off them, and the smoke filled the his nose. He was distracted for a second before he found the next object he could use, and then he launched them forward again.

Henley's grip tightened with every push. Unhindered by gravity, every kick made them faster, until Kit was darting through and around groups of people at dangerous speeds. The Shields were undeterred but slower, more careful of the bystanders. Kit bounced off walls and platforms with reckless disregard for his or Henley's safety. Soft grunts told him when the mage took some of the damage, but his companion kept otherwise silent.

Alarmed voices helped Kit catch himself before he plowed into a trolley full of men and women all wearing the same uniform—for a restaurant, he thought, or maybe a store. He twisted to the side with inches to spare and grabbed for the undercarriage of the car, gasping as the motion tore at his shoulders. The entire trolley tipped sideways with a chorus of yells but didn't overturn. As the Shields tried to stop themselves and change direction, Kit kicked off again, flying straight into the alley between the nearest buildings. The dim light became shadows as the walls closed in.

Fire escapes and hidden porches made him zigzag through the alley and into the next after a sharp corner turn. Lines of strung laundry, drifting like clouds, threatened to trap them at every level as Kit took advantage of a multistory chasm. They went around buildings, between them, under overhangs that were little more than open scaffoldings. With fewer bystanders, the Shields sped up, and Kit started dodging bullets.

"Why aren't they using magic on us?" Henley yelled.

"Shaw wouldn't bring mortal mages into this fight, and Fetters can only channel energy, not direct it," Kit called back, ducking beneath a heavy barge of barrels making its sluggish way through a crossroad.

"Then get me somewhere I can work!"

The Chief Operator tossed a startled look over his shoulder. Henley's eyes were clear and determined, his face no longer sickly pale. Kit grinned, a flutter of wild relief in his chest, and threw them into the nearest open doorway. The building's gravity took hold as they rolled across the floor of a large warehouse, their arms and legs tangled together in a heap. Towers of goods to be transported loomed on all sides, leaving only narrow paths between the shelves and stacks. The warehouse workers stared at them in shock.

"We have to disable them, trap them, slow them down," Henley panted as he pulled himself free. He stuffed his Assignment card in his pocket and rolled to his feet. With a noise of frustration, he yanked his glasses out of his vest. "How many can we expect?"

"At least a dozen, and more will come," Kit panted. "Are you sure about this? It's tight in here, we don't have anywhere to run—"

"We have all the space we need. Better to force them into tight areas. Come on!"

Kit took the hand Henley offered and was hauled to his feet as Henley darted into the aisles. The workers were starting to react, waving their arms and yelling at the pair to get out of the warehouse. They were background noise, uninteresting, until the yelling changed as the Shields entered the building. The workers started running along the tops of the cargo towers, indicating the pair's location to their pursuers.

"That's not polite," Henley muttered, and his grip on Kit's hand tightened as the mage began casting. The Chief Operator tasted an obscure spice, not entirely pleasant. "Five percent, *Silence*. Let no sound penetrate this space, let no voice be raised!"

Kit's ears rang as all sound ceased in the warehouse. The workers could still raise their arms, but once the Shields were inside the narrow paths, they could only see a few workers at a time. He felt more than heard his heavy breathing as he picked directions at random, burying the two of them within the pallets of boxes and burlap sacks. Henley squeezed his hand again. Kit looked back to see concentration on his companion's face before the mage pulled him to a stop. Henley leaned close and mouthed the words.

"Five percent. Create Substance, Web. *Hold fast—"*

Kit couldn't make out the rest of the words, but the intent was strong in the mage's mind, and Kit gave him what he needed in exchange for the feeling of a headache and the smell of a rubber ball that bounced off his skull. Kit had expected a net to block the aisle. Henley layered several enormous spiderwebs at varying angles and distances, making the twenty feet behind them into a nightmare. The Chief Operator stared in fascination until Henley shoved him forward again.

The lack of sound meant they couldn't hear their pursuers or how Henley's traps affected the Shields. Kit ran on hope that they were having any success. As they turned into a new aisle, the Chief Operator's attention was caught by a grinning worker crouched overhead. The worker looked down at them and pointed. Kit released Henley's hand and grabbed a box, chucking it into the air. The worker went down on the other side of the cargo, arms flailing.

His efforts, while satisfying, were in vain. The next intersection boiled with dark uniforms. The Shields, their faces bright with victory, were forced single- or double-file as they made their way toward the pair. Henley grabbed Kit's hand and pulled, yanking the Chief Operator back the way they'd come. Kit felt a slice of pain across his shoulder but kept running, even when blood began to drip down his back. More bullets punched into sacks of rice, spilling it in waterfalls across the floor.

Another crossroads showed them more Shields, this group strung with sections of sticky web that plastered hair to faces and half bound their arms and legs. Henley took another turn. This time the Shields were right in front of them, startled. Kit threw his arms around Henley for support and kicked with both legs, sending an unstable tower tumbling onto the uniformed figures. Henley staggered, set the Chief Operator down, and kept running.

They ran out of luck at the next turn. For a second, the sight of the door at the end of the row filled the Chief Operator with relief. Once they reached it, however, he found it was old and rusted shut. He threw his shoulder into it, frantic as he tried to force it open, kicking it. The door didn't budge.

Henley squeezed his hand. The mage was looking around at the cluttered space, breathing hard. Several buckets and brooms were stuffed into the corner, along with old cans of paint and other maintenance equipment. Kit grabbed a broom and prepared to defend himself. Henley knocked it out of Kit's hand and pushed the Chief Operator's back to the door. He braced his hands to either side of Kit's shoulders and stared into his eyes, then rested his head against Kit's.

"Five percent, *Second Skin*. Stand between me and that which would cause me harm. Fifteen percent, *Constrain Space*. Tighten the air, twist the space, leash it to the shape that I desire." Henley mouthed the words and built spells like an artist. Kit felt each connection open, then close, the elegance of Henley's casting taking his breath away. Henley kept his thoughts and visualizations precise, never offering too much in exchange for his spells. Kit smelled ink and heard a man's measured voice say, *"You have the power within you to make it so. It's up to you."*

Henley wrapped his arms tight around Kit as the silencing spell wore off in a burst of conflicting sounds. "One percent," Henley panted, "*Create Fire*. One spark to bring light!"

Kit tasted the memory of a prick of pain on his hand, then the closing of the last connection, and the aisle beyond Henley exploded. Kit screamed as the pressure forced them harder against the rusted door, threatening to break bones—and then the door gave way as they were thrown into the open.

Brilliant!

Kit howled a gleeful laugh and let the force of the explosion send them rocketing into the Between. He guided their flight as he held tight to the mage. The back of Henley's shirt was burned and crumbling under the Chief Operator's fingers, and Kit's excitement died in a rush of sudden concern. He oriented himself, recognizing landmarks, and pulled his companion into a crowded marketplace. Within seconds they were lost in the traffic.

"We're close—hang on a little more. We'll be safe soon."

"You're sure?"

Kit nodded, skirting clumps of people staring in the direction of the *boom* they had just made. "My place is just ahead."

"Are you crazy? Won't they know where you live?"

Kit looked back over his shoulder, relieved but feeling the melancholy affect his smile.

"Don't worry. No one knows where I live."

Thirteen

Frustration

The barracks were quiet. The only Shields in the area were off duty and had worked twelve-hour shifts hunting for the missing Chief Operator. The usual soft din of human activity, voices chattering and doors opening or closing, was absent. None of them had time to enjoy a casual evening.

Solene was as exhausted as her subordinates, but the day's work had yet to release her from its tension. The officer's level was less populated and more peaceful. She should have been able to rest. Her single room with its metal-frame bed and desk bolted to the floor, windowless and lit only with a single lamp, should have sheltered her from the world. Instead she sat on her bed, back to the wall, still in her uniform, turning the pages of a book.

Water stains and creases marred the book's linen cover, obscuring the title. Glued every few pages were black-and-white photographs, pressed flowers, clippings from catalogs, and notecards of observations in her neat cursive handwriting. Near the beginning of the book, a fragment of an incident report accompanied a photo of a handsome man with a bandage wrapped around his head.

Post-incident update: James Callahan has recovered significantly from the Ethereal discharge event. The physicians say that there will be no long-term effects from his injuries, and he has agreed to testify against the rogue mages who caused the magical overflow. His son Peter was born February 23, 1934, with no negative side effects.

On the next page, a clipped newspaper article listed the best gifts for new mothers. Several items were scratched through, and "bassinet" had been circled. A folded receipt was tucked into a small envelope glued to the page. At the bottom of the opposite page, a photo was tucked into another pocket. Solene slid it free, staring at the smiling couple with their armful of white-clothed baby before turning it over to read the note on the other side.

Investigator Solene, thanks so much again for all your help. Edith and I will never forget everything you've done for us. We sleep safe and sound thanks to your efforts. If you ever need anything, don't hesitate to ask.

She returned the photo to its place with care. Several pages later she had glued another notecard, this one with several baby names that had caught her eye over the years. The ink color and weight changed between names, showing the time passing between additions. *Erika. Theodore. Joaquin. Leslie. Bennet.* An article beneath the notecard discussed the best recipes for picky children. The margins were full of detailed notes and explanations for herself, definitions pulled from cooking manuals for those who had no cooking experience. Page after page passed under her hands, decorated with ribbons and cards and advertisements of smiling families.

Solene paused on the last page, staring at a picture of a mother tucking two young children into bed. The image was one of her favorites, posed with such love and warmth. "Someday, it will be my turn," she whispered. "Someday I'll have a family of my own. As soon as I'm free."

The pounding on her door was so sudden and loud that she levitated a few inches off the bed in surprise. She raised her head with a dark frown. "Who is it, and what do you want?" she called through the door, keeping her voice businesslike as she closed the book on her collection.

"We found the Chief Operator, Lieutenant! He's just fled from the Bureau! The team investigating there is in pursuit!"

Solene leapt from her bed, leaving the book behind. She shoved her feet into the pumps waiting by the door and belted on her uniform coat.

When she yanked the door open, the young corporal on the other side was standing too close and he stumbled back.

"Let's go," she told him, and stalked past. The corporal ran behind her until he caught up, towering over the shorter lieutenant, awkward with his long legs and arms. As they approached the trolleys, more of her tired officers were waiting, straightening their own coats or lacing up boots. At her arrival they fell into order, saluting with little sign of their weariness. She nodded and motioned for them to follow her onto the trolley.

"What updates do we have?" she asked, standing before her team, as the trolley took flight.

"He isn't alone," the corporal replied, standing as well when she gave him a look. "He's accompanied by a human mage. They were getting an Assignment when he triggered his key."

"The same human mage?" she asked, voice sharp. "Were they successful in getting the Assignment?"

"Yes, ma'am. He can cast because of the Chief Operator. I understand there's been a fire at the Bureau."

"Destructive magic is always the easiest for the mages in times of crisis," she noted, looking back at her people. "You heard him. Be aware of every threat and watch each other's backs. We must bring the Chief Operator to justice, and I don't want to lose a single Shield in the process. Remember that mortals are violent and unpredictable."

"Yes, ma'am!" They barked in reply. Adrenaline was kicking in. Her radioman had his head down, muttering into his handset and giving directions to their pilot. The direction of the trolley shifted. "They've got them pinned down in a warehouse, ma'am!"

"They don't have him yet," she replied, turning to face the front windows. "Spread out when we arrive, and help the other unit in whatever way is needed."

Their excitement and optimism died as soon as the warehouse came into view. Smoke billowed from a side door that had been blown off its hinges. A dozen Shields occupied the scene, and every one of them looked pissed off.

Solene tasted the bitterness in the back of her throat as she stepped off the trolley.

"Report, Major," she ordered, and the nearest officer gave her a salute.

"We lost them, Lieutenant. The mage set traps through the warehouse and used a layered explosion reaction to bust them out. We lost track of them at their ejection speed, but I've got a team following their trajectory as best they can."

She exhaled.

"We're dealing with the Chief Operator. He knows the Between like his own face and has resources we'll never match. It's to be expected that catching him will be difficult. However"—she gave him a thin smile—"the call of magic will be impossible for them to resist. They'll expose themselves again. Make sure everyone hears that."

"I will." His shoulders were still tense, but less than they were before she spoke. "What should I tell the Captain?"

"I heard, and it doesn't matter."

Solene and the officer turned as one, raising their hands in automatic salute. Shaw waved to put them at ease as he stepped onto the platform, coat flaring where it hung around his shoulders. He dismissed her companion with a nod.

"Unfortunate that we didn't catch them here, but we'll get them soon." Shaw lifted a gloved hand, holding up an embossed envelope trimmed in gold.

Solene took a sharp breath. "The High Spirits' authorization?"

Shaw nodded. "The second that magic surfaced, they acknowledged the threat. We can't have a mage running around in the Between. It's a huge risk to everyone." He smiled, eagerness bright in his gaze. "This is what we've been waiting for. The Chief Operator has given us the chance we've been preparing for all these years."

Solene pressed a hand to her chest, every one of her precious photos flashing behind her eyes. "What do we need to do?" she asked.

"Gather all of the lieutenants, regardless of assignment," Shaw replied. "Get back to Headquarters and meet me in the central chamber. As fast as possible!"

"Yes, sir!" she replied, and sprang into motion. Shaw took the trolley back with them, leaving Solene to use the radio and summon the division leaders back to the Between. When they arrived at the enormous, columned entrance of the Order of the Bright Shield, dark-uniformed figures streamed into the doors and sirens wailed. 'Iustitiae et Lux in Desperandum,' read the quote over the door, beckoning the Shields to their duty. 'Justice, the Light in Despair.'

Junior officers hurried out of the way as Solene stormed into the building in Shaw's wake. They split up then, delivering the orders needed to keep anyone else out of the way. Then they climbed the stairs, joining the growing ring of bodies on the open second floor around a huge, carved stone sigil cut into the ground.

"All divisions, sound off," Shaw ordered, and hands went up one by one. Twenty-five voices called out with the names and numbers of Actuality-based divisions. In her turn, Solene raised her hand.

"Twenty-Sixth Division, Between," she called. Beside her, a huge man with dark skin and shoulders broad enough to outstretch any doorframe raised his hand, accompanied by the smell of sulfur.

"Twenty-Seventh Division, Ethereal."

The few gaps in their number quickly filled as new bodies arrived. Half an hour passed from the moment of Shaw's order to having the full company of lieutenants present. The Captain examined every face and gave the assembly a slow nod.

"Some of you have witnessed what we are about to do in your time with the Shields," he said. Silence fell in the open chamber; in the area below, a crowd of junior officers made itself known with the smallest shuffles and whispers. "Many of you never have, and you may not see it again. This is the time when we are needed most. The very existence of the Between has been threatened. The High Spirits have entrusted us with the solution, and we will be the summoners of justice."

He held up the envelope, pristine, glittering as it caught the light. "Prepare for the summons."

The lieutenants linked arms, Solene's shoulder straining as she bound herself to the much taller figure at her side. He bent his knees enough that the angle wasn't painful and earned himself a smile from the shorter woman. They braced their feet, ready for whatever came next.

"Seal the portal," Shaw continued. A pair of sergeants saluted as they stood flanking the stairs. The portal the Shields used to travel between worlds was integral to their operations; it was the first time Solene had seen it sealed. Her heart fluttered in her chest. No amount of drills could dull the adrenaline of a real emergency.

"Locking all incoming transport," the first sergeant called. She turned a plate-sized wheel, closing the valve of magic that powered the chamber. The hum that filled the room eased.

"Locking all outgoing transport," the second responded, and the hum died. Several of the gathered lieutenants rolled their shoulders, shaking off the feeling of emptiness that followed. The junior officers fell silent. Shaw opened the envelope, the tearing of paper jarring in the expectant quiet.

"'We the High Spirits, recognizing the threat of Aggressive Parties to the health of the Between, do authorize the Order of the Bright Shield to protect the balance of magic with all Methods at their disposal,'" Shaw read. As he spoke, eight voices overlaid his in a rising echo, and the paper glowed. Pressure rose in the chamber. "'By Our command, the Order must summon the Lineman to guard and defend the Between. Let all in the Order be bound by this Purpose.'"

The Captain held the gleaming paper high above his head.

"I am Shaw, Captain of the Order of the Bright Shield!" he thundered, his voice echoing from every wall. The ground shook. The officers hunched their shoulders, leaning into the pressure together. "By the mandate of the High Spirits, I summon the Lineman!"

He dropped the paper. It fell slowly, twisting and fluttering in midair, but it fell like a bomb. As it struck the ground, a shockwave hit the assembled lieutenants. They stumbled, supporting each other and crying out as a powerful wind tore through the room, flinging hats into the air and yanking at skirts. Solene's hair was ripped from its pins.

In front of Shaw, a glowing figure materialized. His features were indistinct. He was made of light and very tall. The silhouette carried a long blade, hanging low from its right hand. The brighter it became, the more the room was filled with dread, a feeling of terror pressing down on everyone present. This was the world-ender, the only being that could destroy their existence, and it wasn't just the junior officers crying out in fright.

"Lineman," Shaw rasped, his voice raw. "I order you to find Chief Operator Kittinger and bring him to justice!"

The being bowed his head. Then he turned, facing the stairs, and walked through the chain of lieutenants. He disappeared. In his wake, a force grasped every Shield present, filling them with adrenaline and desperation.

Solene gasped for breath, fighting to detangle herself from those around her as they did the same, resulting in chaos. She *had* to leave, she *had* to go and find the Chief Operator, she *had to follow her Purpose*. A stampede blocked the stairs and then the doors. They clawed at each other, climbing over the trampled hands and feet of their fellows. A small voice in the back of her mind railed at the command, helpless to do anything but obey, a slave to the orders of the High Spirits and her Purpose.

She had no will of her own to look backward as Shaw watched them abandon the building with a smile.

Fourteen

Rest

Getting to Kit's apartment was much easier after the explosion gave the pair a big lead on the Shields. Henley harbored doubts about going to the Chief Operator's place of residence, but they faded as the pair left the more populated areas for quiet housing. Henley saw only a few other people as they flew, keeping close to the buildings and low. Those Fetters went about their lives and paid the pair no attention.

He hadn't seen any of the other housing of the Between, but he examined Kit's porch with furrowed brows. It wasn't deep enough for a chair, but a person could sit on the platform and hang their legs between the railing bars. The windows had foggy glass, faded with age. What paint the building face held had faded and peeled away.

Kit looked around with uneasy eyes, but there was no sign of the Shields. He opened the door without need of a key and led Henley into the cramped, cluttered space. The windows provided little light, in part because of the dirty glass, in part because of the shelves that half blocked the second window.

"We need to get a good look at your back," Kit said, turning on a lamp identical to the ones at the substation. After a second Henley realized why—the lamp was by the door, attached to a smaller version of Kit's Switchboard panel. Beyond it was a tiny kitchen, the sink overflowing with dirty mugs and food containers. "Are you badly burned? Does it hurt?"

"It doesn't feel nice," Henley said. "I didn't have time for a real shielding spell, but it could have been much worse. What about you? Your shoulder's bleeding."

"Mmm?" Kit twisted, looking backward at himself. "Oh. I got grazed, I think, but it doesn't hurt. I'll clean it up in a second. Let me help you get your shirt off. And your pants?"

"Everything is damaged, but I'm going to need something to wear."

"Oh, they'll be fine. I can fix them, but you need treatment."

Henley opened his mouth to argue, then sighed. The day had sapped his energy. He couldn't summon the willpower to resist anything Kit wanted him to do. He held his arms out to his sides and the Chief Operator moved close, wrapping his arms around him again. This time Henley rested his head on Kit's shoulder, letting himself lean on his companion.

"You've been through a pretty high percentage of magic today, cumulative," Kit said in a quiet voice as the fabric began to repair itself, rubbing against the mage's skin and too close to his burns. "And you crossed the barrier between worlds, and you were so sick before you got your Assignment. You've got to rest."

"I'm starving," Henley replied, eyes closed. "I'm tired. I just need a little time to recover."

"You'll have it." Kit pushed him upright and unbuttoned the vest, then the shirt. Henley let him take both, watching as Kit turned to hang the clothes over a chair covered in rumpled blankets. By the time they left the Chief Operator's fingers, the burned and warped edges were whole fabric again.

"Kit, your shoulder looks bad. The blood has soaked through your cardigan."

"I promise, it's not as bad as it looks." Kit smiled, then faced Henley again. "Can you get your pants, or do you need help?"

Henley cleared his throat and took off his own damn pants, toeing off his shoes in the process. The fabric left him with scrapes of sharp pain as it brushed his burns. He flushed when he faced Kit, self-conscious in his underwear. "It's a little cold."

"I know, but we have to treat you first. Lay on the bed, okay? This will, um . . . probably hurt, but I'll be as gentle as I can."

"Just what I wanted to hear." Henley looked around. Opposite of the kitchen, in the same cramped space, a bed was wedged into the other end of the room. It was the only furniture aside from the tiny kitchen table and chairs, but large enough to hold the pair. Henley hoped it would do just that sometime soon.

And I'm mostly naked. Awkward.

He shook his head and moved to the bed, pulling the tossed-aside blankets straight before he lay on his stomach. Kit's scent washed over him, familiar and interspersed with the scent of tea, as the thin material of the pillowcase rubbed against his cheek.

The Chief Operator had gone through a door straight ahead from the entrance and was rummaging around in the next room. From the occasional clatter of something falling, Henley didn't think that area was any neater than the first room. The air was stagnant. The shelves by the window held a few books, coils of extra cabling, dust, and empty spaces. It was a storage room for a life, not a home.

"I don't have enough of anything to treat all of you," Kit fretted as he returned, holding a small armload of supplies. He had draped a hand towel over his wounded shoulder. The checkered fabric hid the bloodstain from view. "But I can clean the burns and get the worst ones covered up. Your vest protected your back, but there are a few ugly spots on your legs."

"Just do what you can," Henley replied. "It's better than nothing. Right now, everything feels a little unpleasant."

"You sort of look like unevenly cooked chicken, so that's no surprise."

The Chief Operator crawled up on the bed in little scoots, getting his array of bottles and packets next to Henley in one trip. The bed did fit both of them. Henley smelled blood, stronger when Kit was close, and he resisted asking about his shoulder again. From what he could see when he craned his neck, the stain on the sweater wasn't getting worse.

Kit opened a bottle, poured something onto the rag, and touched Henley's back. With a grunt of pain, Henley clawed his fingers into the blankets.

"What the hell is that?!"

"Iodine. It will be over soon, just hold still."

"Nobody uses iodine anymore."

"Probably because it stings so much. I'm sorry, that's the problem with the Between. Until we're rewritten, we don't grow or change or learn new things."

Henley gritted his teeth and looked for a distraction. Some of the spots on his back hurt less than the others, but when Kit touched them, everything hurt worse.

"What happened back there? At the Bureau. Everything was going fine, but I knew I was in trouble when they told me to use the key."

"Part of the Assignment process is to confirm who you are. For most of the Between, that just means showing your old Assignment card. Operators are different." Henley hissed as one of the wounds protested more than the others. Kit paused, letting Henley relax again before he continued his work and the story. "Because our work is so important, we can't risk someone going on a lark, stealing a key, and trying to change positions against their Purpose. It's rare, but it happens, so we're tested."

"You knew—*ow*—I was going to have to use the key."

"Mmhmm. I snuck in and got close to the Special Assignment room. I've never been Reassigned, but I've been to that area a few times with others or to answer questions from the Bureau. I don't have to be holding my key to activate it."

"So the Shields saw you?"

"No." Kit's treatment stopped for a moment as he hesitated. "They can track magic. The second I activated my key, they knew where we were. There's no other magic connecting to the Between right now, and they were looking for my particular connection."

Henley pushed up on his hands to frown at the Chief Operator. "They were in the *next room*, Kit. That was too dangerous."

Kit met his eyes. They held a quiet determination Henley hadn't seen before—a little bit of righteousness mixed with hope and fear. In his own world, the Chief Operator had more confidence than when he'd been helpless in the Actuality.

"You were going to die if you didn't get that card. What would we have done then? I couldn't fix what was making you sick, but I thought we could maybe be more clever than the Shields and escape. They move around constantly. This area of the Between is my home."

"You should have told me."

"I didn't want you to be nervous."

"I was already nervous." Henley lay back down. Now that he was still and safe, all the ways the situation could have gone wrong screamed in the back of his mind, accelerating his heart rate and shortening his breathing. "Jesus. We were so close to being dead."

"You did so well. You got past your fear of flying, you made explosions . . . that was such clean casting, Henley. You're *really* good. I'm surprised you aren't a Shield yourself, or a Magister or something. You should teach."

"You sound like my dad. He's not impressed with my life choices, either."

"I don't know what a graphic designer does."

"We simplify concepts with visuals so people can understand them quickly. We make words look pretty on paper."

"Oh." Kit went back to work, touching the cloth to places on the back of Henley's legs that made his toes cramp in response. "I think that's impressive. You have to be good at communicating information cleanly and without extra information. That's why you're so good at processing spells."

Henley was silent, ashamed for a moment by the way gratitude bubbled up in his chest.

"Thanks. I think I do my job well, and I like the work. My parents wanted me to be something better."

"Doesn't 'better' depend on what you need to do, and who needs it?"

"Yeah, it does. That's what I think." Henley took off his glasses and rested his face against his arms. The places Kit had touched were stinging less. The Chief Operator set aside his bottle and cloth and began to spread some kind of cream over the worst burns, then covered them with bandages. "It's not that I don't want to do great things. Sometimes I . . ."

He trailed off. He remembered too much, too fast: the way his parents fought not to show their disappointment when he was accepted into the design program, their joy when his sister got her PhD, the way no one wanted to hear about his work at family holidays.

"You wonder if you made the right decision."

He snapped out of his thoughts at Kit's voice and looked back over his shoulder at the Chief Operator. Kit was a pale pastel blur, strawberry hair, vanilla skin, and cream sweater.

"Yeah."

"You can always change it, right? That freedom is the best thing you mortals have. Here, we don't get to decide. The Between and the High Spirits, they decide where we're needed, and what we need to do. If you think you need a new direction, you should just take it."

"My parents would be relieved. Everyone would talk badly about the job I did before."

"Then tell them to stop. You don't have to abandon all your pride to use your freedom. What you've already done is amazing, and what you do next will be amazing—that's how people work."

Henley stared at the Chief Operator, stunned, as Kit put his supplies aside. He slid off the bed and retrieved Henley's clothes, offering them out. "Here. Just be careful how you move until you've had some time to rest. Do you want some tea? I think I have some things to eat here . . . not much, I'm afraid. I always pick up meals on my way home."

"Whatever you find is fine, and yes, please, to the tea." Henley put his glasses back on and took the clothes, easing into them one piece at a time. He left the vest off and didn't tuck in his shirt. Better to be sloppy than aggravate his burns. By the time he was dressed again, Kit had put the medical supplies away, rummaged in the kitchen cabinets, forced an avalanche of tea boxes back into storage, and made tea. Henley sat on the edge of the bed, watching the production.

"Do you have a hairbrush?"

"Mmhmm, in the bathroom. Through that door."

Henley rose to his feet. Walking wasn't too bad as long as he didn't move very fast; the burns weren't as bad as he had feared. The bathroom was consistent with the rest of the house: not filthy, but it was disorganized and as cluttered as the kitchen. He sighed, used the facilities, and washed his hands. In the insulated space protected by tile and peeling wallpaper, weariness began to catch up to him. Henley dug around in the messy drawers until he found Kit's wood-handled hairbrush. With it in hand, he returned to the main room and perched at the foot of the bed with as little of his legs touching the bedding as possible.

"Sit," he said when Kit moved to join him again, pointing with the brush to the space between his feet. "My mom would be crying with how bad your hair is tangled."

"My . . ." Kit reached up to try and touch his hair, but his hands were full of two mugs and a tin of saltines, and a mason jar slipped out from under his elbow. Henley caught it. The rubber-stamped label read "peanut butter." "Really? I should probably cut it, but I always get too busy."

"Really." Henley accepted his mug of tea, too hungry and thirsty to think about all the dirty mugs stacked up in the kitchen. He hadn't seen where Kit had gotten the mug. "I used to have to brush my sisters' hair every morning, until they got old enough. Every time I look at you it makes me twitch."

Kit took the indicated seat, putting his back to his companion. He was tall enough that Henley wasn't going to have to work to reach him.

Henley sipped his tea, a very pleasant orange pekoe, then set his mug on the shelf. Once Kit was comfortable, Henley tugged the long metal pin out of the Chief Operator's hair and unwound the attached cable, making the pinkish mass fall around Kit's shoulders.

"What even is this?" Henley muttered, tossing the "ornaments" onto the bed. He started working from the bottom of Kit's hair upward, brushing out the tangles on the end and finding other small trinkets scattered through the mass. Kit's hair was clean for someone so unkept, unmatted, and the Chief Operator didn't complain like Henley's sisters.

"What is it like, having a family?"

Henley paused, his hands in midair. Then he continued with an exhale of breath.

"Wonderful, and painful."

"Painful?"

Henley worked on Kit's hair for a few minutes before replying. Kit passed him a cracker smeared with peanut butter, giving him another chance to delay his response. The crackers were stale and the peanut butter grainier than the jar in his own pantry, but he was too hungry to care.

"The family disagreement about my life choices has made it hard to talk to my parents at all. My dad and I are barely speaking. It's hard to reconcile what they want, the way we interact now, with the family I love."

"But you *do* love them."

"Yeah." Kit's hair was more blond than pink really, but something about it caught the light and reflected the rosy color. It was no less weird than everything else about the Chief Operator. "I love my sisters so much. I respect my parents; I want to know them and to make them proud. Lately I get angry with myself for not knowing more about my culture."

"You're Chinese, right?"

"Yeah. I was born and raised in the US; my parents immigrated. My parents wanted us to speak English first so we could do well in school. The only phrases I know are *qu xi wan ba* and *hao de nai nai*."

"Your grandmother wanted you to wash the dishes?"

"I was the only one tall enough to reach the sink." Henley accepted another cracker. "You speak Mandarin?"

"Operators speak every language, so we can understand connection requests." Kit glanced back at him and smiled. "Why don't you learn the language then? Why don't you tell them how much it bothers you?"

Henley ate his cracker and stared at the shelf next to him. The dust was thicker than a few years could explain. "It all comes back to my issues with them and my pride, I guess. I wouldn't even know where to start."

"You should start with *wo xiang ni le*."

"What's that?"

"I miss you."

"What if they don't listen?" Henley pushed the words through the sudden heaviness that burned his chest. He could smell his grandmother's kitchen, hear laughter and conversation as his family sat around the table helping with dinner or playing games. "What if we can't come to terms?"

Kit bowed his head. His hair was turning from tangled mass into a shining waterfall down his back. Without tangles it almost reached his waist. "Is that worse than never trying and drifting farther away?" he asked, his voice soft. "You have a family, Henley. It's something worth protecting."

It shouldn't have sounded easy, but when Kit spoke the words they were the clarity Henley had been missing. Even Elryk hadn't distilled it to such simple terms. Henley nudged Kit as he offered the next cracker.

"You need to eat, too," he said, and went back to brushing the Chief Operator's hair. "Why aren't there families in the Between?"

"We can't reproduce," Kit replied. "We can pair up, get married, live together, but the Between decides what new spirits need to exist, and it doesn't benefit the world to lose several years on a Fetter when they can't work or contribute. There's no new life here. Not animals, plants, or people." Kit's eyes strayed to the shelf by the window, and a smile pulled at the corners of his mouth. "Mostly."

"Where does your food come from? It has to be grown somewhere, right?"

"No. It's generated by the Between—ingredients just appear in the warehouses. Really, I'm surprised the Between thinks we need to eat at all, or cook, but I guess we mimic the Actuality so we can understand the mages. That's why we have shopping and businesses, too."

"Good enough point."

Silence fell between them again as Kit made crackers, passed them out, and Henley finished his task. Henley looked around the tiny apartment. It was disorderly, but not that different from his own: empty, impersonal, with the only extra items being remnants of work brought home. Being alone wasn't a fate he wished on anyone.

"I hope you and I get lucky enough to find our families," he said into the quiet, and Kit twitched.

"Oh, don't worry about me. I've got too much work to do to worry about that kind of thing. Besides, I've got a whole crew of operators to be my family."

"That's not what I—"

"It's *okay.*" Kit turned to face him, offering out the jar and crackers. "We're not like humans, Henley. We don't need those kinds of connections. We have our Purpose and our Assignment, and that's why we exist."

Henley leaned forward, elbows on his knees, until he was staring straight into the Chief Operator's eyes. "I'm really good at lying to myself too, Kit. I hope you get it, anyway."

Kit's cheerful denial cracked. It was a small flaw in his smiling exterior, but Henley had seen terrible fear in the Chief Operator's eyes; he knew what the emotion looked like when it slipped through.

"You're very kind," Kit said in a low voice, and slid backward. He set the tin and crackers next to Henley and got to his feet. "I'm going to get cleaned up. We need to rest so we can get a move on tomorrow."

Henley knew when to take a hint. "You have a plan?"

"I know where we need to go. We'll get there and see what happens next."

It wasn't the kind of certainty Henley liked to have in his life, but he was a passenger on this trip. No amount of urgency, no feeling that the Chief Operator was going to fade before his eyes, was going to change what he could do or how exhausted he was. He handed Kit the small pile of trinkets from his hair and the hairbrush.

"Alright. Whatever it takes, Kit—we'll be fine."

FIFTEEN

THE NIGHTMARE WAKES

Kit left Henley and carried his handful of baubles into the bathroom. His collection of coats and robes swayed behind the bathroom door, filling the space more than necessary for a man who could change his clothing on a whim. A hiss left his lips as he leaned against the bundled fabric and pressed against his wounded shoulder. One breath after another filled his chest with the scent of dust and his favorite lavender soap. A few moments passed before Kit willed himself to keep moving.

A rickety shelf holding a pile of unfolded towels half blocked the rust-stained pedestal sink. Habit took over: two steps to the left, a pivot on his right foot, and he escaped knocking the shelf to the ground. The plain mirror over the sink was streaked, evidence of how little Kit stared at his own reflection. He lifted his good hand and wiped the glass somewhat clear with the cuff of the cardigan.

The smaller ornaments Henley had retrieved from his hair—things he'd picked up over time and didn't want to lose—went into a small basket on the counter where he could find them later. The Chief Operator was careful not to lift his arms too high as he slid his hands through the soft strands, marveling at how nice it felt when it was brushed out—and so long, too—before twisting it up behind his head. The metal pin he stuck through the mass, wrapping the cable around it until the pile was secure. His reflection's eyes were sunken.

Whatever it takes.

The mage's words were so loud in his heart. Henley's kind hands, his determined voice, his sharp eyes that looked straight through all of Kit's masks—they broke his detachment. No one had gotten close to the Chief Operator in centuries. No one cared. No one had denounced his words and certainly not with that steady, knowing rebuttal.

I hope you get it, anyway.

"That doesn't exist for someone like me," the Chief Operator whispered to himself. The hand towel was stained with red when lifted it from his shoulder and set it aside. Taking a deep breath, he slid the cardigan off his shoulders, willing the stain away. The garment belonged to him now and it came clean, restored to perfect condition, and Kit hugged it tight against his chest for several seconds before setting it on the edge of the sink.

His shirt was worse. He pulled it off over his head, the motion and the pull of the fabric against the dried blood painful. When he turned to look over his shoulder in the mirror, the "graze" was a nasty line of open red through a sea of old, scarred runes cut into the Chief Operator's skin. The marks distracted him. In concentric and overlapping circles they twisted across his back, shimmering silver if he turned his body just right. The weight of them bowed his shoulders. Splashes of blood, already fading to rusty brown, flaked and cracked over the runes halfway down his spine. How odd, that the itch of the drying blood was almost more bothersome than the gaping wound.

He took several breaths, forcing himself to calm down before he lifted the pile of clean towels and unearthed his medicine box. It was also dusty, but the contents were clean. A needle in the aging wax paper was already threaded and knotted. Kit used the same iodine he'd used on Henley to clean his shoulder, gritting his teeth against the sharp pain. Any agony was better than facing the questions that would come if Henley saw the wound and the scars.

Family is wonderful and painful, Henley had said. How could the mage stand that pain? How could he stand to know that his family was there, waiting for him, and that seeing them would leave him unhappy later? Kit lifted the needle and began the stitches. The angle was awkward but manageable. He bit down on a sound of pain, eyes watering as the thread dragged through his skin.

Does it hurt like this?

He felt empty, the endlessness of his existence stretching out in front of him, with no one he could call family waiting for him. If he disappeared, only a few associates would remember. If he faded away, living out his last days just staring up at his ceiling and refusing his Purpose, no one would know where to find him to check on him.

Henley knows.

"You don't get to keep Henley," he whispered to himself, the words raw in his throat. "This isn't real. Once the High Spirits right everything, he'll go home and be gone. You'll hear his voice on the occasional connection, but he'll never see you again."

Kit tied off the last stitch, braced his hands on the sink, and shook as he stared down at the scratched porcelain surface. The needle dangled over his shoulder. His left hand was covered in blood. It was so red against the white sink, the only vivid color in his world.

Half an hour passed before he left the bathroom, as Kit gave himself time to calm down and clean up. His apartment was quiet. The crackers had been neatly closed in their tin, the jar of peanut butter sealed, and both left in a scrap of space on his crowded kitchen table with their empty mugs. Henley was asleep on one side of the bed, shoes off at the foot, glasses folded neatly on the window shelf. He looked younger without the accessory.

Kit retrieved his cardigan. The fabric was warm as he turned off the lamp and crawled up next to Henley, facing him in the faint light that came from his clouded windows. The mage's black hair was falling around his face, and his collar wasn't lying flat. Kit resisted reaching out to turn the collar corner down. Henley looked good in the fashion of the Between.

He's here right now.

"Goodnight, Henley," Kit whispered, the first time in his life he'd said the words to someone sleeping in the same space. As much as he dreaded the end of this chapter, his little home was warmer for the brief time that Henley was in it.

Sleep evaded him. He was restless, and every time he shifted, he jostled his wounded shoulder. He did his best to stay still so he wouldn't disturb the mage. The shuffle of his thin sheets and blanket was loud in the quiet. He wished for Henley's exhaustion. The mage's eyes twitched behind his lids as he slept. *What is he dreaming about? Does he cast magic in his dreams? If he did, would I have heard it? What keeps dreams from being valid connections if the visualization is strong in the mage's mind?*

The stream of questions kept him awake for an hour, but they became his counted sheep after a while. His eyes drifted closed. He was in his bed, surrounded by familiar scents and safe in good company after the most dramatic day of his long life. His anxieties were no match.

The *sound* woke him.

The *sound* was in his soul as much as his ears, a low *boom* that sounded both like a gong and an explosion, scratching at his ears like static. The air thickened. The floor vibrated up through the legs of the bed. The room was brighter, closer to morning, but his vision flickered with darkness. Kit sat up straight, gripping the blankets through the intense vertigo that nearly put him right back out. Henley was awake beside him, bracing himself against the shelves, his eyes wild.

The *sound* came again. And again. Three times it rattled through the Between, causing raised voices outside as Kit's neighbors panicked. Intense nausea came with muscle weakness and trembling arms. In the center of his chest, a new feeling rose—one that *pulled* him, urging him to leave his apartment. Henley must have seen something familiar in his face because he grabbed Kit's arm.

"Talk to me," Henley said as the air cleared, the sound dissipating. "What was that? What's wrong?"

"He's been released," Kit said, his body heavy with dread. "The Lineman. He's been summoned—he's coming for me. He can find me no matter where I am, eventually. It's over."

"Eventually isn't now." The mage leaned close. He hadn't yet retrieved his glasses. "What was the plan? Where are we going, and how are we getting there? We're leaving *now*."

"Henley, it doesn't matter, the Lineman is everywhere, I—"

"I said *we're leaving now!*" Henley snapped, shaking him. Kit felt the motion in his neck and aching shoulder. "No excuses, no delays—right now!"

Henley moved then, sliding away from Kit to shove his feet in his shoes. The Chief Operator grabbed the mage's glasses from the shelf and followed him, standing helpless after Henley snatched them out of his fingers.

"Where are we going, Kit?"

"Paradise." Kit's bullet wound was a fierce ache now that he was awake enough to feel it again. He hugged himself tight, fighting the way his stomach twisted. The air itself didn't feel right, acrid and bitter to the tongue. His motionless feet tingled. The Lineman's call threatened to force him out into the open the second his attention wavered. "The High Spirits live above Paradise, so we have to get there."

"How?"

"We fly."

"Then let's go." Henley held out his hand and locked eyes with the Chief Operator. Kit felt the gaze in his heart, a life preserver in a storm. He took the hand and let Henley pull him out onto the porch. His neighbors were all in the open as well, both terrified and thrilled as the Between's boogeyman walked among the Fetters. They chattered to each other and looked around, trying to spot the demon himself. Kit didn't follow their example.

"We need to go up," he told Henley, pointing to the glittering array of lights high above. "We'll follow the buildings until we get close, the cut across. We shouldn't be in the open longer than necessary."

"Okay then." Henley marched to the edge of the porch, then threw himself into the open, yanking Kit with him. They didn't get very far as Henley's aborted leap ended in weightless floating. Even in the terrible circumstances, Kit almost laughed at his abbreviated attempt.

"Like this," he told the mage, straightening them. "Visualize a solid step under your feet and push up. Think of yourself as light and full of air."

Henley was pale, and he looked down as little as possible. Once he took Kit's instructions, he made a little progress, but they moved faster when Kit took the lead and pulled him along.

As they traveled, they encountered many more residents of the Between than they had seen so far. Every Fetter not working was out and abuzz with the news. Those who were working craned their heads out of windows and called out to the ones who flew past. Rumors abounded. Kit heard five different versions of what the Lineman would or could do by the time they had passed ten levels. They spoke of him as a nightmare, a savior, the salvation of the Between and damnation to the unknown mages and Ethereals who had damaged the Switchboard.

They're all wrong. He is judge, jury, and executioner.

It took more energy than it should have to reach the levels above them that were closer to Paradise. This area of the Between held fewer residences and more businesses, with hundreds of shops and restaurants teeming with people. Kit focused on flying, kicking away from the weight that seemed to drag his feet down. His labored breathing caught Henley's attention.

"Are you alright, Kit?" he asked, squeezing the Chief Operator's hand. Kit gave him a tight smile and kept flying.

"The longer I'm here without working the Switchboard, the more I deny my Purpose." The words were true, if not completely truthful. "I'm just feeling it more today."

Henley nodded and started pushing off whatever object was closest, helping propel them forward. It was a clumsy effort that would have stood out too much in a less crowded area, but Kit was grateful.

"So many people," he murmured, scanning the crowd. "Why are they all clustered like this? No one's moving."

"The Shields won't let anyone get to Paradise," someone answered at his elbow. The speaker was a plump woman with her hair bound in braids that pulled her face tight. She pointed into the gray. "Individuals are being identified, and the trolleys are being searched. They said the Lineman is coming."

"He'll go wherever his quarry is," Kit agreed, not hiding his concern. Everyone felt something different about the news. "Thank you for your help."

She patted his good shoulder and went back to watching. Henley pulled Kit away, to an area beneath most of those pointing and staring. They stood together, grim and silent, as patterns began to emerge in the crowd: a line of Shields forming a shell-like perimeter around Paradise.

"I don't know how we're going to get in there," Kit said. The weight was getting heavier, and the urgency to flee grew. "They'll spot us for sure if we try to cross that line, but we have to get in there or we won't be able to reach the High Spirits."

"People are still getting in. We just need to disguise ourselves somehow or get in while they're distracted. I can make us invisible, divert their attention."

"If you cast at all, they'll know—and worse, the Lineman will use my connection to pinpoint our location." Kit shook his head hard enough to make his hair shift and almost fall. "We can't, that's not an option—"

"Okay, shh. Calm down, I understand. I'm still thinking." Henley squeezed his hand, staring up at the glow, so close yet so far away. The atmosphere of the people around them was that of a festival. People were excited, celebrating, watching like spectators. Kit wanted to scream at all of them. A shadow fell over the pair as one of the floating food carts drifted past.

"Where are my dishes, Chief Operator Kit?"

Henley turned fast, arm raised to defend them from a threat. Kit moved slower, too startled after hearing the familiar voice.

"Noodle?" he said, incredulous as he took in the familiar red canopy with its swinging lanterns and painted wood panels. All the stools across the front of Noodle's cart were empty, but the aroma of twelve kinds of sauce filled the air.

"Your hands are empty, so I won't expect any of my bowls back today," the chef replied, and turned his keen eyes on Henley. His grandiose mustache twitched. "Almost empty. Who is your friend? Why do you look so miserable? Your Purpose, I suspect."

"Y . . . yes. It's been terrible. This is Henley, a friend of mine." Kit glanced at Henley and offered a small smile, wondering if the title was accurate. "We were trying to get to Paradise on important business, but they won't let operators in."

Noodle took the lie with a thoughtful nod, dropping his eyes to Kit's key. "Mm, I heard an operator was causing them trouble. Do you know anything about it? My business has been poor since the Switchboard went down."

"We're trying to get it repaired, but I need to deliver a message to the High Spirits."

"And the Shields don't trust anyone. I see, I see." The small man dropped down from his high stool and trotted to the end of the trolley, opening the door to the kitchen area. "Come along, then! I have a delivery order for René. If you will take it for me, I can get you to Paradise."

"Noodle, you can't," Kit replied, digging the nails of his free hand into his palm. The small kindnesses of the world were more than he could handle in the face of his growing fears. "You'll get in trouble. They're searching all of the traffic—"

"Thank you," Henley interrupted in a firm tone, tugging Kit along as he stepped through the door. Like the buildings of the Between, the cart held its own gravity, and they didn't float when crossing directly from one to the other. "We're grateful for your help, if you have a way to get us inside. We're happy to help you in return."

"You should keep him," Noodle told Kit, jerking his thumb at the mage. "You need him. Come here, I have plenty of space."

He opened a tall, slender door that should have belonged to a cabinet and shoved on the shelf inside. It slid backward, revealing a space large enough for a few people to sit comfortably behind his prep area. A few boxes were nestled securely in the space, but enough room was left for the pair.

"Good thing you aren't as fat as I am. In with you!"

Henley ducked in first, inching sideways until he could duck his head down and sit facing the opening. Nothing about the action or the position was kind to the burns on his legs. Kit followed, sitting with his back to the wall and his feet braced in front of him, leaning forward enough to avoid aggravating his wounded shoulder.

"Why do you have a space like this?"

"Storage. It's full when people return all their dishes," Noodle replied, giving the Chief Operator a stare. He disappeared from view, then returned a moment later with a pair of bowls. "Eat! You look like a lamppost with no bulb. I'll get you to Paradise in short order."

"Thank you," Kit replied as he took the bowls and passed one to Henley. The chef gave them a warm smile and winked, then pulled the shelf back and slammed the door. Darkness fell over the pair, but as Kit's eyes adjusted he realized light was peeking in through several cracks and joins in the wood.

"Who is this guy?" Henley asked, sipping from his bowl. There was no spoon, but the bowl held a savory cream broth that contained small dumplings. Kit took a sip of his own, taking comfort from the familiar dish.

"Noodle. I order dinner from him almost every night. He's the best chef in the Between."

A sound of approval came from the prep area above them, and Kit gave a rough laugh. Henley set his bowl aside and reached out to grip Kit's arm.

"We're going to be okay, Kit," he said, voice quiet. "We're on our way. We've got help. We're going to make it and then everything will be fine. It won't be long now."

Kit nodded and focused on eating. The soup filled his belly, warming him and helping to control some of his panic. Nothing could make him feel better, but the soup boosted his flagging energy. Eating gave him something to do instead of launching himself out of the cart and toward his pursuer.

"Once we get to Paradise, we'll have to get to the man who runs it, so this is perfect," he whispered. "That's René, the one Noodle wants us to see. We'll have to convince René to let us see the High Spirits. He's known for being um . . . different, so I think he'll listen."

"You're making me nervous again."

"I've only really spoken to him a few times. If nothing else, he's bound to want his meal. What happens after that will be up to us."

Henley watched him in the shadows. All Kit could see of him was the gleam of light across the top edge of his glasses. "Are you going to be okay?"

"I'm scared." Kit forced a smile. "I feel it in every part of my body. My Assignment has been changed, so I'm driven to submit myself to the Lineman. I don't know if he'll find us easier in Paradise, or if it's a protected place like the Switchboard, or if there will be Shields everywhere, or . . . what will happen. But maybe René will protect me until I find answers."

"If he won't, I will."

Kit nodded and drank more of his soup, not having the heart to tell Henley how useless the mortal would be if they were found. They fell silent as they emptied their bowls. Henley shifted to sit in the same position as Kit, with their shoulders pressed together, an inch or so away from the wall. The Chief Operator leaned on his companion and closed his eyes, conserving his energy.

The food cart moved like a swimming whale, floating without making abrupt stops or starts. Kit almost didn't realize they had paused until new voices sounded from the open area of the cart, loud and demanding.

"Open your cabinets and submit to a search. Do you have any staff on board?"

"How many people do they think can fit on these things?" Henley muttered, silencing when Kit shoved an elbow in his ribs. They heard Noodle jump down from the bench, stomping around as he opened cabinets, including the one they hid behind. The shelf was full of utensils and ingredients, but Kit could see through the gaps; he sat frozen as the Shields boarded the trolley and looked through the cabinets.

"No other staff, I make everything myself. Would you like to try? I've just found the perfect recipe for spaetzle. No? When does your shift end? I'll bring the trolley around to the station. You won't regret it, I assure you."

"I don't have time for food, Chef. You're delivering?" One Shield was rifling through the cabinets, moving boxes and bags and dishes aside as the second discussed with Noodle. The first shoved things out of the way, searching as if there wasn't enough time.

"Yes, for René. I'm already an hour late, can you believe it? No one wants to go about their business when they can talk about the Lineman."

"It's not helpful to us, either. Sophie?"

"Clear, sir. Nothing in the cabinets. He's alone." The searching Shield darted off the cart, the weight of it shifting slightly.

"You're free to go," the second Shield said. "Make sure you let us know if you see any operator acting strange. Don't take on any passengers you don't know."

"Yes, Officer, of course," Noodle replied, and the trolley began to move again. Kit sagged with relief, letting himself breathe. He barely strangled a cough, holding his breath for several seconds before he released the sound from his chest.

"You had better not be choking on my gnocchi!" Noodle opened the cabinet and pushed the shelf back again, scowling into the hidden space. "Seconds? You should stay in there until we get closer to Paradise."

Henley reached across the Chief Operator to hand the chef the empty bowls as Kit caught his breath. "I think we're fine, thank you. That was delicious and much needed. Who else have you smuggled in here?"

"Eh?! Smuggled?! I haven't smuggled a single—"

"There are shoe prints on the wall where we're sitting."

Noodle leaned into the space and frowned at the wall. The smell of spices, heavy cream, and strong cologne came with him, the scent leaving its own presence on the small space. When he blocked the light there was little to see, but he didn't argue.

"Well, sometimes people need to get places, or they need to disappear for a little while. I hope you won't go telling stories."

"We won't," Kit assured him, clearing his throat. "We were very lucky you came along when you did, Noodle. I'm going to owe you much more than dishes."

"The dishes are enough!" Noddle squeezed himself back out of the space, then shoved in another pair of bowls, this time holding a solid mass accompanied by forks. "Keep eating and stay quiet."

He left the shelf pushed back so they would have light. Henley sniffed the dish, lifting his eyebrows at the scent of vanilla and cinnamon. "What is this?"

"Kugel. Noodle says he's very avant-garde because he puts pears in it." Kit nibbled a bite, leaning to his right to peek out at the gray world passing by. "It won't be long now."

"So when we arrive, we're delivery boys?" Henley asked around his bites. "We get to René, we beg for his help. How hard is it to get to René?"

Kit turned back to give him a weak smile.

"I guess we'll find out."

Sixteen

Paradise Lost

From a distance, Paradise was bright. The closer the floating restaurant approached, the more the glow intruded on every crevasse and corner of Noodle's kitchen. Within the secret compartment, Henley went from low visibility to enough light that he could see the color of Kit's strawberry hair and his worried silver eyes. Noodle beckoned them out with a few minutes to spare before their arrival. He straightened their clothes, tucked Kit's key into his shirt, and tried to ply them with more food.

The cook threw the occasional look over his shoulder, judging the distance to their destination. Henley watched from where he leaned against a counter. Noodle was friendly and cheerful, but his hands were very still and his eyes wise. He knew exactly when to urge the pair to duck back down out of sight. As they sailed closer to the glittering buildings, they passed occasional floating checkpoints of men and women in black suits with inviting smiles. Noodle gave each one a small nod, and no one stopped his flight.

Once they were out of hiding and could see Paradise in its full glory, the resort did its best to overwhelm. The murky colors of the Between, faded grays and lifeless browns, were countered by opulent gold and shimmering glass. The sound of music and laughter could be heard long before they arrived. Henley tipped his head back as Paradise loomed, shifting his gaze from one detail to the next. It was one building, but many levels which didn't require any base for structural stability. Sections reached out in widely different directions.

He didn't realize he'd spoken until his voice broke the silence. "How big is this place?"

Noodle gave an interested lift of an eyebrow from where he was chopping carrots, and Henley remembered he was supposed to know about Paradise. Kit didn't catch the faux pas.

"As big as it needs to be," the Chief Operator said, turning one of Noodle's endless supply of spoons over in his hands. "Paradise could house the entire population of the Between. The central structure is permanent, but the rest grows or shrinks depending on how many people need to be inside."

"Incredible." The building was a resort hotel crossed with an old Hollywood theater, a shrine to excess. Enough light to power a small city made the place glow. If Henley stretched up onto his toes, he glimpsed open terraces on the upper levels that held a shocking display of greenery. Henley hadn't realized how starved he was for plant life. He'd only caught a glimpse of Kit's beloved plant back at the apartment.

Few other vehicles or individuals moved with them. The traffic was spaced out due to the outer perimeter of Shield inspectors. The checkpoint staff of Paradise gave razor-sharp smiles to the officers, who hovered on the outside edge in frustration. As Noodle guided the floating cart to a platform near the middle of the collection of lights, he spoke to his guests under his breath.

"There won't be Shields inside. René can't stand them asking questions and poking their noses in his business within his territory. His bouncers, though, they'll give you some trouble since you don't have an appointment. And they'll be on guard with the attack on the Switchboard. You'll have to be stubborn to get through them."

"But we have an order for René, right?" Kit looked past Noodle's shoulder to where a cloth-wrapped stack of containers was waiting on the pickup shelf.

"Indeed, but they won't know you. Can you manage?"

"We'll be fine," Henley said, arms crossed over his chest. "We're not stopping now."

The slow passage had given him too much time to think. Too many minutes to consider the risks of what he was doing, too many seconds to think twice, until Kit had rested his head on his shoulder again.

I'm scared, too, Henley wanted to tell his companion. *I don't know if I can do this. I don't know if we'll make it.*

Kit stopped him. The Chief Operator's need for physical contact, his grim eyes, the way his hands clenched when he was left to his own devices. Every time Henley looked at him, he couldn't open his mouth. Henley was afraid that if he voiced his fears, Kit would disappear so Henley wouldn't have to deal with the situation anymore.

If Henley had learned anything in the Between, it was that Kit did everything alone. He couldn't pin down why that was starting to bother him so much. Instead of speaking up, he'd tucked Kit's hand through his arm and patted it, letting his companion sag under the strain of resisting the Lineman's call.

They came to a stop. Noodle settled the hovering cart even with Paradise's landing platform, then placed the wrapped package in Henley's hands. The bottom layer was hard and square, the corners digging into his palms.

"You need to get to the central lift, and take it up as far as you can go," the cook explained. "Then you will be stopped by the bouncers. Tell them who sent you. Then, do your best. If you succeed, they'll allow you to see René."

"You have so much confidence in us," Kit said, and Noodle scowled.

"You owe me, Chief Operator Kit! Failure isn't an option!"

"Okay, okay, I'm sorry." Kit gave the man a little smile, then stepped onto the platform. "Thank you again, Noodle. We'll make sure the order gets to René."

Noodle harrumphed as Henley maneuvered around him. "That's more like it. Good luck to you both—I'll see you again soon, I'm sure."

They stood together on the platform, shoulder to shoulder, as the cart floated away. Noodle didn't look back at them or wave. Kit and Henley were ants in the shadow of Paradise's bulk. As they turned to face the entrance, Henley saw that the shadows had been used to good effect. The noise and excitement of Paradise waited for them beyond a pair of enormous art deco doors.

"Don't think about it," Henley said, eyes forward. "Just go."

Kit looked at him, took a deep breath, and walked forward. The movement triggered a response from within the resort. A pair of smiling young doormen opened the huge doors for them, battering the pair with a sudden shock of laughter and spritely jazz music. Light reflected off gold accents and crystal chandeliers with hundreds of lightbulbs hung two stories overhead.

Their first steps were on carpet so thick Henley's feet sank into the plush fibers. A woman waited for them at a reception podium, dressed to the nines in a long, straight dress, with feathers pinned in her hair. She had the same smile as the doormen, bright and perfect.

"Are you making a delivery, sirs?"

"Yes, we are." Kit's smile was just as bright, just as fake, his back and shoulders too stiff. "René ordered from Noodle. The Shields held us up, so we need to get to him as soon as possible."

"The Shields?" The woman looked past them and pursed her ruby lips, pulling her delicate beauty mark off-center. "Of course, right this way. Just go straight through the lobby to the bar, you'll see the lifts—take the one on the left to the seventh floor."

"Thank you," Kit replied, and started walking. Henley stayed a few steps behind, looking as stoic and boring as possible. The grand hallway stretched out before them, dotted with tables holding small plates and drinks. A waft of rich, buttery caramel under Henley's nose almost broke his focus. He counted himself fortunate that too many people occupied the hall for him to find the source of the scent.

The hall wasn't crowded, but enough people were present to contribute to the festive atmosphere. No one but the staff wore anything less than a ballgown or tuxedo. When Henley passed too close, a woman's fur stole stroked against his sleeve. She shifted her weight enough to be out of his way, but never looked at the pair. Only the staff gave them those bright, flawless smiles. The feeling of nonexistence clawed at Henley's shoulders.

"Why aren't they looking at us?" he whispered to Kit after the third couple swept to the side just in time to avoid colliding with him. "Can they see us at all?"

"In Paradise, you only see what you want to see," Kit whispered back. "Unless you work here. This place soothes the mind and encourages rest. Since we're not here to enjoy ourselves, we don't fit into the fantasy."

"I don't like it." Henley hovered protectively behind Kit as the Chief Operator led the way to the lifts. A new crowd of partygoers occupied the bar, this time to enjoy a live band and a dance floor. The glistening flow of fabric, the dazzling glitter of jewelry and glasses of expensive alcohol—it was a silver-screen view of the 1920s that called him to step into the dream.

"This way." Kit's voice snapped Henley out of his reverie. A set of gilded lifts with wrought iron doors waited, another smiling attendant inside ready to close the gates and pull the lever that led to the seventh floor. Henley tightened his grip on the packages as his heart hammered his chest. *Now comes the lie.* Paradise's bouncers could ruin everything. After all the pair had been through, to be stopped now by some overzealous bodyguards would be—

Kit glanced at him and offered a brave smile. There was fear in the expression still, but also hope . . . and trust. His face wasn't as creased with exhaustion. The Chief Operator leaned a little against Henley's shoulder, and he made himself smile back before he focused on the doors.

When they opened, the attendant bowed and motioned for them to exit. A windowless, round lobby waited for them, claustrophobic after the multilevel spaciousness of the floors below. Henley was too aware of the lower ceiling. The glitz and music of the main area had given way to uncomfortable silence.

Henley stepped out first, making sure that the package was held where it could be clearly seen. Kit placed a hand on his arm as the lift doors closed behind them. Henley had been in funeral homes more welcoming than the cluster of wingback chairs, end tables, and guards in the room. Five doors offered exits, each flanked with a pair of suited figures half again his size.

No one moved to greet the newcomers. Did he want to be greeted by those hard faces? *Not really.* When they weren't in motion, the smell of cheese from his package hung in the air around him, and his stomach twisted. "Go ahead," Henley whispered to his companion. "If they don't want to let us in . . . make a scene."

Kit darted another look at him, nodded, and stepped forward.

"We have a delivery for René," the Chief Operator said, his voice only shaking a little.

Bitter cold laced the voice of the woman who answered. "You're not Noodle." The perfect tailoring of her black pantsuit complimented olive skin and the palest green eyes Henley had ever seen, almost glowing against her complexion. She wasn't one of the ring of guards, and Henley didn't know when she had appeared in the room.

"Noodle sent us. It was very difficult getting through the Shield barricade." Kit laughed, voice a little too high. "The spaetzle isn't very good cold, you know."

"René hasn't changed his order in two decades," the woman replied. How her voice dropped a few degrees in temperature, Henley had no idea. "You may leave."

"I'm sorry I don't know his order. I didn't see Noodle pack it, but I just tried the spaetzle and he's been pushing it on everyone. He's always so proud of his new recipes." Kit was starting to babble. Henley looked around the room. There were far too many guards for them to get past, magic or no magic.

"You may *leave*, or you will be escorted."

"We have to make this delivery!" Kit's voice rose, and so did the tension in the room. The guards dropped their hands to their sides and straightened. "Noodle is counting on us, I promised him we would make it as soon as possible. It's already cold! We were delayed, it's not Noodle's fault!"

Several of the guards left their posts and approached. Kit took a step back against Henley but kept pressing, his voice rising in a dramatic wave.

"Don't you understand what's happening? If I don't do this I'll be like the operators, my Purpose—"

"Your Purpose isn't our problem," the woman replied. Kit took a deep breath and clenched his fists.

"Your Purpose isn't MY problem!" he yelled. His hair was coming loose from his bun as he gestured wildly, the strands flying around his head. "You don't get to decide who delivers *food* from a business that isn't yours! Do you even know how precious this is? Noodle puts all of himself into these dishes, he's a *master* at his work, he—"

"Rosetta!"

The crack of the voice was sharp even through a pair of doors. Henley wasn't sure which doors hid the speaker, but everyone froze, including Kit. The Chief Operator was panting but stood still while everyone listened.

"If that is my lunch then do not keep me waiting further. This day has already been too long."

The guards took a step back. Rosetta pressed her full lips into a thin line, then turned and walked to one of the doors. She opened it a few inches.

"It isn't Noodle. It's someone posing as delivery boys."

"Two of them?"

"Yes, sir."

"Then I've been waiting for them. Let them in—unless they don't have my lunch. Then you can throw them out."

The woman looked back at the pair. Henley lifted the wrapped package in his hands. The smell of cheese and butter wafted to his nose.

"They have it, sir," she sighed, and pushed the door open. "Go in. If you do *anything* unwise, remember how many of us are waiting to show you the error of your ways."

"Thank you," Kit replied, brushing his hair back out of his face. He summoned his dignity from where he'd thrown it and walked forward, through the open door. Henley followed. Rosetta's gaze stayed unfriendly as she closed the door behind the pair and left them in silence. The lighting in the office was brighter than the rest of Paradise. No, not brighter—whiter. A stack of magazines with current Actuality dates was in a haphazard mail pile on the table by the door: *People*, *Cosmopolitan*, *Vogue*. An enormous desk dominated the space, clean of everything but a laptop and a gold-accented coffee cup. The fantasy of Paradise popped like a bubble.

"What on earth—" The whisper left his lips before it could be stopped. Was that a handheld food processor next to a bag of coffee, squeezed into a shelf with a cheap souvenir snow globe? The trinket sat on a carved wood stand, given a place of honor among the trappings of Actuality conveniences. Henley's traveling eyes caught a warning look from Kit, and Henley shook himself back to attention.

Behind the desk sat one of the most beautiful men Henley had ever seen. He was in his mid-thirties with a trim build suitable for a Parisian catwalk. Flawless skin almost glowed under long blond hair that spilled over his shoulders in glittering curls.

"You should have changed his glasses, Chief Operator. That's a very modern look." When the stranger rose to his feet, he straightened a burgundy suit as tailored as the one Rosetta wore, and he was shorter than Henley by a few inches. The light caught on cufflinks set with impressive gems.

Kit went still. Hands still full of Noodle's delivery, Henley stepped between his companion and their host. René arched a single, cynical blond eyebrow over blue eyes that were as clear as a summer's day.

"What do you expect me to do to him, Mr. Yu? Bite him? Set him on fire? Cry and cause a scene?"

"You know who I am?" The room, the man, and the name left Henley off-balance. Behind him, Kit shuffled to the side, and Henley moved to stay in front of him.

"The Shields released your details in the Actuality. Your face is all over the internet. I have business in all realms, because Paradise is the center of all worlds, and I keep up with the news." René motioned to the chairs in front of his desk. "My order, if you please. It's gotten cold enough."

Kit nudged Henley's arm with his elbow, giving him a gentle push forward. Henley complied, wary as he walked closer and offered the package.

"It's good to see you again, René," the Chief Operator ventured, and received a grunt in return.

"You didn't come here to flatter me or exchange niceties, Kittinger. Tell me what you want so you can be faster out of my office." As he spoke, the blond unwrapped the package, setting the covered bowl aside. Beneath the dish, the square shape Henley had felt was one of the boxes stored in Noodle's hidden compartment. This René set aside.

Kit coughed as he took one of the seats. He had grown paler as they moved through Paradise, complexion turning gray. The scene in the lobby had taken too much out of him. Henley stayed on his feet, hovering behind Kit's shoulder. On the wall behind the desk, a framed copy of the *Dark Side of the Moon* album cover was hung upside down. Focusing on the conversation was a struggle.

"We need to see the High Spirits." Kit kept talking even after René made a sound of amusement. "The Shields have been corrupted. They've been siphoning the magic of the Switchboard substations. That's why I disabled the Switchboard. They came to No. 28 and killed my patrol officer. I think they were going to kill everyone."

Something in his words got the man's attention. *They'd better,* Henley thought, uneasy with how direct Kit was being with their information. René sat down and closed his laptop, thoughtful as he examined the Chief Operator. He ignored Henley.

"You know for certain they're the reason for the dead zones in the Switchboard?"

"I do. I saw them. I heard Shaw myself. They've been chasing me ever since I ran to the Actuality."

"I see." René uncovered his bowl of pasta. It was bright orange: cheddar-covered mac and cheese. "If Shaw himself is involved, the situation is very complicated. What do you plan to do about it?"

"I want to plead to the High Spirits. I'll tell them everything and get them to disband the Shields."

"There are two problems with that statement. One: the Lineman has been released, which will prevent you from doing anything as soon as you submit to his call. Two: there are many, many more Shields than High Spirits. Do you think the Spirits can do anything to control such a large group? How do you expect them to stop the Lineman?"

"They can reassign the Purpose of the Shields." Kit had clenched his hands in his lap. Henley rested a hand on the Chief Operator's uninjured shoulder, giving it a squeeze.

"That removes the peacekeeping force from the Between. The Fetters will be defenseless. The mages in the Actuality won't be overseen either, and who knows what they'll get up to."

"It's better to have chaos than to have destruction," Kit pleaded. "Isn't it? The Shields can be rebuilt. They have to be *stopped* before the balance of magic is shifted beyond repair."

René leveled those cold blue eyes on his guests.

"There's always a method of repair, and it's hunting you right now. The Lineman will force your obedience and the Shields will be judged as the High Spirits see fit, but not before your fate is decided. You know how this is destined to end. What do you plan to do to forestall the Lineman?"

Kit floundered. The tension rolled off him, traveling up Henley's arms, and he lifted his chin.

"He can't capture Kit if he can't find us," he said, firm. "If we stop the Shields first, I'm sure there's a way to stop the Lineman. The High Spirits can call him off."

"You don't know a damn thing about the Between, Mr. Yu, and you should take your ignorance into account before you speak."

"I haven't let that stop us, and I'm not going to stand by and *be ignorant* while everyone else ignores the problem. The Lineman isn't here. The Shields have almost caught us three times, but they haven't succeeded once."

René tilted his chair back and stared up at him over a forkful of mac and cheese. "I hate mouthy mages. Every one of you mortals thinks you know everything."

"I know there's no reason for the Between to exist without the magic. I know that you hold the key to letting us try the one thing that might work to keep all of this from crumbling to dust. I know that if this isn't resolved, the Actuality will get worse and worse until thousands of lives are lost or disrupted by the magic backlash."

The blond gave him a sour look before he turned his attention on Kit again. Henley rubbed Kit's shoulder, never taking his eyes off René.

"And what about you, Chief Operator?" René asked. "Are you willing to take the risks this mage is suggesting? Does he speak for you?"

"Henley is the only one I can count on right now," Kit said. "I never would have made it this far without him."

"That doesn't speak very well of your chances." The blond paused between bites. His attention was heavy on Henley, a somber weight that countered his over-dramatic personality. "Why are you here, Mr. Yu? What do you stand to gain from this?"

Henley said the first thing that came to mind. "I found a new Purpose."

"Your smart mouth does not make you more endearing," René grunted. "Why shouldn't I have you both thrown out?"

"You don't have any reason to help us, but you have more to gain if we succeed and the Between isn't rewritten." Henley stared at the shorter man. "Besides, you knew we were coming. You made your decision about helping us before you told Rosetta to let us in."

René sagged back in his chair, examining his guests with hooded eyes. "I would love to say otherwise, but reality interferes. Very well, Mage and Chief Operator. I will grant your request, but whether the High

Spirits will see you is another story. They've been quiet for a month. It took something as extreme as your actions to have them speak again, and the Captain of the Order had to go to them in person to beg for their assistance."

"What do we have to do?" Henley asked as he stepped back to his former position.

"Since you aren't the Captain or the Lord of Paradise or the damned Lineman himself, you must request admission. The High Spirits will discuss your request, then either send the lift for you or reject the proposal." René waved his fork at Kit. "You could go alone of course, without restriction, but your mortal friend is the problem. Given your circumstances I admit that you are vulnerable without his assistance."

"You won't let us in?" Henley asked.

"No." The growled word carried plenty of force. "This is your fool's errand, not mine. I will not risk the safety of the souls under my charge without good reason. You could be a worse threat than Shaw, for all I know. If the High Spirits see the urgency—and they see *everything*, Kittinger—then you will be allowed to present your case."

Kit looked up at Henley with determined silver eyes. Henley gave him a tight smile.

"That's why we're here," he said. "You know this is real, and I know they'll listen to you. It'll be fine, Kit."

The Chief Operator gave him a nod, and René waved a hand.

"Get out of my office, then. Rosetta will give you what you need to prepare your request and deliver it for you. Don't cause any trouble while you wait."

SEVENTEEN

BETRAYAL IN PARADISE

This isn't going to end well for any of us, René thought.

"I've sent their message to the High Spirits," Rosetta said, framed in René's office doorway. Her frosted personality was marred by the smallest movements of her hands. All the Paradise staff were nervous. "The Chief Operator and his friend are waiting in the Sapphire Parlor. The Shields have demanded entrance again."

"Keep telling the Shields to piss off until Shaw himself shows up, then send him to me," René replied. His lunch bowl was empty and set aside, the flat box open in front of him. The black velvet interior cradled a dozen imperfect crystal points, each pulsing with magic. He plucked them from the velvet with a pair of platinum tongs, delicately placing them into individual bags. "Have the transporters arrived?"

"Yes, sir. I don't know how we're going to get them out through the Shields."

"They don't need to leave. Get them their orders, then have them enjoy Paradise until you have an opening." René hesitated, then tucked one of the small bags into his inner coat pocket before pushing the tray toward his assistant. "Did you see the High Spirits with your own eyes?"

"No, sir. I sent the message and heard no response. I've got one of the boys watching the lift."

"I don't like this," he said, glaring at the surface of his desk. His attention was drawn again by the empty bowl. "If their story holds true, the entire Between is going to collapse. Business will be severely disrupted until the rewrite is complete."

"You should be charging more right now, then, sir."

René barked a laugh. "This is why I keep you on my staff, Rosetta. Go on. I'm going to check on our guests."

She took the box. He retrieved his cell phone from his desk and slid it into his pocket as he left his office, giving a nod to his guards. The vaults, hidden behind the other doors, were secure. Paradise was still his domain.

Then why do I feel as if a noose is tightening around my neck?

He took the lift down to the main floor, taking a deep breath when the atmosphere of revelry and enchantment wrapped around him. He saw through every illusion. The beautiful people were normal Fetters under their fancy clothes, working people who had earned their chance to enjoy a little Paradise and keep their minds stable. There was more to it, of course. There was no need for a place like Paradise in the Between, unless it served another purpose.

René could see that purpose. Flowing through every member of his staff was a thread of magic, glowing soft silver. The visiting Fetters glowed as well, in varying stages: those who had been there the longest were bright, while the newest had flickering, weak lights. They danced and laughed, unaware of the massive, crackling pillar of energy that tore through the center of Paradise and recharged their fading energy. The Between renewed itself. The magic was always in balance.

"And that's why my business is so good," he murmured to himself, and stepped up to the bar. The bartender bowed to him, reaching under the counter to retrieve a cup of coffee. The scent was far stronger, more real, than anything in Paradise. Several dormant crystal points rattled on the saucer.

"Any message?" he asked the bartender. The man nodded.

"He said to tell you he's still not interested."

"Bastard." The word was mild on René's lips. He pocketed the crystals and lifted the cup to his lips, breathing in the rich steam. The faint bitterness to the taste told him more than any message. "He won't last much longer. If he responds, open the way to him immediately."

"Yes, sir."

Confident in his work and his plans, René put his back to the bar and surveyed his domain. His people were paid well and did good work. His guests were happy. The coffee in his hand was hot enough to slow his sips. His shoes were new and expensive. Paradise was his playground.

So what in the Hells is that sound?

He slid a glance to his left, toward the main entrance of the resort. Raised voices nearby carried alarm and concern. Neither of those emotions were acceptable within his walls. His heartbeat sped up as the noise carried through the open promenade, causing a ripple effect of worried guests in its wake. René put his coffee cup back down.

"Code Four," he murmured to the bartender. He received a small nod in return before the man stepped back and walked from behind the bar, carrying René's instructions to one of the other staff. It was subtle, but René knew what to look for: an intricate dance as staff members switched places, left the area or entered, and made their way through the guests. The Paradise personnel knew their priorities. The guests came first, but then Paradise itself would be protected at all costs.

A shuffle of expensive fabric told him that his assistant had arrived at his elbow. "Sir, do you want the lifts restricted?"

"That depends, Rosetta," he replied. "Who is causing that racket?"

"The Shields, sir. Captain Shaw is on his way to speak with you himself."

René unbuttoned his coat. "Entertainment for the guests in the East Ballroom—make it big. I want the promenade cleared. Summon the guard team to replace the staff along the route the Shields will take. Anticipate violence. Send the Chief Operator and his friend directly to the High Spirits—the Shields are here for them."

"We aren't turning them over, sir?"

René snarled at the words, glaring toward the main doors. "No one takes a guest under my roof. Those barbarians can cut my throat before

I'll hand over a damn thing at their demand. Shaw has no authority over *me*. Hurry."

She nodded and disappeared. He took one last look around the bar, smiling at the worried guests, and spent a few minutes distracting them with the promised entertainment. Only once the crowd was drifting toward the East Ballroom did he make his irritated way to the entrance.

A block of black uniforms was a barrier between him and the outside world. A lovely black woman in uniform with victory rolls in her dark hair spoke to his harassed-looking doormen. The Captain was nowhere to be seen.

"Lieutenant Solene, I'm very disappointed in your rudeness. You know the Shields aren't permitted in Paradise—you're upsetting my guests."

Solene inclined her head to him, crimson lips still and emotionless.

"The Captain has business with one of your guests—a confirmed criminal. If you continue to keep us from our duty, we have been authorized to use force. You may take it up with the High Spirits later."

Bitch. René exhaled.

"Where is he?" he grated, rage flickering at the edges of his judgment.

Solene's lips curved up at the corners. "The Captain expected your stubbornness."

"Code Seven!" René shouted, and the staff that had clustered behind him surged forward as he moved back. They didn't display weapons—nothing that would cause alarm among the guests—but they had other means of fighting. The Shields didn't show as much consideration. As René ran for the lifts, he heard the first shots.

"Damn fools!" he hissed, motioning for the grim-faced lift attendant to close the gate. "Take me to the Terrace—that's the only other place that bastard could get in."

The lift rose, and he fought to keep his breathing calm. Paradise hadn't been assaulted since he had taken over as its lord and master. There were only two people who could break that sanctity, and both of them were imminent threats.

At least the Lineman doesn't sneak around.

The sounds of invasion met his ears before the lift doors opened. Fired shots pinged off the ornamental metalwork of the gardens and tore through the painted walls. Glass shattered. René gritted his teeth.

"Do these cretins not understand how hard it is to maintain a greenhouse in the Between?" he growled, and then launched himself out of the elevator as soon as the doors opened. His people were being pushed back into the building from the open, greenery-filled spaces beyond. Shields were stomping through the flower beds as if they didn't exist.

"That is the limit of what I am willing to accept," he said, tension rigid in his shoulders, fists clenched as he stepped up behind his people. "All restrictions lifted! I want this trash out of my resort!"

A stunning array of weaponry was produced in short order from sleeves, boots, vests, and pantlegs. His people didn't carry firearms—how *uncouth*—but everything else was on the table. The Shields cried out in surprise as they were suddenly faced with Paradise's teeth.

"Call them off, René!" Shaw's voice cut through the conflict. He stood behind the Shields, waiting for them to clear a path. He and René could have been brothers in coloring, but one wore arrogance where the other wore righteousness. "This is your last chance. I don't think you want to see Paradise fall."

"Go fuck yourself, Shaw." René lifted his chin, staring across the battlefield at his nemesis. The Captain stood in the center of the Terrace and smiled, hands held out to his sides.

"It's a shame you have to be like this." He raised his voice. "Focus on René! Bring him down!"

A chorus of determined officers answered. "Yes, sir!"

René fought the urge to send one of his knives straight between Shaw's eyes. That would really be uncivilized. As his people converged on him, however, he knew he was running out of options. He had warned Kit about the numbers the Shields possessed. No amount of training or planning would disable them for long.

He ducked back into the lift. "Parlors," he said between gritted teeth. The lift started moving before the doors were closed, showing him flashes of other floors as they passed. Black uniforms were visible on far too many.

The lift lurched to a stop, and he squeezed between the doors before they could fully open again. The Parlor Level contained two dozen small nooks and private rooms suitable for pleasant conversation, card games, or intimate moments. Rosetta stood at one of the doors, the Chief Operator and his mage framed in front of her. The woman turned as the lift arrived, a baton snapping to full extension in her hand.

"How the hell did they know?" René yelled, throwing his hands in the air. "Shaw is here and he wants blood. Has there been word from the High Spirits?"

"I don't know, sir—and no." She stepped aside, and he beckoned sharply to his troublesome visitors.

"They'll deal with the headache on their own terms, then. Keep stalling the Shields, Rosetta. Let's go!" The trio ran together and crowded into the lift. "Top floor!" he ordered, the poor attendant pulling the appropriate lever in the few inches he had to spare. Kittinger coughed, his thin body shuddering with the movement. René's hopes for their success dropped a few more points.

"When we get to the top level, you'll have to take the lift the rest of the way," he said, watching Kit. "I'll stay behind to buy you time, but it won't be enough. You must get in there and make your case before he comes after you."

"They'll know something is terribly wrong when you send us—they have to," Kit said, and René shook his head.

"The High Spirits do as they like. Even I don't know what moves them. Just don't waste this chance now that all of Paradise suffers with you."

"What happens if—"

The lift slid to a stop before Henley could finish his question. The doors opened on half a dozen revolvers raised in their faces. "Oh, Hells!"

René swore, panic clawing at his throat. There were only two available paths, and both were full of Shields.

There's no way we can—

Steady and sharp, the mage's voice cut through the rising voices of the Shields. "Ten percent, *Magnetic Force*! Submit to the law of Earth, drawn together without failure, bound by the force of nature!"

René gawked as the spell slammed into the officers. It had little effect on their bodies, but their guns went flying, stuck to the ceiling with their badges and whatever other metal they carried.

"Twenty percent, *Hold Fast*. Bound by my will and removed of your freedom, I forbid you the grace of your own control!"

René turned his head and stared at the mage. Kittinger was clutching Henley's arm, eyes just as wide. Henley flicked his gaze at René and nodded toward the open lift doors.

"I can't believe that just happened in the Between. Thirty percent and you aren't even breathing hard," the blond said, and ran forward, winding his way between the Shields. They couldn't even move their eyes to follow the group as they ran for another set of lift doors. These were ornate and set with thousands of small glass tiles, shimmering in the golden light of the hall. As they approached, the doors slid open in welcome, the lift beyond covered in mirrors that reflected a dozen views of their anxious faces.

"Go!" he ordered them, motioning the pair into the lift. "There's only one lever and it only goes one place. Once you reach the highest level, you'll be among the High Spirits—watch everything you say and do!"

"Are you sure you'll be alright without us?" the Chief Operator asked, leaning on his partner. A heavy, omnipresent bell sounded as he spoke. Gravity increased. The air thickened, sending a shiver of dread down René's spine as the sense of something terrible approached. Kittinger grabbed for the lift wall to keep his balance as his knees buckled. His already-pale face twisted with pain.

"I'm sure you don't have any other choice!" René said. Henley was looking past the blond, and his eyes widened. Already cursing fate, René turned to face the other end of the hall. The original lift doors had opened again to reveal Shaw and more of his people. Rosetta was among them, pointing at the fleeing pair.

Oh, I'll come for you next.

Thirty feet separated René from the first lift and his enemies. The heaviness in the air increased until the Shields and their prey struggled to remain standing. Only René and Shaw stood with their shoulders unbowed, privileged by their positions and not subject to the Lineman's overwhelming presence. Behind René, Henley forced the doors shut. Their lift jerked into motion. As the pair raced away, the heaviness lifted.

The Lord of Paradise focused his gaze on the Captain of the Order and gave him a vicious smile.

"Come on then, Shaw—let's see how long you last."

Eighteen

High Spirits

Too close. That was too close. Thirty seconds more and—

Kit's breathing bordered on hyperventilation. Claustrophobia set in as he was trapped within the tiny elevator with no way to run, no way to escape. The fact that the lift was taking them to supposed safety didn't alleviate his desperate need to do something to save himself.

Henley's arm was still tight around Kit's shoulders, supporting his weight as the Chief Operator got his legs back under him. Kit could feel the race of the mage's heart, as grounding as it had been the last time Henley had comforted him, sharing the fear and adrenaline.

"He's gone, Kit," Henley was saying. "He didn't get you. He's not *going* to get you. We're okay."

The entire world still felt too heavy. The weight that dragged at Kit's arms and legs called to him, as if he were still bound to the levels of Paradise that fell away beneath them. Bad enough that the Lineman had been so close. His Purpose screamed in the back of his mind, trying to cripple him after such a close encounter.

"It's calling me," the Chief Operator said, his voice rough. "Every time you use magic, he'll get closer. My Purpose has changed. Now I have to submit to the Lineman—I can't get better unless I surrender."

"Yes, you can," Henley replied, rubbing his other hand against Kit's back. "You can, if the High Spirits call this whole thing off. That's why we're here. We're going to force them to listen to us, and we're going to settle this right now."

Kit focused on breathing. He coughed, but not bad enough to send him to his knees. Yet. Henley supported him, eventually pushing Kit back enough to look into his face.

"Feels bad, huh? I know. We're going to handle this soon, so hang on. Can you do that for me, Kit?"

He had softened his voice, talking in gentle words as if to a child. Kit didn't care; he appreciated the comfort and special treatment. With a nod, he straightened.

"I'm sorry, I was just—"

"You don't have to apologize to me, Kit. For anything—ever. Unless you eat all my lunch in the refrigerator. Then we're going to fight."

Kit looked up in surprise. Henley had a little smile on his face and nodded when he knew he'd gotten Kit's attention. "Lunch theft is the worst. If you do that, we can't be friends."

A weak smile made its way to Kit's lips.

"Are we friends, Henley?"

"Yeah, we are." Henley squeezed the Chief Operator's shoulder before dropping his hands. "Since it looks like you and I have about the same number of friends, we need each other." He tucked his hands in his pockets and met Kit's eyes. "And I don't forget *anything*. Or anyone."

It didn't matter that they had just met. It didn't matter that Henley didn't understand how the Between worked, how the magic would ripple through the mages and change the perceptions of anyone who had ever dealt with the Between. There was such confidence in Henley's words that Kit was forced to accept them, forced to believe that this single mortal mage might remember him in defiance of the natural laws. Emotion tightened his throat.

Do you even know what that means to someone like me?

"Thank you," he said, instead of speaking his thoughts out loud. "You did it again. You were so fast with those spells. No one knows what to do with you."

"I'm glad it was worth it, if it also made your situation worse. Wait until you meet my sisters, they're faster than I am at casting. Not the best thing when you're the only brother. Lianlian has this one spell she likes that makes my socks try to eat my feet. They can't, but it's so *weird* it breaks my concentration."

Kit managed a rusty laugh and leaned against his companion's shoulder again.

"I'd like to meet them," he said, and Henley smiled.

"You will. When all of this is over—when you're safe. I'm already an exception in the Between. You can be one, too."

The Chief Operator nodded, relaxing one breath at a time as the lift made its slow ascent. Henley didn't push him away. "It's getting better," Kit told him, still taking slow breaths. "The Lineman can't reach me in the High Spirits' Palace unless they summon him themselves. Do you think René will be alright?"

"Do you think that Shield guy will be alright? René looked like he was ready to claw his eyes out."

"He might." Kit stared at his haggard reflection. "That's Shaw, the Shield Captain. He's the one that would have summoned the Lineman."

"Great, I hate him already."

They were quiet for a moment before Kit spoke again. Forcing the words out of his chest was harder than he expected, even with how much they had endured together. Maybe it was hard because they had been through so much. He stared at the floor.

"Henley, I'm so grateful or this—for everything. You're so strong and if you weren't here I couldn't have made it this far."

"I don't think that's true."

Henley elbowed Kit and looked up at him. His dark eyes were clear and determined, unwilling to accept the worst-case scenario.

"I think If I wasn't here, you'd do what you had to do—just like when you took the Switchboard down. You're right to be afraid, this is scary as hell. However, that doesn't make you weak. I think you're already one of the strongest people I've ever met."

Kit didn't understand the tightness in his chest. It was different from the constriction caused by the Between. This was warm, frightening, and as painful as it was pleasant.

"Henley, I—"

The lift came to a stop. Silver eyes and black lifted to stare at the doors. They could hear nothing from the other side. Henley straightened his shoulders.

"You ready?"

Kit drew himself up as best he could, then nodded. Only then did Henley pull the lever to open the doors. They braced for an attack, staring ahead, but the hall beyond the doors was silent. Together they crept out, looking to either side and up at the vaulted ceiling that rose four stories above them.

The hall was built on the same scale, made of gothic gray stone with inset carvings. No rugs or furniture softened the echo of their steps; there were no windows or doors immediately available. The silence was that of complete emptiness, with no living beings to make small sounds except for them.

"Have you been here before?" Henley whispered, and even that echoed. Kit nodded.

"I've communicated with them by message a few times, but I'm here in person more often. It's stale, like no one has been here in a while. It changes every time I visit so it's hard to tell if anything is out of order."

A strange smell hung in the air, faint and organic and unpleasant. Henley stayed close to Kit. "Let's see if we can find someone, then. As long as that lift is up behind us, they shouldn't be able to follow, but we should still move fast. It feels too strange in here."

Kit nodded. "Magic doesn't work the same way in the Palace. The High Spirits are the manifestation of the Between, its spirit in essence, and what liberties I can take are curtailed by their presence. If something doesn't feel right, don't force it."

"Warning taken."

They crept forward, the hallway so wide they couldn't reach the walls even if they stretched their arms to their farthest length. Sconces were lit along the way, spaced in perfect intervals; the clear globes provided plenty of light, but the ceiling above remained in shadow. The endless nature of the hall made tracking time difficult. *How many lamps have we passed? Ten? Twenty? Did I start counting at the first or somewhere along the way?*

"Kit, there's a door."

He blinked and found himself facing the end of the hallway. It hadn't been there a minute before, he was *certain*, but now the hall ended in a high wall. A pair of doors waited, three times their height, massive wood planks with iron finishings. They were cracked open.

"Maybe they knew we were coming?" Kit said, and Henley shook his head.

"I think I know what that smell is," he replied, grim. "I don't think we're going to like what's on the other side of that door."

Kit looked behind them, far down the hallway where the elevator glittered in the distance. The doors were closed.

"The elevator is gone. We can't go back anymore, Henley."

Henley looked back as well, exhaled, and then returned his gaze to the heavy doors.

"Alright."

They stepped forward together, and Kit pushed the doors open wider to allow them both to enter. A small foyer waited on the other side. It was made in the same fashion, with high arches and dark stone, but held several chairs and a large desk. Kit smothered his shock behind his hand as he saw the slumped body behind the desk and the dark stain on the floor.

"Smells like *rot*," Henley said, fine lines of stress appearing around his eyes and mouth. "That's not fresh blood, Kit. She's been dead a long time."

A door waited to their left. As much as Kit didn't want to open it, he *had* to know, had to see with his own eyes. He pulled Henley along as he pushed it open wide. The stench of death increased tenfold, making them gag as they faced the huge circular room, set with thronelike chairs.

There were bodies everywhere.

Two were in their thrones, slumped with heads lolling to the side. Three were on the floor, sprawled in tangles of arms and legs and flowing robes. Elegant hair accessories and circlets were scattered across the ground. A cluster of three bodies was piled near another door in the back, bloody handprints staining the stone where they had tried to escape and been mowed down.

"The first two were shot," Henley said from behind his hand. Kit turned to stare at him, preferring anything over looking at those corpses and the blood that smeared and splattered across every surface. "I don't know how long ago, but everything here is dry."

"They're all dead?"

He couldn't be right. People didn't die in the Between. They had crime, but not *murder*.

"I'm going to be sick," Kit announced, and turned away from his companion as his stomach rebelled. Another body waited for him, however, and he gasped as he flinched away again, backing up into his companion.

"Kit—"

"I know, I'm trying, it's just—how could anyone do this? The High Spirits! They're benevolent rulers, they don't cause any harm, they're—"

"*Kit.*"

He froze. Henley had grasped his wrist tight enough to leave bruises. As Kit turned, slow and careful, he met the mage's furious eyes before looking past him to the arm that held the pistol to the mortal's head.

Shaw's hand was steady, even though his face was a mess of small cuts and blood had splattered onto his uniform, the fabric torn and sliced in the same fashion. He didn't spare any attention for the bodies. Behind him, Solene covered her mouth with both hands, eyes wide with disbelief.

"This man will die if I pull the trigger, Chief Operator," Shaw said. "He won't come back as another Fetter. He might not even go on to *heaven* or whatever the mortals believe these days. He'll just be a pile of skin and blood on the floor. Let go of his hand and step away."

"Shaw, he doesn't have anything to do with this," Kit said, dropping Henley's hand as fast as he could. Henley resisted, fighting him, forcing Kit to yank his hand away. He stepped back, hands raised, facing the Shields. "Send him back to the Actuality. Let him go."

"He has everything to do with this," the Captain replied. "And if he ensures your cooperation, then he's not going anywhere. Solene, take his card."

The woman didn't move, deaf to his command until he called her name again. Then she hurried forward, face ashen, and fished the Assignment card out of Henley's pocket. Henley curled his shoulders, bowing his head as the sickness washed over him again. Shaw tapped the back of Henley's head with his gun.

"Walk. Back to the lift. Kittinger, the slightest wrong move on your part ends his life."

"I understand. Please—I'm coming. Don't hurt him." Kit kept his eyes on Henley as they were escorted back to the hallway. Every corpse they passed had the mage's face in his mind; every bloodstain was Henley's.

Shaw's officers waited for them near the elevator, far from the sight of the massacre behind closed doors. Kit stayed as close as he dared, keeping his eyes on Henley's stiff shoulders. None of the Shields looked unscathed, but few had the level of injuries Shaw displayed.

Two of the waiting Shields stepped into the lift with them, both sporting rank pins on their collars. They positioned themselves between Kit and the others, pinning the Chief Operator face-first against the back wall. Henley was given the same treatment, shoved against the mirrors, glasses pressed awkwardly into his face, and Shaw's pistol still held against the back of his head. The ride to the lower floors was silent.

The doors opened on the bar, the main promenade laid out in front of them in a warfront of broken furniture and grim-faced officers. Kit heard sounds of fear and alarm in the distance, but there were no civilians or Paradise staff present. René was nowhere to be seen. One of the waiting Shields stepped up to Shaw, offering a folded pad of gauze for his face. The Captain took it, holding it below his eye.

"Sampson, take the mortal and secure him at Headquarters. Solene, find us an empty trolley—we'll be taking the Chief Operator to Substation No. 28."

"Yes, sir." One of the Shields drew his service weapon and leveled it at Henley. The fear of not knowing what would happen next sent Kit into action. He threw himself at Shaw's gun arm, wrapping his own around it and yanking on the man with all his weight.

"You can't! He's going to die if you don't give him back his card. Shaw, he's not at fault for this! Please, you can't harm a mortal innocent—"

Too much happened for Kit to follow the movement. His legs were kicked out from under him and he went down, his arms pried off the Captain, a boot to the stomach leaving him gasping, then coughing violently as his weakness was exacerbated. He heard Henley's raised voice and the sounds of a scuffle. When he looked up, the mage's arms were pinned behind his back and his glasses were cracked, a bruise starting to bloom over his right eye.

Shaw was furious. "*One* more move, Chief Operator, and I stop being generous." His voice shook with his willingness to carry out the threat. Kit was yanked to his feet to stare at Henley, helpless.

"This isn't over yet, Kit!" Henley told him, his voice carrying a different kind of anger. "Stay focused. You're here for a reason—"

Sampson shoved the barrel of the gun into the mage's mouth and pushed his head back.

"Walk," he said, and marched Henley backward away from the group. Kit smothered a curse in the back of his throat as his friend left his line of sight, swallowed up by a sea of black uniforms. His struggles against the hands that held him proved pointless.

"Where were we?" Shaw asked, once again in control and calm. Solene lifted a hand. The woman was still pale, Kit thought, but he was barely thinking about anything.

"The trolley, sir. It will be an hour or so before we can leave due to the evacuations, but I'll detain the first one that returns."

"Fine. Has there been any luck getting into René's office?"

"Not yet, sir. The informant isn't in any condition to help us."

"Keep trying."

"Yes, sir. Will we be calling the Lineman?"

"Yes, when the Chief Operator fixes what he destroyed."

Shaw looked around, then walked to the bar and took a seat. He shoved aside a half-empty cup of coffee and motioned for Kit's captors to bring him close.

"You're causing me too much trouble, Kittinger, but I have to thank you for your efforts." Kit stared at him, unable to connect the words to an explanation as he was forced onto one of the other barstools.

"Thank me?"

"Yes. Without your mischief, summoning the Lineman would have taken decades. Now we can bind him to our Purpose and the entire Between will benefit."

"Bind—you can't bind the Lineman, Shaw. He's not subject to anyone's control or reason, only the High Spirits' orders."

"Anything can be bound with enough magic." Shaw's smile was dark and unpleasant. "Before you disabled the Switchboard, we would have had to gather an astronomical amount of magic to both summon and bind him. Now he's here. All I have to do is force him to obey my commands."

A sinking sense of horror settled into Kit's stomach. "Why? What could you possibly want with him?" he asked. "His only purpose is to protect the Between and destroy anything that threatens it with harm."

"And when the Between itself is the threat?"

Kit blinked, shaking his head in confusion as Shaw stared at him.

"The Between is a nightmare, Chief Operator. You probably haven't seen very much in your flight, but we Shields see it every day. The mortals, the Ethereals—the freedom they enjoy is so much more than we get. We can't have families—we can't even have pets! This place is a prison. And what do the mortals do with their great privilege?"

He gestured sharply with the hand not holding the gauze to his face. "They squander it with careless disregard. They make war upon each other, tearing at their neighbors like animals. The Actuality suffers under their control, a beautiful world corrupted by their manufacturing and their poisonous ways of life. They take for granted every blessing they have been given while we must watch from a distance, never experiencing that joy ourselves."

Shaw took a breath, pulling himself back together. Several Shield officers had gathered around them to hear this speech, their eyes glowing with the same zeal.

"When I bind the Lineman, I'll force him to cut all Fetters free of the Between and let us live as we please," the Captain continued. "The Between will no longer exist. We'll channel the magic ourselves. We'll become the power the mages have corrupted. That's the only way we can be free."

"You're insane," Kit said, hands shaking. He clenched them tight in the cuffs of his cardigan. "The Fetters don't exist without the Between. The Lineman doesn't have that power. You're living in a fantasy!"

"That's what you've been trained to believe. What the High Spirits *wanted* you to believe, to keep you under control." Shaw gave him a small nod. "You'll see for yourself soon enough. When the Lineman cuts your thread, you'll wake up in a better world."

"It won't be better. It will be different, it will be empty and hollow and fake, rebuilt into a new incarnation where you won't remember any of this—"

"That's enough." Shaw took a deep breath and turned away from his prisoner. "Save your speeches for when I give you proof."

Kit fell silent, the pit in his stomach deeper. As he looked around the area at the gathered Shields, he saw no doubt in any eyes.

It's all for nothing.

He rested his head on the bar and fought to keep from passing out as the pull in his chest threatened to drag him out of Paradise.

Nineteen

Turning the Page

As the goose egg over his eye swelled, Henley's field of vision shortened. A series of cracks across his glasses' lens blocked portions of his view and made him vulnerable to objects in his path or doorframes he couldn't see. He stumbled, was dragged to his feet, and kept walking. Broken glass scraped and slid under his shoes. Gouges from knives and the impact of bodies had been left in the gold wood accents. The air was unnaturally still, giving Henley the heightened clarity of someone waking from a bad dream.

Wet stains on the lush carpet swam in and out of focus. The sickness of having no Assignment was worse the second time, when he knew it was coming, when he'd already felt the relief of being free of the nausea and shortness of breath. Henley's limbs wouldn't obey his commands. His heart rate was too high, but that had nothing to do with his Assignment. As he was half carried by his escorts, panic twisted his stomach.

They'll kill Kit. They'll give him to the Lineman. Then they'll kill me.

Sampson wore more cologne than most civilized people. It flooded Henley's nose and mixed with the lingering scent of gunpowder. Henley couldn't make out the details of the officer's face. Sampson kept his service pistol pressed against Henley's head even when he was cooperating to the best of his ability.

"You!" At first, Henley thought Sampson was talking to him. They had left the bar area and traveled down the wide main hall. Clusters of Shield officers dotted the entryway, blocking the doors that hung open in the distance. The Shield who was the object of Sampson's command rushed to straighten himself. His right arm was held tight against his ribs.

"Yes, sir?"

Sampson pulled Henley up next to the new Shield. Only then did he lower his weapon, but he kept it free at his side. "Shelly, Shindry—"

"Sidney, sir."

"Of course. Put the mage somewhere while I arrange his transport back to HQ. See to his security personally."

The officer stared at the major, then at the Shield holding Henley's right arm, then back at Sampson. "Major, I'm on the injured list. I've been ordered to the infirmary."

"Am I to understand that a Shield officer can't handle one powerless mortal mage?" The polite disbelief in Sampson's voice was marred by the way he stepped forward to stare the officer down. His words were met by a stiff shake of Sidney's head.

"No, sir. I'll take him. There are several rooms down this hall where he can be secured."

Sampson relaxed his hold. He was taller than Henley, and his shoulder ached where it had been forced a few inches too high. "Good. I'll return for him when the second trolley arrives. If he does anything to give you trouble, shoot him."

"Yes, Major."

Sampson turned on his heel to stalk back the way they had come. A moment of awkward confusion followed as a second Shield nearby assessed Sidney's injuries, then traded places with him so the injured side wasn't holding Henley. The grip that resulted wasn't as strong as when Sampson had been present, but Henley had nowhere to go and too many enemies in the hall if he broke free.

"This way, past the balcony. The civilians have been cleared from this wing." Henley's new escort spoke in short sentences over his bowed head. The trio turned off the main hallway and into an area with less lighting and fewer marks of the fight to control Paradise. A few doors had been left open, the rooms beyond indistinct through his cracked glasses.

Dozens of doorways lined the endless hallway, but Henley counted only ten doors before he was led into a library.

Floor-to-ceiling bookshelves lined the walls and loomed half again Henley's height. No windows threatened to fade the book covers, and the space was instead lit with small electric lights on panels tucked between the shelves. Sofas sat against the left and right walls with a long table down the middle of the room. The same carpet that had softened the mage's steps hushed every sound. Henley's captors walked him into the room and deposited him on one of the sofas.

"You heard the major," Sidney said. "Don't give me a reason to shoot you."

Henley looked up at him, lips pressed thin and headache growing by the second. He sagged in the embrace of the leather sofa, without the energy to sit up straight and glare. "I'm fully aware of my circumstances." It wasn't a promise of good behavior, but it was close enough. The Shields backed away from him and moved toward the door. After a short conversation, the uninjured guard helped Sidney out of his uniform coat, then disappeared back down the hall. A palm-sized crimson stain was spreading across the guard's ribs through his white uniform shirt.

Sidney positioned himself where he could block the door and continue to watch Henley, then proceeded to pull up his shirt and wrap the cut on his ribs with bandages and gauze from his coat pockets. Henley evaluated the man in silence. Sidney was middle-aged, with gray in his close-cropped hair and lines etched around his mouth. He was fit enough, but desk work or easy assignments had given him softness around his belly and thighs. His service pistol hung in a harness under one arm. Getting it away from the officer would be too dangerous.

What are you thinking, Henley?

Disabling an officer would require more than accidental impact. Nausea rose in the back of Henley's throat. Sampson was casual in his cruelty, but Sidney was just doing his job.

What would happen if he didn't stop the Shields from carrying out their plan? Shaw had been clear that the Lineman would be summoned and his twisted "justice" would be served to the Chief Operator. *How will they do it? What does it mean to be given to the Lineman? Is it painful?* Kit had seemed sure that Henley would forget about him. Henley was used to sorting through his memories, using what wasn't important for his magic, and reserving those too precious to lose. The idea of losing Kit from his mind, forgetting what they had endured together, the color of his odd hair, the way he had huddled against Henley's chest for reassurance, was a violation he couldn't bear.

Seconds ticked by as his thoughts raced in a circle, a state of mind that served no purpose. As he had been taught as a child, Henley grounded himself using his senses, identifying points around the room. He could see hundreds of hardcover books, lamps with brass pull chains and gold shades, and a bookmark someone had lost under the table. The smell of leather from the sofa mingled with the scent of old paper. In the distance he could hear the low din of voices. Sidney swore under his breath as he pulled the bandages tight. The cushions were cool through the fabric of his slacks. Henley tasted blood where his teeth had cut into his cheek.

By the time he had finished cataloging his surroundings, the rush of adrenaline had slowed, but clarity of thought only made his options stark. He could find a way to get free and rescue Kit, or bad things were going to happen to the Chief Operator and maybe Henley as well.

Get to the point, Henley. You've got much more to lose by sitting still than you do by taking action. Think. What can you use?

Henley stopped his examination, staring with blank eyes at the wall. Something had caught his attention, but it took a few seconds for him to realize what he was looking at. To his right, one of the panels between bookshelves didn't hold a lamp, but it had a doorknob. From where he sat, he couldn't tell if it was a closet or a door to the next room. If he didn't know where it led, it was doubtful that Sidney knew, either.

What if this plan doesn't work?

What if the first trolley came for Kit while he was sitting there considering his options?

The *what if* pushed him to his feet. His struggle to breathe returned. Sidney stopped what he was doing to monitor his charge. Henley ignored him and shuffled to one of the bookshelves. As he approached, the books shifted and changed positions, their spines transforming into those of familiar volumes in another display of Paradise's magic. The first to meet Henley's eyes was one of his favorite suspense thrillers. On the shelf above rested copies of his preferred design manuals. The one he used most often was a tall book thicker than his thumb with black-stamped lettering; the copy on his home desk held an inscription from his mother. Her handwriting was nowhere to be found when he pulled it down and opened the cover.

Book in hand, Henley moved to the next shelf. Fiction stayed at eye level, as if Paradise wanted him to lose himself in the fantasy. The design manuals turned into reference books and then into books about productivity and time management. By the time he brushed his fingertips across the bedtime stories he read to his niece and nephew, Henley stood only steps away from the door. The light shone gold across the grain of the polished wood, then sank into the aged knob. Sidney went back to his slouched lean against the bookshelves. Henley kept his eyes on the book titles and reached out with his left hand to turn the knob with the smallest movements he could manage. The door was unlocked and eased open a crack.

Henley took a breath that filled his chest until he strained to hold the air, then released it in a silent rush. Sidney was watching him when Henley slanted his eyes in his guard's direction. Henley waited another beat, then yanked open the door and darted inside.

It was unlikely that the door would be anything but a closet in a library, but Sidney couldn't know that for sure, and he couldn't ignore the way Henley threw himself into the space beyond. The Shield yelled, his boots hammering the floor as he ran across the room to give chase. The closet was only big enough to hold three or four people, but that was more room than Henley needed. As soon as he was inside, he stopped and faced the door, the design manual ready in his hands.

When Sidney came through the door Henley swung the book with every bit of energy he had left. With a loud *slap,* the smooth black cover impacted his opponent's ear. The Shield cried out and staggered to the side. Henley dropped the book with a silent apology to the author and grabbed Sidney's arm, yanking him deeper into the closet. The few seconds Sidney stayed off-balance were all Henley needed to throw himself out of the closet door, slam it, and shove one of the wooden chairs under the knob.

Within seconds, Sidney was back on his feet and pounding on the inside of the door. The heavy wood shook and the chair vibrated, but it held. Henley stared at the arrangement in delirious shock at his victory, panting for breath. He was free, but for how long?

Decades of mage training pulled him through the moment. He closed his eyes, slowed his breathing, and filed the new memory away for later use. The cautious planning. The rapid execution. The spike of adrenaline and the rush of victory. *Worth at least thirty percent, maybe more,* he thought. With a forceful exhale he opened his eyes.

Ignoring the noise of the trapped officer, Henley crossed the room to where Sidney had hung his coat over a chair. The Shield uniform coat was knee-length, black, and heavy in his hands when he shook it out. A shoulder patch held the Shield insignia of a lantern with the number 2642. The hem was a little too long for Henley but not enough to be noticed, and the shoulders fit him with some room to spare. Henley's black pants finished out the look. His head, however, was uncovered and too visible. Sidney had left half a roll of bandaging on the table. Henley removed his cracked glasses, tucked them into his coat, and wrapped the gauze around his head to roughly cover his good eye. The swelling over his right eye would help to make his face harder to recognize.

He hoped.

As disguised as he was going to get, Henley left the library and closed the door behind him. Sidney's pounding was muffled, the sound a soft echo in the wide, gracious hallway. The world was blurred and indistinct without his glasses. Doorways loomed in dark rectangles spaced along the gold-brown wood, which was in turn broken with splotches of color from paintings that held little detail until he was within arm's reach.

The hush of the hallway stayed absolute until the moment he placed a foot onto the wine-red carpet of the main entrance lobby. Then the sound returned in a wave of voices and activity, accompanied by the smell of expended ammunition and blood. Black uniforms with unfocused faces blurred together. Henley kept his eyes on the ground as he eased himself through the milling officers and toward the door. A line of Shields had formed before a pair of uniforms that bore white-and-red armbands. One by one, the queued officers shuffled between the pair to be evaluated. The medic on the left claimed Henley as he approached. Up close her features sharpened into dark skin and a button nose.

"Injuries?" Her voice was brisk but not without sympathy.

"Got thrown into a wall. Hit my head," Henley replied.

She nodded, gripping his arms and pressing down, then moved the same firm pat to his chest and ribs. "Let me know if anything hurts. Name and unit number?"

Henley looked to his right. The other medic was giving the next Shield in line the same treatment. No one had any attention to spare for him. "Stewart, 2642. Nothing hurts but my head."

She patted her way up to his shoulders again, pressing on his neck in a few places before she gripped his chin in one hand and held up a finger on the other. "Follow my finger. Good. You'll be alright. Stand ready on the platform. You'll be part of the escort team to Substation No. 28." Henley took a breath of surprise, and the medic arched an eyebrow. "Scared of the Chief Operator, Stewart?"

One day soon his luck was going to run out, but until then he counted his blessings. "No. Of course not. I'm sure the Captain will keep him in line."

"That's *your* job, so don't make the Captain's life any harder than it already is." She jerked a thumb over her shoulder. "Go on, trolley will be here in ten minutes."

He wasn't sure if he should salute, but the medic's attention was already on the next Shield in line. Henley mumbled his thanks before continuing forward to cross through Paradise's ornate doors, propped open with their smiling doormen missing in action. A sensation like a dozen soft hands on his arms and shoulders pulled him back in an attempt to keep him from leaving the building. *Don't you want to stay?* the feeling asked. *Wouldn't you rather be here?*

Henley shook himself free, looking back over his shoulder. Paradise was beautiful and warm even in its damaged state. The Between was gray, the endless empty space at his back, and the infinite wall of floating buildings looming before him in an oppressive shadow. The wonder of the strange place had crumbled into unease. When he joined the small group of officers on the platform, they stayed silent, only shifting enough to make space for him in their ranks.

The minutes dragged past. A few of the Shields talked among themselves in low voices, nothing Henley could hear. Occasionally an officer would walk out to join Henley's group, until a dozen Shields were prepared to escort the "criminal." Enforced inactivity made it all too easy to think about his nausea and his chances of survival. Henley kept his head bowed and held himself together.

The stated ten minutes passed before a new wave of murmurs caused him to lift his head. A trolley was approaching—a real trolley, black with gold trim, and the same lit-lantern logo, looking like it had just left the train tracks. The seal was too busy for Henley's taste, the details hard to make out, and he hated the bulky lettering that spelled out ORDER OF THE BRIGHT SHIELD. What he did like, however, was that it held enough seats for two dozen people.

The trolley settled next to the platform. One of the Shields by the door ducked back into Paradise to spread the word. Henley stayed still, holding his breath. Within a few minutes Shaw and Solene came through the doors, escorting Kit through a wave of hostile silence that fell over the Shields with the heaviness of a velvet curtain. Kit's hands had been bound in front of him. His hair was coming loose, the metal pin half-falling, and his key had been pulled out of his shirt to dangle around his neck like a brand. When he was led past the assembled escort, the Chief Operator kept his eyes forward and his shoulders straight. Henley hid the curl of his fists within the cuffs of his stolen uniform coat.

The trio boarded the trolley, and Solene paused at the door to speak to Henley's group. "Half of you in front of the prisoner, half behind. Be on your guard, especially once we reach the substation." Henley couldn't tell if her dark face was still ashen, but there might have been an unsteady edge to her clear voice. Without further instruction, she followed Shaw and Kit into the trolley, leaving the escort team to board in her wake.

When they were settled, the trolley was silent, and Henley was sitting directly behind Kit and Solene. He could have touched Kit's hair, fixed it, reassured the Chief Operator he wasn't alone. Instead, he stared out of the window and willed his tired body to keep fighting.

Twenty

Doubts and Demands

The trolley shifted under their feet as the Shields boarded, rocking back and forth. Solene counted the movements, numbering the officers out of instinct. Fourteen wounded, one sergeant, two corporals, herself, Shaw, and one prisoner. The uninjured would deal with the Chief Operator. The injured would be treated and back to work in a few days, but in a few days none of it would matter.

It was much easier to think of the minute details: the count of Shields, the way her skirt was showing wrinkles after a hard day, or the way she wished she had eaten a heavier breakfast. She didn't want to think about the High Spirits. Her thoughts were a tangled mess.

When did he do it? How long have they been dead? Does that mean the Captain wrote the Lineman order himself? How is that possible?

Have I been wrong all this time?

She couldn't be wrong. It was true that the Between was a prison for Fetters, that they had no freedom and so little control of their own fates. The only job a Fetter could choose was to be a Shield, if they could manage the training. For everything else they were Assigned their Purpose and settled for a life with no family, empty and meaningless. She wanted freedom. She wanted a family.

But the bodies. They died in fear, they died in a massacre. Did he kill them all himself? Was he hiding this from me? The Chief Operator—

As if her thoughts had summoned his voice, Kittinger glanced her way with those somber silver eyes. Shaw was in the seat across the aisle, his injuries being treated by one of the medics. Solene was closest to the prisoner, and he hadn't given up.

"This isn't going to accomplish what you think it will," he said, his voice low and tense. "The Lineman can't do what you think he can do. His blade cuts threads, that's it. Everything will restart, and we'll all still be in the same circumstances."

"Isn't it enough to try?"

He paused at her sharp response. Solene was sure it was the first anyone had given him, aside from telling him to shut up.

"What?"

"Isn't it enough to have made the effort, to *try* and be free? You don't know anything more than the rest of us—what will happen, what can and can't be done. The chains that bind us are made of magic, manufactured. There must be a way to break free."

"But we'll all be lost, all forgotten," he said, clasping his hands tight in his lap. His voice was heavy with frustration, and she gave him a strange look.

"The memories people have of you aren't real. You barely exist in this place; your life is made up every time the Between is reset. It doesn't matter if someone forgets you. Their lives are meaningless, too. That's the point."

"They aren't all meaningless," he said.

She pressed her full lips to a thin line and looked straight ahead. It was so much easier to reject his arguments than it was to face her own turmoil.

"That mage—do you realize how short his life will be? He will only live sixty, seventy more years at the very most. You've interacted with him for a few days, and in that time, you've risked his life multiple times. He'll be better off forgetting you."

"No," the Chief Operator said, his voice unsteady. "No, he won't forget. He's my friend, he's helped me so much—"

"He's helped you. Not the other way around. If you think of him as a friend, then you should want the best for him without being selfish."

He was quiet for several minutes, and Solene thought she'd finally won until he spoke up again. He coughed before he replied, the sound crackling in his chest and shaking his thin shoulders.

"What do you get out of this?"

This time she dug her fingers into her palms, her manicured nails threatening to cut through the leather of her uniform gloves. "I want to be free," she whispered, the muscles of her neck tense, a headache starting at the base of her skull. "I want to have a family. I want to go home to a man I love and our children and grandchildren. I want to live my life and know I meant something to someone."

He was quiet again. Solene had time to cool from her readiness to strangle the Chief Operator before he once more broke the silence. His voice was even softer than her whisper, almost escaping her ears.

"That's what I want, too."

Twenty-One

Reactivation

Kit dreaded their arrival the closer the trolley floated to Substation No. 28. The threats had already been delivered. The more he resisted, the more harm would come to Henley. He would be forced to choose between his friend and the fate of all magic.

I'm so sorry, Henley. I can't do it.

What was he apologizing for? Being unable to save the mage, or unable to sacrifice him? The cuffs of his cardigan had grown dingy in their short time together, and Kit didn't have the energy to clean them. His calloused fingers caught on the soft fabric. He dragged one fingernail over the rows of knitting, feeling it gently pop over each ridge. Henley had given the sweater to him because he thought Kit was cold.

The world went in and out of focus. Kit was falling apart under the influence of the looming, terrible decision and the persistent drag of the Lineman's call. Never in his long life had anyone shown him the kindness he had experienced in the previous few days. He yearned for it, like a plant wilting out of direct sunlight. He wanted to show Henley the rest of the Between, to let him experience the wonders of Paradise when it wasn't under attack. Kit wanted to see the Actuality and listen as Henley explained all the strange details. He wanted to meet Henley's family. The Shields would kill the mage, or Kit would lose him when the Between was reset.

Wasn't one of those worse than the other? How could he contemplate the alternative? The one thing Kit wasn't, was mortal. Death didn't feel final to him. As much as he knew the reality, forcing himself to accept it was difficult. Henley *might* die, he *might* be gone forever, if Kit couldn't figure out what plane his energy had gone to after he was killed. Energy wasn't made and erased. It existed in a constant state, expended and renewed, so human spirits had to go *somewhere*.

If the Lineman reset the Between and forced everyone who had touched it to forget, there was no going back. Kit hadn't had the chance to introduce Henley to his plant.

The trolley pulled to a stop at the platform of No. 28. Kit rubbed his eyes, looking up at the face of the building where he had spent decades of time making connections to mortals he had never appreciated. He had experienced thousands of first spells from mortal children testing their clumsy wings. *Lift Object, Breeze, Sprout,* and even the occasional dangerous *Create Spark,* all one percent flickers that meant nothing in the long view of time but everything to the young casters. No matter how much he had cherished those connections, it wasn't as much as they deserved.

"Let's go, Chief Operator."

Shaw was on his feet, and Solene stood at his side. They and the other officers were staring at Kit, waiting for him to stand. Rising slow wasn't enough to keep the world from spinning. His knees were weak as the pressure to comply with his Purpose tried to drive him to the ground. He grabbed for the back of the seat in front of him, and hands from behind kept him from falling. The air was so thick.

When Kit thought he was stable, he pulled away from the grip on his arms. The Shields said nothing. Kit edged past them down the aisle and stepped off the trolley. They stayed close, ready to snatch him out of the air if he tried to fly. He didn't have the energy to run.

With his escorts close at his shoulders, he walked across the broad platform and pushed open the doors of the substation. The silence inside was heavy and still. The old wood floor creaked under his steps as he walked forward, stopping next to the stain on the floor. It had been mopped up and the body was gone, but the wood was still marked.

"Why did you have to kill Sandoval?"

Shaw stepped up next to him and lowered his eyes to the stain on the floor. The bootsteps of the other officers were the only sound for a moment before the Captain exhaled.

"Officer Sandoval's death was not in our plan, and it is a tragedy. I knew there would be casualties. I never imagined my people would fall at the hands of our own." The words echoed in the silent lobby, where Sandoval's cheerful voice had greeted Kit every morning. "He gave no offense but being honorable, which is hardly a fault in the Order."

Kit swallowed. "So you killed him for doing his job?"

Shaw's face fell half into shadow as he turned away. "Keep walking, Chief Operator."

The substation was as he and Henley had left it, including the line of lamps that led the way across the big, open room. Kit brushed his fingers over the desks and panels as he wove through them. Each one belonged to faces and voices he knew, histories and habits and foibles. They were real to him. To each other.

He reached the ruined wiring of his panel and looked up at the mess he'd made. Half a dozen Shields spread out around him. His desk was littered with reminder notes for tasks he would never complete. *Remind Kelley about the orange juice. Take dishes back to Noodle. Get more tea—rooibos?* The papers and wood were smeared with ink from his faulty pen, which he would never replace. A few forgotten scraps of copper wire peeked out from under the mess.

"It would take days to fix everything," he ventured, looking back at the overhead wires. "I can only fix my panel. See, that thick wire there, that goes to this desk. I'd need a full team to—"

"Get to work."

"The Lineman can't find me here, you know. The magic of the Switchboard is too warped."

"He'll know when you make your first connection." Shaw's voice was cold, so cold it made Kit's jaw ache with tension. "Fix it."

Kit bowed his head. He could stall, maybe giving the Shields time to deliver Henley back to the Actuality. All he needed was a few hours. That had to be enough. He retrieved his wire shears from a drawer. Taking a deep breath, he climbed onto his chair, then onto the desk, crumpling his notes. The thick dangling wire was heavy in his hand as he stripped it, hunting behind his panel for the matching wires. They were short. It wasn't the first time his panel had been disconnected and repaired. The Switchboard knew he was trying to help. The magic surged against his fingers, gentle and terrifying. One by one, he split the wires apart and bound the tiny strands together.

The drive to kneel and offer himself to the Lineman made concentrating difficult. The Shields were even less helpful to his painstaking efforts. They idled in the Kit's vicinity, poking at the desks of his comrades, examining photographs and rummaging in drawers. Shaw kept his eyes on Kit and let his officers do as they please, regardless of Kit's resentful stares. Half an hour into his work, one of the uniformed figures began setting chairs upright and neatening the disrupted panels. His productivity shamed his companions into assisting. A small knot untwisted in Kit's shoulders.

"This would be faster with some tea," he said, and was ignored. The blood had drained out of his arms as he reconnected the hanging wires. Shaking out the pins and needles in his fingers, Kit risked a glance toward Shaw and Solene. Her dark skin was still a sickly shade. When she asked questions, Shaw answered with a grave expression. He stood close enough to her that their conversation was quiet but made no gestures to seek her sympathy.

At least he isn't making excuses for himself. Solene clutched at the front of her uniform blouse, wrinkling the pressed fabric. Whatever pleading she offered her superior summoned a tired smile from the Captain before he turned back to the main panel. For a moment, Shaw's eyes met Kit's. Weariness lingered in that blue gaze before the feeling was wiped away, replaced by a hard stare. Kit got back to work.

He could only stall so much. His panel went live after an hour's work and a twist of his operator key into its socket. Kit was relieved despite the situation, his splitting headache fading. The darkness of his dormant panel had been worse than unsettling.

"I could really use that team," he said, looking back up at the other wires. "Just a dozen operators could make short work—"

"That's unnecessary. Get down." Shaw nodded to the waiting chair. "With one panel up, others can be wired in. We know that much. Once the Lineman comes for you the rest won't matter."

"But the Switchboard—"

"Will be rewritten, like the rest of the Between. Or it won't. That doesn't matter for you."

Kit ground his teeth. He stepped down, awkward with no assistance. Standing before his chair and looming panel, he tried one last time.

"Shaw, *please*. What you're trying to achieve is impossible. The Switchboard won't even respond to you without an operator to guide it."

The Captain gave him a thin smile that held none of the patience Shaw had shown his officers. "Stop stalling and make a connection."

Kit's stomach roiled. He had torn the Switchboard down without a second thought. One mage, one mortal, challenged his willpower. His hand trembled and hovered over the plugs.

Before he could touch the cables, the panel crackled with energy. A string of silver lightning arced from the baseline up to F28. The magic answered a call from *within* the Between, and Kit was close enough to his panel that the call was connected without his intervention.

"Twenty percent, *Call Lightning!*" The voice was so loud, so close that every Shield took a step back. Kit spun. The diligent Shield who had redirected the others lifted his hand and clenched it into a fist, sparks captured in his fingers. "Strike with no mercy, scorch the earth, drive back all who would threaten my allies!"

Time slowed as matching lightning splintered through the room, striking every uniformed figure except for Henley, with Shaw himself forced to stagger back into the nearest desk. Henley stood among them as they were blown off their feet, unbandaged eye wild with no glasses to block his face. His ill-fitting uniform was the most unkept Kit had ever seen him dressed. People were shouting from every angle. Henley pulled out his glasses and flipped the legs open with a contemptuous flick of his wrist before sliding them back on over the bandages. One black eye met Kit's silver gaze, and Henley smiled.

Time jerked back to normal speed. The floor vibrated with pounding steps as the Shields who had stayed outside heard the noise and came running. Some of the Shields were motionless, but Shaw didn't stay down. Kit felt the Captain's fury as pressure in the air.

"Get the mortal under control!"

Gunfire snarled through the room, bullets pinging off panels and punching through the walls. Shrapnel from furniture burst into the air. Kit flinched, feeling the shots pass too close before Henley was *there*, standing in front of him, blocking the attacks with his body and his magic.

"Twenty percent, *Shield*. Five percent, *Create Fog*. Ten percent, *Stench*. Five percent, *Create Shadows*." The spells and their corresponding incantations flew from Henley's lips. Kit spun back to face his panel as he was given time to react, pressing a hand flat to the ports to stabilize the flow of magic. Memories flickered under his fingers, across his nose, through his ears before they passed to the Ethereal.

The Lineman's deep, heavy bell echoed through the room. The presence was like claws dragging up Kit's spine, a near-physical pressure that terrified him more than anything in the world. He smothered a sound of panic behind gritted teeth, and Henley reached out to grab his shoulder.

"He's not here yet, Kit. There's still time. Where can we go?"

Kit could see Henley within the barrier that surrounded them, but he couldn't see any of the Shield officers. He couldn't smell the stench, either, the sounds of retching and gagging came from all over the room.

"I don't know, with the Switchboard up he can find me—"

"Not while I'm here!" The force of the mage's words brought Kit's voice to a stop. "I'll throw fire down his throat. Pick a direction and let's go!"

"We can go back to the Actuality, the same as before!" Kit grasped the spark of hope in one hand and a trio of cables he had repaired in the other, ripping the cords out of the panel. They tore the fabric of the Between. A muted glow appeared in the fog, rippling and shifting. "Your spirit is connected to the last place you touched in the Actuality. Go now! Hurry!"

Henley dropped his hand and grasped Kit's. He took a step toward the foggy portal. Then a *bang* echoed through the room, half-gunshot, half-thunder, and Henley jerked before falling to his knees. Kit went down as well, patting his hands over Henley with a cry of alarm, trying to find what had brought him down. When he reached Henley's leg, his hands grew wet and warm.

Shaw's voice came through the fog, distant and muffled after the roar of his weapon. "Give me another mage-killer." In a direct line from the Captain to the pair, a tunnel of clear space had been cut by the shot. The pistol in his hand hadn't changed. Solene handed him a bullet that shimmered with silver light.

"Take him out by whatever means necessary," the Captain continued, slapping the round into his revolver. "Don't let them leave the Between."

Kit stood. His hands were red with Henley's blood, mortal blood, his ears full of the mage's labored breathing and muffled curses. Henley was trying to get to his feet. Trying to drag himself to the portal. Trying to form new spells through the incredible pain. Shaw lifted his gun again.

They'll kill him, or I'll lose him.

One was indeed much worse than the other.

"You wanted this, Shaw," he yelled. He ripped the metal pin and the cable out of his hair, smearing blood across the pinkish strands. With precision born of terrible knowledge, he turned and stabbed the pin into one of the ports on his panel, the end of the cable grasped tight in his red fingers. The bell tolled again, and Kit began to glow.

"No!"

Henley's scream was quiet under the roar of magic in Kit's ears. The entire world pulsed with it, warping his vision and all his senses. The structure of the Between was laid bare to him in threads of magic that glowed at varying intensities, reaching out to every object, every person. Henley's thread was different from the others, glowing brilliant blue to their faded silver. The color of his magic was so *beautiful*.

Kit dropped his hands from the panel and let the cardigan slide off his shoulders onto the mage's prone body. Cloth slithered across his skin as his clothing changed, heavy robes falling around his slender frame, the fabric leaving his back bare. The runes carved into his skin glowed and brought with them fierce pain. Kit gasped. The agony was sharp, but as he surrendered to his Purpose he could breathe without effort. The pull that had dragged at his body for so long released Kit and left him light. He tipped his head back as the color and moisture leeched out of his skin and hair, leaving him a dull alabaster statue. The long blade, so much heavier than his shears, formed in his hand.

He looked down at Henley. Fear and shock warped the mage's face. Kit met his eyes with the last of his clear thoughts.

"I won't let them hurt you," he said, and then his consciousness was forced into darkness as the Lineman took control.

Twenty-Two

Lineman's Awakening

The fear in the back of Henley's throat choked him, cutting off his ability to breathe or scream. The Lineman's aura overwhelmed the pain of his wound. Sounds of terror—not screams, for the Shields were affected in the same way—rattled through the room as every sane person tried to flee. Only Henley stayed where he was, staring up at the being who had been his friend seconds before.

Kit's worries were gone. The Lineman's silver gaze was devoid of emotion. His ritual robes, dusty white edged in red, hung from his thin frame and clawed tight around his throat. The runes that had glowed were now aggravated red, old wounds on his skin. His presence pinned Henley to the ground. The blade in his hand, as long as his arm, had an ivory hilt and reflected no light.

"My Assignment proceeds," the Lineman said in a horrible parody of Kit's voice, **"yet I cannot rest. You do not belong here, mortal."**

The pale entity lifted the hand that held the blade. With one forceful strike, he cut downward, and something inside of Henley snapped. All the magic in the room died. The Shields who could now see the Lineman screamed in terror. Henley felt so sick, so weak, that fear became secondary. The Lineman put one foot in the middle of his stomach and shoved him through the portal.

Henley rolled and fell, impacting a low table and crashing to the ground. The fluorescent lighting disoriented him. Hands were on his shoulders, a clamor of voices exclaiming as the smell of his blood mixed with the fragrance of coffee. Henley saw a flash of the portal closing, Elryk's concerned face, and Fine Ground's tiled ceiling before he blacked out.

Twenty-Three

Return to Fine Ground

When Henley opened his eyes again, everything was quiet. The room was dark aside from the glow of a lamp to his far right. His thoughts were clouded and slow. *Where am I? What happened?* His leg hurt but the pain was distant, like something stood between him and the ache. His stomach churned. Overlying everything was an intense feeling of loss.

He smelled coffee.

He heard soft voices.

Someone else's pillow and bed were under his body, unfamiliar and hard.

Kit is gone.

The thought struck hard and he sat up, or tried, flailing as his immobilized leg prevented him from following through. No one stopped him or caught him, but the voices ceased. He fell back against the pillows, gasping for breath. Elryk spoke up once he was still.

"I'd definitely advise against trying that again."

"I have to go," Henley grated, fists clenched. The pain poked through the barrier when he moved, giving him a slice of the true anguish waiting. "I have to get to Kit. The Lineman got him."

"The Lineman didn't get him, Mr. Yu."

Henley blinked at the ceiling, then lifted his head as much as possible at the new voice. The world was fractured through the cracked lenses of his glasses. He was laying on a bed in a small studio apartment, the furnishings shabby and out of date. The quilt that covered him was made in big squares of earthy tones, and the fabric was fraying around the edges. Across from him, René sat on a sofa with a small kitchen light to his back, holding an ice pack to his swollen left cheek. His blond curls were a ragged tangle. His burgundy suit was torn.

"I saw it. He glowed and he changed, it took him over—"

"When the Lineman *gets someone*, they have their thread cut. Did he disappear in front of you?"

"No," Henley replied, swallowing around his dry throat.

"Kittinger didn't get taken over. He *woke up*."

Henley put his head down, breathing in short bursts through his mouth. Hands scooped under his shoulders, and Elryk's face was grave as he helped Henley to sit up and stuffed a pillow behind his back. The lingering burns from his flight with Kit didn't have the same agony as his leg.

"What the hell does that mean?" Henley asked when he was able to lift his head. He was wearing a shirt, the same one he'd been wearing before they left Houston. Kit's magic had left him. René sighed.

"Kittinger is the Lineman, Mr. Yu. That is his secondary Assignment and Purpose. He ran from it until he no longer could, I assume."

"He told me if the Lineman got him he'd be forgotten, that he'd cease to exist. It terrified him."

René rubbed at the uninjured side of his face, a frown settling on his lips.

"Those facts are no less true given his position. I suppose that means he remembers all the rewrites of the Between, while he has always been forgotten by the rest of us. I don't envy him that existence."

Henley stared at the Lord of Paradise, the details sinking in. *Could Kit disable the Switchboard because he was the Lineman? Was that why he could connect me to magic even without the Switchboard? Was that why—*

"Did you know who he was? Is that why you helped us get to the High Spirits?"

"I did, but that wasn't my reason. One does not 'speak' with the Lineman or 'know' him. My encounters with Kittinger as Chief Operator have been few and limited to his scarce visits to Paradise for rest. He has the right to go where he pleases, and I had no reason to bar his path. That is all."

Henley dropped his head back against the pillows, eyes closed. His thoughts were still a disoriented mess. Elryk was still next to the bed, a somber sentinel through the conversation. The scent of coffee lingered on the man's skin. Aside from their voices, Henley could hear nothing but the occasional hum of the AC.

"El, is it raining?"

"No," the coffee man said. "It tapered off to a drizzle a few hours ago. The magic is still unstable according to the trackers, but the storms are dissipating."

"What happened to me?"

"You were shot."

Henley opened his eyes and stared at his friend. Then he lowered his head and lifted the blanket, drawing in a hiss of breath when he saw the brace bolted around his naked leg. The skin around the edges of the support was vivid red and mottled with fading bruises.

"How long ago?"

"You fell into my workroom this morning, raving mad. I disabled you and called in some favors with local doctors to accelerate your healing. Dr. Yu did the best she could to block your pain. You took a mage-killer to the femur; you're lucky it was off-center and didn't shatter the bone. Or puncture the artery, for that matter."

"What time is it?" Henley didn't blink at the mention of his sister, too focused on the conversation.

Elryk leaned over to check the alarm clock on the side of the bed. It was an old digital model with a fake plastic wood exterior and glaring red numbers. The nightstand surface bore multiple water stains and coffee rings.

"Four."

Henley gritted his teeth. His fingers were white-knuckled where he gripped the blanket.

"So it's been hours since the Lineman was released? I have to *go*."

"It's too late, Mr. Yu," René spoke up. He lowered the ice pack, revealing thick bandages and swelling over the left side of his face. "The Lineman has been summoned. The Between crumbles with the death of the High Spirits. The magic is unregulated and out of balance. The rewrite of the Between has already begun."

"Nothing you said tells me I can't stop this."

"Henley, you have to let it go," Elryk said, brow knit. "The Between must be in balance, it's the only thing that keeps all the worlds stable. The Lineman is doing his job. It's unfortunate but necessary. This is our circle of life."

"Not mine." Henley hooked both hands under his injured leg and swung it to the side. His knee was part of the brace, forced immobile, and his foot stuck out into the room before he eased it down to the floor. He was wearing underwear, at least. Moving hurt, but the pain was dulled and distant. Minglian did good work. "Shaw is making this happen outside of necessity. He's killing everyone in the Between. I'm not going to sit here and do nothing while he gets away with it."

"Shaw is an asshole, and he deserves a higher punishment, but there's no one left to deliver it," René grunted. "The High Spirits would censure him and send the Lineman for his thread, but they're gone and the Lineman will cut us all anyway. Within a few days I won't rule Paradise anymore, and you won't remember us at all."

Henley stared down at his injured leg. His body screamed to run, to fight, to take action, but that emptiness still lingered in his chest.

"El, can I seal my memories of Kit somehow? Keep them from disappearing?"

"Why are you asking me? I'm no mage—"

"Bad time to play stupid, El." Henley looked up at his friend. "I know you're not human."

"*Fantastic* job keeping that secret," René snorted, and Elryk's eye twitched.

"Alright, fine. But the answer's no." The coffee man took a seat on the edge of the bed, serious as he met the mage's eyes. He spoke with the careful, gentle tone of a man bringing news of death. "Can you feel what happened to you?"

Henley lifted a hand to rub against his chest, the feeling of dread rising. "The mage-killer?"

Elryk shook his head.

"Mage-killers are bullets that punch through magic. That's it. I'm sure you were fighting Shaw with spells, so he used a weapon that would negate your advantage. The Lineman cut your connection to the Between, Henley. He took your ability to draw on magic at all in order to force you back to the Actuality. Without that thread, you can't use magical relics, cast spells . . . anything."

"Even with stored magic?" Henley stared across the room at René, who narrowed his eyes.

"You think we have something that valuable available?"

The box we delivered from Noodle. The shoe prints inside the hidden compartment. Elryk's silent early-morning customer who grabbed something from his saucer when I walked in. "What else is going to be smuggled in and out of the Between—with deliveries out of Elryk's coffee shop?"

René sat back in disgust.

"He's annoyingly clever."

"*Now* you think he's annoying?"

"More annoying than he was." René waved a hand. "Noodle said he noticed a few things during his transport to Paradise, so it should be no surprise." The blond pulled a pouch from his suitcoat pocket and tossed it across the bed to the mage. It landed on the quilt, small in the sea of fabric.

"Try it for yourself."

Snatching the pouch from the folds of the blankets, Henley opened it and poured the contents into his palm. A single raw topaz point, clear and mellow gold, fell into his palm.

It felt like a rock. Henley looked between the other two, closing his fingers around the stone.

"I haven't used stored magic in forever. What's the trigger?"

"There's no trigger," Elryk said, placing a hand on Henley's shoulder. "If you could use magic, it would be waiting for you, and you could use it to cast without requesting a connection or making a sacrifice. You're just a normal man now, Henley."

Henley tightened his grip and debated throwing the gem across the room. The concerned looks on both of their faces made him rethink the action. He dropped it back into its pouch.

"Shit."

Elryk squeezed his shoulder at the despair in his tone.

"I'm sorry, Henley. It's possible the connection will return when the Between is rewritten. The ties that bind mages are part of the Between, after all."

"I can live without the magic. I need to help Kit." The words were a lie that Henley accepted for the moment. The thought of losing his magic was a screaming fear in the back of his mind. Everyone in his family used magic, from his aunts and uncles to the babies and oldest grandparents. To have it and lose it, to be crippled, was—

Not now, damn it.

"You are intensely stubborn, Mr. Yu. Kittinger is gone. The Between is gone. *I* will be gone, soon enough, though I expect he'll get to me last."

Henley took a breath. He took another. They filled his chest, pushing down the panic. He had conquered problems since his childhood by facing them with logic. He sat in silence for several minutes, his head bowed, neatly filing each piece of the catastrophe into its own box.

"Why would he get to you last—because you're here, or because you run Paradise?"

"How ignorant you are." René looked up at Elryk. "This calls for drinks and something in his stomach, I think. How convenient that your shop is just downstairs."

"Are you trying to get rid of me?" Elryk asked, but he was already on his feet. René smiled.

"I have no secrets from you, my dear, but my cup is empty, and Mr. Yu's body has done too much healing in too short a time. As if you don't know the answers already!"

"Alright, alright. I'll be right back."

Elryk left. The room was quiet. The blinds were closed, but weak sunlight slanted across the floor around the edges. Henley wasn't sure when he had last seen the sun. The small apartment was one large room holding the bed, sofa, some bookshelves, and a small kitchen area, as if a stage had been set for their conversation. The Lord of Paradise let the silence gather for several seconds before he spoke.

"The Between is as much an entity as a place," René began. "It is pure energy, manifested in the forms of the Fetters and the buildings and the connections. It regenerates itself by calling the Fetters to Paradise where their energy can be restored. However, where it interacts with the planes of the Actuality and the Ethereal, it warps. It requires management. Three forces rule the Between: the Judge, the Arbiter, and the Balancer. The High Spirits act as the Judge in this incarnation, aided by the Captain of the Shields. The Lineman is the Balancer. He is eternal, apparently."

"And the Arbiter?"

René inclined his head.

"The Arbiter speaks for the Fetters and those who would be punished by the Judge. He or she is also the Lord of Paradise. It is our responsibility to ensure the health and stability of the Between."

"Sorry to be blunt, but you're really letting the Between down right now."

René pursed his lips.

"I wish I could disagree. This happened under my nose, and when I lose my position, it will be a just sentence. In a normal trial I speak to the Judge and request leniency if I believe it is warranted. The Lineman stands before them, silent. He doesn't have much mind of his own, from what I've seen. A decision is made, and he follows his Purpose."

"He has to have some thoughts. Otherwise, how could he function without the High Spirits giving him orders?"

"His function is to balance the Between. If it is out of balance, then he will restore stability even without orders."

"Do you know that for sure, or are you making an assumption?"

René opened his mouth, then closed it with a click and a glare, but it was Elryk who answered. The tall man stepped back into the room with his hands full, crossing the space to hold out one hand.

"Are you fighting against the injustice, or because you're attracted to the Chief Operator?"

Henley's thoughts stumbled to a halt. He stared at the protein bar Elryk was offering, unable to get past the word *attracted*.

Kit's desperate eyes. His tangled hair. The way he held my arm so tight.

"I've never seen you involved with anyone, and I've never seen you like this," the coffee man continued. He kept his voice even and calm. "I think you need to consider the possibility that your emotions are making you irrational. What you're suggesting is the same as deciding between one day and the next that gravity shouldn't work anymore."

Henley took the bar in numb fingers. Elryk stepped away to offer the coffee in his other hand to René. The room was silent until Henley began to open the package, the crackle explosive in the quiet.

"I've never been attracted to another man before. It doesn't make sense that I'd start now."

"Unless you hadn't found the right one."

René's comment cut deep. Henley thought about Kit's messy desk, his effortless flight, and the small potted plant he'd talked about with such love. He cleared his throat.

"It's still wrong, no matter what I'm feeling. Justice doesn't prevail because of apathy. If we don't do anything, what keeps the cycle from repeating?"

"There's never been an incident like—"

"How would you know?"

Henley barked back at the Lord of Paradise, sharper than intended. René and Elryk watched him like he was a cornered beast. Henley realized he was breathing harder.

"Alright." Elryk spread his hands. "You have to eat, and you have to rest. You *will* do both, or I'll knock you out again. Take a couple of hours to think about it and recover. I'll see what I can find out about what's going on in the Between. There are millions of threads to be cut. The Lineman will be working for days. A little time spent being logical is worth the minutes lost."

"Elryk—"

"No." The coffee man stared Henley down. His eyes glittered in clear tones, like light through cut gems. "You're badly hurt. I'm still willing to listen to your thoughts, but if you cause yourself more harm I'll put you out until this is all over." He pointed to a set of crutches next to the bed. "Use those. Bathroom's through that door. Let's go, René."

The blond was watching Elryk's efficiency with raised eyebrows. He rose from his seat, gathering his coffee and his ice pack, giving Henley a better look at how tattered and scorched his suit had become. He'd given Shaw an impressive fight. The Lord of Paradise gave Henley a small incline of his head before both men left the room. Henley was so infuriated by the sound of the door closing that he crushed the protein bar in his hands. The grainy texture helped to refocus his thoughts.

Because you're attracted to the Chief Operator.

Henley hadn't been in a relationship since he was eighteen. She'd been a friend, someone to go to prom with, someone who needed a shoulder to cry on when her mother passed away from cancer. College had made them distant. They were still friends, but he'd never felt the same intense need to protect her and fight the world on her behalf that he felt for Kit. It was a bad time to be questioning his sexuality.

Am I even questioning? What does it matter? He wanted to help Kit because Kit was important, because no one else would ever help, because he had seemed so alone when they were huddled in Noodle's compartment, *because he can't be trusted to brush his own hair*—

The emptiness of his lost magic was so shallow compared to the agony that came with his memories of Kit.

"I don't want to lose him."

He said the words out loud. They startled him; his voice was strained and rough. When he tipped his head back to stare upward, the ceiling was tiled with old decorative panels. His parents would like Kit. His sisters would love him. What concerns his parents had wouldn't be as severe as the fights Henley'd had with his father about his career, no matter how they reacted. He thought about meeting Kit for coffee at Fine Ground. He thought about spending nights sitting with the Chief Operator on Kit's balcony, legs dangling, watching the Between go by.

"Damn."

He lowered his head and ate the protein bar in small pieces, licking the almond butter and chocolate from his fingers. The food gave him the energy to calm his swirling panic. The pain of his leg was still separate from him, allowing him the mental space to deal with everything else. Kit's cardigan finally caught his eye where it was rumpled within the blankets he had tossed aside. Rust-brown bloodstains around the cuffs showed where Kit had tried to help the mage, before he sacrificed himself to save Henley.

Henley didn't know what it meant to be in love, or if what he was feeling counted. He thought he might love Kit as a person loved their family, someone they cared about and wanted to keep close. If it was an infatuation he thought he would be more blind and more scared. *Would I even be able to tell? Would my mind be clear when I'm so caught up in emotion?* All he knew was that he'd found someone he liked, and he didn't want that person to disappear.

He could figure out the details after the dust cleared.

Twenty-Four

Cutting Threads

Substation No. 6 went down with the same brutal efficiency as the previous five stations.

With the reactivation of the Switchboard, every operator was once again on duty. The operators were a different breed from the Shield officers who had shown such fear at No. 28. They knew, better than anyone in the Between, how the Lineman worked and what his appearance meant. There were no screams. When the Lineman appeared in a column of light in the center of each substation they stood, trading brave smiles and sometimes holding hands as they waited for their new future. The blade came down and they ceased to exist, as did the substation itself.

Only one operator made a move: the Stationmaster sent out a call to their peers. This time the woman's calm voice contained a note of wistful regret.

"Substation No. 6, going dark."

The Lineman felt no emotion as No. 6 disappeared, fading in broken pieces, leaving a blank space in the fabric of the Between. The substation was a box to be checked on his list. Thousands of homes and businesses were arrayed with No. 6 as their central hub. He got to work one Fetter, one building, at a time, cutting huge swaths of emptiness into the Between. The Fetters who weren't operators were as frightened as the Shields. They saw him, felt his aura, and fled screaming as if it would do them any good. He would find them all, in the end.

Kit screamed with them. He clawed at the Lineman's control of their mind as No. 6 went down and Kemah's voice sounded for the last time. Every time he had spoken to her in the past, she had told him to eat a little extra for her on his next break. She had a full, boisterous laugh that could be heard throughout the area around his panel. Within a breath she was gone. He railed against his alter self, beating at the barrier holding back his control of their body to no avail.

The Lineman was still Kittinger, at his most basic level. They walked the same way, gestured with the same hand, and shared the same memories. The ominous figure was Kit's distilled consciousness, his logic and emotionless rationale. The Lineman was consumed by his Purpose. Kit was a prisoner to the same, fighting for control in a battle he would never win.

He could suggest and remind. Kit could *suggest* that they visit the substations first, then attend to the surrounding area, thus delaying the fall of the entire magic network. The Lineman could be *reminded* that Paradise had been evacuated, making it a lower-priority target and protecting its beautiful halls from destruction. It didn't matter. Like every rewrite before, he would delay and delay but the Between would still fall.

Still he *suggested* and *reminded*, while his heart broke, while the people and places he had known for a century vanished from existence. *Please*, he begged, fighting to rationalize every heartfelt desire. *Please don't hurt anyone else. Please leave them intact. Please fix the balance but leave the people alone.*

The Lineman's cold voice countered every passionate request.

The people destroyed the balance, it said.

Only a few of the people!

A few became many. Shaw did not work alone. If the balance must be restored, then everything must be reset.

But it isn't their fault. They will be punished for nothing. Their lives, their stories will be gone—

They will feel nothing, remember nothing. They will have new lives and memories.

But they won't know what they've lost.

They don't need to know.

Every response was scientific. Practical. Ruthless. Kit's resistance was battered and broken until he could do nothing but sit and watch as his world was once again taken from him. He was the one left grieving as every single person he knew died.

Just like they always did.

TWENTY-FIVE

BACK TO THE BETWEEN

Whatever makes mortals so stubborn should be bottled and sold on the open market. The substance would cause so much to get done on other planes.

René sat at Elryk's pitifully small kitchen table, watching the coffee man and Henley barter for their next course of action. Elryk was a man made of stone, literally, yet Henley Yu was wearing him down. René could almost see the edges being carved away. Elryk crossed his arms. He paced across the aging floor that creaked under his steps. He waved his hands in the air. He raised his voice. Henley sat on the edge of the bed with his crutches close to hand and refuted every argument with force. *All we really did was give him time to gear up for the fight. I doubt he rested at all.*

René sipped his coffee. The windows were dark—it was almost midnight by Houston time. He needed the caffeine. Cut off from Paradise and his Purpose, his body moved slower, his energy low, and every action seemed to take so much more effort. In combination with his Shaw-delivered injuries, the Lineman's arrival was starting to sound like a relief.

"No matter what you say, you can't get past the immediate problem," Elryk argued. "The Between will reject you. You'll feel ten times worse than the way you did before you got an Assignment card, and that's if the Between doesn't just spit you back out."

René spoke up, tearing off a corner of his croissant and popping it into his mouth. "It won't." The pastry was handmade by Elryk; the man had a godly effect on anything edible he touched. The ice had done its magic, reducing the swelling in René's jaw enough that he could chew without agony. Elryk and Henley turned to give him matching, doubtful stares.

René swallowed and licked his lips. "The Between won't reject him out of hand. It will attempt to understand him and figure out where he should go. He'll have a chance to bargain his way in."

"René, please don't tell me you're cooperating with this plan."

He lived for that frustrated look on Elryk's calm face. *Payback for all the times you told me to be patient with my orders.*

"My future is set, darling, unless something dramatic changes. I'm very fond of my life and the way I've arranged my circumstances. If Mr. Yu can do something about the Lineman's rampage I only stand to benefit."

Elryk pinched the bridge of his nose and breathed in. Henley leaned forward.

"What does that mean—that I'll have a chance to bargain? What do I have to offer?"

"Why do you think memories have value to the Ethereal?"

"*René.*"

"Hush, Elryk." René waved a hand. "He's so deep in the secrets of the world now it doesn't matter if he knows one more."

Henley didn't answer for a long moment. René liked that about the mage. The way he thought through every answer was reassuring. Even when he spoke in anger his mind was sharp. Reliable. *What a comfort.*

"I always thought—and I was taught—that the Ethereals wanted our memories because they couldn't experience the memories for themselves."

"Yet here Elryk sits, making his own coffee, living his own life. Why does the taste and smell of his coffee have value *even to him*, if it comes from the mind of a mortal?"

Henley gave a slow turn of his head to stare at the coffee man as René outed him without restraint. Elryk found something on the ceiling to hold his attention.

"Because mortals impart something into the memories that can't be duplicated?"

"So clever. I see why you like him, when that cleverness isn't getting him into trouble." René picked up his neglected cup and sipped more of his coffee. It was a deep, dark blend with hints of chocolate. *Bitter. Too strong.* He shivered with pleasure.

"What mortals have that everyone else lacks is *mortality.* The time you spend gathering your memories is finite. That makes it rare and gives it a special sort of energy that magnifies a hundredfold when delivered to someone like me, or like Elryk. Power is easy to come by in the Ethereal. It takes a massive amount of energy to rise above whatever rank someone in the Ethereal holds, so the Ethereals are always eager to bargain with humans."

"I'm not sure why that should matter to the Between itself, but alright." Henley rubbed one hand across his bandaged leg. "What about you? If you're the Arbiter, the Lord of Paradise, why do you need power?"

"We all defy fate in our own way." René exhaled, blowing steam across the top of his cup. "The Arbiter, as you may have inferred, is not a permanent rank. It moves and is Reassigned as the leadership of Paradise is distributed by the High Spirits. I went from knowing nothing to knowing everything. I have never felt such terror. I wanted to control *something*, and mortals are as greedy for 'free,' 'untraceable' magic as the Ethereals are for memories."

He smiled over the rim of the cup, eyes cold.

"The Lineman sees much but also very little. The Between is a broken creature, an ancient spirit something like an Ethereal. I don't see how that will change with a rewrite, so I am willing to encourage you. If you can face the Between, give it enough to satisfy it, then it may allow you entrance. If you gain entrance, then you may face the Lineman. If your belief is strong enough . . ."

Elryk's voice was low. "You think he has a chance to stop the Lineman?" He walked away from Henley and placed both hands on the table, leaning close to speak just between them. René lifted his chin and met the coffee man's jewel-like eyes. In the night hours they had blood-red depths.

"I think it doesn't matter, but if he does then it might bring great change," he whispered. "Damn them both for giving me a hope that I might remember your name next Tuesday, my friend."

Elryk breathed out through his nose in a rush. He pushed up from the table.

"Your leg's barely working, Henley. Even if the Between accepts you, you won't have the connection you need to move around as you should. You'll be reliant on René to get you where you need to be. The pain block your sister put on you isn't going to last forever."

"Doesn't matter."

"And if you run into Shaw again? Not if, *when*. I'm sure he'll be lurking near the Lineman."

"If you're so worried about it, maybe you should go with us."

René choked and put his coffee aside before he could spill it all over himself.

"What a fascinating thought. Elryk, in the Between?"

"If I didn't know better I'd say you planned this just to get me to Paradise." The coffee man ran both hands back through his hair, gripping the strands tight. "Fine, I'll go. I have to get you there, anyway, since the infrastructure is falling apart." He turned, pointing a finger at the mage. *I wonder if we should stop calling him a mage, considering.*

"It's going to be dangerous," Elryk said, stern. "You're already wounded in multiple ways. Shaw will kill you if he gets the chance, and there's no telling what will happen if you're in the Between when the rewrite takes effect. Your plan is what—to reason with the Lineman? What good do you think you can do?"

"I think I can assess the situation and take action as I see fit." *Damn, if he doesn't look so sure of himself.* "I'm going to find him and face him and at least—at the *least*—I'm going to make Shaw pay for what he's doing."

"Have you ever seen such arrogance?" René murmured, hiding his smile behind his coffee. "High Spirits save us from mortals and their endless optimism. He might even do it, Elryk."

"Shut *up*, René," Elryk sighed. "Henley, you ate right? How do you feel? If we're going to do this, we might as well get moving."

"I ate." Henley grabbed the crutches and rose to his feet. His leg was stiff and awkward. He was wearing the stained cardigan, out of place with his clean attire and simple style. Pants from the bag he had left with Elryk pulled as they draped over his leg brace. Every movement looked painful when he took a few experimental steps forward.

"If you fall down the stairs, we're not going," Elryk grunted. "Make sure you call your sister when you get back. She almost wouldn't leave after she patched you up, and I promised her I'd keep you in one piece." He held open the apartment door and waited as first Henley, then René, eased past him. Henley handled the steps with all the grace of a drunk flamingo, but he made it to the first floor.

"No one will be grieving today," the wounded mortal panted, rubbing the sweat from his face against his shoulder. He eased around corners and didn't put any weight on his bad leg. His complexion was paler than usual. *Already in so much pain. So brave, yet so foolish. Do you know what will happen if the Between takes every memory of your pain and forces you to experience the agony fresh once more?*

Fine Ground was closed at that hour, the chairs on the tables, the floors sparkling clean. Relics drained of magic had been taken down, leaving brighter patches on the wall. The big coffee pots were cold, aside from the one Elryk kept hot at all times. It gave off intermittent burbles to break the quiet. With only a few lights lit, every shadow was deeper, longer, and René understood why mortals could be so skittish.

The coffee man opened the door to his workroom. It had changed little in the years René had visited the coffee shop, the recent events having little effect on the comfortable furniture. Henley's eyes, however, lingered on the new scrapes on the coffee table and the faint reddish stains on the floor.

"Why does this work?" Henley asked, once everyone was in the room and the door was closed. "Why can Elryk send us to the Between if he's not a mage or an operator?"

"It's less what he can do, and more what he is *allowed* to do," René explained, unbuttoning his suit coat. He retrieved pocket fodder from various places before tossing the abused fabric aside. His shirt and vest were in better condition. "I cannot use magic as you know it; I control only Paradise and certain aspects of the Between. Elryk can handle pure magic. In this place, where the veins of energy converge, he can seal and unseal the rifts they create."

"How is that different from making a portal?"

"I don't make it." Elryk continued the explanation, pushing the table out of the way. "It's already here—it's been here since there were enough mages in the area to force it open. I just bought the shop in the right place. I can cover it up, so no one sees and abuses it, or uncover it. I can't use it to go to the Between without René—as proxy for the High Spirits—allowing my presence."

Henley exhaled. "And Kit?"

"He tore a hole in the fabric of magic, forcing himself into the place he chose. That's the prerogative of an operator—they can see what the rest of us can only sense. What the Lineman can see, I can only imagine."

Elryk stood in the center of the room and lifted his right hand. Around the cluttered workspace, crystals in a seemingly random configuration began to glow. His eyes lit from within. The air pressure in the room shifted, the energy rising to his call. With his left hand, he pushed down.

To René, the magic twisted and unwound like a spring forced straight. The discomfort scratched at his mind, an *improper* use of magic he couldn't ignore. Henley showed no signs of noticing the shift, the poor bastard.

The rift yawned open. The view on the other side was not the comforting image of Paradise's bar René expected. The bar was dark, the counter splintered, glasses broken in the background. He clenched his fists.

"What's going to happen when we go through, René?"

"I have absolutely no idea, Elryk," he murmured. "I assume you and I will pass through into Paradise. From here, Mr. Yu is on his own."

"Last chance to change your mind, Henley."

The mortal didn't look at either man. He shuffled himself forward on his crutches, passing through the rift and disappearing. The portal flashed, warped, then stabilized. Elryk sighed.

"Alright then," he said, placing a firm hand on René's shoulder. His touch was warm, so warm though the fabric of the thin shirt. "We're doing this. I'll be counting on you to protect me."

"Aren't you supposed to be coming along to protect us?"

"This is your realm, not mine." Elryk tightened his grip. "But I'll be watching your back."

"Excellent."

They stepped forward together, Elryk shortening his strides to match René's steps. The rift tugged at René's skin as he crossed over, pulling at his hair and fingernails and his eyelashes. Electricity danced across his nerves, raising the fine hairs on his arms. His teeth ached. Then he was through, and the Between *welcomed* him, the bar beginning to repair itself, the lights flickering back to life.

The pain of his home radiated against his mind, striking him with the destruction and the shrapnel that had been blown off the walls. Golden wood paneling showed bullet holes and huge cracks. The plush carpets were littered with glass and blood. A few of the chandeliers were hanging off-center or lying shattered on the floor. Paradise was silent. His people were likely all dead, captured, or evacuated. *But High Spirits, what a relief it is to be home.*

Elryk staggered out of the rift. He was still gripping René's shoulder, and that warm hand trembled. "I hate this place," he wheezed, doubling over with both hands on his knees. "The restrictions the High Spirits put on Ethereals are too much. God, the air is so thin here. I'm going to starve, drown, and asphyxiate all at once."

"Two of those are so similar. Be more creative, darling." René took in the fallen barstools, the broken chandeliers. The ever-present sound of spritely music had ceased. They were alone.

"Mr. Yu is gone."

Elryk stopped his groaning and straightened. In Paradise, his eyes shimmered green and gold, but his lovely gaze told René nothing as he searched the room.

"Do you think he'll survive?"

"His odds are better than ours at the moment. Let's get to my office before anything exciting happens."

Twenty-Six

House of Mirrors

The Between did not welcome Henley.

He had a few seconds to recognize Paradise much as he had last seen it—broken, faded, neglected—before the ground dropped out from under him. He plummeted, spinning end for end, his crutches ripped from his hands and tossed in the air. When he faced "up," they tumbled in slow spirals overhead. The world was gray and empty in every direction.

The fear controlled him, and it didn't release him for several minutes. Mortals knew that when they fell, they would land, and the landing would bring pain. Freefall with no ground below meant almost certain death. He was going to die. *He was going to die.* Grasping hands closed around empty air, and his scream was lost in the nothingness.

After a while, the fall lost its impact. Why did it matter if he was falling, when there was no ground, nothing at all to hit? Then he was dizzy from the spinning and faint from the adrenaline. In fits and starts, he found his focus and brought it into himself.

The outside world can't change your inside. His father's voice came to him through the panic, and Henley took a deep breath. Then another. With every breath his heart rate slowed. The memory left an ache in his chest as he regained control. It had been years since he sat with his father and practiced magic, and they would never share those moments again.

With as much force as he could manage, he shoved the terrible thought out of his mind. The Between allowed him no *time* to deal with those consequences. His parents and sisters were safe from the storms. They would find a way through his loss, together. Kit needed him first.

In a battle with gravity that strained his muscles and wrenched his battered leg, Henley brought his feet together, and then twisted himself to point his feet "down." His fall accelerated. He stopped spinning. The fear returned. However, like the first time, the fear faded when nothing else changed. What the hell was he supposed to bargain with? He had connected to the Between using magic, but his magic was gone. He didn't even know how he would bypass the operators and reach the Between itself. *But doesn't the Between allow the operators to exist, and decide what is needed to support their work? Isn't the Between then, in its own way, sentient?*

If he thought of the Between as an entity, everything changed. He could communicate with an entity and send a message to a person or hear their voice over long distance. Could he do it without magic?

What else am I going to do?

The magic didn't respond when he began casting his spell. Like a performer, he stretched out his hand and went through the motions that should have opened him up to the flowing energy of the worlds. The complete lack of *anything* rising to meet him hit him in a surge of pain and loss.

"Fifty percent," he said through gritted teeth. He figured it would take a massive spell to make that kind of connection. He'd never used more than forty for a single spell in his life. "*Call.* Target: the Between. If you're listening—you and I need to talk!"

The memory of his first job was wound into his demand: the impact of the stapler in his hand as he stapled receipts at his cousin's store, the smell of the cleaning solution when he mopped the floor at night, and the sound of the entry alarm dinging every time a customer entered. It was the least elegant spell he'd cast in his years as a mage. His parents would have been mortified, but *something happened.* As he fed it the memory of his first, exhilarating paycheck, the memory was sucked out of his mind.

Pain bloomed, and the wind was knocked out of him as the ground slammed into his left side. It was a short fall, no more than a few feet. The crutches clattered to the ground next to him. Disoriented again, he panted, feeling the burn of his injury clawing at his leg. Familiar nausea rose in the back of his throat. His chest was too tight to draw a full breath.

When his body recovered enough, he sat up and looked around. An old hardwood floor, scuffed and marked by years of use, extended before him and to both sides. Blank gray space took the place of walls. Enough illumination came from unseen light sources that he could see clearly.

"Hello?" he called. The sound didn't travel far, swallowed by the gray. "Is anyone listening? I have to get to Kit—to the Lineman. The Shields have betrayed you!"

Silence. *No surprise.*

"Alright, it's better than falling," he muttered. One of his crutches was close enough to reach. Muscle clenched in Henley's jaw as he stared at the other where it lay several yards away. Precious minutes were wasted as he used the first to hobble to the second and tried to get it up to his hand without falling over. He was sweating again, and the crutch had knocked into his wound three times. The pain block was fading fast.

One crutch at a time, he turned himself to face the rest of the platform. Movement at the edge of his vision made him yell, sending a shot of panic through him when he saw dozens of figures standing behind him. He backed up several hasty steps, almost falling again, before he realized he was looking at his own reflection. The platform behind him had changed. It held dozens—hundreds?—of mirrors in thick wooden frames, placed in alternating rows. They stood unsupported on the floor, twice as wide as his shoulders and a few feet taller.

Henley drew a breath that turned into a coughing fit. His reflections coughed with him, but not all at the same time. Some covered their mouths, some didn't. Some wore cracked glasses. Some wore different shirts. Some walked without crutches. Some looked confident, some terrified.

All moved forward when he did, more careful of his leg. In the first mirror, his reflection returned his scrutiny. That version of Henley wore his arm in a sling instead of using crutches. Henley reached out to touch the glass. It shocked him, painful, burning his fingertips. The reflection didn't change.

"Okay, I won't do that again," he said, shaking out his zapped hand. A shuffle to the side brought him to the next mirror. Certain patterns began to establish themselves. If he could find a reflection with the right color shirt, the mirror beyond it would have the same shirt, and maybe also wear cracked glasses. When he came to a mirror with an incorrect trait, he looked around until he found the next most accurate depiction, then continued his path.

After twenty minutes, he was panting louder and the urge to rest had grown. The mirror in front of him had the most accurate reflection yet. Same shirt. Glasses. Crutches. Kit's cardigan. Desperate. What next? The reflections stared back as he looked around. Only his labored breaths and limping steps broke the silence.

"What am I supposed to do?" he called. Nothing answered.

Henley coughed again, then braced himself for the pain. When he lifted a cautious hand to touch the glass, it didn't produce a shock. The reflection rippled, changed, and the glass melted away to reveal a closed white door that could have come from any suburban house. The platform shrank, empty of mirrors between one moment and the next.

He turned the brushed-nickel doorknob. It didn't budge. When he knocked, nothing happened, and the sound was solid. "Okay," he said, rubbing his sweaty face on his shoulder. "Maybe you want something in return?"

An unlocking spell required little magic—five percent for the most stubborn lock, if it was a lock and not an entire security system. Henley pressed his hand flat on the door, fingers spread, and released the memory of hitting the ground on the platform.

The door opened. He exhaled in a rush. More gray waited through the white-painted frame. "Thank you," he said, and hefted himself through, careful of the lower frame edge. His head jerked around to stare as the door closed behind him and disappeared.

A new platform of mirrors waited. Every four-letter word he knew, in any language, rolled across his tongue in rapid succession. The crutches dug into his armpits with bruising force, but their support was welcome. The scuffed hardwood floor offered no sympathy as he ignored the ache growing in his shoulders and moved forward.

This time, the reflections didn't move with him. They played on their own, showing a hundred versions of the same scene. He heard the music before he comprehended the memory. The Gavotte from *French Suite no. 5*, by Bach. The sound, slower than the proper tempo and dotted with mistakes, punched him in the stomach as he moved closer to the first mirror.

His younger self, age ten, sat at the piano on a pair of cushions. The heavy brass foot pedals, burnished by his father's slippers, would be out of reach for a few more years. The boy's shoulders were too tense. Furniture and people crowded his family's front sitting room. Two curio cabinets full of dishes and carved jade statuettes were spaced around the sofa, an armchair, and the piano. Minimal floor space was occupied by his sisters—Minglian listening with a solemn expression, Rulan playing with her little horses, too young to care. Henley's piano teacher sat to the left of the piano, her face impassive. His mother stood behind the sofa with her arms crossed over the front of her plain green sweatshirt. On the sofa, Henley's father was listening, lips pressed in a thin line and eyes narrowed. His jaw twitched at every mistake.

No, that isn't right. Dad always listened with his eyes closed.

Remembered anxiety knotted his stomach. He hadn't eaten anything that morning, and he'd thrown up what little was in his stomach after the small recital. The mirror to his left showed his father sitting with his eyes closed. Something was still off about the image, but several seconds passed before Henley noticed his sister was playing with a teddy bear. Rulan had been a horse girl until she realized they smelled and meant being outside. The plastic horses reappeared with his father's closed eyes five mirrors later. The toys were a different color from those in the first mirror.

Bile rose in the back of Henley's throat. He backed up a few steps to look at the first mirror again, comparing the scenes. Four measures later, Rulan trotted one of the horses up the leg of the piano closest to the player. Minglian hurried to pull her away before their parents offered a scolding, but Henley remembered the sharp contrast of the light gray horse against the ebony wood out of the corner of his eye—not the bay shown in this reflection.

"It's memory," he whispered to himself. "You can remember. Everything is in your mind. You've been doing memory exercises for your entire life. Put them to work."

He let himself go back into the recollection, feeling the ache in his hands, the vibration of the sound in his legs, the weight of those eyes watching. The scent of the untouched cup of tea at his teacher's elbow. Rulan's annoyed voice, quickly hushed by their sister. The anxiety of not being able to redirect her himself or distract his strict parents from her antics. *Big brother always had to watch out for his little sisters.*

Young Henley finished the song. The room was silent. He rose from the bench and bowed to his small audience, then waited. Henley remembered the sweat on his palms and the gold-and-white pattern of the rug under his feet.

His father's voice was quiet gravel. Raising his voice was the utmost loss of decorum, but he had ways of making his displeasure known. Henley remembered reading every possible nuance into the words, real or imagined. "This is what you have been working on, that you would not let me hear?"

"Yes, sir."

"How long have you been studying the piano?"

"Six months."

"How many songs have you learned?"

"Three songs." A tiny shuffle signaled his teacher readjusting her feet.

"Why only three songs in six months?"

"Because—" His young voice cracked. It was a small tell, but everyone in the room focused on the sound. Even Rulan ceased her playing. "Because I wanted to get this one right."

"Do you think it is complete?"

"No, sir."

"Why not?"

"Because my fingers won't reach the keys the right way. They're too far apart."

"What have you done to fix that?" An impossible request, but not unexpected.

"I stretch my hands five times a day. Last month it was worse."

His father was silent. The entire room seemed to hold its breath, including the furniture and the frosted glass light fixtures. The piano itself felt on edge. Henley's father rose to his feet. He stepped forward and placed a hand on Young Henley's bowed head. A smile warmed his quiet voice.

"Very good work."

Henley gritted his teeth over the emotion those words had brought. His younger self had been shocked to learn that his father hadn't expected him to play the piece to the end in the first place. The family had gone to dinner that night to celebrate the accomplishment. Henley's father had been in a good mood for days. They had played the piano together, with the elder Yu showing his son tricks to reaching the farther keys. It was one of his most precious, most terrifying memories.

Letting himself drown in the past made finding the correct mirror easier. As the thoughts wrapped around him, he cast aside images where his mother was wearing a dress, where his sisters weren't present, or where his teacher drank her tea. By the time he found the mirror where everything was in place, with Young Henley being squeezed between his two excited sisters, he had wiped his eyes more than once. His chest ached with much more than the Between's rejection.

He touched the mirror. It turned once more into the waiting, locked door. Henley gathered himself, recovering from some of the emotion, and fed it another small memory.

Nothing happened.

Henley had never struggled with magic. Even when he was very young, his spells had always done *something*, even if they didn't finish his intended purpose. *Nothing* wasn't something he could comprehend. He looked around, expecting a different door to appear. The area stayed the same. When he tried the doorknob it felt solid—too solid.

His mother's restrained smile. His teacher's reassurances that there would be many more songs, that Young Henley was just a perfectionist. The cold water he used to rinse his mouth after he'd been sick in the bathroom. The way his father had hugged him close and rubbed the back of his head. Was that what the Between wanted?

Another memory was offered, stronger than the first. Still nothing. The memories remained in his mind, rejected without consequence. Tension ached in his neck as Henley exhaled.

"For Kit," he said, and let the memory go. It drained out of him with physical pain, so many prized details ripped away, leaving him emotional and weary with no knowledge of what caused the sensations. He'd never released such a high-value memory; there were some memories too precious to even consider using for magic. A lingering sense of joy and loss settled in his chest. The door opened. He stared through it, seeing nothing but gray in the frame, and dreaded the next price he would be asked to pay. Would it be the death of his grandmother, or the birth of his youngest sister in the same hospital? Forcing himself to walk through was unpleasant medicine.

The smell of Korean barbeque hit him, and he would have backed out if the door hadn't closed behind him. Behind the sound of raised voices was the whisper of old country western music. The air was cold with the bite of Houston's short winter. Untouched food filled the white kitchen table. His sisters sat in their chairs, spines straight and faces grim.

Twenty-seven-year-old Henley and his father were on their feet, yelling. His mother hovered by the sink, gripping a dishcloth tight.

In the blink of an eye, he was that younger man again, pushed past his limits of tolerance. The same despair clouded his thoughts. The familiar shame made him clench his jaw. His throat was sore with the force of his snarled replies. A part of him recoiled from his words, the mere suggestion of yelling at his father horrifying. That hadn't stopped him.

Henley closed his eyes, resting against the crutches so he could cover his ears with both hands. He didn't want to hear or see or smell or feel the smooth wood of the table under his pounding fists. He hadn't touched Korean barbeque since the night of the memory, and his stomach turned at the thought of eating it. The scene still hurt after so many years.

He cringed as he lifted his head to watch the mirrors. He and his father looked so much alike. His father shook a finger in Henley's face, and the younger male slapped it aside. His sisters flinched. His mother tried to step forward to intercede, but the anger between the two men had exceeded reason. The words grew harsher. Henley didn't have to hear to remember every single word, the breaths between them, or the expressions that punctuated the anger.

"You were born to a bloodline with the strength to shoulder the burdens of those less fortunate. The least you can do is step forward when others cannot. You have a responsibility to your community—"

"I don't owe you or the community anything. This is my life, I'm going to do what I want in it, and if you aren't paying my bills it's none of your business!"

The Henley in the mirrors stalked away from the table and slammed the door as he left the house. No one had chased him. His sisters dreaded his parents' disapproval as much as he had, right up until that moment. He hadn't spoken to anyone in his family for a week after the fight, and it had been most of a year before he had gone home again. They still thought he was a poor son, he was sure.

The memory restarted. Henley took a deep breath and hobbled through the mirrors, focusing on the small details instead of the shouted words. The closer he got to the true reflection, the more painful the memory became, until he was fighting his own emotions. He stared at the final mirror, every detail crystal clear and accurate, and his eyes were reddened by the loss of his relationship with his father.

Wo xiang ni le. I miss you.

He raised a trembling hand to touch the glass. His father's hand rose in a strong gesture, as if to force his hand away. Henley yanked back, but the mirror had already accepted his acknowledgement. The scene faded, leaving him with another door.

"This should be easy," he said, "but it's not."

No memory had caused him more grief. No memory was the source of so much damage. To relinquish it, however, meant giving up the protective barrier that insulated him from his family. It meant giving up the reason for the distance. He would remember later conversations with his sisters and the tension between him and his father, but he wouldn't be able to remember why it was so important. His father would remember. Henley would be subject to whatever his father felt about the fight, without enough memory to defend himself.

He grasped the handles of the crutches so hard the grips squeaked. To give up the memory meant he would be weak, out of control, vulnerable.

You don't have to abandon all your pride.

Kit's voice came back to him with such strength it made him gasp. Those silver eyes stared in his memory, calm and sad. *Your family is worth protecting.*

"Dammit," he swore. "Take it, then!"

Henley gave it up—all of it, every sensation, every word, every sob that had died in his chest as anger ruled. He forgot the smell of Korean barbeque. He surrendered the slammed door and the silence that had stretched out for days. He let go of the pain and the self-doubt, the worry that his father was right, as he had always been right before. His shoulders shook as he rested his head against the door, tears streaming down his face.

And then it was over.

He knew what memory he had given up when he lifted his head, but he couldn't replay the scene in his mind. That was the nature of memory; giving it up didn't mean one forgot all the other times it had affected them, or how it had affected the other people involved. He still remembered that first careful phone call from Minglian six days later, on his way home from work. The impact of the moment had lessened. For the first time in years, he thought of his father and remembered only how tired the man had looked when he had sent the volunteers home. Had he hurt his back safeguarding the house against flooding again?

A watery laugh sounded in his throat at the thought. *Stubborn old man.* It was impossible not to see where Henley had gotten it from. He was light, the tension he always carried in his shoulders lifted. Free. He tipped his head back and stared up at the endless gray.

"Thank you."

Henley breathed. He rubbed his face dry. Then he looked back down at the open door and shuffled himself through.

Rain hit him in the face, negating his efforts of moments before. This time he was in the scene, not hunting for a perfect memory in a mirror. Thunder crackled overhead. The air was full of the scent of wet, hot concrete. The gray sky cast everything in oversaturated colors. Henley stared through the torrential curtain at the two figures huddled in the doorway of Fine Ground.

I don't want to disappear.

It was different now. Every space in his chest that had been left empty by the loss of the previous memory filled as Henley watched himself refute Kit's fears with force. He knew then what that soft hair felt like in his fingers. The fears were real. Kit's desperation came from an eternity of loneliness and being forgotten. As he watched himself pat Kit's back, he longed to do it again properly, to hug him so tight and promise him that Henley would never, ever forget. That Kit would never be alone again. If he could just have one more chance to put aside his frustration and exasperation and see how much Kit needed him, how much they needed each other—

He was shaking his head as the words found their way out of his mouth. "You can't have this one." This was where it had all begun. That moment, even more than the scene in his kitchen as Kit crawled out of the cabinet. The interaction he watched was where his life had changed, unable to ignore the cry for help placed at his feet.

"I'm not going to forget him," he continued, raising his voice to yell at the endless sky. "Not one single memory—you can't have it!"

The pain that followed was swift. It knocked him off his feet, sending him awkwardly to his unbraced knee, his wounded leg sticking out to one side. His hands scraped on the rough pavement, wet and slick with motor oil. His nerves were on fire. The pain block was gone. Henley screamed and writhed on the ground as the lightning arced through him, silver and blinding. The memory-selves of Fine Ground and their conversation disappeared from in front of him, but the rain didn't cease, adding cold and wet to his misery.

The memory started to drain out of him against his wishes. Was the pain in his body or his mind? He couldn't tell, because the pain was *everywhere*, and the memory was only one facet of what he endured. He clawed his hands against the ground, shredding his fingernails and using the feeling as a focus. He had never fought to keep a memory, and he didn't know how to hold it fast, but he didn't give up trying. He formed mental barriers with the same speed and decisiveness he used in spellcasting.

In desperation he battled the Between with other memories, with nonsense, with the names of every software he had used on a project in the last ten years. He threw Elryk into the mess, then René and Paradise, then the substation, and the terror of falling that came with flying around the Between. He refused to give up any memory of Kit, forced to divert and correct on a second's notice when his rebellious heart and mind returned to his friend again and again.

The Between was gaining.

Henley hid behind his childhood, his excellent grades, his lectures when his sisters snuck into his room to play with his things. His grandmother's dumplings. The countless dance recitals where Huiying had gone from awkward duckling into delicate swan. The sound of his mother humming a traditional song while she balanced her checkbook and paid the family bills. It wasn't enough. The pain surged, pushing him past the point where his mind broke, and he could do nothing but scream.

Twenty-Seven

Collapse of the Between

"And the Elderhouse Market? Where am I going to get decent pepper now?!"

Noodle bemoaned his fate as he hustled his floating restaurant away from the collapsing buildings that rattled, imploded, then disappeared as they died. The cart shook with the strain of outrunning the death of the Between. Most of the Fetters he saw in his flight were too shocked to make a move. They disappeared with the same speed as the buildings, sliced out of existence by a tall figure made of light.

"Why couldn't I have started with the ramen?" he cried, throwing his weight into the steering wheel. The cart spun almost on end, sending dishes and ingredients flying. He still wore his clothes from the day before, as if anyone could sleep in that chaos. His mauve pants were *such* yesterday's fashion. His stoves were cold. No food waited for customers, because there would be no more customers. "I'm so close! I have to finish it—this is unacceptable!"

Despair threatened to overcome his boundless good nature. "What will happen to us now, Chief Operator Kit?" he asked as he sent the cart into a nosedive to avoid a large cluster of rubbernecking Fetters. They scattered like bugs in his wake, as if his crashing path had reminded them that they were about to die.

What is death to us? We will be reborn. I won't remember this. I won't remember my progress!

He gasped at the thought and craned his neck to find his next location. If he ran fast enough, could he avoid the rewrite? Could he keep his precious knowledge? Around him, on all sides but the endless gray, massive sections of the Between disintegrated. Whatever order the Lineman was following, it didn't take a linear route through the Between. The wall of buildings was becoming a patchwork of emptiness and fragments of the soon-to-be past.

A flicker caught his eye. High above the perishing Between, Paradise still hung in the air. It had been dark for hours, its glorious music dead, its joyous halls abandoned. As he watched, light returned to one room at a time.

"Yes. Yes, a lovely idea," he muttered, and jerked the wheel upward. The cart's internal gravity shifted, and it was a few seconds before his feet were back on the floor again. "A vacation would be excellent. I'm sure there will be answers in Paradise. Do you hear me, René?!" He leaned out of his window and screamed the words into the gray.

"You had better have a plan!"

Twenty-Eight

End of Paradise

"Can you make it?" Given René's determined independence, it was an indicator of how severe the situation had become that Elryk would even ask the question.

René opened his eyes. He stood on the stairs of the third level, his hand on the wall, and he was sweating. The damp, over-warm atmosphere made his blond curls tangle. It was a sense of general misery that made him enjoy his wounds even less.

"This is not my fight, my dear," he said to Elryk as the Ethereal peered at him in concern. Elryk's hand was under René's other elbow, offering quiet support. He didn't look up or down the stairs, or around, only at René. *What a good man he is*. René took a deep breath.

"I am weary, but I provide nothing to Paradise except stability. It is . . . uncomfortable. The entire Between is uncomfortable."

"Is that why it's moving so slow?"

He nodded. He lifted his eyes, scanning the walls, the stairs, and the chandeliers overhead. Paradise rebuilt itself at a crawl. In his immediate vicinity, the golden glow of the resort returned. Ahead, where they had yet to arrive, the wallpaper peeled and rotted. The lights were dim and cracked. The doors hung open at strange, eerie angles.

"Right now, the Between knows the Lineman's intent. It is unnatural that Paradise would attempt to heal, knowing that the end is near. However, her master's will has not ceded to the Lineman, thus she struggles to stay alive." He gave his companion a tight smile, then moved forward another ten steps. Elryk stayed close, lines of tension creasing his olive skin. "I am displeased with these events. They are certainly the most unpleasant in my tenure as Arbiter."

"I'm not going to argue that, but if we don't move faster, we're not going to make it."

René gazed up at the top of the current flight of stairs. The lift was out of the question, given the instability of the upper levels. The highest stairs he could see were still gray and cracked.

"We have four more floors to reach my office and look at the condition. If we rush, we will outrun Paradise and likely fall to our deaths."

"Do you want the Lineman to beat us to it?"

René exhaled through his teeth. "I hate your practicality," he muttered, and shook off the supporting hand. "Let's go, then, but I've warned you. Watch your footing and where you put your hands. When we reach the dead areas, this is no longer my Paradise."

They continued the climb and outpaced the healed areas in moments. With every step, Paradise was leeched of color and splendor. Peeling paint turned to cracked walls, then gaping holes, then rotting wood. René put his foot through a soft stair. Elryk caught him before he could fall.

"Test before you put your weight on something. Maybe closer to the edges—"

"Elryk, it has me."

The coffee man raised his head sharply at the strange tone in René's voice, tense and harsh. Then he threw his arms around the René's waist and yanked him back. René cursed. The stair fought the release of his ankle, the broken wood gouging into his flesh. Pain lanced up his leg while blood dripped into his expensive shoe.

Elryk's voice sounded inches from René's ear. "What the hell is happening?"

"Paradise houses all the exhaustion, sickness, and injury of the Between." He hung in Elryk's arms, testing his wounded ankle. It held. "Without her master, the poison seeps into the very furnishings. We have less time than I thought."

The sound of creaking, groaning wood filled the air around them as Paradise began to warp. The walls bent and broke, then rejoined, individual boards fitting into place. Clawing limbs stretched out from a central core. What they became defied words, but they struck René as scarecrow-like: tall, too thin, inhuman.

The arms around him lost their soft human muscle and gained the hardness of stone. Elryk released René and drew his arm back, following the motion with a savage punch into the broken stair. The "teeth" of wood crumbled or drew back in pain, René wasn't sure which, and he didn't stop to find out. With his foot free, he launched himself up the stairs, the boards cracking beneath his weight.

"René, what are you doing?!" Elryk's voice held a note of panic as the Ethereal followed. The staircase curved around the walls, a windowless, cylindrical tower that stretched the entire height of Paradise. The creature made of Paradise's corpse was waiting before them, turning its gangly body in their direction. It had no eyes, only empty black holes in its head.

"Death waits for us behind and before, my dear—I choose forward!"

Elryk started swearing, an impressive array of words René would have admired in any other situation. He clung to the rusted handrail, using it to drag himself upward and over the soft boards until they disintegrated. The creature was waiting. It swiped at him with giant claws made of broken fixtures.

"Useless, useless," René muttered, hauling himself up the last few steps to the next level. He darted several glances at the monster over his shoulder, staring at its claws, its elongated body, its disturbing face. "There's nothing I can work with here. In we go!"

"What's useless?" Elryk yelled as he scrambled to follow. René rolled to his feet, ignoring the slight limp and the burn of pain in his ankle as he threw his weight against the door to the fourth level. He had expected it to be soft. It was not, and his shoulder protested as the door burst open.

"Keep moving darling, we have too much ground to—"

René cried out as gravity flipped. He stepped through the door and fell to his right, landing in a heap on the righthand wall of one of the less ostentatious hallways. Elryk knocked the breath out of him when the man followed, landing on René. Every part of his body vowed vengeance until Elryk rolled off him.

"This place isn't damaged," Elryk panted, eyes wild. "How is it safe?"

"It's not safe, it's just not as exposed, but that is over and we need to keep moving!"

René dragged himself to his feet and started running across the wall. To the untrained eye the hall was fine; he could see the tarnish on the glittering features, the fade of the carpet, the gathered dust. The hall was silent of music and empty of people. When the creature ripped open the wall that held the door behind them, the decline accelerated.

"Wrong door, wrong door." René counted doorways under their feet as they leapt across, identifying each room by glimpses of their contents. The furniture maintained its original gravity. Sofas, painting easels, tea tables, and hatstands protruded at angles strange to his ninety degree–different gaze.

"Here!"

He didn't stop to consider his actions as he dropped through one of the doorways when it showed him a smaller set of stairs. This time he was at least prepared for the fall—he thought. He expected to slam into the wall opposite the door. Instead, the room twisted again, tossing him onto the ceiling. He rolled anyway. Elryk made a more decorous entrance, checking the gravity before he dropped in. The groans of the creature followed. As René watched from his new position on the ceiling/floor, the wall around the doorframe turned gray, then spotted with black mold.

"Another stairwell?"

"My private stair!" René said, scrambling up once more. He blinked, then drew a shaking breath, struggling to orient himself. "Down! We must go down to keep going up!"

"I am really hating Paradise right now, René!"

"This is not the hospitality I expected to offer," he panted, taking the upside-down stairs in twos and threes. His shorter legs made the task reckless. Every time he stumbled, Elryk was there to catch his arm and hold him steady. The Ethereal's expression was grim, but unafraid.

Wood cracked. Splinters and thrown nails filled the air. The rug ripped, fragments raining down from above. They passed the door to the fifth level as claws scratched at the stairwell behind them, too numerous to belong to one monstrous creature. Clicks and harsh, high-pitched shrieks filled the air.

"René—"

"I don't want to hear it!" he snapped as the first step creaked under him. The decay of Paradise crawled up the walls, faster than they could run, his repair work outpaced by the destruction. His breath stabbed at his chest. As Paradise weakened, so did he, and lifting his feet grew harder with every step.

A little more, he snarled to himself. *Don't you dare end your existence eaten by a conglomeration of boards and wallpaper, you half-baked snake oil salesman!*

He fell anyway.

The entire section of stairs beneath them was ripped out of the wall. The creature had grown as it traveled, sucking up bits and pieces of Paradise until it could barely fit in the stairwell. Its massive arms crawled with smaller creatures, each as inhuman and misshapen as the first. Together, they grabbed for the stairs and ripped them out of the wall, up to its gaping maw. René's weight dropped as he plummeted toward the upper levels.

Elryk's grab tore René's shirt and wrenched his shoulder almost out of its socket. The coffee man hung by one hand from the hole he had punched in the wall, the other swinging René over the endless drop. "Where is the door?"

René gasped for breath, frantic, as he searched for an exit. The reversed stairwell prevented him from seeing the doors. As he swung, he caught

244 CHRISTINA K. GLOVER

glimpses of what lay above the broken area, and almost screamed when he saw the crooked *L* of the seventh floor.

"Left!" he cried in response, flailing a hand in the appropriate direction. "Ten o'clock!"

"Brace yourself!"

Elryk gritted his teeth and flexed the impressive muscle hidden under his simple clothes. His grip was iron, removing any fear that René would fall. The Ethereal swung them back and forth a few times, then dropped them, sending the pair tumbling down another set of stairs. They landed on the underside of the platform for the seventh floor.

"How do we get inside?" René asked. Above them, the creature raged as its prize traveled out of reach. The smaller creatures latched on to its arms, making them stretch closer.

"The same way we got here," Elryk replied, rolling onto his stomach. He was sweating as well, which was damn gratifying considering how much of a mess René was looking. "You have to drop in. Take my hands and go—I won't let you fall."

René crawled to the edge of the platform and stared over the side. Paradise only had so many levels, but the stairwell went on forever, an endless tight spiral. He fixed his eyes on the next platform down, which would surely break his fall. As if he could ever doubt Elryk.

"I hate this, I hate it," he rasped, and faced Elryk on his side. The coffee man gave him a tense grin and gripped his arms. With a deep breath, René gripped back until his fingers could have left bruises on his friend's arms, then rolled his weight over the side.

They both grunted as Elryk took the weight and René dangled. He kicked at the door. It held fast, and he screeched his own cry of rage.

"What's wrong?"

"The door is locked—this is a secure floor. Of course it won't just open. Damn every damn thing!" He kicked over and over at the surface, drawing labored breaths as his arm muscles protested. "Damn you, open—open! Your master commands it, I said *open!*"

Whatever he had thought would happen was not the result. The stairwell spun. Gravity returned to normal. René fell onto the platform, dragged to the edge as Elryk began to fall. They both yelled as René dug in his feet, fighting to stop the momentum. Elryk released him, hauling himself up to snatch at the edge of the platform with one hand. When René had stopped moving, he reached for the Ethereal's other hand, helping him to climb up to the platform. Below them now, the sound of groaning boards turned confused.

"To hell with this job," René swore, lying flat to catch his breath as Elryk collapsed next to him. "I'm moving to the Actuality. I'm taking your spare room."

"Welcome to it," Elryk groaned, and pushed himself to his feet. "Come on, move!"

The door stood wide open. René gave it a baleful stare, then staggered to his feet with Elryk's assistance. Together they stumbled through, into the sitting room outside of his office. This place was still pristine. For the moment.

"Now it can come," René panted, dropping into one of the elegant chairs. He ignored how he bled and sweated all over the nice upholstery. "Stand aside, my dear. I will deal with our uninvited guest."

Elryk stayed on his feet, fists clenched as he stared at the doorway. He didn't look as though the shifts in gravity had addled his equilibrium. *He barely looks winded. When he sweats, it is artistic.* René pushed the thought aside as the first long, broken-board fingers clawed into the doorway.

The fingers absorbed the wall around them, growing in size and length. René exhaled in relief. Elryk threw him a concerned glance.

"I told you I would handle it, Elryk," René murmured, eyes on the incoming threat. "Paradise is a big place and full of treachery at the moment, but this is the immediate domain of the Lord of Paradise. *Here* I cannot be touched."

He lifted his chin. He could see every board that the creature had taken, the finish, paint, or paper different depending on where it had been located. He let the creature take what it wanted. As it tried to shove its huge head through the doorway, Elryk took a step back.

"René? *René—*"

"That's about enough."

He lifted a hand and pointed an imperious finger at the gnashing "teeth." "I command you to return to your place."

The first rotting, warped board snapped straight, its finish glowing warm, shiny gold. A second followed. The creature roared in pain, its heinous breath blasting René's hair back from his face and shoulders. He gave a savage grin as another piece returned to its former state, then ripped away from the monster's face, flying across the room to rejoin the broken wall. Claws scrabbled at the surfaces, rending the entire length of the wall that separated them from the threat. René kept his eyes locked forward as the creature penetrated the vaults on either side of the stairwell, tearing open the thick walls and sending a shower of coins and paper notes into the air.

Sweat slid down his spine. In alternating waves, he felt glorious, then weak, as Paradise faltered and healed. His fingers dragged over soft upholstery as he fought the battle of his will against the dying resort. Elryk stepped back to stand behind him, gripping René's shoulders. The touch was warm, pulsing with limitless energy. His vision snapped into focus. Flickers of red and orange and green light danced at the edge of his vision as the Ethereal fed his power into the Between, soaking it into René's skin.

The healing of the walls accelerated. The creature's screams grew louder and higher in pitch. Furniture flew. The pressure was sucked out of the room as the stairwell door reset itself with a satisfying *slam*, and the pair was left in silence.

". . . That was amazing," the Ethereal said, lowering his hands. The fountain of energy faded, leaving René sagging and out of breath in his chair. "Why couldn't you do that in the lower levels?"

"Time. This is where I spend my days, so I know it down to the smallest details. Give me a few days and I could reclaim all of Paradise, but we don't have that kind of time." A faint, exhausted smile curled René's lips. "That, and you just proved why Ethereals aren't allowed to go where they please in the Between, even under strict limitations. Thank you, my dear."

"Don't mention it. Really, don't." Elryk shook his head. "I'd prefer not to get arrested when this is over. Can you keep going?"

The thought of continuing their journey filled René with displeasure. The chair called him to sit still, to hurt, to sweat, to breathe for a while without expending more effort. Unfortunately for the chair, René was too stubborn for his own good. He took a deep breath, then hefted himself up. The air was still thin, but the breaths came easier as he turned and limped toward his office.

"I apologize for my lack of hospitality. My assistant turned traitor, and I can offer you no refreshments."

"I'll bring coffee next time. What do you need me to do—anything?"

"No, my dear, this I can do alone." René crossed the room to stand in front of the window. "The Between will let me find any Fetter and observe. Let's hope this is enough to find Mr. Yu."

"How can you track him if he's not a native of the Between?"

"That does pose some complications, but there are ways." René reached into the front of his vest, locating the small plastic bag tucked next to the pouch that held his emergency gems. "That lovely doctor you found for him provided me with some assistance." He held up the bag for his friend to examine the contents. Elryk leaned close, then frowned.

"Is that the bullet from Henley's leg?"

"It is." René opened the bag, fishing out the warped metal. It sparked and sizzled, rejecting his touch. "Nasty things, mage-killers. Designed to get under one's skin and cause all sorts of lingering problems. They bind to the blood of their victim."

He tossed the bag aside, then turned back to his window. He held the bullet with the tips of his fingers and pressed it against the glass. The window rippled with light. They saw nothing, but the sound of Henley's cries of pain and madness flooded the room. René hissed as the sound tensed aching muscles.

"How much faith do you have in this man, Elryk?"

The Ethereal moved to stand with him, brow knit, one hand resting warm on René's shoulder.

"More than I have in any other mortal."

"Let's see if that trust is well-placed."

René reached through the glass. It was *thick* under his fingers, like jelly, but it gave under his command. Blinding white light obscured the glass and hid his hands from view once they passed through the barrier. He squinted against the brilliance, grasping, finding nothing with his fingers. He stepped closer until his chest brushed the glowing surface.

"Make sure I don't go all the way in."

Elryk's grip latched on to him so fast he had to have been in motion before the words were said. René chuckled, then resumed his search. The screams were louder. He kept his expression calm so Elryk wouldn't suspect how the raw, whipping winds of the Between were lashing at René's hands, flaying his skin and shredding his sleeves. The pain fractured his focus, and his hands shook. *What a horrible path he has taken.*

His hands found an arm, a chest, tense with agony and writhing. René gripped what he could and pulled the figure closer. Something fought him—the Between itself? His vision started to fade.

"I have him," he said, slurring his words. "But he is so far, and it fights me—"

Elryk tightened his arms around the Arbiter's waist and *yanked*. René knew the Ethereal was strong. He had no idea how powerful his friend was until Elryk hauled him and Henley out of the grip of the Between, flinging them halfway across the office. The light died. Two prone figures decorated the carpet. René's arms were steaming and bloody. When he rolled his head to stare at the mage, Henley was limp and unconscious, no less disheveled than the other two.

Elryk loomed over René, his shadow blocking the light. That was fine. René was grateful to have less light as he recovered from his efforts. The Ethereal crouched, grim and disapproving.

"I'll get something for your arms in a second. Are you alright otherwise?"

"I am flawless, as always," René croaked. Elryk grunted in disagreement before he rose and moved to check on the mage. He rolled Henley on his back, touching the mortal's throat and chest, then finally held his hand in front of Henley's nose.

"Weak, but still breathing. I'm not sure he's up for a fight."

"He must." René squirmed until he could sit up without the use of his arms. "He's dead either way, but I'm not giving up without making him—"

The sudden lurch of Henley's body curdled René's words into a high-pitched yell. Henley sat up and grabbed Elryk in one smooth motion, then threw the Ethereal to one side. Elryk was off-balance and had no chance to stay on his feet. The mortal opened his eyes, his stare wild, breath heaving in his chest, wounded leg stuck out to one side.

"Ow," the Ethereal complained from the floor.

"I remember," Henley said. "The coffee shop. Paradise. We came here with Noodle's order. Before Shaw found us. The High Spirits were dead."

"Did you expect to have forgotten?" René asked. He attempted to rest his arms on his knees and yanked them back up again when the pain struck.

"Surprised I remember anything." Henley swallowed, his eyes haunted, his words ragged and weak. "Where's Kit?"

"The Lineman's doing his work," Elryk replied, shaking himself out. He sat at the third corner of their triangle, watching as the steam cooled on René's arms. "Paradise is disintegrating. You think you can manage hunting him in your condition?"

"I'm going to—Jesus. What happened to your arms, René?"

"The same thing that happened to you. I will heal. Focus, Mr. Yu."

Henley pulled off his cracked glasses and rubbed his face. René tilted his head to the side, wondering how angry he'd made the Between that Henley was bruised and beaten but not lashed like René's arms.

"If the Between wanted you dead, I think you would be dead. You may feel the opposite, but congratulations are in order regardless. We can give you only a few minutes to gather yourself. We have taken too much time to get this far."

"I'll be fine." The mage's breath wheezed in his chest. René traded a grave look with Elryk.

"Then we must get moving. Your crutches seem to have been lost to the Between—Elryk, please assist Mr. Yu."

"In a second." The Ethereal looked around the office, then retrieved a pitcher of water from René's coffee station. Elryk made efficient work of cutting away the shredded sleeves with one of René's concealed blades, exposing the lashes the Between had delivered. Once they were rinsed clean, the wounds proved numerous but shallow.

"No bandages?"

"I cannot remember the last time I was injured. I will survive with this, thank you."

Henley was quiet while they worked. René watched the mortal out of the corner of his eye. Henley slouched forward, hands in his lap, staring at the lines of his palms with intense focus. *Whatever his injuries, whatever his thoughts, he is ready for a fight.*

René stood, straightening himself with care. Elryk moved to the mage's side and offered his hands, hefting Henley to his feet. With his arm around the shorter male's waist, he made the pair mobile, though lines of strain still showed around Henley's eyes.

"Where are we going, and how are we getting there?" Elryk asked. "We can't run like we did with Henley this hurt."

"The space I need to control is much smaller," René explained, cautious as he opened the office door. The lobby outside was as they had left it, undisturbed. "There is one place the Lineman must go, to reset the Between—the place where this world is the most fragile. It is called the Main Line, the central thread that binds the Between to the Ethereal and the Actuality. My elevator reaches between it and the High Spirits."

"You said the elevator was a bad idea," Elryk countered.

"We are leaving Paradise. This lift will be one of the last pieces of the Between to fall."

René stepped aside to allow the pair to hobble past. His lift doors were closed, and no sounds came through the walls to indicate the state of Paradise. A dull vibration met his lacerated palms when he crossed the room and pressed them against the control panel. The agony and loss of his home echoed under his fingers, as loud as any cry of grief. *Someone, anyone, I beg of you—end this trial and let Paradise rest.*

The doors slid open. The elevator beyond was pristine, the carpet fresh, the mirrored walls glittering. René stepped inside.

"Prepare yourselves, gentlemen. Our reception is unlikely to be warm."

Twenty-Nine

Solene's Choice

Solene's heels were too loud on the marble floor as she hurried after Shaw's longer strides. She held her clipboard with white-knuckled fingers, the edge jabbing into her ribs. The uniform belt on her coat was coming loose. So were the pins in her hair. There was no time to stop and correct her appearance.

The facility that housed the Main Line spread out before them, an expansive train station built to move hundreds of people a day. It was empty save for the pair, neglected and faded with lack of use. Like ants, they hurried down the decorative steps, tiny intruders disturbing the rest of the sacred space. A large set of wooden doors waited at the opposite end of the terminal. Shaw was headed for them at full speed.

"Captain, I thought you could control him," she said, her voice a little too high, a little too sharp. It echoed back at her from the cold stone walls and the high, vaulted glass ceiling. She dodged a pair of wooden benches with peeling varnish. "We've lost touch with all divisions. The communications team itself has stopped responding. How are we going to survive this?"

"If you have so little faith, Lieutenant, then why are you here?"

Shaw stopped and turned. Solene skidded to a halt, so close her skirts brushed his legs before she took a hasty step back. Like Solene, his uniform showed signs of his hurry: a missed button, a fallen strap. The marks the Lord of Paradise's knives had left on his face were still hidden under bandages. "The Lineman is an otherworldly creature, unpredictable and savage. He will do what is in his nature until he is confronted here."

She listened. She breathed. Then she straightened her spine.

"Sir, since the moment he appeared, the Lineman has not listened to a word you've said. He has severed the threads of hundreds, thousands of Fetters. Can the Between be salvaged like this? What is the point if we will lose everything—"

"We have known from the beginning that there would be risks—that what we attempted was nigh impossible," he said. In the distance, muted thunder echoed his words. "We strive to unbalance the established order of the world. There is nothing else we can do but move forward."

"He isn't here!" she answered, spreading her arms to indicate the empty station. "What good can we do? What is this place?"

He stepped to the side, half turning to point at the distant doors. "This station is a placeholder. It exists only to house one thing—that room. Within it, the Main Line burns like a sun, supplying all the energy that connected the Ethereal to the Between, and then to the Actuality. The Lineman must come here at the end to sever the Main Line and reset the Between. If he succeeds, or the Chief Operator's allies get to it first, we have lost."

"Captain, if that is the last stop on his list, then what do we have left to save?"

Shaw clasped her shoulder with the firm grip that had often meant his approval. The action was jarring without his accompanying wide smile. The Captain's blue eyes were somber.

"You have worked so hard," he said. "You have come so far from that determined new recruit who was a head shorter than everyone else in her class but with twice the determination. Even now you are wise enough to question me with courage. Only you, when everyone else failed or disappointed me. Can you give me a little more time to justify your faith?"

He was her *Captain*. He had believed in her, mentored her, and supported her for years. "Sir, do you believe, without reservation, that we can still succeed?"

Shaw nodded. His voice was heavy with finality. "I do."

Solene tugged the front of her uniform coat straight and shook out her shoulders. He dropped his hand. "Then we'd best get back to work," she told the man, and received half a smile in return.

They continued their walk across the open concourse. Dull sunlight filtered in from the high windows. As Solene followed Shaw, they left footprints across the dusty ground. *Just a little longer.* No one would control them again. No one would enslave them again. *I will be free.*

The Lineman arrived in a crackling beam of light that silhouetted Shaw's form. The Captain stopped, holding out a hand behind him to halt her as well. She leaned around him to stare at the figure as the glow receded. Kittinger had seemed so defeated when he was captured. Now his skin was the same color and texture of the dust, but his posture was regal, his shoulders back, his head high. His cold, evaluating eyes fixed on the pair.

Solene thought of that desperate Chief Operator, begging them to reconsider their actions. *What if he was right about everything?* The Lineman sucked every emotion out of the open space, leaving only fear behind.

Shaw spoke before the figure had a chance to pass judgment on the pair. "Lineman, do you know who I am?"

The voice that followed made Solene's knees lock with flickers of panic. How could such a nightmare be real? **"You are Shaw, Captain of the Order of the Bright Shield."**

Perhaps how Shaw could talk to the being before them was a better question. The Captain showed no sign that he felt the terrifying aura. "I am in pursuit of a criminal, and you must allow me to finish my work. The mortal mage Henley Yu has threatened the Main Line. It is imperative that you make sure he can't reach it. The rewrite can continue once the Main Line is secure."

"**Henley Yu has been expelled from the Between.**" The voice was so empty, so alien. The blade didn't waver, its tip hovering a few inches from the floor.

"He will do anything to reach the Main Line, and he has powerful allies. The Arbiter has been corrupted."

"**The Arbiter will face the High Spirits if he has betrayed the Between.**" The Lineman adjusted his grip on his blade and took a step forward. Shaw retreated by the same amount. "**The Between must be rewritten.**"

"If you cut the Main Line now, the mortal will remember too much." Shaw spoke faster, his gloved hands raised in self-defense or warning. "The Arbiter has Ethereal allies, as well. I must be allowed to investigate. My Purpose is to protect the Between, especially when Ethereal influence is at play."

A frown crossed the Lineman's face—an expression Solene prayed wouldn't be directed at her. "**You have stalled enough. The rewrite will sever all ties to the Ethereal and the Actuality. Henley Yu has been expelled, and his memory will be corrected. He—**"

As the officers watched, the Lineman tilted his head. A ripple of energy tore through the terminal space, forcing Solene to windmill her arms to maintain her balance as the floor heaved. Motionless and steady, the Lineman stared into the distance and lowered the dull, engraved knife against his thigh to be lost in the folds of his robes. His eyes glowed, the shimmering silver filling the room as the runes carved into his skin blazed to life.

"**Henley Yu has returned to the Between. I will attend to the mortal first.**"

He turned and walked in the direction Shaw had been heading without another word, taking that brilliant light with him. Solene's breath came in sharp gasps. The room felt empty of oxygen. Shaw didn't relax his shoulders before he turned to face her.

"This is as far as you go," the Captain said, and she stared at him in confusion. He gave her the smallest smile, just a hint of it on the corners of his lips. Shaw took her hand, pulling a scrap of paper from his coat pocket and placing it in her palm. The scrap of crossword puzzle, torn from a newspaper, bore messy handwriting and fine splatters of blood. "I wanted to keep you safe as long as possible, but since he's here the final act must begin. Succeed or fail, I will be held responsible for all that happens next. The Order will need you. This is what you have trained for, and the reason I have kept you at my side. *Remember,* Solene. Remember everything for which we have fought, and the sacrifices that must never be made again."

Solene grabbed the front of his coat to keep her balance. The dizziness and fear that came with the Lineman tangled her thoughts. "Captain, what are you saying? We have work to do. You can't take on the Lineman alone, I don't know how you could even converse with him—"

"I know." His hand was on her shoulder again. "It's going to be hell, but enough of us have suffered for this cause. You'll be free next time I see you. I promise, I will take care of everything."

He struck her temple with the edge of his hand. The clipboard hit the ground with a clatter before she followed.

THIRTY

THE MAIN LINE

Henley couldn't tell if the lift was moving up or down. All the buttons had disappeared from the inside of the car. Once they had entered and the doors were closed, the lift had moved, but he could swear it had changed directions. He knew the High Spirits had been "up." There was nothing under Paradise, from what he remembered, but he didn't remember seeing anything above it either.

It hurts. It hurts. The pain block had broken. With every harsh breath drawn into Henley's chest, the weight of Elryk's worried stare grew heavier. Putting any weight at all on his bad leg made his vision go white. Even the greatest of mages would have struggled to do magic in his state, but that was no longer Henley's concern.

Will the magic come back if the Between is rewritten? Will it come back if we stop the Lineman? René and Elryk left him to his frantic thoughts as they rode. Henley could hear too much of their fidgeting, smell too much the strange metallic scent that rolled off Elryk under the familiar hint of coffee. The small distractions worsened his focus. His father's voice echoed in his mind, telling him to clear his thoughts and focus on the smallest problem he could resolve. Free of his past, Henley missed the man so much, craving his steady presence and guidance.

He leaned on Elryk, sweating with the effort of working through the pain. None of his problems were small: his magic was broken, his leg wasn't functioning, and the Lineman was going to rewrite the Between

258 CHRISTINA K. GLOVER

and take away his friend. That was the only problem he might be able to solve.

Henley exhaled, then took a deep breath. He held it for ten seconds, then did it again. Elryk mimicked the pattern as Henley took a second deep breath. René stared at the pair with narrowed eyes.

"Focused breathing techniques," Elryk explained when he saw the look. "They help manage pain as well, from what I've heard. Still with us, Henley?"

"Still here. I'm going to confront the Lineman, put a stop to this, and then pass out."

The Arbiter made a sound of amusement and faced forward again. Elryk's arm tightened around Henley's waist. The lift slowed to a stop.

Nothing else happened.

"René?" Elryk's question was met with René's frown. The blond stepped forward to touch the doors, pressing his bloodied hands against them. A hiss of displeasure left his lips.

"They are sealed. The Lineman has beaten us to the Main Line; the Between is preparing for the end."

"Have we reached the right place? We're not just floating in nothingness, are we?"

"No, my dear, the Main Line waits for us on the other side. I can feel it."

"Take Henley, then."

René quirked an eyebrow, then moved to do as he was told. He was two inches shorter than Henley, a relief to his over-stretched shoulder. Elryk stepped out of the way and then up to the door.

"Elryk, you can't do anything with it. The will of the Between is—"

"It's just energy, René." Elryk rolled his head from one side to the other, then shook out his shoulders. "Energy can be molded and directed. That's my job."

"But you have a fraction of your strength. This is the *Between*—"

Elryk ignored the worry in René's voice and braced his feet. When he lifted his hands, digging his fingers into the seam between the doors, the coffee man's body rippled with growing muscle. Rough mottled browns of raw stone shifted across his skin. His hair melted into shards of crystal. The seams of his shirt split, torn apart by spikes of translucent citrine and outcroppings of granite. Henley had never seen an Ethereal with his own eyes. Reality itself warped to release Elryk from his mortal form. The basic shape of the man remained, now embraced by the element of earth.

And the doors began to open.

Elryk growled under his breath, muttering something that sounded curse-worthy to Henley. The doors fought him. He changed his footing. As the doors opened, the vast gray space of the train terminal came into sight. Elryk got a foot between the doors and wedged them open. His chest heaved and his arms shook as he pressed himself to one side, his arms pushing the opposite door against its frame.

"Go," he said, his voice rough. "I'll follow when I can. You don't have time to waste."

"I am *very* upset with you for worrying me like this," René snapped, but he was already moving. He eased himself through the space Elryk had made, then supported Henley as he stumbled through. "Don't you dare let those doors crush you!"

"And he still has time for the last word." Elryk laughed, his voice thin and strained. "Go!"

Henley nearly fell as he made it through the opening. René caught him, both flinching as Henley gripped the Arbiter's wounded arms. The shorter man threw one last worried look over his shoulder, then moved Henley's arm to drape around his shoulders. The best speed they could manage was a weak hop. Henley slid from time to time on the dust-covered ground.

The same dust showed him the marks of others who had passed before—multiple sets of footprints. "He's not alone, René."

"Shaw, I would assume," the Arbiter replied through panted breath. The station was a silent sentinel to their efforts, their voices echoing off the bare walls. "I will deal with him. Keep your focus on the Lineman."

"Feels like a trap."

"A bit late for those concerns, now."

René kept his head up and his eyes fastened on the path ahead. The large doorway at the opposite end of the terminal loomed before the pair. The blond looked back only when they reached the doorway, hesitating as flashes of light reflected from the stone floor. He didn't comment on what might be happening to Elryk behind them. "Are you ready?"

"Yeah."

The doors were ajar. When René kicked, they swung open, washing them both in blinding light. When Henley could see again, he stared in awe at the molten pillar, crashing and flickering, that poured through the center of the room. The train station's waiting area held benches and a few desks, all bleached white from exposure to the radiance. It made no sound, but it generated wind and energy that blasted through the room. The column of energy extended through the floor and the ceiling into infinite space. Henley wasn't sure if he was tiny, or if the Main Line was gargantuan.

The silhouette of a tall man with long hair and robes waited for them. Henley's pulse raced. Kit was right there, *so close*, with nothing separating them but distance and the Lineman himself. The figure turned to face the pair. A bullet chambered into Shaw's pistol inches from Henley's head.

"You have brought yourself to your doom," the Captain said. When Henley turned his head to stare down the barrel of the gun, Shaw's blue eyes shone with reflected light at the other end. "Now the Lineman can finish his work in peace."

"I withdraw my endorsement from Shaw, Captain of the Order." René raised his voice, and the certainty was wiped from Shaw's face. "I submit him to judgement for the crime of betraying his position and using his power for personal gain."

"You can do nothing without the High Spirits, Arbiter—"

"**Noted,**" the Lineman's steady voice interceded. "**Captain Shaw's Purpose and Assignment shall be suspended until his trial before the High Spirits.**"

Shaw's face turned red, then purple. He choked on words, then gasped for breath. He lowered the gun. He stumbled back and fought to breathe. Henley gave him a tight smile.

"Feels bad, doesn't it? Don't move around too much. You'll make it worse."

"**Henley Yu has been expelled from the Between. He must be returned to the Actuality.**"

His triumph at Shaw's predicament faded as fast as Shaw's expression had changed. The Lineman had moved as fast as light, and he loomed before the hobbled pair. His hair was long, brushed, beautiful. His colorless skin was that of a corpse.

"I permit this mortal to enter the Between in order to testify before the High Spirits." René spoke fast, spilling the words into the tight space between them. "The trial of Captain Shaw must be completed before Henley Yu returns to the Actuality." He shuffled them backward until Henley could grab the frame of the doors. The Lineman remained where he stood, his cold gaze unchanged.

"**I will accept his presence.**"

The tall figure turned and walked back toward the Main Line. Even his long, dull blade reflected the brilliant light. The Main Line seemed nothing more than a thread before him in one second, but in another the blade was godlike and huge.

"You can't!" René left Henley at the door and ran forward. "If you rewrite the Between, the trial cannot continue!"

"**The trial cannot continue without the High Spirits. The High Spirits must be rewritten.**"

René grabbed the Lineman's arm. The Lineman rolled his shoulder—barely shifting—and sent the Arbiter flying across the room. He didn't stop until he met the nearest wall. When he collided with the surface, it crumbled beneath him. His body bent at unnatural angles, slid down the broken wall, and was still on the floor.

Henley sucked in a breath. Panic rose in the back of his throat as he looked from the fallen blond to the thin figure framed in light. The Lineman raised his blade again. A strong hand grabbed Henley's shoulder from behind, and another pressed something thin and metal against his palm.

The lift doors crushed Elryk, applying more pressure than he had encountered in deep crevasses of the Actuality. The edges dug into his spine, into his palms, making his bones creak. The boot he had lodged against the opposite side slid an inch, then two. *The Between is winning.* He tried not to be fatalistic, but he needed a solution or the situation was going to get ugly.

The metal didn't respond when he tried molding it, melting it into place. Metal never did like him very much. It was fickle, less practical than stone and somehow more stubborn. He couldn't apply the heat needed to force it to obey. The lift was lined with glass mirrors, however. Glass was more useful. It was fragile, though. *Can I make it hard enough with just pressure and no heat? Doesn't seem likely. What if—*

He severed his attention from the problem and focused on the train station beyond the lift. A sound caught his attention, then faint movement. Something had fallen. Something else fell, then several more somethings.

The ceiling?

He scanned the upper reaches of the station. The glass skylight was too high for him to make out the details, but the soft crash of exploding glass told him enough. The warping of the walls, bubbling in and out in slow waves, told him the rest. *We're in real trouble. Holding the lift isn't going to be worth a damn if the whole Between collapses.*

Elryk eased himself sideways until he was facing the station, the lift doors beginning to close as his strength moved away from his task. Gem-like eyes focused on the distant doors that still framed his companions. He launched himself out of the lift and nearly lost a foot when the doors slammed closed. From his new position on the ground, he watched as the lift doors turned to stone and blended into the wall. The collapsing, unstable wall.

"Damn it all," he growled, and pushed himself up to his feet. Getting across the main concourse was slow going. Falling glass was bad enough, but the floor twisted and moved as well. Cracks formed in the marble, spreading into large rifts. He jumped small breaks and ran to the side to avoid those too large to cross.

He stumbled over the woman behind a rotting bench, crumpled on the floor, her uniform coat sparkling with splinters of glass. Her hair had escaped some of its pins, a tangled mess. Dust streaked her dark skin. He knew the uniform. It wasn't going to make his life easier to stop, but he stopped anyway and rolled her onto her back. A nasty bruise on her temple was decorated with a trickle of blood.

"Captain?" she said, her voice slurred.

"Afraid not. Let's go, you're going to fall through the floor."

"The Captain—the Lineman isn't listening, he won't cooperate—"

"That's what he does, from what I've seen." Elryk got his arm around the woman and hefted her to her feet. Her heels were troublesome, but who was he to judge? She was steadier on her feet than he had expected once upright. Staring at her shoes led his eyes to something else on the floor—a clipboard, and the glitter of flat metal.

"Is that Henley's Assignment card?"

A pane of glass fell perilously close to his face. He jumped back, then forward once it had shattered, snatching the card from the ground. The mage's name was punched into the metal surface, over the word OPERATOR.

"He's gone," the woman said, eyes out of focus as she moved forward. "He was sent back to the Actuality when the Lineman appeared. That's when everything fell apart."

"Time to fix it, then. Keep up, officer."

She was moving on her own, and he felt less guilt as he sprinted toward the doors. For a few moments he had lost sight of Henley and René. They came into view again, backing toward the doors. Then René was gone, only to fly across his vision seconds later.

I'm done with staying in my place.

Before Henley could follow the Arbiter's fate, Elryk grabbed his shoulder with one hand, then shoved the card into the mage's other palm.

"Time to see what an operator can do. Get moving!"

The Between welcomed him back. Henley felt the cold metal, the strong grip, then the blast of raw energy that poured into him from all sides. His exhaustion disappeared. The pain remained but it faded, pushed back to something he could manage. The colors and sounds brightened as if he had been seeing everything from behind foggy glass.

And the *magic* crackled in his fingertips.

It was different from what he had used as a mortal. It wasn't potential anymore, it was lightning waiting to be thrown, something he didn't have to summon. His eyes glowed silver. In a moment he took in the huge room, the figures trapped within, and he focused on the Lineman. His voice was so loud Elryk flinched away from him.

"Thirty-five percent, *Hold*! Restrain and restrict, prevent motion!"

The Lineman's arm halted before the blade could be dropped. He turned his head slowly to look back over his shoulder, far from the frozen state the spell should have enforced.

"That's not good," Henley muttered, then pointed down at his leg. "Ten percent, *Brace*! Secure and support!"

Bands of glowing metal wrapped around his leg and forced it straight. The sensation wasn't pleasant but he was stable, able to move without falling. He limped forward, aiming his spells at the Lineman again.

"Fifteen percent, *Weight of Stone*. Five percent, *Rush*. Twenty percent, *Open the Earth*!"

The Lineman's blade faltered, forced lower by the additional weight of the spell. The marble tiles beneath his feet became liquid, wrapping around his legs and making him sink. The pale figure lifted one foot and planted it on the ground, dragging himself out of the mire.

"It's not working—he's too strong!" he yelled, throwing a frantic look to where Elryk was crouched over René. The Ethereal pointed to the towering cyclone of the Main Line in exasperation.

"All of the magic in the Between is right there—find a way to use it!"

"The Between must be reset." The Lineman had turned to face the mage, his blade lowered to his side. **"Your efforts are futile. Your thread must be—"** The pale figure paused, knitting his brows in mild confusion. His face had lost Kit's natural expressiveness, a robotic parody of the Chief Operator's emotion.

"You do not have a thread."

"Who's fault is that?" Henley asked, and stretched his left hand toward the Main Line. He gritted his teeth and he *called* the magic, summoning it as he had back home. Ponderous and heavy, the Main Line responded, moving toward his hand. Then it stopped, a foot away from his fingers, stretched to its limit.

"Henley!" Elryk's raw voice tore through the big room. The Lineman was right in front of Henley, still puzzled, but raising his blade anyway. His presence was a heavy weight, pinning Henley in place with fear and ominous intent.

He stared into the Lineman's eyes and saw grief in the silver depths. The pale being's mouth was neutral, his eyebrows low, but his eyes alone held emotion.

"Ten percent," Henley panted. *"Elastic."*

The magic yanked the Lineman through the air, sending him flying back to the edge of the Main Line. Henley got moving in a frantic hobble across the cracking ground. The Lineman was still on the ground when Henley reached the edge of the tiles around the Main Line. As the Lineman shook himself and pushed back up to his feet, Henley stared at the thundering, shimmering glow, praying his plan would work.

He threw himself into the Main Line.

The magic was forced into his skin, his eyes, his teeth, his mind. The power burned the ends of his nerves, leaving him numb to pain. He didn't know if he still had hands or feet or clothes. He didn't know who or what he was supposed to be. He was a conduit, unable to affect the magic, but able to direct the flow.

Caught in the stream of all magic in his universe, Henley saw thousands of points of connection, all mages across the Actuality calling for magic that wouldn't respond. He saw confusion and fear. Doctors in hospitals swore, children at their lessons tried again and again, and mundane mages in every corner of the Actuality changed their wording to see if they had said something wrong. He felt each and every one and knew how to give them what they needed. Right then, he needed it all.

He directed his attention to the Lineman, feeling more than seeing the presence. The Lineman's energy was blood twisted with silver, the color of sacrifice and loss. It was *wrong*. Kit's colors should have been faded cream and pink and green, the colors of life and spring. Henley lifted his hands, feeling the magic spill over them like water.

"*Be still.*"

He dropped every part of the incantation he didn't need. Who cared about percentages when he had all the magic at his fingertips? Who cared about the words when he could direct the magic to do exactly what he saw in his mind? The Between had already taken everything he had to give. The Lineman froze in place, held fast by invisible chains. His blade stopped in midair. He could not move to finish the job of cutting the line.

"Now," Henley continued, his voice reverberating through the room, "make it stop."

The Ethereal had left Solene just inside the door. The wall offered feeble support as it wavered and crumbled. In the middle of the cavernous room, a battle raged, but she was outside of the swirl of violence and energy. *Where is the Captain?*

Her thoughts were still fragmented, her vision unclear. Her head was pounding. Shaw had hit her hard enough to cause real damage. The thought brought growing concern instead of anger. She hunted among the benches and decorative railings, seeking a uniform much like hers.

She found it to one side, prone. Shaw's legs stuck out from behind one of the benches, his boots dragging on the ground as he writhed in pain with what little energy he could muster. Solene struggled to get to his side, her disoriented vision making it difficult to walk in a straight line. She stumbled over low steps and her own feet. When she fell to her knees, it was a relief to be on solid ground.

"Captain?" she asked, leaning forward to meet his eyes. Shaw's breath wheezed and rattled in his chest. His shoulders and fingers were growing transparent. The Captain opened his eyes to stare at her and closed them again as he rolled his head away.

"You weren't . . . supposed to see this, Solene."

"Captain, what happened to you?" She ignored his words. His eyes were sunken and his hat was gone, knocked halfway across the room. "What do I need to do?"

"Can't do anything . . . now." He reached up, motor control failing as he pawed at her hand, finally getting it within his and bringing it to his chest. "Damn the Arbiter. Didn't plan for him. I'll be judged. He won't—" The Captain broke into a coughing fit. She pressed her hand against his chest, feeling the erratic beat of his heart. "—won't let me escape. So sorry. I wanted . . . better for you."

"It isn't over," she replied. "You'll be judged and rewritten. You can try again. We'll be alright. Just rest."

He opened his eyes and stared at her. In his weakness, he managed a smile, just the corners of his lips pulling up as he gazed into her eyes. She was struck by that image, the confident Captain, the carefree and certain man who had made her so sure anything was possible.

"Not after this," he said. "Can't. Even if . . . rewrite continues. He won't let me come back. I failed you S . . . Solene. I'm so . . . I'm so sorry. Everything depends . . . depends on you, now."

Even if it continues? She looked up as Henley stepped into the flow of the Main Line. The light exploded in the room, blinding as it washed over the occupants. He was an avatar of magic, holding the Lineman fast. Preventing the rewrite. Freezing the collapse of the Between and forcing the destruction to stop. Just as Shaw had warned, Kittinger's allies would ruin everything she had fought to achieve.

She looked back at her Captain. As the seconds passed, he grew as pale as the bandages across his face, and the vivid blue of his eyes faded to washed-out gray. His gaze moved across her face, trying to fix on features he struggled to see.

"It's not over," she repeated, and caught his hand. The words were rough in her throat, and her breath was held tight in her chest. With precise care, she released the Captain's hand and rose to her feet, ignoring the questions he barely had the strength to ask. As she walked toward the Main Line, her mind was crystal clear, the ripple of energy and time moving so slow around her steps.

She drew her standard-issue pistol and raised her hand.

Thirty-One

All Falls Down

The Lineman heard the sound and felt the release of the bullet that sliced through the air. He was bound in half a dozen ways, unable to avoid the shot, but it wasn't directed his way. The mage-killer warped the Between as it traveled. Mage-killers had a single, nasty purpose. This one, like its predecessor, punched into Henley's body and severed his connection to magic. The mage—*operator?*—was overwhelmed as the pulsating energy rejected him and threw him out of the Main Line. The room crackled with magic, and the Lineman was free. Voices raised around the room, but they were unimportant to his Purpose.

Order restored, he straightened and lifted his blade again. The rewrite of the Between was natural. It was a wounded creature in need of resurrection. The relief that followed his release was the closest the Lineman came to emotion. Soon he could rest again. He moved to cut the Main Line and discovered his arm hadn't lifted at all. Once again, he was puzzled as he looked at his lowered hand.

No.

The Lineman had never felt pain. He didn't know what it was or how to make it stop when it tore through his mind. It drove him to his knees. The pain extended to his throat as his involuntary screams pierced the air. His left hand clutched at his skull, but his right hand was out of his control.

Kit dropped the blade and fell forward, supporting their weight on his right hand. He had been ravaged by pain and loss, and he fought through those emotions as he scraped control away from the Lineman one inch at a time.

"I can't accept this," he panted, his voice lacking the formal tones of the Lineman. "He doesn't belong here. None of them belong here. You must reconsider—hnnng!"

The Lineman was a savage machine as he took control again. Blistering pain rose and crashed over them in waves. They fell on the floor, spine arching up from the ground as they writhed. Their head whipped back and forth as control faltered between the personalities.

"The Between . . . *must* . . ."

"There has to be a way! We can find—"

"I cannot defy my Purpose. All the Between depends—"

"*Henley!*"

The final cry shook the room. The skylight panels overhead rained down and shattered around them in great bursts of glass. No one escaped the impact. The smell of blood rose in the air from dozens of wounds. Cracks split the marble tile.

"*Kit!*"

Silver eyes snapped open. The familiar voice was filled with pain and rough with heavy breath, but clear.

Henley is alive!

The mage-killer missed vital areas. He is still a threat.

"Stop it, stop it, stop it—" Kit howled, banging his head back against the ground. "Leave him alone—"

With staggering steps, Henley fell to his knees next to them. "It's okay, Kit! It's okay."

The smell of blood was stronger as the mortal leaned over the fragmented Lineman and his trapped passenger. He held their left hand in his own, the grip slick with blood. Exhaustion darkened the circles under his eyes. There was no sign of his broken glasses. Blood dripped from his lips and soaked through the chest of his white shirt, where a hole ripped through his body.

"I need you both to listen to me, okay? Kit? Lineman, can you hear me?"

"Y . . . yes." The pain in Kit's chest had nothing to do with his war against the Lineman.

"I am listening, mortal."

"Good." Henley closed his eyes, gathering his strength. The floor shook again. Kit was aware of more voices in the background, a conflict as Elryk restrained Solene. He didn't take his eyes from Henley's weary face.

"I can't feel the Main Line anymore. I'm right here and I can't . . . I can't feel it at all. I don't think I can do anything else to stop this." Henley opened his eyes again to stare down. "Maybe I shouldn't. Maybe we never had a chance."

"I can't lose you, Henley," Kit said, and tears coursed down the right side of his face. "I can't do this again, I can't be alone—"

"The Between *must* be rewritten," the Lineman interrupted. **"Every soul within depends on the stability of the Between."**

"Shh, Kit. Shh . . . it's okay." Henley slid his other hand under their head, supporting it in his palm. His slouch had shadowed the bullet hole through his chest, but now Kit could see light through his body. The threads of the Between flickered around him, unable to determine whether he was mortal or Fetter. More than being wounded, he was being *unmade*. "Lineman, I want . . . I want to be here. With Kit. Can you let me in?"

"Unsanctioned mortals do not belong in the Between. I cannot determine the outcome of your request."

Henley nodded. "Can you ignore me then? Don't expel me, just . . . leave me here. Let whatever happens, happen."

The Lineman was silent for a long second, his spirit still against Kit's struggle.

"This is acceptable."

"Okay." Henley exhaled, rubbing his thumb against Kit's temple. "Kit, everything's cracked. Even if we want to stop it, there's no Between left. The magic is broken. My people, they need the magic. We have to fix it." He leaned down, resting his head against Kit's.

"I swear to you, I will never forget you," he whispered. "You are the memory I won't sacrifice. No matter what happens, I'll be waiting for you. I need you to trust me."

"I don't want to be alone again."

"Can you *trust* me?"

Kit stared up at the human, fragile and mortal and caught between worlds. He didn't want to just be remembered. He wanted *this man* to remember him, and Henley promised him the world. Kit nodded, jerking his head, and Henley smiled.

"I'm not the only one, Lineman. Can you spare the others here too?"

"Only those who are not Fetters. Those who belong in the Between must be reborn."

"That's the best I can ask. Do you need help?"

"No."

The Lineman sent the order to his right arm to lift the blade. Kit stared into Henley's eyes and allowed the motion. Henley watched him and gave a small nod.

"Together, Kit. We're going together."

The Lineman's blade was either very long, or the Main Line had appeared right next to them. The sharp edge sliced through the silver flow. It shredded into a million strands. A gaping hole in the fabric of the Between appeared, then disappeared where Elryk had stepped through a portal. The walls dropped and took the Between with them.

Free of Elryk's hold, Solene scrambled to reach Shaw as the Between collapsed. She was still several feet away when the floor vanished, leaving her to watch the Captain's motionless body drop into nothingness in a rain of dust and rubble and broken glass. Try as she might, she couldn't reach him, and she tumbled out of control through empty space.

"Try again."

She knew the voice. It was devoid of emotion, but not compassion. The Lineman stared back at her from one of the falling glass panes.

"Come back. Look harder. Try again."

Solene gave up her fight, and then she knew nothing at all.

The Between tore at René, strangling him. Paradise was ripped away. The feeling of control, his power, his position, everything was plucked from his hands. Pain followed. His skin burned, his scalded arms a weak shadow of the agony that flared through his soul.

So this is how the end feels.

The Arbiter fought with all his strength. He resisted the threads that attempted to tear him apart. The pain reached a blinding point as all color and shape faded from the world. He forgot Kit. He forgot Henley. He forgot Elryk. He forgot himself. He forgot the moment when the Ethereal's strong hands pulled him away from the pain and into the Actuality. He forgot everything for a long, long time.

What buildings remained in the infinite wall of the Between disintegrated. The people had disappeared, leaving behind belongings and fragments of life. The noodle cart broke apart, the pieces fading with the shell of Substation No. 28. Paradise fell in a shower of glittering particles. The Between was wiped out into a space of gray emptiness.

And then it began to rebuild.

THIRTY-TWO

BEGINNINGS

The bell over the coffee shop door jangled, but Henley didn't lift his eyes from the depths of his fresh coffee. He could no longer feel the surge of magic that would have told him when someone stepped across the shop's wards. The white mug made a pristine frame for the liquid, surrounded by the mellow gold of the wood coffee bar. It was a nice aesthetic. Fine Ground was filled with the babble of voices. Elryk had taken fifteen minutes to take his order.

Henley's leg ached, but it no longer burned with infection. Magic had returned in full force. The end of the storms meant extensive repairs to flooded homes and businesses, but the doctors were back in business. He was surprised his sister was letting him off with physical therapy only three times a week.

Minglian had been his second phone call after waking up on the floor of his apartment. His first, to Fine Ground, hadn't gone through. The pain hadn't allowed him to worry more about Elryk's state. His sister had appeared within ten minutes to block the pain again, help him get into bed, and clean off the blood of wounds that no longer existed. Only his leg injury remained. She was a damn good doctor and hadn't pressured him for explanations before he rested. She was a better sister, and Henley hadn't woken up alone until he could walk again.

"Did you put in your notice?" Elryk was racking mugs behind the bar. His assistant—only one, so Elryk could watch her closely—bustled to refill one of the big pots. Sunlight poured through the windows. At the far end of the bar, Henley sat alone.

"Yeah. I told them I'd finish all of my current projects, so they took it well."

"When do you start training?"

"Two weeks, when my notice is up. Then I'll be back and forth to the Between, but I'm keeping my apartment."

"Will your leg be up to the training?"

"We'll find out. They said I can focus on the procedures first and get through my physical training when I've healed a little more. My sister will kill me if I push it too hard."

"You still staying with your parents?"

"For now. They've accepted that I can't tell them everything that happened, but they don't like it, so they feel better where they can keep an eye on me. It's nice to have someone there to make tea when I can't sleep."

Elryk glanced up from his work, his eyes a heavy weight on the center of Henley's chest. Henley rubbed the spot where the bullet had pierced him with his free hand.

"Still no sign of that shot. I dream about it, though. I wake up feeling it."

"I guarantee no one else in the Order of the Bright Shield has had your experience with mage-killers. At least you'll use them with caution." Elryk braced his hands on the bar. "I'm still surprised they took you. At least they were *kind* enough to rescind the search order they broadcast with your information while you were wanted."

Henley sipped his coffee, then exhaled a breath that blew hot steam back into his face.

"The rewrite handled that. No one remembers me being hunted—I had to make my request to the head of the local Observer division before anyone even knew what I was asking about. The Shields need mortals who can go between worlds without trouble, and you don't need magic to arrest people and keep order. I'd rather be there, doing something, than acting as damaged as my family thinks I am."

"They have a point."

"Not one I like hearing over and over." Henley set his cup back down and lowered his voice. "You've heard nothing? Any news from René?"

Elryk fell silent, letting the noise of the shop roll over them. One of his regular customers called out, and the shop owner waved, then sighed. "I hate getting your hopes up. I've heard . . . something. It might not mean what you want to hear."

"It's been three weeks, Elryk." Henley shut out the sight of the coffee shop with his hands, rubbing his eyes under his new glasses. "I understand it's questionable. Give me something, at least."

"Our messages are getting more consistent. He's still the Lord of Paradise, but it took a while to find a solid communication channel. He sent this back to me this morning."

The Ethereal slid a paper napkin across the table. The small cream square was decorated with gold at the corners, and an art deco logo. A message scrawled across the paper in burgundy ink.

You are invited to Paradise on the condition that you bring my usual coffee order and a box of quality tea. I may need to bribe my way in to see the Chief Operator.

The stab to his chest was like being shot again. Henley lifted his eyes from the napkin, fastening his gaze on Elryk, but he didn't see his friend. He was thinking of silver eyes and strawberry hair and a wistful smile instead.

"That has to be Kit."

"I don't know why he'd say it like this if it wasn't." The coffee man leaned forward. "Henley, this doesn't mean it's the same Kittinger. It doesn't mean he remembers."

"He will." He unclenched his fists, smoothing the napkin he had crumpled with his reaction. Like Henley, it couldn't go back to the way it had been before, but it still did its job just fine. If only his heartbeat would calm down.

"You've got two weeks to find out how I contact René once I get to the Between. Just give me that much, and I'll figure out the rest. I *know* Kit's waiting for me." Henley met his friend's eyes and offered a determined smile.

"I've got a promise to keep."

Henley and Kit will return in
THE MAGE-KILLER
December 2024

KEY CHARACTERS

The Actuality

- **Henley Yu (Yu Xiatong)** – Mortal mage, Gulf Coast Mage Council

- **Elryk Seldriksen** – A simple coffee man, owner of Fine Ground

- **Haotian Yu (Yu Haotian)** – Henley's father, mortal mage, High Magister of the Gulf Coast Mage Council

- **Dr. Minglian Yu (Yu Minglian)** – Henley's middle sister, mortal mage, Gulf Coast Mage Council

The Between

- **Kittinger** – Chief Operator of the Switchboard, Stationmaster of Substation No. 28

- **Kelley** – Operator at Substation No. 28, Kittinger's second-in-command

- **Shaw** – Captain of the Order of the Bright Shield

- **Solene** – Commanding Lieutenant of the 26th Division (Between), Order of the Bright Shield

- **Sandoval** – Patrol Officer assigned to Substation No. 28, 26th Division, Order of the Bright Shield

- **René** – Lord of Paradise

- **Noodle** – The best pasta chef in any world

Acknowledgements

This book sits in your hands thanks to the incredible patience of the best family in the world. I am so lucky to have them putting up with me through every frustrated rant, every tear shed over my own characters, and every tangled plot element that needs to be re-woven. To my wife Chu (forever René's true inspiration) and my dearest Abi (president of the Captain Shaw fanclub): at this point I can't crawl out of your debt, so you're stuck with me forever!

I've been wildly fortunate to have supportive parents who told me I could do anything I put my mind to, as well as teachers and mentors who guided me into confidence. Thank you to every precious English teacher who fostered my creativity instead of killing it, SCC ("You need to do better for yourself, go back to school") and RW ("Believe in yourself, even when others don't"). My eternal adoration for Shawna, who could have just seen this project as a job, but instead became one of my loudest cheerleaders. Endless appreciation also for Shiye, who volunteered to help with translation and ended up completely saving me when it came to the names of Henley's family. (*Whew*, that was close!)

And finally, to the Twitter writing community: *they can't kill us if we all refuse to die*.

O brave writer, I pass this torch to you.

About the Author

Christina K. Glover (she/her) is an accountant determined to prove that crunching numbers doesn't crunch creativity. She lives in Houston, TX with her family, including two incredible housemates and a menagerie of pets. Her bucket list items are learning Japanese/visiting Japan, learning to pick locks, and flying in a hot air balloon. When not writing she can be found buried in a pile of manga or playing phone games (Stardew Valley, anyone?) long past her bedtime.

She would be delighted to hear from you, either via review or through email at the Lies and Bees website: www.liesandbees.com/books

Made in the USA
Columbia, SC
24 June 2024